THE HOLLOW WORLD

MICHAEL KACE BECKUM

The Hollow World is a work of complete fiction

Based loosely on the public domain version of
At The Earth's Core
originally printed in *The All-Story Weekly*
in April of 1914
written by Edgar Rice Burroughs.

The characters, incidents, situations, and all dialogue
are entirely a product of the authors imagination, or are
used fictitiously and are not in any way representative
of real people, places or things.

Any resemblance to persons living, or dead
is entirely coincidental.

First published in the United States of America

by Wild and Woolly Press, Inc.

3 5 7 9 10 8 6 4 2

© Michael Kace Beckum 2015

The Hollow World / Michael Kace Beckum

DEDICATION

To my dear friend, Steve
Who gave me my first job
And was the best of friends
when I needed one.
Thanks for being patient.

CONTENTS

THE MACK INTERVIEWS

"So Mack left the boy bleeding out all over the sidewalk, and then came back to... what? What happened next?"

"We don't really know. They asked, but the only useful thing Mack said was that he got into Alvarado's Borer. After that he vanished, and then just reappeared out of nowhere on the platform. Everything in between was... well... his story... everything he told them was just crazy. I mean, totally fucking nuts. But it's the only explanation we have for where he went, and where he is, now. Where Mizellier, Pompaneau and the cop are. Unfortunately all we have are these recordings, and all they show is Mack talking, but I guess... here. Let me turn this one on, and—see? He's just sitting at a table with the camera locked off, so we can't be sure who he's talking to, or who else was in the room, though we have some good ideas about a few of them."

"But we have the other security camera footage, right."

"We do. Yes. But it's recorded and stored in a separate area, there are clearances we're going through to get them..."

"Jesus, I hate bureaucracy. Do we have a full interview, here? Does Mack ever get to it? What happened to the mole? All that hollow earth bullshit? From after he killed that kid?"

"Yes."

"All right. Let's watch."

Onscreen, Brandon Mack runs his hands through his hair.

"I'll explain why I... how that... um... you know... how that guy was killed. I didn't mean to. It was an accident. So I shouldn't go to jail, right? And then you'll help me? You'll send me back to Pangea? It's important. You have no idea... You think there's plenty of time—we always think there's plenty of time—but there really isn't. Time is an illusion."

There's a pause as Mack waits.

"Did you hear me?" Mack asks someone offscreen.

"I heard you," a voice replies. Pompaneau, most likely. "Did you hear ME? I can't help YOU if you don't help ME. But if this guy insists that you start at some arbitrary and non-specific point in the past, so be it. Just tell us whatever it is you're going to tell us, already, and get the fuck on with it."

Another pause.

"Why is Pompaneau being such a dick?"

"He needs an excuse?"

"Good point. But even for him..."

Onscreen, Mack glares, and then speaks carefully.

"Yeah. Right. Well... I guess... it started because of my last date with Jessica..."

Someone sighs very heavily, off-screen. Mack glares past the camera, and snarls.

"Just roll with it, asshole," Mack snaps.

"Did... did you..." off-camera we hear sounds of someone shifting around. "Did he just call me an asshole? Did you just call me an asshole?" There's another pause, as Mack simply stares. "Don't call me an asshole... asshole."

More silence. Mack looks furious, his eyes never seem to blink, and eventually he continues.

"We'd been on a date..." Mack says, "Jessica and I... we... and it seemed to go really well. So I was expecting certain things, you know? Hoping for certain things, I guess."

"Don't be coy," Pompaneau snarls, "Just say it straight out so we can get through this shit faster."

"I wanted to fuck her." Mack says, staring silently again, off-screen. "Direct enough for you?"

"Perfect."

YOU HAVE TO START SOMEWHERE

JESSICA'S KISS WAS PASSIONATE and deep, but too damn brief. She seemed to re-think things once my hand cupped her breast, and pulled away, pushing me off. It wasn't the first time.

"I don't want to move too fast," she said, trying to sound playful, but inflecting it more like a warning.

I sat back in the driver's seat and let the passion evaporate from my lips, my hands... and other places. She was already reaching for the door handle.

"All right," I said. "We'll keep taking it slow."

"I think that's best."

"I'm sure you do."

She studied me for a minute, and though she still smiled, her eyebrows crunched together in the middle.

"I don't want to make a mistake," she said, as if answering my unasked question.

"How—exactly—would it be a mistake?" I returned, losing my veneer, sincerely wanting to know. "We've been dating a month. We have a lot of fun together..."

"We're at different places in our lives, and sex *always* complicates things."

She said it as if I already knew, and was intentionally annoying her by making her say it.

"How are we at different places in our lives?" I asked.

"Well, I'm focused on my career, and you're..."

"You're a *receptionist*."

"Don't say that like it's nothing! I'm going to school at nights! To study law! And you're a *janitor*!"

"So we finally get down to it. And sex between a receptionist and a janitor..."

"It's more than that. When two people are at different places in their lives, one of them always gets too clingy, or needy, and the other..."

"*One* of the them?"

She sighed and folded her arms. Definite body language stuff going on.

"Relationships are always unbalanced," she said.

"Are you seeing someone else?" I asked.

"*Brandon!*" she snapped, angry that I could even suggest such a thing. But I noticed she didn't actually answer my question.

I looked around at the neighborhood. A nicer one than mine. With nicer cars. Nicer trees. Nicer lawns. Nicer curbs, and drains, and mailboxes. Nicer garbage cans. I couldn't help wondering if that had something to do with keeping me at arm's length. Not just my 'career' as a night janitor, but also where I came from. My blue-collar upbringing.

The evening had been romantic and fun. Jessica seemed to enjoy herself, appeared genuinely interested in me, her attention rarely wavering, and the conversation never seemed to lag. She wasn't my intellectual equal, but saw herself as superior, and that was okay. All good, or so I thought, especially only a month into the 'relationship'. When we were out, we never seemed 'at different places' or 'incompatible'. And yet...

Once we'd finished this date—our fifth—we'd been sitting in my car in front of her house, chatting and laughing, when we hit a lull in the conversation. I'd studied her—carefully—she seemed to want it, so I haltingly leaned in, and she'd responded, passionately. Very passionately. At least for a moment. Then suddenly she wasn't passionate any more, and now we were here.

I didn't understand any of it.

"Don't play games with me, Jessica. I can handle it. Just be honest. Are you seeing someone else? Are you not interested in me?"

She scowled, then softened, and after a moment of studying my face leaned closer to give me a quick kiss, then stared at me from only inches away. She looked down at my crotch, and 'Hmmm'd' a little. Then she gave the bump in my jeans a quick squeeze.

"You're hard," she said, evidently pleased.

She certainly knew how to change the subject.

"If you like it that much," I said, "why don't you let me come in?"

She looked as though the question actually angered her a little. But she shook it off, and smiled.

"Let's wait," she said, hotly, rubbing me in a way that was only going to make it *more* difficult for me to do this *her* way. "Trust me. I'm worth it."

She waited for what felt like a minute or more, rubbing me, eyes unblinkingly riveted onto my eyes—like a challenge. Then her smile fell, she patted my crotch like it was a nice dog for staying where it was, opened the car door, leaned in to give me another, quick, soft, and surprisingly sensual kiss before exiting.

"You're so sexy," she said.

Wait—what? Sexy? But—what? Not sexy *enough?*

She got out, worked her cute little ass straight up to her apartment, and didn't even glance back as she strode quickly through the front door. I shook my head, and drove away.

I STUPIDLY CALLED HER again a couple days later, thinking I had waited long enough to not seem 'needy', but really being exactly that and unable to take her silence for what it was—a stake through the weakening heart of our 'relationship'.

"Hey, it's me, Brandon. Just wanted to chat before tomorrow night. I'm looking forward to *Beasts*," I lied. "Hearing great things about it. I was hoping we could grab some dinner before. Let me know."

When she didn't call back, I went in to work early one evening so I could catch her at the reception desk. If I didn't make a special point of it, we almost never saw one another even though we both worked for APL—Avionics and Propulsion Laboratory. I got there just as she was packing to go, and the look she gave me was less 'Oh! It's so nice to see you," and more 'what does *he* want?'

"Hey, Jessica."

"Hey," she said, not looking at me.

"Sorry. Don't mean to bug you at work. I just came to make sure you still wanted to go to the play tomorrow night."

"Yes," she said, coldly. "Why wouldn't I?"

"I don't know, I just... hadn't heard from you."

"Classes keep me busy."

"Is something wrong?"

"No." she asked. "Why?"

"You just seem... you know... distant."

"No," she said, flatly. "I'm not."

"Did I do something to upset you? You don't feel like I was pressuring you too much the other night, do you?"

"No. If anything, you weren't pressuring me enough."

"I.... what? Wait. I'm in trouble because I didn't push *harder*?"

She clutched her books tightly against her chest, leaned closer and spoke with an edge in her voice.

"A girl needs to feel like you really *want* her."

"But... what about: 'no means no'."

"I'm not asking you to *rape* me. Just be a man and show me you *want* me."

Glaring at me, she walked out the front door, leaving me more lost than I'd ever been before.

I ENDED UP SEEING *BEASTS* alone. A waste of expensive tickets for something that wasn't really my kind of thing; dancers in animal costumes, and people who sing their way through life's tragedies. But I didn't want to feel like I was missing out on something because of Jessica, her last minute text making me all the more determined to live life without her.

Sorry. Can't make tonight. Hope you'll be able to give my ticket to someone else. Really busy these days, but it would be great to see you. Have fun! Call me when you get a chance!

I *had* called her. Repeatedly. And I *had* given her ticket to someone else— a gay man who'd been waiting with friends and was thrilled with the gift—and disappointed that I was straight. I wish I hadn't been so pigheaded and given *mine* to someone else.

I re-read her message and noted that it was polite, impersonal, and easily defensible if read by another man.

I DROVE HOME IN a fog, my mind swimming over elements of the play that paralleled my own life.

The story had centered around a couple stranded on a deserted island that won't give in to their animal passions because they're committed to other people. They spend hours dancing around the subject—literally—only to give in to their passions in the third act, and immediately regret it.

I pulled slowly to a stop and parked on the street in front of my house—or, rather, my *parent's* house. I sat quietly and thought about Jessica—how beautiful she was, how funny, how desirable, and knew she must have better offers. I lived with my folks, and as a prospect was only one step above a jobless, homeless transient. We were both young—I was only twenty-three, and really couldn't do any better—not yet, anyway—so it didn't seem that big a deal to me. But it obviously was to her.

Variations on the theme of 'what was I doing wrong' seeped into my soul like a slow acting poison as I reluctantly got out of the car and walked inside to face the inevitable 'pep-talk' with my father.

"Hey, dad," I said, entering the family room, trying to hide my depression behind a smile. "How's retirement?"

"Good," he said, sitting comfortably in the shifting glow from the television. "Great, actually. Watched eight hours straight of *Walking Dead* and no one complained."

I laughed.

"How was your date?" he asked.

I shrugged. "Wasn't a date. Jessica blew me off."

"Ah!" Dad said, shaking his head. "Girls. Well, just ignore her. Play her little game."

"Play her little game?" I asked, confused.

"Yeah. Girls play these games. Just go along and be patient."

"What kind of games?"

"The 'are you worthy' games."

"And why should I play?"

"Good things come to those who wait."

I stared at him, unsure.

"You're young," he continued. "Kids always want everything *now, today, right away.* You think the world will end if you have to wait two minutes for something. But sometimes the best things in life are worth waiting for."

"Dad. It's not like that..."

"I waited for your mother. Waited a couple years for her. And I waited for the right job. I waited for retirement. It's the waiting that makes what you want all the sweeter when you get it. If things are handed to us, we don't appreciate 'em."

"And how long—exactly—do I wait?" I asked. "At what point am I just waiting for something that's never going to happen?"

My father shrugged.

"Depends on the woman," he said. "Just remember: it's always darkest before the dawn, and tomorrow is another day."

I stared at my dad and *really* wanted to believe his string of clichés. *Really* wanted to. Clichés become clichés for a reason, right? And what did I know? I was just a kid, comparatively. He'd lived, at least. But...

"Yeah," I said, deciding I just didn't want to talk about it anymore. "Let's see what tomorrow brings."

"Ignore her. Make her want you."

"Okay."

"Hang in there."

"Night dad."

"Night, Brandon."

My father had been a tool and die fabricator in New York who retired to Connecticut after moving the family there before I was born. He saw the writing on the wall as his profession gradually became outsourced to computer-operated machinery, when pride and

9

craftsmanship alone were no longer enough to hold a job in a business that increasingly required accuracy down to a microscopic level. He kept talking about starting a business, getting into another line of work entirely, maybe opening a bookstore, or a video store, or—I don't know—something.

A week before our conversation he'd taken early retirement with the hope of finding a new direction in life—whatever that might be—so he could finally do all the things he'd wanted to do when he was young... after a couple weeks of relaxing and watching TV, that is.

That night he died.

I won't get into the details—my mom awakening me with tearful screams, images of my father's pale, overweight body being loaded onto the gurney, the gawking neighbors, the long night in the hospital waiting room—let's just say it hurt.

Of course, I wasn't ready for it, and went into a tailspin for several weeks before regaining myself. And did some stupid things when I hit bottom.

"Hey, Jessica. It's me, Brandon. Um... I was hoping I could see you. I really need someone right now, and you're tops on my list, so... please call me."

"Hey, Jessica. Not sure if you got my last message, but I could really use a friend right now. Please call me. It's Brandon, by the way."

"Jessica. It's Brandon. Uh... in case you hadn't heard, my dad died, and I... I don't know. I'm not sure why I'm calling you."

"Really? How heartless are you? Can't you even send a text, or respond to me at all? My fucking dad died! Jesus."

"Hi Jessica. Sorry about that last message. Been a little rough. (PAUSE) Take care. (PAUSE) Bye."

DEPRESSED AND ANGRY, lost, and confused was my complex emotional state the night I ran into her, and pretty much why I killed her boyfriend.

HOW TO KILL A MAN WITHOUT REALLY TRYING

I PAID FOR THE pizza I intended to share with Milton Alvarado, a scientist friend of mine at APL, and as I stepped out the front door folding my receipt with the number they would call in about fifteen, twenty minutes, I nearly bumped into Jessica walking down the sidewalk toward me. She was with some guy. They had their arms around each other, and were cuddling like old lovers—which they probably were. The affection she showed him made me doubt that the end of their evening would leave *him* 'waiting'.

It shouldn't have surprised me—or hurt me—but it did.

I saw them before they saw me, and was so stunned—especially because she was so much happier with this asshole than she'd ever seemed with me—that I just stood in the shadows of the restaurant awning and stared at them, kind of idiotically.

He was one of those ridiculously handsome guys who probably slept in Tupperware so he awoke perfect and handsome every morning, ripped, tanned, coiffed and ready for the day at precisely seven.

They were laughing, he a little less joyfully than she. I noted that the 'unbalance' in *their* relationship was all on her side, he a bit cool and distant, she, clutchy and adoring, never taking her eyes off him which is why she didn't notice me. At one point he made a joke, she laughed

11

harder than any joke could have warranted, and gripped his ass in a quick gesture of appreciation and promise.

He clearly didn't want her as much as she wanted him, which made me the door prize if he ever came to his senses and moved on. Something he most likely would do, if she ever told *him* he had to wait for sex.

He smiled at her little grope, and seemed pleased with where the evening was going right up until he saw me staring at them.

For some reason our eyes locked. Mine unblinking, and unfocused. His curious, and slowly angering.

"You got a problem?" he asked.

"Oh, my God!" Jessica said, finally seeing me.

"What?" Ridiculously Handsome asked. "Who is he?"

"That's the guy from work," she said under her breath, quietly enough that I could still hear. "I told you about him, remember?"

"Oh," he said, relocking eyes with mine. "Yeah."

And what—exactly—had she told him?

Still not blinking I shifted my gaze over to Jessica, whose cheeks had flushed bright red. She said nothing, and continued leaning against her 'beau'.

"Did sex complicate things with *him*?" I asked her.

She remained silent, only swallowing, nervously.

I turned my attention back to Ridiculously Handsome.

"She make *you* wait before she fucked you?" I asked in that intentionally vague way that makes it sound like I had fucked her.

I really don't know why I said it. Really don't know why I was pushing it. I'd long suspected Jessica was sleeping with someone else—someone she was into way more than me. Maybe several someones. And I had... well... this wasn't... I was angry—I admit—about her blowing me off without so much as an explanation, angry about my dad, angry about a lot of things.

But I *wasn't* angry enough to start what happened next.

At the moment I was just feeling bad, hurt, stupid and used, and all I really wanted was to not feel that way, anymore. And getting in the face of the dick who'd beat me out in competition for Jessica was perfect for making me forget the pain. Petty, I admit, but perfect. So I asked my jerky little question, and stood there not letting either of them off the hook.

"You make him wait, or did you fuck him right away?" I asked Jessica, making her gasp, and look afraid for her life.

It was all good fun right up until Ridiculously Handsome took exception to me saying dirty words to the girl-he-sort-of-liked-because-she-would-have-sex-with-him, and began to puff up, insisting that I 'take it back.' Take what back, asshole? I asked her a question. I didn't call her names.

So he kept insisting, having crossed the line over into protective, dominant male, while I simultaneously crossed a mental line of my own and decided—internally; *I'm taking nothing back, fuckwad, and in fact if you keep pushing it, I'm going to make you eat shit.*

See, I'd studied some karate, and worked out a little. Enough to defend myself, anyway. In most circumstances a little karate is plenty because the percentage of guys who actually know how to fight is really low. So when Ridiculously Handsome stepped up to me and got in my face, trying to intimidate me, I was all fine and good—completely comfortable with my manhood. But when he shoved a finger in my face and started pushing on the tip of my nose, while, for emphasis, slapping my cheek to punctuate each word in his sentence—well—things got a little out of hand.

"You…" *slap,* "…don't…" *slap,* "…talk…" *slap,* "…that…" slap, "…way…" slap, "… to her!" *SLAP!*

The last slap was strong enough to knock me back against some guy's car, and that's when people finally seemed to notice something was actually happening close enough to them to potentially be a problem. I heard a gasp, some shuffling feet, scooting chairs, and felt the masculine shame of being manhandled by an asshole.

I started to get up off the stranger's car, but Ridiculously Handsome shoved me back onto it, with a kind of grunted warning that I should stay put, keeping his palm on my chest for emphasis as he turned to Jessica and snarled.

"Did you fuck this guy?" he demanded.

"*NO,* I…"

And that's when he punched me. If you've ever been punched, bare knuckle, you know it hurts like hell. Pain sears into your face, blood thumps the wound, and your brain takes a minute to stop jello-ing around inside your skull so you can think straight.

"Are you, *sure?"* Ridiculously Handsome growled.

"Josh, *NO!* I *swear! I barely know him!"*

"Don't lie to me, *cunt!"* He screamed, as he punched me again. Clearly taking his anger at her out on me.

Well, I guess I *had* implied something, so I'll take some of the blame, but not all of it. What happened next wasn't *just* my fault, right?

See… in karate the *first* things they teach you go entirely toward handling situations like this. Typical bully, typical bar fight nonsense. So even though I never got beyond a green belt, I could handle this. And suddenly I was *really* motivated to handle it.

Very calmly, and very quickly, I reached up and grabbed Ridiculously Handsome's non-punching hand off my chest with *my* non-dominant fingers and twisted his arm around until he was hurting, really hurting, and off-balance. Then—while he was unsteady and just struggling not to look like a puss, though pretty much helpless and already practically crying—I punched him in his fucking face.

Unlike him, I knew where to aim. Bridge of the nose, first two knuckles between the eyes.

Blood gushed like a fountain from both of his nostrils, and I was amazed at how fast his face started swelling up. It shocked us both. Him maybe more than me.

I wasn't shocked enough to stop, though. Because now I was pissed.

Still twisting his hand I hammered him again in the side of his head, and watched the skin on his face flop around like it was slo-mo water I'd thrown a brick into. Then I let go, drew back the hand I'd held him with, clenched it into a fist and slammed that into the opposite side of his face—you know—just to balance out the bruising.

Unexpectedly for both of us, the impact toppled him over and back, right through the pizza store's plate glass window.

Jessica was screaming, glass was exploding all around us, and a piece of crystal razor guillotined down and ripped through the guy's arm and chest. I guess it must have severed an artery. I've never seen so much blood rush so quickly out of a human being. He went completely pale, looked like death, and held out his arm to stare at the wound as if he couldn't believe what had just happened. He began to moan, incoherently, his eyes widening with fear and horror. Still in a rage, feeling no sympathy at all at that point, I stepped up to pop him once again in his pleading, begging, wimpy fucking face. The fight was way beyond over, but I wanted to punch him again anyway.

But my mind cleared before I popped him, and I began to feel empathy, so I paused, and suddenly someone was pushing me off him, while someone else was yelling to call nine-one-one, a third guy was screaming to apply pressure to the wound, and Jessica was just shrieking nonsense, kneeling beside the lover boy she hadn't made wait, while I stood there, the anger draining out of me the way his blood was draining out of him.

Jessica turned suddenly to me with tears in her eyes she would never have shed for me, and screamed.

"What is WRONG with you?"

I honestly didn't know. I just knew she hadn't told me the truth, it had made me angry, that guy had started it, and now everything was a mess. I walked away thinking how us not having sex hadn't made this any *less* of a mess.

GUNS DRAWN

I GUESS I SHOULD have helped. I guess I should have stayed around. But my mind was a cyclone. For a moment I wondered if it was over with Jessica, and then laughed at myself.

No, Brandon, no! Any minute now she's going to realize that what she wants more than anything is a violent sociopath who slices men up and then leaves them bleeding on the street! Then she'll come running!

I shook my head in a vain attempt to clear it.

"Fuck," I said quietly to myself. "What have I done? My life is over."

My phone buzzed. My mom. I stared at the glowing screen and decided to ignore it.

I had driven up to APL because I really didn't know what else to do, and sat there in the parking lot for a long, long while. What if the guy died? Would there be a trial? Would I go to prison? Even if I was lucky enough not to, would I lose my job? APL was a hi-tech facility that required security clearances, and background checks. Even just for emptying wastebaskets and vacuuming rugs.

Eventually I got out of my car and headed for Milton's office thinking the guy was going to be starving, which is when it hit me that I'd left without the pizza.

Crap. No going back for it, now.

No going back for *anything*, now.

I WAS WALKING toward the elevator, heading down the sidewalk past Lena's...I mean, Dr. Mizzelier's office. The path was almost completely blocked by a pile of broken palette wood; apparently fragments left over from some crate that had been destroyed removing whatever had been inside. I thought for a moment about how it was probably going to be my mess to clean up, and then realized I'd probably be in jail, and wouldn't have to clean up anything at APL ever again.

I was just stepping around the debris when Dr. Mizzelier opened the door to her office and startled us both.

Her perfumed scent drifted lazily in the air, and when she turned to me I noticed she wore mascara, her lips redder than usual. She is, in not just my opinion, a very beautiful woman, but usually more plainly made-up because she didn't need to impress anybody when she spent most of her time alone in those rooms of hers. So it stood out that tonight she looked ready for a special evening.

"Brandon!" she said, startled, and then checked her watch. "You're early."

"Oh, uh..." I said, trying to sound casual. "I have to see Milton."

"You and Milton," she said, smiling. "I hope there's nothing going on between you two?"

"No, I just..." I flinched a little. "He's been a good friend, lately, is all."

"Do you need a good friend?" she asked, smiling.

I lowered my head and avoided the question. I hadn't told her my dad had died, and she had been the one to set me up with Jessica, so I never felt comfortable discussing my relationship—or lack thereof—with her. And now seemed like a bad time to start.

"Well, what's Milton going to do when you aren't around any longer... because you're spending all your time up at UMPA?"

I stared at her blankly for quite a while, until slowly—very slowly—it sunk in. On my behalf she'd offered to talk to the chancellor at the university where she taught, and he'd apparently agreed to help get me into the school. It was the longest of long shots for a poor kid like me; with the crappy grades I'd had in school and not even enough money for the application fee. But Dr. Mizellier had come through. My mind began to wander with thoughts of attending classes while I was in prison.

"They're willing to grant you admittance," she said confirming my train of thought. "More importantly, I think you've got a shot at that scholarship."

Her smile fell, as she saw no change in my expression. I continued to stare at her blankly; overwhelmed with a deep sadness about how completely I'd just fucked up my life. She was offering me the sky, but one moment of anger, a second of lost control, and it was all gone. Completely blown. College, a scholarship, a future, a life beyond being a loser janitor. Maybe Jessica. Maybe... maybe everything I'd ever wanted... flushed like the shit my life had so suddenly become.

16

"Aren't you excited?" she asked, obviously reading my mood.

"You, uh..." I said, struggling to find coherent words, "you have no idea."

I couldn't focus. I only wanted to *not* think about the ruin I'd just made of my life.

"Are you okay?" she asked.

"I don't... I just..."

My phone buzzed against my thigh like an angry swarm of bees, and wanting to avoid a conversation with Dr. Mizellier anyway, I finally gave in, took it out and answered the damn thing.

"Hi, mom," I said.

She was crying. Sobbing. She sounded like she was in fear of her life.

"Mom...?"

"Brandon, the police were just here. They got your address from the credit card company off the number you left at some pizza place. What's going on? They said you killed someone!"

"I... what?" My voice fell almost to a whisper. I was shocked to my core. "He *died*?"

"You mean you DID kill someone?"

"No, Mom, I was just..." I held a finger up to Dr. Mizellier, she nodded understanding and I walked away.

"Mom," I continued, turning away, whispering as Dr. Mizellier stood watching me from her door. "I was just defending myself..."

"Brandon, what happened? I know you're a good kid, honey... the best! But since your dad died..."

"This has nothing to do with that, mom. The guy was being a jerk to this girl, and..."

"So you *killed* him?"

"Oh, Jesus."

I heard sirens coming down the long road up from town and fear ripped through me.

"Mom? Did you tell the police where I worked?"

"They wanted to know where you were! I figured it had to be a mistake!"

The sirens stopped, but I could see red and blue flashers out near the main guard shack.

"Mom, I have to go..."

"Brandon, what happened?"

"Nothing! It'll be all right! I promise! But I have to go!"

"Bran—"

God, I wanted to cry. One stupid mistake, one idiotic moment of passion, and my life was now completely fucked.

My head swam, its thoughts a turbulent morass of uselessness. I thought of giving myself up. I thought of running. I thought of... everything stupid and nothing smart.

My brain was a mess. I needed help. I needed advice.

Milton.

I began walking toward the elevator as Dr. Mizellier called after me.

"Brandon?"

Ignoring her, I ran the rest of the way to the elevator and rode up to the next floor, and Milton's office. The lift stopped, the doors opened, and filled with a man in uniform. My heart stopped.

"Got your pizzas, buddy," the delivery guy, said.

"Holy crap, you scared the *shit* out of me," I said laughing, but still an emotional wreck inside.

"You left 'em at the store, so I brought 'em up. I knocked at the office door, but the old guy didn't answer."

"He gets focused, sometimes," I said, calming down a little. "Sorry."

I'd paid for the pizzas at the store, so I tipped him, then took the boxes and drinks.

"What's going on?" he asked me, looking in the direction of the flashing lights of the cop cars pulling into the parking lot.

"No idea," I said.

"Big night for the cops. Some dude got killed tonight right outside our store. So gross. Blood everywhere. It's gonna wreck business."

"Really?" I said, trying not to sound like the person who'd killed the guy—and worse—wrecked business. "Wow. Well... thanks again."

"No problem, Brandon. Anytime."

The guy remembered my name. Of course he remembered my name. He delivered pizza to me and several other APL night owls probably every night of the week. I shook it off and walked away from the patrol cars toward Milton's office without looking back, fearing eye-contact might make the cops recognize me, or something, and come running right away. I felt a shiver of fear run down my spine and goose my ass.

The pizza guy rode down in the elevator, and I used my janitor's passkey to let myself in to Milton's lab. As expected the older engineer sat motionless at his desk, but instead of working, his head was down resting on his arms. He didn't so much as twitch when I came in.

"Hey, Milton," I said, trying to sound cheerful.

No answer. He just lie there... as dead as Ridiculously Handsome. I stared for a while at my old friend, a little worried, but saw that he was still breathing and let it go. Maybe he was taking a nap... or maybe he was just being Milton. Since he wasn't talking I took the opportunity to go to the window and peek out onto the parking lot below.

Down near the cop cars I watched as the pizza guy stepped over to a uniformed patrolman, and one of the armed security guys who worked the night shift. They were all talking calmly in short bursts. The pizza guy was gesturing vaguely and nodding, then he looked right up at me, and pointed. I felt certain he and the cop both saw me—they must have—then the cop reached down to unsnap the holster covering his gun, already moving at a fast walk in my direction. He was followed closely by the security guard, who was also opening his holster. Both men spoke excitedly into their little shoulder talkies as they broke into runs.

They were coming after me with weapons drawn.

"Oh, my fucking God," I whispered.

"Wake up, Milton!" I said, smiling fakely and trying not to sound as terrified as I was. "Take my word for it, whatever it is, I bet my day's been worse."

I set the pizzas down and began to pace like a lion in a circus cage, desperately trying to figure out what to do next.

"Is that right?" Milton asked, simply, without lifting his head. "They've killed my mole. What comparable horror has happened in your life?"

"Killed your what?"

"My mole."

"What do you mean, 'killed' it?"

"Killed it. Scrapped it. Junked it. Made it redundant." He lifted his head and finally turned to me. "Choose a euphemism, Brandon. Any will do."

"That was today?" I asked, feeling like a bad friend.

"That was today. It all ended today. I'm sorry," he said, returning his head to his desk. "I don't feel like pizza tonight."

I waited a moment, until a sad realization finally hit me.

"Just the project?" I asked, gently.

"No," he said, weakly, "the man, as well. So tell me how has your day been worse?"

"Oh… well… I murdered someone, and the cops are coming up here right this very second with guns drawn."

"Very odd joke, Brandon, but all right. If you really murdered someone…"

He stopped mid-sentence. Very slowly he lifted his head and turned to me, a stunned expression melting his face into weirdly shifting patterns of horror and disbelief. He studied my eyes very seriously for a moment and apparently saw truth in them, somewhere.

"Brandon," he said, carefully. "What's happened?"

"I accidentally killed a man—in self-defense—sort of—and the police are…" I heard a familiar noise. One I didn't often hear this time of night. Motors throbbing to life in a hollow, concrete shaft. "And they're coming up in the elevator right now, armed."

Milton continued to look at me as if he'd never seen me before. He glanced at the door, then back at me.

"Brandon?" he asked.

I sat on the edge of the desk across from him and felt nearly as low as he did. I was scared, genuinely terrified, and I know he had been, too, before I came in. He was older in a world that favors the young. We were both looking at a kind of end to our lives. But at least his didn't climax in prison ass-rape.

"Put the pizza down and help me with something," he said, suddenly, getting up and walking toward me.

"What?" I asked.

"Quickly, quickly," he said.

He climbed a small, metal ladder and removed a hatch from the full-scale model he'd been constructing, and handed it to me.

"Take this," he said, and I did. "Put it on the table, there."

He began pulling out modular components, handing those to me as well. I placed them alongside the hatch.

"That should be room enough. Now, get in."

"What?"

"There's no time, Brandon. Please. Quickly. Get in."

I did as he suggested, and he pressed me into place with a shove, carefully tucking in my stray bits of clothing. Then he grabbed the lid off the table and replaced it over the hole in the mole's hull.

"Ow! Fuck!" I said, as he pinched me.

"Sorry," he whispered. "Now remain completely silent."

Latching the hatch with a couple bolt twists, he climbed down and went back to his chair, replaced his head on the desk, and waited.

The wait was short. Almost immediately there was a loud knock on the door, and one of the cops yelled; "POLICE! OPEN UP!"

"*Open up, yourself!*" Milton answered, angrily.

Something swiped and clicked, and the door burst open. I couldn't see it, but I assumed the cops were entering with barrels held out threateningly before them, clearing the room.

"Why didn't you open the door?" one of the men asked after a substantial length of time searching.

"I thought it was a joke," Milton said. "I thought Brandon was being funny, and I'm not in the mood for funny."

"Brandon Mack?" The cop asked. "The janitor?"

"Yes," Milton said. "What's this about?"

"We need to ask him some questions."

"With guns?"

"Something happened tonight that warrants caution."

"But..." Milton asked, nervously, "*guns?*"

"So... you haven't seen Brandon tonight?"

"No."

"Then how did this pizza get here?"

I cursed inwardly. If Milton had only told me what he was doing...

"Maybe he left it," Milton said.

"But you said you hadn't seen him," the cop asked in that suspicious, cop way.

"And I haven't. When he came in before, I had my head down and never picked it up."

"Why not?"

"I've had a rather bad day," Milton responded tiredly. "And just so you know, this isn't making it any better."

There was a moment of silence, and I heard feet moving around. Coming closer.

"Why has your day been bad?" The approaching cop voice asked, his sympathy sounding pretty genuine.

"Well," Milton began, "first thing this morning I was told that my last five years of sweat and toil have been a waste of time and money, and my dream project was shut down. Just for good measure I was told that I—personally—was a waste of time and money, and was also shut down—with severance. I was supposed to be cleaning out my office, but mostly I've just been sitting here, with my head down, contemplating the cruel nature of existence."

"I'm sorry," the cop said, still sounding sincere.

"And now you've come to tell me that Brandon—someone I care very much for," Milton said, sadness cracking his voice, and I felt touched, "someone I've enjoyed many hours of pizza and beer with—is in trouble with the law, and that only makes my day infinitely worse."

"You two have been very close since his father died?" the cop asked.

There was a silence. When Milton spoke again, his voice was barely audible.

"I... suppose so."

I had never told Milton about my father.

"You okay?" The cop asked Milton.

"I just..." Milton began, and I heard the confusion and pain all too clearly, "it hadn't occurred to me that... yes. We've been close. I like Brandon. He's a good man."

"Did Brandon help you with your work?" Another voice asked, and I had to force myself not to jump. The voice was inches from me, just the other side of the mole's hatch.

"Only in that he listened when I needed someone to listen. Brandon was the janitor—but he's so much more than that. He's too smart to be cleaning floors."

"Did he ever talk to you about a girl named Jessica?" The more distant voice asked.

"Often. Usually with considerable sadness."

"Did he ever mention getting even with her—or her boyfriend?"

"Never. I'm fairly sure he didn't even know she *had* a boyfriend. He never mentioned one to me. Only Jessica... and he was beginning to move on from her."

"Move on with whom?"

"Ummm... no one. Just... you know... move on."

"So running into her with another guy," The cop beside me asked, scaring the shit out of me, again, "might that cause him to become unexpectedly jealous? Or violent?"

"Brandon?" Milton asked, astonished. *"Violent?* The man was a lover, not a fighter. Just ask... uh... I mean... if he fought with *anyone, they* must have started it."

There was silence while the cops digested that.

"This your work?" the closer cop asked, again jolting me.

"Yes," Milton said. "It's a mechanical mole for mining on Mars. Or Venus. Asteroids, possibly—that would require no tripping of the system. At least it was."

"Tripping of the system?"

"You wouldn't have to remove the drill assembly to replace cutters, remove cuttings—things like that."

"It just keeps going?"

"Ideally, yes."

"Kind of sharp?"

"In places."

"So... you cut yourself on it? There's blood here. Pretty fresh."

My skin electrified. As silently as I could I touched the arm where Milton had pinched me, and felt the wetness there, dripping down, and apparently out of the mole. I grimaced and applied pressure to stop the flow.

"I'm afraid I did," Milton said. "The hazards of working with custom-fabricated metals."

"Can we look inside?" The cop asked, and my stomach tightened into a solid knot of fear. The door beside me began to shift and wiggle, slightly.

"Why would you want to do that?" Milton asked.

"Just to look," the cop answered, forcing a jaunty sound in his voice that I didn't buy for a second.

There was an extended silence. Fairly long and drawn out. Was Milton coming closer? Was he going to open the hatch? As if in response, it wiggled beside me with more vigor.

"You're not hiding Mack in there, are you?" the cop joked, but he wasn't joking.

"It's filled with computer components," Milton responded. "There's no room for a man in there."

"Really?" I heard hands testing the fit of the latch beside me; I watched it turn, slightly, and my hair stood on end. "Looks to me like you could fit a *couple* guys in there."

"Trust me," Milton said, trying not to sound agitated, and failing. "There's no room."

23

"So… can we?" The cop asked again, still forcing 'casual', the latch still jiggling beside me. "Have a look?"

"Do you have a level five security clearance?" Milton asked.

The cop laughed.

"Pretty sure the answer to that is a 'no'," he said, I heard the latch settle back into place, and footsteps moving away. "But I'll look into getting one."

That last sounded like a warning, but after a few more questions, and a request to notify them should I return, the officers left.

Milton stayed where he was for a good long while, and said nothing. Eventually he moved to a window and looked out at the parking lot very close to my car. He told me later the policemen spent a considerable amount of time there just talking amongst themselves and to the APL security detail. Eventually another officer who had apparently been searching elsewhere joined them; they jumped in their cars and left at high speed, with no lights or sirens.

An APL guard remained close to my car.

It was almost another half hour before Milton felt comfortable opening the hatch for me.

"Well, Brandon," he said, smiling. "Why don't you tell me about *your* day?"

"MILTON, I'M SO SORRY I got you into this," I said.

"I'm not '*into*' anything," he told me. "Unless they come bursting through that door. And if they do, I'll tell them you threatened to kill me if I talked."

I laughed, and so did he.

I hadn't gotten out of the mole, just in case they *did* come back, and he had listened to my story while leaning against the equipment-covered table.

"But of all days to bring this kind of craziness to your doorstep," I said.

He waved it off as though it were nothing, got up and moved to stand near me, and his giant digging machine.

"It was a wonderful distraction. Very entertaining," he said, smiling, leaning against the mole while speaking to me in a very fatherly way. "But I'm afraid at some point you're going to have to go to the police and face this."

"I know."

"It *was* self-defense, Brandon. Even if you used too much force. How could you know to stop? The man assaulted you."

"Let's talk about something else," I said, sighing, and gripping a strut before me. "Tell me why they killed… er… shut down your mole?"

"Ooooh, I could never conquer overburden pressure," he said, dismissing it as something he had known and expected. "The deeper you go, the harder it is to keep from being crushed. Just like with anything, I suppose. In the end, it's the outside stresses that kill you."

I flinched, and he saw it.

"Why didn't you tell me your father had died?" Milton asked.

I shrugged.

"You have problems of your own," I told him.

"I'm your friend, Brandon."

"And you've been a friend, even if you didn't know how much of one, just by being there and helping me to forget."

"Well, I certainly did have problems of my own."

"Why would they do this to you after all your hard work?"

"I can't really blame them," he said, sighing, looking around at the full-sized, practical drill. "People are starving on this world, why waste money trying to dig dirt on some other?"

"But your dreams…"

"Dreams are fine. But shouldn't I be putting my mind to more practical use?"

"Asteroid study *is* practical, Milton! One of those things hits the earth and it's goodbye human race! Or most of it, anyway."

"My studies had nothing to do with mass extinction, Brandon. This was about going deep under the Martian polar ice, and finding signs of life—or at least the essential chemical components of it—not the prevention of potential death."

"Can it be re-purposed?" I asked, standing up and looking the huge metal mole over as if I knew the slightest thing about it. "Maybe turned into a prospector for use here on Earth, or something?"

"I suppose it's possible. But it's hardly cost-effective. It has busloads of unnecessary equipment because it's designed to be run remotely, from millions of miles away in extreme conditions, without human contact. And anyway, beyond that… I don't own the rights," he said, sighing. "Those, the prototype, here, and the underlying concept are all owned by APL."

"But there has to be a way!" I said.

"Why is this so important to you, Brandon?"

I looked at him, sadly, and forced a smile.

"Because I like you, Milton. And I want to see you achieve your dream."

"Why? Because you watched your father fail to achieve *his* dream?

"And when he finally retired, all his kids were grown, he had a chance to achieve it…"

"… And then he died," Milton said, with deep sympathy.

"Yes."

"I'm not going to die, Brandon," he said, smiling sadly.

"I know. Because we're going to find a way to achieve *your* dream."

He placed a gentle hand on mine.

"My dream was to find life in the universe, Brandon. Not gold in South Africa."

MILTON AND I SAT until the early morning hours, essentially back-to-back, drinking beers from a small fridge he kept beside his desk, talking about everything from the best cannoli we'd ever had to what it would mean for society and religion if he *had* been able to find life on Mars. At some point during the night he'd finally climbed inside the thing with me so he didn't have to keep craning his neck up to talk to me.

"I don't think religion would collapse and implode, as many have theorized," Milton said. "Instead I believe it would grow, and expand, becoming more inclusive, deeper, stronger, and more accepting of divergent points of view. God will *still* have created it all, Brandon. Just not with a snap of His fingers."

"In your opinion."

"You don't believe in God?"

"Not one that robs men of their lives and dreams. Or lets children starve in Africa, or get cancer, or die in car crashes…" my voice became quieter, and more somber, "or let's someone ruin his life simply because he lost his temper."

I tore at the label on my beer bottle and thought of my night. Milton was respectfully silent.

"Will you visit me in prison," I asked, smiling.

"Can we eat something besides pizza?" he replied, and I could hear the grin in *his* voice.

"My dad used to say that everything was *more* intense for the young," I said, "more dramatic, more immediate, the consequences apparently greater. We know—because older, more experienced people keep telling us this—that life ebbs and flows, goes up and down; but at our age, we only know that the ups and downs are *so* intense that they couldn't possibly get any *more* intense. So, when a dream is taken away from you, or an opportunity is lost..." I paused, and thought about it. "When a girl doesn't want you the way you want her, you think 'I'll never love this way again.' The emotions are *so* powerful that you can't conceive of any love greater, or stronger... or better. It's just horrifying to contemplate there being something *more* passionate than what you feel now—because a pain *that* big would destroy you."

Milton didn't answer for a while, and I just picked at my bottle.

"Believe me," Milton finally answered, kindly, "the ebb *will* end, life *will* flow, and you *will* feel that way again, someday, Brandon. Only next time—she will reciprocate."

"Did someone ever reciprocate for you?"

"Oh, HELL no!" he said, and we both laughed. "But you're younger and better looking than I. You still have time. God will provide."

"But there will always be games," I said. "Codes, and indirectness that I will never understand."

"Not when she's the one who's right for you."

"And will God provide an outlet for you and *your* dreams, Milton?" I asked.

Milton didn't respond.

"Maybe you can get someone like that Virgin trillionaire guy to finance you," I said. "On an all new mole that APL *doesn't* own."

"Yes," Milton said, his voice telling me he didn't think he ever could, not in a million years. "Perhaps."

I wanted to say more, to encourage him further, to make him know that this wasn't the end as it had been for my father, but a click at the door silenced me. Someone was using a card key.

The two cops from earlier burst in, guns drawn, aiming them pretty much at my face. Obviously they hadn't bought Milton's story about no one being inside the mole.

Scared shitless, but thinking I was glad it was actually over, I raised my hands and told them not to shoot.

That's when Milton's mole suddenly rumbled to life, shaking like an earthquake. In fact, at first, I thought it *was* an earthquake.

"What did you do, Brandon?" Milton yelled.

"I don't know! Nothing! Maybe I bumped this switch!"

"You turned it on?"

"What do you mean, 'I turned it on?' **This thing is functional?"**

"Of course it's functional!"

The noise was deafening. The movement terrifying. I tried hitting whatever buttons I'd hit before, but nothing happened. For a full minute neither of us could do anything but cling with the absolute desperation of drowning men to the inner walls of the screaming, whining, drill machine.

"SHUT THAT THING DOWN!" The nearest cop yelled to be heard over the noise.

"WE DON'T KNOW HOW!"

He pointed his gun more forcefully, as if he needed to, and yelled louder.

"SHUT THAT DAMN THING DOWN!"

And suddenly we dropped!

I watched as the floor rose up past the half-closed hatch, and slammed it shut. The mole instantly ripped through tile, sub-floor, wood, wires, and whatever the hell building materials were between us, and the room below. A bullet exploded through the shell of the mole and scraped my cheek. Then another, and another!

"SHIT!" I yelled.

Damn those fast repeating police Glocks!

After a minute of deafening grinding, we suddenly fell, the drill lurched sideways, there was a horrible grating screech, and a massive flash of light as we ripped through something electrical that seemed to blaze through my eyelids, pierce my brain, and rip open my soul. As quickly as it struck the light faded, the inside of the little vehicle began to smell horribly, musty and dank, as we—I had to assume—drilled headlong through the ground floor and into the earth below!

"Are you okay, Milton?" I asked.

"Fine!" Milton replied.

"Not shot, or anything?"

"I don't believe so!"

"How do we stop this thing?" I asked.

"With the controls in my office!"

"I don't think I can reach those from here!"

"I'd be surprised if you could!"

"There's no way to turn this off from the inside?"

"Not from where we're sitting!"

*"Milton! **What do we do?**"*

*"**I don't know!**"*

The vehicle rumbled for a while, grinding and ripping its way into the planet, God only knew how deep under the hills below APL.

"How far can this thing go?" I asked the old man, calming a little.

"As deep as it needs to."

"And how deep is that?"

"I don't know. Until it hits bedrock, I suppose. But that might not even stop it. Just slow it a bit."

"Will people be able to get to us?"

He didn't answer right away, and I knew he was thinking the answer was 'no'.

"Can we turn around?" I asked.

"Not without those controls."

"So what are we going to do?"

Again, silence was my only an answer.

"Just getting laid off," I said, trying to lighten the mood, "isn't looking so bad right now, is it?"

Still nothing. Then a slight snicker.

"How much oxygen do we have?" I asked. "Will those bullet holes be a problem?"

"Your guess is as good as mine."

"I'm so sorry, Milton."

"I know, my boy. I know."

We sat in silence as the thing drove us God only knew how deeply into the seemingly endless earth. Once or twice the thing popped, or lurched, and I thought we'd reached the end of our journey, but the damn thing was too well-designed, I guess, and before long the sound of the engine returned to its steady drone, the rasping of dirt and grit once more scraped upward along the outside walls surrounding us, and we continued inexorably down.

We were going deeper and deeper into the Earth, further and further from people who might be able to rescue us, essentially inside a self-burying coffin.

MY CELL PHONE stopped working less than five minutes into the journey, and it was too dark for Milton to read his watch, so I had no idea how much time had passed. Hours? Days? Weeks? I was beginning to get hungry, and wondered if it was more than just psychological.

"Will it run out of power?" I asked.

"Of course," Milton said, then continued in a half-whisper. "In about five years."

"Seriously?"

"It is *very* well-designed."

"Damn you, Milton Alvarado."

He laughed, a little.

"We're probably beyond anyone's reach by now, aren't we?" I asked.

"I'm afraid so, Brandon."

Milton was a quiet, somewhat religious man, and I'd often interrupted him in prayer as he asked whatever God, or gods, he thought might help him with a particular problem or concern. As time dragged painfully on, I assumed he would do something similar, now.

But to my astonishment—with death staring him in the face—Milton Alvarado was transformed into a new and completely different man. From between his lips flowed—not a prayer—but a clear and steady stream of undiluted profanity, every word directed at the grindingly stubborn, unyielding machinery surrounding us.

"Not exactly what I expected to hear from you at a time like this," I noted.

"*Fuck that!*" he snapped. "I've prayed my entire life, Brandon, and if anyone had been out there listening—a god, a deity, or even just a semi-intelligent hamster running in a wheel that powers the universe, this would *never* have happened! I hoped to one day wind up in heaven, and instead I'm currently on a collision course with the eternal fires of *hell!*"

"Or the Earth's core."

"Same thing!"

"What can we do?" I asked, hiding my concern and fear behind a low and level voice.

"Nothing!" he snapped, and I heard him fidget in his seat. "At some point I have to believe our air will run out, long before *this* Goddam thing ever stops drilling!"

"Because of the bullet holes?"

"No, the bullet holes are meaningless unless one of them damaged a part of the mechanism, somehow. This thing doesn't need air to run. It's because we could end up miles below the surface, very far away from a free-flowing oxygen supply."

"Oh. So... we'll suffocate, probably," I said, my voice betraying my fear.

"Well," Milton said, softening, his concern for me tempering his tone, "perhaps we have a slim hope that we'll hit a layer of stone that will deflect us, and turn us back toward the surface. But suffocation does seem most likely," he continued on, forgetting to be comforting, and building up some emotionless, analytical steam. "I suppose it's possible that we could be cooked to death slowly as the temperature rises, or perhaps we'll actually make it deep enough to be crushed by the extreme pressures of the earth's crust and unceasing gravity, just as the review committee believed. But, no... more likely I think we're simply going to suffocate to death very, *very* slowly."

"Nice." I said.

"Not really."

"I was being sarcastic."

"Oh."

We dug along for quite a while before speaking again.

"I'm sorry, Milton."

"I know."

And, again, more silent traveling.

"It's getting hot," I noted. "Is it possible we could hit lava?"

"No, Brandon."

"Oh. Okay."

Grind, grind, grind.

"You said we might cook to death..." I said.

"Temperatures rise the further down you go... upwards of a hundred forty degrees—no lava—or rather magma—required."

"Oh."

We traveled for a while longer with nothing else to say, so I started repeating myself.

"I'm really sorry, Milton."

"Please stop saying that."

AFTER WHAT MIGHT have been another hour of total quiet, Milton surprised me with a potential out.

"We could hit water," he said, sounding hopeful. "At least then we would drown, instead of suffocate."

"Oh," I said, surprised. "That would be... something to look forward to."

"Statistics show that drowning is the most pleasant way to die, you know."

"More pleasant than dying on top of a naked woman?"

Milton laughed.

"Perhaps the study was done by scientists who go the other way," he said, giggling, and I laughed, as well.

"Then wouldn't they prefer to die on top of a naked *man?*" I asked.

"Okay, *asexual* scientists, then!"

Now we both were laughing, so hard I thought we'd pass out. Eventually we both settled down and became serious again.

"So... in theory... this thing could keep right on drilling long after we've suffocated."

"I think that's pretty likely, actually."

"And eventually we could hit something, rebound, then come up somewhere weird, a giant, spinning, mechanical mole, with two, cooked dead guys inside."

"It's possible."

"Be funny if we came up in the middle of someone's party."

"Are you getting light headed, Brandon?"

"Maybe. Either that, or I'm just losing my mind."

"Perhaps the air is getting a bit thin."

"Is it on a diet?" I asked, and laughed hysterically.

"Don't talk, Brandon. You should conserve your air."

"I'm tired of conserving. Green this, green that. Now we have to conserve air? Where's the oxygen recycling bin?"

"Brandon, please."

"God, it's so *hot!*" I yelled. "So *fucking* hot! *Will you please turn down the thermostat?* I keep telling you, I'm not made of money!" I laughed like a giddy lunatic. "And close the front door. What are you trying to do, heat up all of the great outdoors? *Jeez!* Letting all the flies in..."

In my delirium, I hadn't noticed Milton's voice getting quieter, and weaker, so I continued rambling on senselessly for several minutes more until it finally penetrated my non-oxygenated skull that Milton was no longer responding.

"Milton?" I asked. "Yo! Miiiiil-*ton!*"

Nothing. I tried a few more times, and then it hit me that the old man had actually succumbed to the lack of air. My dear friend, dead. And I'd killed him.

Inexplicably, I began to sob.

"Oh, God, Milton. I'm so sorry. So, so, so, so, so, so soooooooorry."

Against my will and all my efforts, my eyes closed, my brain dimmed, and darkness enveloped me like a hot blanket, making me comfortable for a sleep that would go on forever.

And ever.

I OPENED MY EYES and struggled to keep them open.

Breathing was difficult. I gasped and sucked at the nearly nonexistent air around us, my head fuzzed—my limbs heavy.

"Milton?" I asked, hopefully.

Nothing.

I struggled to stay awake. Or, rather, to become *more* awake. To not die.

I was still a young man. There was so much I had never done, or tried. Prison now seemed like a preferable alternative to death. I didn't want to let go of what little life I'd had.

I struggled to pull my head off of the floor where it had become wedged between metal struts, when it suddenly dawned on me that my head shouldn't be *on* the floor. I pulled myself around, and noticed Milton, slumping similarly, only a few inches from me. I wriggled nearer to him, and heard raspy, little, panting breaths.

He was alive!

And I wasn't on the floor. I was on the ceiling, and so was Milton. But why were we stuck on the ceiling?

I managed to scooch myself around and get my butt against the metal of what had been the top of the mole and looked around. Other than the stench of urine and shit because we'd both apparently lost control of ourselves while asleep, nothing had changed as far as I could tell, not that I understood any of the lights or displays blinking around me. Even so… something seemed different.

Wait.

We were turned around.

Somehow the mole had reversed itself and come back around, heading toward the surface. And I was alive! And so was Milton! We might make it out of this after all!

It was all I could do to keep from shouting and shrieking with joy. As it was, I did a little happy dance, bouncing up and down in my seat before realizing I was still almost out of air, and had no solution for that little problem.

Suddenly the mole rocked and shuddered, and fell over on one side, throwing me practically on top of Milton. The drill above me roared and rumbled, moving very fast against nothing.

It had broken through the surface! Spinning madly—running loose—in *air!* I could feel it rushing in through between the seams of the mole! Air that filled my lungs, energized my body and what was left of my brain!

We were safe! *We were going to live!*

As air gushed in, I gasped it down, waving some over to Milton, who was now breathing more normally. But suddenly, unexpectedly, I realized I was once again getting light-headed, feeling faint and exhausted, and before I could wonder why, I lost consciousness.

WEIRD WORLD

I WAS OUT FOR LITTLE MORE than a moment or two, because as I fell, I slammed into a metal crossbeam that hurt like hell, and startled me back to a fuzzy, light-headed form of consciousness.

"Son of a…"

Regaining my senses, my first concern was for Milton. I was horrified at the thought that right on the very tip of salvation he might actually have died. Tearing open his shirt I placed an ear to his chest. I could have screamed with relief—his heart was pounding, healthy and strong.

I searched around against the walls of the mole, but couldn't find a lever or handle to release the hatch cover, so leaning back a bit I raised a leg and kicked hard at the damned thing. It took four or five tries, but I was eventually able to bend it outward until it flew off and landed with a clank and a thud somewhere below.

Sticking my head out I looked around for water, or anything else that might help revive Milton, assuming he might be dehydrated. A small, stream fed pond rippled nearby, but it turned out to be unnecessary.

"Brandon," he said, weakly, and I turned to see the poor old guy trying to do what I'd done minutes earlier, attempting to right himself in the now flipped around digging machine. I bent close and helped

35

untangle his shirt from a bolt it had become hung on, and within a few seconds we'd gotten him around and upright into a sitting position.

"I'm sorry," he said.

"Why?" I asked.

"I seem to have… em…" He pointed vaguely at his crotch.

"Don't worry about it. We both have. Doesn't matter. *We're alive!*"

"The air," he said, weakly. "Where's it coming from?"

"Out there," I answered, pointing vaguely.

"Out… where?" he asked. "Where are we?"

"Back on the surface, somewhere," I said; "where, exactly, I don't know. It looks like a jungle, or a forest, or something."

"We turned?"

"Apparently."

"You said 'a jungle'? What jungle?"

I shrugged. "Your guess is as good as mine."

"How long have I been unconscious?" He checked his watch.

"No idea," I said. "I'm just glad you're all right. You gave me quite a scare."

"Three days."

"What?" I asked, not believing he could be meaning what I thought he was meaning. "You've been unconscious for three days?"

"No. We've been in the mole for three days. I have no idea how long we've been unconscious."

"Three days! That's insane!"

"It does seem unlikely."

I stared at him, completely lost as to what I should say next.

"Let's get out of this damn, stinky box." I said, finally.

He grinned appreciatively, and together we stepped out to stand in silent awe of a landscape both weird and beautiful. Behind us lie the forest I'd seen, and the small lake. Stretching out beyond that was a low, level shore that spread down toward a calm, incredibly clear, blue sea. Apparently we'd narrowly missed coming up in the middle of an ocean, or enormous lake, which I can only imagine would have been very bad. Or good, I guess, if you're looking for a pleasant way to die.

As far as the eye could see the surface of the water was dotted with tiny islands—hundreds of them—some made of towering, barren, granite, others draped majestically with gorgeous layers of tropical vegetation, dotted unevenly with magnificent blooms of vivid color.

Near us, at the outer edge of the forest sprouted up the same beautiful, colorful blossoms that glorified the islands. Beyond them lie that dark, and forbidding forest of giant ferns, heavy trunked trees, dense foliage, and thick, emerald grasses. Huge creepers hung low, drooping from tree to tree over a closely packed under-brush knotted and tangled around a mass of fallen trees and roots. The thick packed foliage created dense shadows within the jungle, a darkened gloom as inviting as a grave, the shade untouched by the noonday sun pouring unfiltered radiance from a cloudless sky.

"It was night when we came down," I said, staring up at the sun directly overhead.

"So… in three days…" Milton said, his mind trying to understand it all. "No, it should be late evening."

"Then how can it be noon?" I asked, turning to him. "Did we change time zones? Where on Earth could we have gotten to?"

For some moments the old man didn't reply. He stood with his head bowed, buried deep in thought. As he focused on whatever preoccupied him, I took the opportunity to get out of my disgusting clothing. Eventually he looked at me, his expression confused, and twisted with concentration.

"Brandon," he said, "I'm not so sure we're *on* earth."

"What?" I said, nearly laughing. "Where else could we be, Milton? You think we're on Mars? Maybe Venus? I know your mole is good, but…"

"No, not another world," he said, shaking his head, "what I'm thinking is—and I know this sounds ridiculous, Brandon—but what I'm thinking is: we've crossed a few parallels and are actually in another hemisphere."

"Another hemisphere?" I asked. "Like… where? Hawaii?" I gathered my clothes and looked around. "I'm not sure I follow you. You think maybe we angled through the earth's crust, and an ocean, and came out on some tropical island that's…?" I looked back at him and stared. "I don't understand, Milton."

He just shook his head, and suddenly noticed I was naked.

"Brandon, what are you doing?"

"Milton," I said, patiently. "Take a sniff. We're revolting, and need to get clean."

I headed toward the waters, while he sniffed at his armpits. Wincing as if in pain, Milton followed.

"What if someone comes?" he asked.

"I think they'd prefer we were clean, too."

I reached the ocean, tossed in my clothes, and dove after them. The waters were clear as glass, warm, and felt good against my bare skin. I broke the surface, grabbed my shirt and pants, and began scrubbing them out.

"*Feels* like Hawaii," I told Milton. "Come on in. The water's great."

Slowly, and cautiously, he did. After getting up to about his waist, he crouched down until the crystalline surface was up to his neck.

"Certainly smells better this way," he admitted.

"So… where do you think we are?" I asked him.

"It's hard to explain, Brandon," he replied, bobbing about in the sea, and removing his own garments. "It doesn't seem possible, based on what we know of the planet's crust. But I have no other answer. I think…" he looked at me, and apparently thought better of what he was going to say, lowering his eyes. "Never mind. I suppose the best thing for now would be to do a bit of exploring up and down the coast. Maybe we can find a native who will enlighten us with something more than my ridiculous speculation."

"Like a Hawaiian?" I asked.

"That would answer all questions, now wouldn't it?"

I agreed, and finished beating out my clothes.

"Let me get the stink out of this stuff, first," I said. "I'm not meeting any native girls with poo on me."

The upside of our crazy situation was that it had completely distracted me from Jennifer's dead boyfriend, and I began to feel like my old self. Milton looked at me with mischief in his eyes, and suddenly splashed me like a five year old. I returned the favor, deluging him with a wave that could have drowned a smaller man. He stared at me in horror, and I just smiled.

"Don't look at me like that," I said, pointing accusingly. "You started it."

But his expression didn't change. Only his mouth moved—open and closed—like a fish through a bowl.

"What's the matter?" I asked, then realized he wasn't looking *at* me, but *past* me.

"Brandon, *RUN!*"

I turned to see what he was looking at, horrified to find a smooth, black shape moving rapidly through the crystalline waters, directly at me.

"Holy, *SHIT!*" I said, and tried to do as Milton asked.

But I was in up to my armpits, and walking was *not* the best way to move in water that deep. So I dove into the translucent liquid, and swam for all I was worth. Milton was already scrambling back up onto dry sand, with me close behind him. I turned to see if the thing was still coming, and nearly shit myself again when I saw hundreds of white fangs inside an alligator-like head come thrashing up through the roiling sea, snapping only inches away from my bare ass.

In my terror, I stumbled over Milton, and fell onto some patchy grass along the shoreline. The beast behind me lunged and snapped, barely missing both me and my older friend, dragging itself from the surf on flippered proto-limbs. Luckily for us we were just out of reach, and while the monster seemed capable of walking a bit on its awkward appendages, it apparently preferred not to, and scuttled backward into the gentle waves, to slip once more beneath the clear surface.

We watched as the thing thrashed around through our floating clothes, ripping them to shreds, and ingesting parts of them. What little that remained would hardly be worth retrieving—not that we'd be brave enough to enter *this* ocean again.

Having finished its miniscule meal, the black monster circled once, then twice, and finally drifted off into the depths again in search of—I'm sure—a more fulfilling meal than our filthy pants had been.

Milton and I looked at one another in absolute amazement.

"What the fuck was that?" we both asked as one.

FOR NO PARTICULAR reason other than that it meant getting away from the mole and that thing in the water, we headed off down the shore, both of us now completely naked, except for shoes. Milton had stopped to grab a palm frond for propriety, but I'd decided to just let it all hang out. What was the worst that could happen? I could go to prison for indecency? Hardly a threat. I was already a murderer, after all.

As we walked along the sand Milton gazed intently, and very seriously out across the water. He was evidently wrestling with something, and finally reached a point where he couldn't contain whatever it was any longer.

"When you have eliminated the impossible," he said quietly to himself, "whatever remains, however improbable, must be the truth? Isn't that right?"

"What are you whispering about," I asked.

He repeated it, louder, so I could hear.

"I've heard that," I said. "Who said that? Einstein?"

"Sherlock Holmes. Have you noticed anything unusual about the horizon?"

I looked in the same direction he did, and slowly began to understand the strange feeling I'd been having since exiting the mole, a sensation that had haunted me since first kicking my way through the thing's door—*there WAS no horizon!* As far as my eyes could see the ocean continued outward and upward, dotted by those tiny islands and shoals, all fading to mere specks in the distance; but beyond them—beyond all—continued the sea, upward, ever upward as though lying against the inside of a bowl. I was looking *up* into the distance—a distance that faded gradually away in a haze of blue atmosphere that blurred together with the azure of the water. That was all. There was no clear-cut edge marking the dip of the Earth below my line of vision, only the gradual disappearance of the ocean into a mist of sky.

"I feel as though a great light is slowly igniting inside my mind," Milton continued, again looking at his wristwatch. "I believe I have partially solved this puzzle. It is now eight o'clock Pasadena time. We've been here two hours. When we emerged from the mole the sun was directly overhead." He looked up. "And where is it now?"

I turned my eyes upward and found the immense, burning ball of superheated plasma still motionless in the center of the sky. But... the sun! I hadn't noticed it before! The thing was at least three times the size of the one I'd lived under my entire life, and apparently so close I could reach up and touch the damn thing.

"Oh, my God, Milton." I said, completely awed. "Where the hell are we?"

"I think I can say quite positively, Brandon," he began, cautiously, "that we are—" but he got no further. From behind us, near the mole, came a thunderous, heart-stopping roar. Whatever it was sounded as though it stood ten stories high and ate Cadillacs. As one we turned to witness the source of that terrifying noise burst from the darkness of the forest, and into the brightness of that oversized sun.

If I—after what had nearly eaten me, and after all I'd just become aware of—still held some tenuous belief that we were still on good, old planet earth, what exploded from the forest before us would have crushed that notion completely. Bursting from between the gnarled trees and twisted roots of the jungle was an immense, monstrous creature that looked like a bear gone wrong. It was larger than a goddam elephant and covered in a thick coat of shaggy black hair, its enormous forepaws armed with massive, lethal looking claws as big as my arm.

But more shockingly still, right behind it came charging an actual fucking dinosaur! A living, breathing, running, twelve foot tall T-Rex, or some shit, racing madly after the bear-thing, and both charging hotly in our direction.

Roaring horribly the two monsters stampeded our way, one trying to catch lunch, the other hoping not to *be* lunch. Unfortunately for both Milton and I, we were 'wrong place, wrong time'. I turned quickly to the old man to suggest that it might be in our best interest to seek new surroundings—but he was gone, his back to me, a good fifty yards from where I stood, and moving like a gazelle. I would never have guessed he had it in him.

Milton's palm frond had been tossed aside, and his bare bottom was rippling crazily toward an outcropping of forest that fingered in the direction of the sea along a small spit of sand. One tree in particular looked big enough, and sturdy enough to hold us both and hopefully get us high enough to be out of reach. Feeling the tremors on the ground from the things behind me, and practically sensing their breaths on my back, I kicked it into high gear in an effort to catch up to the lightning legs of Milton Alvarado.

While the massive beasts pursuing us didn't seem built for speed, the adrenaline rush of both predator and prey was pushing them toward me at a pace that was faster than comfortable. At my hardest sprint I wasn't sure I'd have enough time to make it to the tree and safety, so—like Milton—I flew.

As I neared the trunk Milton was already monkeying up, I nearly fell over with laughter at his frantic attempts to climb, naked. His horrified glances back over his shoulder, his wide eyes and gaping mouth, coupled with his jerking, squirming attempts to get up that gnarled conifer—all without any clothes—was pretty fucking hilarious. He looked more like he was trying to have sex with the tree than climb it, and terrified its dad was going to come into the room at any second. By the time I reached the trunk myself I was laughing so hard I could barely get a grip to lift myself.

"*BRANDON!*" Milton shrieked, pointing.

And I turned just in time to see the bear-thing tumbling right at me, the jaws of the dinosaur clamped tightly around the back of its neck. I was about to be crushed by them both.

THE NAKED CAVEGIRL

I SPRANG UP TO a low branch just as the two creatures slammed hard into the base of the tree, jolting it and nearly ripping the old evergreen out by its roots. The bear screamed, struggling crazily, dino teeth sunk deep, and already drawing blood. I tried to regain a grip so I could continue my climb, but the thrashing bear again hammered into the tree's base, sending violent shudders all the way to the top.

Milton nearly fell on top of me as my fingers clawed desperately to grip a branch, and I almost dropped, my legs dangling too damn close to the heavy, thrashing bodies, flashing claws, and grinding teeth below. The old man's horrified face was now very close to mine, as his terror-stricken shrieks awakened other monsters in the grim forest that howled and rumbled all around us.

I was no longer laughing.

Getting a solid enough grip that I could finally pull myself up, I swung a leg over the branch Milton clung to, and lifted my body beside his. Holding tight to secure us both, I then helped him to his feet. Together we clutched the tree's trunk desperately as the struggling beasts continually rocked and shook it, claws now and again ripping splinters from our fragile perch. Fearing we were still too close I hoisted the flailing, old man to the next branch, getting both hands under his bony, little butt and shoving for all I was worth. He managed to roll atop the next limb, arms and legs wrapping around it with all the strength his skinny muscles could manage, and once settled, he—bless his heart—reached down to help me up.

41

But in that instant the monsters below collided violently against our little shelter and sent me flying. I landed hard, right atop their squirming bodies; the dinosaur snapping angrily in my direction, and fortunately for me I was falling away from him, and so narrowly missed losing an arm. The bear—not realizing its attacker's attentions had been distracted—bit the dinosaur on the chest, and the two turned back again on one another, which gave me a much-needed opportunity to sprint away.

"*Brandon!*" Milton called, and I looked up to see the poor, old man's anguished face staring at me with fear and concern.

"I'm fine!" I called back. "Go higher, and jump to the next tree! I'll distract them!"

"Don't be *insane!* Get yourself to safety!"

"Once I know you're out of danger!"

"*BRANDON!*"

Once I'd sprinted a good forty or so yards away I grabbed a rock, and turned on the flailing monsters, hurling the stone with everything I had. I hit the dinosaur in the eye, and it turned on me, furiously. It was about then that I realized—if I'd just left the thing alone, it probably would have killed the bear and ignored Milton and I completely while it ate.

Stupid, stupid, stupid.

Because now the thing was leaving its weakened prey where it lie, and charging at me, picking up speed rapidly with every thrust of its powerful legs.

And I had nowhere to go.

The tree Milton hid in was behind it, I was exposed on the open shore of the beach, and the nearest secondary line of trees was about thirty yards away. Not sure what else to do, I bent to pick up another, larger rock and waited, trying to figure out if I might be able to duck aside, out of range of teeth and claws, and smash it in the head.

I sighed. The instant I considered the plan, it already seemed hopeless.

Ten yards, five yards—I raised my rock, my arm now shaking—two yards... I was just about to make a sideways dive when the neck of the thing was pierced clean through by a spear that took it down, knocked it on its side, and caused it to slide to a sandy stop at my feet. It flailed and squirmed, blood gushing from its mouth and throat, but something important must have been severed by the stone-tipped javelin, because it didn't thrash long, and eventually spit a last gasp of steaming breath and lie very still, its twitching eyes the only thing to betray any sign that it had ever been alive.

Astounded, and grateful to whoever had thrown my salvation I looked in the direction from which it had come, and was even more astounded.

She would have been beautiful by any standard of measure back home. Long, wild, black hair flowed crazily over her shoulders and down her back; blue eyes as bright and clear as the sea behind me pierced hotly into mine from beneath those raven bangs; other than a few decorative necklaces, a pair of hide sandals, and a tiny loincloth, dirt-streaks and sand were all she wore to cover skin bronzed by an apparently never moving noonday sun.

Her scowl was the deepest and most confused I've ever seen on a human face, and she stood silently for what seemed like hours on the low branch of a nearby tree, staring at me as if I was the stupidest creature she'd ever seen in her life.

"Shah toonga wa noot!" she said.

"I'm sorry, I... what?" I asked.

"Shah *toonga*...!"

When I continued to look confused, she rolled her eyes in what must be a universal gesture for 'why do I bother?' and waved her hand dismissively, apparently too frustrated with my stupidity to make any further attempt at communication.

She leapt from her perch, walking quickly and forcefully to where I stood. The motion made her breasts jiggle in ways that made my knees weak, and when she stuck a foot on the neck of the dinosaur to retrieve her spear, I was astonished—and I have to admit rather thrilled—to see pubic hair peeking out from under the tiny flap of leather dangling before her privates.

Holding her foot and the spear in place, the dinosaur twitched and attempted to raise its head, but before it could pose any threat girl pulled a stone knife from her waist strap, leaned down and expertly sliced open its throat. It spasmed once, then lie completely still, even its eyes.

Wrestling the spear from the dinosaur's neck she again began speaking to me in whatever language was her native tongue, none of it making a damn bit of sense to me. Once her javelin was free she bent to wipe the blood in the sand, so I—and I admit to feeling guilty about it—took the opportunity to drink in that magnificent, nude body of hers, and the delightful way that both inertia, and gravity made the best parts of it dance.

She gestured in Milton's direction, and I looked over to see the bear-thing struggling to its feet, most of its neck ripped away, blood flowing in rivers across its sand dusted pelt. For a moment it didn't seem sure what it wanted to do, snorting and howling fiercely in our direction.

The naked savage girl lifted her spear defensively, and held out a protective arm for me to stay back. I nearly laughed at the caring gesture, but did as I was ordered and remained behind her, mostly appreciating her incredible bare behind. No loincloth back here, just a completely visible magnificent ass on either side of a tiny leather thong.

After a moment, the bear-thing snorted a few times, then lumbered off to—I have to believe—die alone somewhere in the forest. I didn't see how it could possibly survive the wounds it had received.

The pretty savage girl turned and smiled at me, saying something charming, I'm sure, with her native tongue. Her words were still a mystery, but her smile, and gestures seemed to mean, "Damn, that was a close one, wasn't it?"

I laughed and nodded, hoping she hadn't actually said something like "you'll be tasty with the right seasoning."

We both continued grinning as she looked me up and down, taking in my naked manhood with amused curiosity. For a moment she looked startled, then shook her head.

"Nashka duron doe," she said.

"If you say so," I responded.

That's when I noticed Milton was missing.

"Oh, shit," I said, running in the direction of the tree where I'd left him.

BEHIND ME THE GIRL was racing to keep up, saying something I still couldn't understand. I reached the base of the tree Milton and I had climbed, and looked up, then into the neighboring conifers, then all around on the ground. Nothing. Not even a *hint* of where he might have gone.

I turned to the girl who was scanning the area, as confused as I had been, her eyes and gestures making clear that she had seen Milton and also had no idea where he'd gone. Then she suddenly looked terrified and pointed behind me.

"Nyame!" she screamed.

And I turned to see the bear-like creature galloping back toward me, a pack of long-toothed dog-things biting it on all sides. In its mad fury, the 'Nyame' was crashing our way, blind and maddened by the vicious, almost orchestrated attacks of this new predator.

I felt my arm being yanked, and before registering everything fully, was running alongside the savage girl, trying to escape the snarling carnage behind us. But instead of running down into the soft, loose sand, the girl had taken us into the dense thicket of jungle, and—attempting to leap over a fallen branch—she hooked her foot in a vine and went sprawling over the dirt and grasses along the jungle's edge.

I bent to pick her up, but she was too twisted and tangled, so I took her spear and turned to defend us both as best I could. She shoved me away from her, gesturing for me to run, but I shook my head and scowled. She'd protected me, this was the least I could do in return. The look of surprise, and gratitude on her face was priceless.

I pointed the spear with one hand, wedged its end into the ground, and wrapped my other arm around her, pulling her to me, protectively. As the sounds of animal furor and breaking underbrush raced nearer I felt her head tuck in against my chest, and her arms wrap tightly around me. Something about her touch made me feel invincible.

The black, snarling, bleeding, frothing bear charged closer, the brushwood near me jerking and twisting fiercely from its raging battle with the dog things. I aimed my spear as best I could, and waited for the inevitable.

The 'Nyame' was nearly overwhelmed by the snarling pack of about ten leopard spotted, wolf-cat creatures—wild, earless beasts—that rushed growling and snapping at it from all sides, sinking their vicious white fangs into the slow brute, then leaping away again before it could reach them with its massive claws and sweeping tail. I followed the action with the tip of the spear, hoping to at least deflect whatever came our way. Then suddenly the bear struggled no more, and stumbled right at us, dragging two of the attached wolf creatures down on top of us.

I set the spear and pointed it at the center of the monster's mass, instantly feeling the wood flex with the sudden impact if its massive weight. Its body slid the length of the spear nearly to my clenched hand, and I shoved hard to one side, angling the momentum away from the girl and I, so that it fell on the dirt and not on us, snapping the spear as it collided with the ground.

The two leopard creatures thrashed to pull loose from the dying beast, the one closest to me already biting at me, ferociously. I shoved the broken piece of spear through the neck of my newest attacker, and as it struggled against me, the second, and then a third rose up over the heaving body of the bear monster and stalked—growling—directly toward the us.

She was working with her knife to hack away the tangle of vines pinning her ankle, and I continued to struggle with my broken piece of spear. It didn't look like either of us would get free in time.

I turned and looked at the cave girl, feeling responsible for having gotten her into this. If she hadn't become involved in my mess…

We stared at one another for what could have only been a moment, but felt like a week of frozen time.

"I'm sorry," I said, knowing she wouldn't understand me.

In the background I noticed a sudden chattering and gibbering through the lower branches of the nearby trees, and we all—the girl, the leopard creatures, and I—all turned to see a cluster of humanlike monkeys covered in light, sandy fur that seemed to be urging the wolf pack to stop. They were thin, wiry creatures with teeth sharpened to points, and prehensile tails gripping nearby tree trunks and overhanging branches.

The 'Nyame' gave one last shudder beside me; its massive body spasming in agony, and the wolf-creatures turned from us, to it, and began to feast. As they did I felt myself lifted, sandy hands gripping tightly under my armpits, a pair of tails wrapping securely around my waist. I saw the savage girl look up at me in surprise, and before being enveloped by branches and leaves, I watched as she, too, startled and struggling, was gathered up by still more monkey people.

With surprising skill and ease our captives set me on a large, high branch, and began to study me, carefully. Their eyes wandered curiously over my naked body just as the girl's had, lingering on my shoes, and my private parts. One reached out and touched the skin where my manhood joined to my body, and that sent a signal to the others, who began reaching in for a similar feel, and nearly knocked me from my perch. In an effort to avoid being tossed from the tree to what I guessed was a good fifty-yard drop, I slapped them all away, and even kicked one for good measure. A female went nuts trying to fend off my slaps, and reached out viciously to grab hold of my dangling member, nearly crushing my balls in her grip.

"Hey, hey, hey!" I yelled, smacking her away.

Suddenly—in her apparent defense—a monkey man punched me—surprisingly hard—and once I was addled, he yanked off my shoes, tossed them to her, then gripped my pits and lassoed me with a tail, lifting me once more into the open air. Joined by two others on either side, we took off at a horrifying speed through the treetops.

Holy shit! A rollercoaster can make your balls ride up practically inside your chest, but this brought mine nearly to my throat.

From tree to tree the agile creatures bounced like flying squirrels, first this way, then that, then another, as a cold sweat slowly spread over every inch of me. Any misstep by one of my carriers and I was certain to plunge to my doom on the distant jungle floor below. As they slung me along, I tried to distract myself with a thousand other thoughts, the best of them having to do with the naked cave girl.

What did these monkey-men want? Where were they taking me? Where was Milton? Would I ever see him again? And what about the girl? Was she all right? Was she flying along through the forest with two other monkey-people scaring the shit out of her? Would I ever see *her* again? *And where in the crazy fucking hell was I?*

For some reason, as important as the question of where I was might seem to have been, the question about the girl had become surprisingly much more vital to me.

I *wanted* to see her again. I considered how lucky I would be if I *could* see her again. How lucky I'd be if I survived long enough to, in a world as insane as this.

MONKEYS AND BUGS

WE MUST HAVE TRAVELED for miles through the dark and overhung woods when we suddenly emerged into a clearing, and a dense village built high among the branches. As we approached the little town center my escorts erupted into wild shrieking and shouts, which drew immediate responses from the many huts and buildings. A moment later a swarm of monkey-people poured out to meet us. Some were tall, some small, there were obvious males, and equally obvious females—clothing apparently determined by need, rather than modesty.

We dropped to a large, central platform where I once more became the center of attention for the wildly chattering horde. I was pulled this way and that. Pinched, pounded, prodded and thumped until I was practically black and blue. I don't think they were being either vicious or cruel—I was simply a curiosity, a freak, some new plaything that everyone wanted to investigate for themselves. It only became a problem when one of them once again grabbed hold of my junk.

What was the fascination?

I slapped the grabby hand away; the monkey-man recoiled and hissed angrily, offended and visibly upset. I smiled and wagged a finger at him, smiling, and faking a grab at his crotch.

"Unh, unh, unh..." I said, jokingly.

A few of the others laughed, and shoved him, one even grabbing *his* member as he had done mine. The little ape-man slapped his teasing friend's hand away exactly as I had done his, and then laughed a little as he realized that maybe he *had* gone a step too far.

With gentle force they dragged me into the heart of the village, an open area made up of several hundred fairly sophisticated huts all clustered around a massive, communal fire pit that even now burned with a large, open blaze. Overhead we were sheltered by branches and leaves that covered the community and kept us protected from the continuous heat of the perpetual summer sun.

Running between the huts were a series of crooked bridges made of planks, and logs, and dead branches, all of which connected the huts of one tree to those of adjacent trees; a complex network of rooms and pathways that formed an almost solid flooring more than fifty feet above the ground.

I wondered briefly why creatures so agile and clearly able to bridge the distances between trees even needed paths, but then a monkey man pushed a little wheel barrow into view, and another rounded a bend rolling a cart, followed by pack-animals, a couple children, and some four-legged pets; among them smaller versions of the snarling, earless cat-wolf things that had attacked the Nyame. There were also little dogs, small monkeys, and fat-uddered goat-things alongside something utterly bizarre that looked like a kangaroo crossed with a fat fish.

The monkey-man who had carried me here guided me to one of the larger huts, and indicated for me to stop and wait. I did as ordered until—responding to a chattering summons—another, larger monkey-man stepped out along with his female companion to study me carefully from top to bottom. He—like the rest of us—was entirely naked except for some decorative arm and leg bands. He was similar to the other monkey-men in every way, except that his eyes gave the sense of a sharper mind than any of the rest. He finished his inspection of me with a focused glare at my crotch, and then shook his head in seeming disbelief.

Suddenly the chattering and shrieking rose up again, and all eyes turned as one toward something behind me. I spun on my heel, just in time to see the pretty cave girl who'd saved me arriving in much the same way I had—two monkey-men supporting each armpit. They tossed her rudely to the deck of the central platform, apparently less enthusiastic about her than they had been about me. I moved to help her up, but before I could even offer her an arm she was already on her feet and shouting, eyes scowling furiously as she barked something in her local language that I wished I understood.

"Shoo sopa manteka wont!" she shouted. "Foo doh! *Foo doh, sint!*"

Then she made a rude gesture that only made her captives laugh.

Ignoring their obvious disrespect of her, she turned to me and smiled, patting my chest as if she were glad to see that I, too, was still alive. I could only smile in return, and nod, hoping I had understood her meaning. As she grinned and checked me over to see that I was all right, I saw her brows fold together in a scowl, and she bent forward to look at something below my waist.

"Shalla seppa fweet?" she asked. "Na tekka seppa fweet?"

Then—like the monkey-man earlier—she reached out and grabbed my penis, moving it around as if checking for bruises, or venereal warts.

"Na tekka seppa fweet?" she repeated, rubbing her hand up the length of it to my lower stomach where it attached to the rest of me, making a swiping sound with her other hand. "Shoop! Shoop!"

At this point, things went suddenly kind of wrong.

She was rubbing me in a way that would make any man react, but add in the fact that she was now entirely naked, likely having lost her tiny loincloth somewhere along her journey, and that her gentle rubbing movement was making her bare breasts sway in delicious ways; throw in her lustrous hair, her beautiful eyes locked on mine with the most sympathetic, caring expression any woman has ever shown me, and you can't really blame me for what happened next.

I got hard.

She noticed, and was surprised, though clearly not offended. Instead she actually seemed rather delighted by it. She glanced at the others, trying to gauge their reaction. As she did, I backed away in an effort to force my 'pointer of interest'... em... to angle itself the other way. But there was no stopping it. I can't begin to explain how incredibly overwhelmed I was by this stunning, naked cave girl and her sensual touch, other than to say that within seconds I was as hard as a tree trunk, and equally upright.

My fellow captive smiled at it, now more obviously pleased, and I had never felt more aroused. Then she made things worse by gripping it and giving it a couple quick jerks to test its firmness. I nearly spurt on her fingertips.

"Wee nagga jo-hatta," she laughed. "Yunda, yunda."

Whatever she'd said made our captives laugh, as well. With no other options, I stood there and tried not to look as humiliated as I felt with all eyes on my reddening member, and everyone laughing.

The monkey-man with the intelligent eyes smiled broadly, and motioned to the cave girl, saying something in his native language, then gestured vaguely to me, which made her laugh even harder in response. She waved her hands and shook her head as if to say "no, no, no", then pinched her tangled bush of pubic hair apparently explaining why she couldn't do whatever he'd asked. She pointed to my crotch, and I finally realized it was my lack of fuzz, and possibly a foreskin that had brought on all this unwanted attention.

Then she stepped closer to me, seemed to measure my erection with her open hands, one near my testicles, the other near its throbbing tip, moved her hands over to her genital area and shook her head, making fearful faces, as if explaining that the thing between my legs would never fit through her small opening. Having definitively made her point, she laughed again, and was once more joined by all the others.

"Oh, God," I said, humiliated.

As the laughter continued, the tent flaps on the hut behind the lead monkey-man parted, and Milton's face poked through with a look of total surprise, and absolute joy spreading out across his entire body.

"Brandon!" he said, stepping toward me, as naked as the rest of us.

"Milton!" I called. "Oh, thank God, Milton!" I yelled. "I'm so glad you're safe."

His face fell.

"Why… are you erect?" he asked, glancing down and wincing.

"Oh. Uh…" I looked down, then over toward the still smiling savage girl.

Milton looked her way, his eyes widened, and his mouth fell open.

"Oh," he said, getting it, instantly. He was old, but he wasn't dead. "I understand perfectly."

He turned back to me and grinned ear-to-ear.

"I'm so glad you escaped!" he said. "You'll understand if I don't hug you, in your condition."

"Later," I said, winking charmingly, which made him laugh.

"I saw you and some girl…" he turned and looked at the female in question, waving, politely. "Her, I suppose. I saw the two of you fall, and the bear creature run over to you with that pack of wild lycaenops swarming like bees…" He turned back to me and his face softened with an expression of deep emotion and concern. "I feared you were dead."

"No, Milton," I said, comfortingly. "In fact—I'm a little more alive than I want to be." I joked, nodding toward my still stiffened rod, and we both laughed.

"Well," he said, taking in a very appreciative view of the savage girl, "I can hardly blame you." He tore his eyes away from her beauty, and scanned the crowd, his expression becoming stern. "I wonder what these creatures intend to do with us, Brandon."

"That's got me worried as well. They don't seem to be really savage, or threatening. But—I don't know. We're not exactly guests, either. Maybe I'm expecting too much from these guys, but… what do you think they are? Where the hell are we Milton?"

"I have no certain idea."

"What do you mean, 'no *certain* idea'?" I asked, becoming even more concerned, which was—fortunately—making my erection drift downward. I avoided looking at the girl to make sure it continued that way. "You were about to tell me where you thought we'd come out of the ground when all hell broke loose."

"Yes, Brandon," he replied, "I was. Because I think I *do* know where we are. And if I'm right, we've changed the world, my boy! We've overturned *decades* of scientific belief! I believe—in all honesty—that we are at the *center* of our *Earth*."

"At the center of what, now?"

"Inside the hollow Earth!" He said, proudly. "We've proven that the planet we live on, is hollow—like a ball! And we have passed entirely through its crust to a world within our world."

"Milton," I said, gently. "That's not possible."

50

"Isn't it, Brandon? Isn't it? I estimate we bored down about two hundred and fifty miles in that mole, right through the crust of the outer world. There's no other explanation."

"There has to be. There's molten lava at the center of the Earth, Milton, everyone knows…"

"Magma."

"What?"

"Magma. Not lava. Lava derives from magma, but it is technically different."

I sighed.

"Okay, magma. There's magma at the center of the earth…"

"No, there isn't," he said, giddy with his weird thoughts. "There is a bright, gaseous star."

He pointed up.

"Milton…"

"Look at the strange fauna and flora which we've seen and in some cases nearly been eaten by. What does it take to convince you that we're not *ON* Earth anymore, but *IN* it? Remember the horizon—what other explanation do you need that we are—indeed—right now—standing upon the inner surface of a sphere?"

"But the sun, Milton!" I urged. "How can a sun just be hanging in the sky—at the center of the world?"

"How can there be dinosaurs, and cave people, and monkey-men, and a sun that *never changes position in the sky* no matter how much time elapses?"

I looked around. There was no doubt that this place defied all explanation. Things had happened so fast I really hadn't had time to process it all. I looked at the girl, she smiled at me, and I immediately regretted it. My hanging vine popped upright again, and everyone returned to laughing. All except the girl. She looked at it, then up at me, and tilted her head with such a sly, feminine, amused expression of pleasure that I nearly walked over to her and showed her that it *would* fit, dammit.

I studied the creatures near her—and me—the still fidgety monkey-people. As Milton had suggested I thought of the T-Rex and the bear and the black crocodile thing in the sea—all the weird creatures we'd seen since exiting the mole. We certainly weren't anywhere on the known surface of the Earth. Was it so unbelievable that we were actually *inside* the planet? It certainly explained the upward curve of the horizon.

"Okay, Milton," I said. "I have no other explanation for this… for *any* of this. I really don't. So let's just go with your idea and see where that takes us."

"It's really all very simple, Brandon. Edmond Halley proposed it in the 17th century. You see, the earth was once a nebulous mass…"

"I really don't care. It doesn't matter. We're surrounded by monkey-people, the horizon bends upward, and women don't shave their pubic hair. Whether we're at the center of the earth, or in a big bowl somewhere near the south of France, all that matters to me is staying alive."

"Excellent point."

Milton glanced down at my hardened dong, which bobbed up and down with my overactive heartbeat.

"You should probably stop looking at her," Milton whispered to me, quietly.

"Thank you, Milton," I said. "Good advice."

The monkey people had talked long enough, or perhaps they'd simply given up on the idea that I was going to entertain them by using my hardened, shaved manhood on someone. Whatever the reason, the chief gestured and chirped at some of his men, who immediately walked over and grabbed we three captives.

"What do you think they plan to do with us?" I asked.

In answer, the chattering returned, explosively, the monkey people swarmed as one, and we were again seized under our arms, each by a pair of the powerful, tailed people, then lifted effortlessly into the air, and slung along between the treetops. All around us, and trailing in our wake raced a chattering, jibbering, grinning horde of sleek, brown, monkey-creatures.

A couple times while flinging me around through space they nearly dropped me, but recovered almost instantly and snatched me up before I could become a lifeless pulp on the forest floor. The fact that they'd slipped seemed no bigger a deal to them than the stubbing of my toe might be to me while crossing a city street—they simply laughed riotously and kept right on moving. The upside was that my erection shriveled down to nothing, my balls yanking up to somewhere behind my eyes.

How long we flew through the treetops I'll never know because—as I was finally starting to understand—time is not a factor in the lives of the people in this inverted world. Once there is no means for measuring it, the concept of time really ceases to exist. Milton's watch was gone, and we were trapped under a motionless sun. I was already completely baffled as to how I could even compute the amount of 'time' that had elapsed since we'd burst through the crust and into this madhouse. It might be hours… it might be days… it might be no time at all.

Eventually the forest ended, and we dropped from the trees to land lightly on a level plain. Not far ahead of us rose some low, rocky hills, and our captors shoved Milton, the girl and I forward, up a path that fed into a narrow pass. After a short period of hiking through the constricted, winding crevasse, our way opened up onto a wider trail that led down into a tiny, circular valley.

The attitude of our captors changed instantly as we entered this natural arena. Their laughter stopped. Their faces set, and their eyes shot about nervously. They moved quietly, as if on tiptoe. The happy-go-lucky personalities had gone, and were replaced by aggressive ferocity—bared fangs, threatening growls, and vicious snarls.

We were shoved down an incline toward the center of the amphitheater where another captive man and woman had already been herded, as afraid as we were. As we descended, the entire tribe of monkey-men and women spread out around us into flowing rings of mounting hostility. No more laughter, no more jokes. I don't know what had changed, but it was making the group of us anxious and uncomfortable.

We five 'performers' exchanged nervous glances, then stood together at the center of the ring, backs to one another, facing outward defensively, waiting uneasily for whatever might be coming next.

The floor of the arena was pocked and uneven, as if it had been dug up and refilled many times over many years, and I wondered if the mounds scattered around us covered past captive's decaying corpses.

The cave girl and Milton both jumped when the monkey-men suddenly began to pound on drums that had appeared from nowhere, a unified, rhythmic beat that seemed to thrum its way right into our bones. The dirt beneath our feet even vibrated with the rising volume of the drums.

The monkey crowd parted abruptly at one end of the arena, and several of those earless, sabertooth wolf-cats were prodded into the theater at the opposite end. The things bodies were as large as full-grown Great Danes; dark, spotted, leopard-like hair decorating their backs and sides, chests and bellies a snowy white. They fanned out in pack hunting style, eyes partly focused on us, partly on the vibrating earth beneath their paws. They padded carefully in our direction, powerful legs and foot long fangs making them the obvious odds-on favorite in the ensuing match-up. As they approached, their lips curled back away from strong jaws packed with seemingly endless rows of ivory, razor edged teeth.

Whatever show we were expected to perform, it was certainly no contest.

Milton began to pray, dropping to his knees and folding his hands together before him. The other man backed up, and moved closer to us, carefully putting the two girls between him and danger. I scowled at him, then glanced at my cave girl friend. She saw my annoyed reaction to the stranger, rolled her eyes, then turned back to face our predators, grumbling under her breath, probably saying all the things I was thinking.

I stooped and picked up a small stone, testing its weight in my hand. She saw what I was doing, looked at the rock, then at me, then at the cat-things, and finally back to me with an expression that spoke volumes.

Yeah, that worked so well against the T-Rex, she seemed to be thinking.

At my movement two of the things veered off a bit and began circling us slowly. Evidently they had been a target for stones in the past, and were cautious, but hardly intimidated.

Our captors were now dancing up and down on the theater benches in their chittery, monkey way urging the wolf-cats on with vicious whoops and cries. Perhaps encouraged by this, when I didn't throw, the nearest wolf-cat charged.

Like any kid growing up in America I'd played my share of baseball. If I'd been any good, I'd have made that a profession instead of becoming a janitor at APL. I wasn't terrible, and I'd never been chosen last in pick-up games. More importantly, I had no other weapons options, and I'd never been as motivated as I was now.

I tried to remember everything I'd been taught about throwing with speed and accuracy, then tried to forget it all when I recalled a pitching coach telling me not to get too lost in my own head. Keeping my eye on the nose of the leaping beast I let fly, throwing with all the strength I had—and a little more.

I startled even myself when I hit the thing hard in the eye. It yelped, jerked its head to one side, and fell beside me, scrabbling and scratching in the dirt, closing both eyes as it flailed away from us, screaming with a furious hiss. Righting itself, it began to rub at its injury madly, as if trying to scrape away the pain, when suddenly the ground erupted beneath its feet, and a monstrous, armored centipede creature exploded up out of the earth to envelope it whole.

Milton shrieked, leaped to his feet, and my cave girl and the other spun to see what was happening.

We watched the centipede coil around the now panicking wolf-thing, wrapping it tightly inside an iron ball of legs and chitinous plating. As it twisted and rolled closed around the terrified cat-creature, we caught a glimpse of a central mouth filled with razor teeth of its own. Its captive began to scream horribly from inside the now solid casing.
All we could do was watch, knowing that once it had finished with the wolf thing, we were next.

CHANGING MASTERS

"ARTHROPLEURA," MILTON WHISPERED. "At least I would think so."

"What?" I said, not really wanting an answer, just more surprised at the timing of this particular paleozoology lesson.

"The largest known land invertebrate," he answered. "Kind of a Jeopardy question. But it's supposed to be an herbivore."

Blood began to leak from between its interlocking plates and the wolf-cat stopped shrieking.

"Yeah, not so much," I said. "Do you know how to kill it?"

"No," Milton answered, awed.

"Fat lot of good you are," I said, teasing.

"It shouldn't even be able to *live*. It existed at a time in Earth's past when the air was over oxygenated, and…"

"The sun never moves, the horizon goes up!" I snapped.

Milton sighed. "Point taken."

Another of the horrible centipedes exploded from beneath the ground near us, antennae at one end twitching in the air, as if searching for us.

From nowhere, one of the monkey people jumped in and scrabbled in the dirt, searching desperately for God knows what. He threw up his hand with a *'Eureka!'* yell, and the centipede instantly enveloped him, crushed him, and munched him bloody. His extended hand fell free of his body to the ground near me, and I saw it held a fistful of dirt flecked with small lumps of gold.

55

Is that what this was about? Some bizarre, otherworldly mining expedition?

"Goot na sama," my pretty savage girl said in awe, then bent to pick up a stone of her own.

The crunching centipede stopped chewing, turned instantly in her direction, antennae flicking frantically. I grabbed the girl's arm and held a hand to her mouth. She looked at me with wide, terrified eyes, and got my message. She then turned back to the searching, monstrous, plated insect, and remained silent. Our newest predator continued to face our way, rising up on multiple back legs, segmented body twisting this way and that, antennae scanning furiously. Its central mouth began to chew again, absently, on a last, bloody piece of monkey man while it searched, and presently the creature's legs moved in unison, carrying the beast slowly toward us.

The other male captive who had tried to hide behind us made some fearful, guttural sounds, bent to grab a rock of his own, suddenly deciding for some inexplicable reason that it was time to communicate with us. He said no more than three or four words when the centipede-thing honed in on him, and struck.

We had only enough time to watch in horror as the damned thing sunk a dozen, spiky, segmented legs into his soft, pink flesh and yanked him almost directly into the buzz saw mouth at the center of its abdomen, curling around him as it did. Before its legs and plates had fully closed to trap the man inside, we saw his head and right arm ripped from his body with a single, vicious twist of the segmented, giant insect.

I wanted to scream, absolutely horror-struck, but managed to bite it down. Unfortunately the cave girl in my arms couldn't do the same.

"Dia sima godessi," she whispered, and the ground beside her exploded upward.

Another of those goddam centipedes rose up out of the dirt, higher than my six feet, and was already diving toward her. Bravely, she shoved me aside, and I nearly tripped over a panicking wolf-beast. Thinking faster than I thought I was capable, I lifted the leopard skinned predator and tossed it directly into the mouth of the newest centipede just as it was about to envelop the cave girl I was beginning to think of as mine.

The newest arthropleura gratefully accepted the alternate offering, and clamped viciously down on the poor wolf-cat, spraying blood all over the girl, Milton, and the other woman captive.

On all sides rose a deafening roar of shrieks and howls from our circle of spectators, I assumed because they were pleased with the way the 'show' was playing out, or they were seeing gold nuggets that I was too busy to appreciate. But I quickly realized that the monkey-things weren't reacting to us, and were all breaking in different directions, rushing from the small arena and out toward the surrounding hills as one of the enraged cat-creatures tore through them looking for an avenue of escape. Two more of the armored centipedes burst up near the carnage, and immediately encased two monkey-creatures. I took my cave girl by the arm and pulled her in the opposite direction, then bent and yanked Milton to his feet.

"God answered your prayers, Milton," I said. "We're all still alive. Now, let's get the hell out of here."

Milton opened his eyes, and clearly relieved, jumped up to follow, as did the other woman. Together, the four of us raced for a nearby exit, but my stupid jokes, and our stomping feet must have focused the remaining insectoid attention because two of the chitin plated monsters ripped from the ground before us, right in our path, the first one making an immediate dive for me.

The cave girl bravely leaped between us and threw her stone dead center of the thing's mouth, apparently striking some kind of nerve. It immediately recoiled, and curled up nearly closed, like a pill bug. But only for a moment. Recovering quickly, and with a horrifying roar, the thing spread out wider, and rose up higher than any of the monsters had so far, to nearly ten feet tall, and four or more feet wide.

Its gaping, gash shaped, fang rimmed maw blew wide with its scream, froth and mucus spewing out in glops and streams. Its many legs spread open as if crying to the heavens, and fortunately for us, all the noise it made seemed to distract the second, blind centipede into near immobility.

We froze, trying to prevent being 'seen', as the confused insect raised its antennae slightly, and twisted them as though searching, opening and closing its legs in a rolling, finger-drumming sort of way, its mouth snapping absently open and shut. Not thinking clearly—mostly acting on instinct—I pounced on one of the extended, twitching legs and twisted as I had Jessica's boyfriend's arm, and to both our surprise, the leg snapped loose in my hand. As the thing screeched, and flailed—still not having formulated an actual plan—I spun and jammed the spiky appendage with both hands right into the still screaming mouth of the first centipede.

Black goo and saliva gushed forth, sliming across my arms and down the thing's 'chest', and both centipedes were now rendered useless from agony.

Trying to remain silent, I signaled to the others to follow me.

As a unit we hurried quietly out of the arena, and up along a narrow aisle dividing the stones forming the general seating area. Behind us the monkey-men scattered from both centipedes and angry wolf-cats. There were a few stragglers in front of us blocking the way, but a couple well-placed shots from the stones my cave girl and I had picked up sent them all fleeing for safety. Once an escape path had been cleared we could see before us the ridge leading out of the tiny valley, toward freedom, and we all smiled.

But we shouldn't have.

As we hurried to escape, an entirely different type of man came over the lip of the canyon riding on the back of a good-sized, two-legged dinosaur. The rider was tall, almost black in color, and resembled a panther more than anything. One of our monkey-man captors had been focusing too much over his shoulder on the carnage behind him, didn't see the newcomer's arrival, and ran right into the open mouth of the panther man's mount. The thing ripped him instantly in two, sending legs, tail and a hand flying in three different directions, then quickly swallowed the remaining bits.

The rider didn't react at all, and never took his eyes off me.

Two other panther-men rode up alongside the first, and one of their mounts finished the bloody legs and tail of the previous kill. The cave girl grabbed my arm saying something I didn't understand, pulling me anxiously in another direction.

"*Angara*," she said, pulling me hard in the opposite direction, the fear in her eyes obvious, and we ran as fast as we could away from the new arrivals.

But now we were moving in the same direction as some of the panicked monkey-people, and they were forming a wall between us and safety. Bodies piled atop one another, crushing the ones further down. With no nearby trees for them to leap into, they were just a normal crowd trying to escape a burning theater.

I tried scrambling over the squirming pile of our terrified and dying captors, pulling the girl up by the hand behind me, Milton helping the other woman to keep pace.

Behind her, streaming in our direction through the pass, which led in from the valley, came a swarm of the huge, hairy panther-like 'Angara' on their weird mounts. Armed with spears and axes, and protected by oval shields they descended like demons on the monkey-people, spearing them viciously, slicing off body parts, and splitting skulls. One 'Angara' went down, attacked by a wolf-cat thing, but the leopard spotted creature was soon dead inside the mouth and belly of the rider's long-toothed dinosaur 'steed'.

Racing past us in every direction flowed the pursued and the pursuers, the hairy ones giving us nothing more than a passing glance as they chased down their tailed prey and slaughtered them mercilessly. With the chaos and insanity now spread all around us, we very soon had nowhere to go and little to do but wait until it was all over.

Trying to avoid the bloodbath we carefully and quietly moved back to the center of the amphitheater to watch and wait. Finally—all monkey-people now dead or escaped—the attacking horde returned to us, an apparent leader riding up close to stop before us, studying me with more than casual interest. After a while he motioned around his groin and again near the top of his head, looking at the others and laughing. Apparently they were amused by my choice of hairstyles— both above and below.

After a moment of staring and laughing, the leader motioned disinterestedly that we be brought with them.

One of his men grabbed the cave girl and reacting instinctively I punched the guy in the side of the head, then moved her behind me for safety. I'm not sure what I was thinking. I was going to die in the mouth of some wolf-cat just moments ago, and these guys handled them—and all my captors—quite handily. I was obviously no match for them.

The Angara all stopped what they were doing and turned back to look at me in complete surprise. The guy I'd punched touched his cheek as if it tickled, and was wondering what had caused it. All their expressions told me this must be the absolute last thing they expected from me—or anyone.

The leader reigned his mount in my direction and stopped right beside me. We locked eyes, and he studied me as carefully as I had been studying him. His hair was graying, and a scar split the right side of his face as if he'd been hit with an axe that had been stopped by his orbital bone before reaching the underlying eye—and he had just shaken it off. I began to feel stupid and afraid, until the cave girl placed a gentle hand on my shoulder from behind, leaned closely to me until I could feel her cheek against my back.

Suddenly I felt as if I could fight a hundred of these guys, and spit on them when I was done.

That's when the lead Angara snapped his foot out, kicked me in the face and sent me sprawling in the dirt. So much for confidence.

I rolled on the ground, holding my head, my eyes feeling like they were going to burst, hoping he hadn't caved in my skull. Through the fog that surrounded my brain and eyes I heard the panther man bark something harsh and guttural. Two of his companions leaped down from their saddles to clank a cuff and chain around my neck, then yanked me to my feet with it, and linked me to both the girl, and Milton. They then fastened Milton to the other woman. Our captors performed their function with a lot less gentleness than they might have had I not foolishly punched one of them.

Suddenly the ground burst upward very near where I had fallen, and another chitinous centipede threatened to bite off my head. But the Angara who had kicked me simply raised an axe and split the thing nearly down to its clacking maw. It was dead before the two pieces hit the arena floor.

I have to admit, I was impressed.

Once the four of us were linked together—Milton, the cave girl, the older woman who'd been with us in the arena, and I—the panther men dragged us all up one of the paths and out of the small enclosure, heading back toward the great plain. Shuffling over the rise we saw a caravan of men and women—humans like us—and for a moment hope and relief filled me with something like joy. Even though they were all as dirty and wild and naked as the girl who'd saved me, they were at least more human than anything besides her that I'd seen since arriving in this bizarre, bowl-shaped world—and it made me hope I might be able to communicate with someone, and through them find out *just what the fuck was going on!*

Sadly, none of them spoke any more intelligible language than the cave girl, or the older woman. Milton made a few attempts, but most of the other slaves wouldn't even look at us. We both sighed and moved to the end of the line as instructed by an Angara, where we were chained to the others, me first, then the girl, then Milton, then the other woman. One of the panther-men stepped over with an ornate box, and carefully removed its contents. I became concerned when the eyes of my pretty savage girl widened in horror, and she began to back away, shaking her head in what was obviously a fairly universal gesture of fear and refusal. I stepped forward to block the Angara, but another guard—probably the one I'd punched—yanked me nearly to the ground with the chain around my neck. As I watched helpless, my dark-haired savior—still shaking her head, eyes closed and pulling tightly against the length of chain that connected us, began to scream, horrifyingly, as whatever the panther man had removed from the box was pressed tightly against her face and forehead.

I yanked hard against my chain, and to everyone's surprise managed to jerk my antagonist to the ground, but too late. Whatever the device in the box was, it had knocked the girl unconscious, and to keep from choking her Milton and I had to move quickly together to slacken the links and lower her limp head so it could rest against the carpet of sand and matted grasses.

Then the panther man turned the thing from the box toward me.

"Brandon," Milton said with deep concern.

I considered resisting, perhaps testing my strength against all of them, but even the slightest of movements placed tension on the link of chain surrounding the girl's neck, and rather than risk her life, I knelt motionless and waited as a weird, grasping, slithering, organic, metal squid-like-thing was pressed over my face. There was an instantaneous blast of horrifying pain in my forehead and through my temples that went deep into my skull—my brain—my mind—and screaming like a dying man, I—mercifully—blacked out.

NOVA THE BEAUTIFUL

Someone was kicking my head.

"Get up, fuck-face," a voice commanded.

Scrunching my eyes against the light, I slowly lifted myself off the ground, and struggled back to consciousness.

"You're still alive," a female voice said, sounding grateful. "I'm so glad. Milton was getting worried. Not that I was. I knew you wouldn't die. Not yet."

I opened my eyes and saw the dark-haired savage girl, squatting near me, grinning, mischievously.

"What did you say?" I asked.

"I said I couldn't imagine you dying, yet," she repeated. "The gods had brought us together for a reason. I refused to believe it was just so I could watch you die before being able to even speak with you."

"I understood you," I said, amazed. "How can I understand you?"

"Ah," she said, realizing, her face falling and darkening with unexpected sadness. "The thing in the box. It steals our language and fills us with the words of the Grigori. We now speak only the language of slaves. We will never be able to return home—never be able to speak to our loved ones, again—not in a way that they will understand."

I looked up at the panther man who had kicked me awake.

"Who are they, these Grigori?"

She studied me for a long beat, her brows furrowing deeply at the center. Then she glanced up quickly at Milton.

61

"You weren't kidding," she told the old man. "You two really are from someplace very far away. I never imagined there was a place anywhere in Pangea where people had not heard of the Grigori."

"Trust me," I said. "There's a place. And what's 'Pangea'?"

She snorted a sudden laugh.

"Now I know you're joking."

"No," I said. "Really…"

"It's the name of the world we're in," Milton interjected. "That's what they call it. 'Pangea'."

"Oh," I said, "So… these Grigori …" I gestured toward the panther-men nearby.

"No, not them," she said, seeing where I was looking. "They're slaves, as well. But more trusted than we are. They are the Angara—a stupid but very strong, very violent race of people. They are the muscle for the Grigori who can't do things for themselves, for obvious reasons."

"Obvious to you," Milton said. "Not to us."

She studied him carefully, then shrugged. "Weird," she said. "Someday I would like to go to this place with no Grigori. I think I would like it there. Except for the way you shave your bodies. Especially your genitals."

She grinned and glanced down at my bald penis.

"It's—uh—kind of the fashion where I come from."

"*Crazy* fashion," she laughed. "Sharp objects scraping away at people's most sensitive areas? We thought maybe someone had tortured you."

I laughed, and finally understood the fascination back at the panther village.

"*You* do not shave, Milton," the woman said to my friend.

"I have no one to shave *for*," the old man admitted with a smile. Beside him, the older woman from the arena laughed a little into her hand.

"Ah," she replied, turning toward me, and seeming to deflate a little. "You do this for the benefit of your woman. Interesting kind of 'fashion'. I wouldn't want my man to do it for me, though, and I think I'll leave my fur the way it is, if you don't mind."

"I won't mind at all," I said, becoming hot with the impression that she seemed to be talking about me as if we'd be sharing our fashion choices on a more intimate level. "What's your name?"

"Nova," she said, glancing down, shyly. "Nova, the Beautiful."

She smiled, as if she'd made some joke I didn't understand.

"You're well-named," I said, smiling back at her.

She studied me carefully, turning her head a bit to the side as if waiting for something, then she smiled and seemed to melt a little.

"I'm glad you think so," she said, finally.

We sat like that a moment, just smiling and staring at one another, and I became overwhelmed with the sense that this woman wanted to kiss me. But I also had the distinct impression there was something going on underneath the surface of our conversation that I didn't understand—along with everything else I didn't understand—and before I could ask, or explore the kissing thing, we were distracted by the snarls, threats and jabbing spear-points of the panther-men letting us know it was time to get moving.

And moving.

And moving.

The journey itself to wherever we were going felt endless, the never moving sun giving you the sensation of having made no progress—none that could be judged by time, anyway. The upside was the seeming 'perpetual time' it gave me with Nova. I was never bored, so other than the chains and the obvious drawbacks of being a captive, I was content to just walk and talk and laugh with her.

I'd never known a funnier, sexier, more charming girl, and she seemed to enjoy me as much as I did in her. In spite of the fact that she was a naked savage in some backward world of cavemen and dinosaurs, she honestly seemed smarter than any female I'd ever dated on the outside world—short of Lena. Not that I'd ever *dated* Lena, though, so I guess the comparison still holds. Simply put: Nova's obvious intelligence and zest for life made me wonder about my choices in the past.

We would stop occasionally, and the panther-men—the Angara—would feed us an unpleasant mixture of fruits, nuts, and raw fish. We were all so hungry we devoured it instantly with no complaints. Afterward we were given time to relieve ourselves along the side of the trail, or just relax, and even sleep if we could manage it.

Occasionally, ahead of us in line, other prisoners would come together so they could engage in sex, apparently unconcerned about privacy. The others took it all in stride, and I wanted to ask Nova if this was how things were done in Pangea—shameless public fornication—or was it only because we were captives. But I was too nervous about the topic to even bring it up. She would often watch the couple, amused and apparently pleased, then look at me with a questioning—perhaps hopeful—look in her eyes while she fidgeted nervously with her hands, but I was too fearful of the possibility of offending her that I refused to even ask. The silences that fell between us when I ignored her interest were the only unpleasant times we shared.

I could never make myself fall asleep, mostly because I never wanted to miss a second with Nova. She did sleep, occasionally, and I took pleasure in just watching her doze. Eventually the Angara awoke all slumberers, broke up the rutting pairs, and forced us back into a marching line.

Once moving again, the awkward silences ended, and we returned to the fun relationship I was beginning to need more than food. As we talked, I rubbed my chin, feeling the stubble thicken, and Nova laughed at the sight of it.

"I saw a sharp rock back there," she said, smiling sarcastically, "if you want to shave yourself. Or maybe an Angara will lend you a blade. We wouldn't want you to not have fashion for your woman."

"I think I'll pass," I said, wondering if she even knew what the word fashion actually meant.

"The growth of my beard makes me realize there probably *are* ways to tell time here in Pangea, after all." I said, looking over at Milton, sadly realizing that I sometimes forgot he was even there. His face had become as grizzled as my own. "What do you think, Mr. Alvarado?"

"I think in a place with no night… time will always be malleable," he said, "but you're right. There will be ways to measure it, if we learn to focus on them."

"What is 'time'?" Nova asked, sounding almost poetic, but intending to sound simply confused.

"You two say that word a lot," the older woman beside Milton asked, "and I feel I should know what it means, but I don't. It's very confusing."

"The word is in this new Grigori vocabulary," Nova added in an effort to be helpful, "but I don't understand its complete meaning. It is… the measurement of age?"

"That's a way to put it," Milton answered. "A distance along an arbitrary line that moves—not in a physical direction—but a temporal one."

She looked at him, blankly, as did the older woman.

"Yeah, you're probably not helping," I told Milton with a grin.

He shrugged, dismissing it as their problem, not his.

"It's a way to measure…" I said, then thought about it for a moment, realizing I had no idea where I was going with my answer, "…how much of your life is being used up."

"Ah. Because life lasts for so little in the stream of existence?" Nova said. "I understand. Pangea goes on, but we do not. Like how much of our life is being wasted on this march, or in talking, or in anything."

"Well, not necessarily *wasted*. Not for *me*, anyway." I said, grinning.

"But time we could spend in living our lives, playing together, mating, loving…"

"Uh… yes. Those things."

"Time is an amount of life," the older woman beside Milton said, contemplatively. "How much life it takes to go to a place, or grow a beard, or urinate, or defecate, or before a woman next bleeds."

"Yes," I admitted. "Those are all amounts of time. Some consistent, some… I don't know… more arbitrary, I guess."

"Time is good to know," Nova said happily, turning to me and smiling, arms out as if inviting the noonday sun to worship her lovely, nude body, so inviting and beautiful. "We should always be aware when we have wasted too much time in a world that gives you so little."

None of us saw it. It was waiting in a row of trees and bushes for us to pass, natural greens and browns masking its massive presence.

Before I even realized it was happening a giant mouth filled with teeth was opening around Nova, hot breath blowing her hair around her smiling face. I reacted quickly, and maybe too violently, yanking the chain that connected us, and pulling her out of the way before the monster's gnashing teeth could slam closed into the softness of her bare flesh.

"I'm sorry," I said, as she grabbed her neck, and fell into me.

My rash motion had jerked the prisoner just ahead of her into the path of danger, and faster than it takes to tell, the Tyrannosaur had re-opened its mouth and crushed the poor man to pieces, twisting it's head sharply and spraying us all with blood, an arm flying loose and nearly hitting me in the face.

The T Rex lifted its neck, craned upward twenty, thirty feet, and opened its mouth to allow the pieces of its victim to be pulled by gravity into its gullet.

Appetizer devoured, it returned for more.

Our chain had been snapped by its clenching jaws, which meant we were free—but far from safe. The tyrannosaur strode from its hiding place and again lunged for the tasty Nova. She was still holding her neck where I'd nearly broken it, and I had to jerk her violently to my left once more to keep her from becoming the dinosaur's second course. Grabbing a spear from a horrified and frozen Angara, I thrust it deeply into the Rex's snout near an eye, which released a surprising flow of blood. It screeched and reared back, and after considering the situation for less than a second, changed its mind about Nova, turned abruptly aside and clamped onto two other prisoners and an Angara, the three having become tangled in some roots, vines, and one another.

While the thing was distracted the Angara I had disarmed was able to focus in on what had happened and grabbed me around the throat. The spear was too long for me to pull back and angle inward to defend myself, so though I struggled furiously, it wasn't long before I felt the fugue state of unconsciousness creeping in and eating away the edges of my brain.

Crunch! The panther man's grip suddenly loosened, he fell over, his head caved in, his throat gushing blood all over himself and me. He was dead and sprawling on me before I could blink. The Tyrannosaur dove quickly my way, I turned, and shoved the lifeless Angara corpse into its path. The bite snatched it, and not me.

Milton stood nearby, apparently having thrown the stone that saved my life, and Nova was pulling at my arm, a knife in her other hand, red to the elbow with Angara blood.

"We must go!" she yelled. *"Now!"*

We had been the end of the line of prisoners, most of our Angara guards had fled, and confusion reigned as the tyrannosaur took its time chewing through the easy pickings of exhausted men and women bound awkwardly together, so our escape would have been easy.

Would have been. If Milton hadn't fallen.

Though keeping an eye on the still raging tyrannosaur, three Angara fell on the old man, and pinned him to the ground. They were too far away to reach Nova and I. But I still stopped.

"Go," I told her, pulling the length of chain out of the band encircling her lovely neck. It hurt to see she was already red and bruising where I had jerked her. "I can't leave my friend."

She stared into my eyes, deeply horrified and momentarily lost. She turned and stared off into the distance, across the open plain we'd just traveled as prisoners, now beckoning us both to freedom. Slowly she turned back to me, her expression having fallen to one of deep sadness. Then she closed her eyes and wrapped her arms tightly—lovingly— around me.

"I can't leave you," she said, her voice barely audible. "Ever."

I began to argue, intending to force her, but by then we'd been discovered, the tyrannosaur apparently having eaten its fill and moved on. Several Angara grabbed us roughly and shoved us back in line where we would once again be chained to the others.

No Nova and I were thrown roughly to the ground and told to stay there as the remainder of the slave chain was brought back down along the path to re-link with us. The two men at the other end were thrown to the turf on our right, Milton and the older woman shoved down beside us on our left. Then the Angara hammered recklessly on the chains and collars to open links, fasten, and pound them closed again. As we lie there, grimacing against the rough hands and disgusting breath of our captors while they pounded on our necks furiously, and thoughtlessly, brutally fastening us back together again with the rest into a single line, Nova reached out to take my hand, and held it tightly.

I saw a tear in her eyes, and felt an overwhelming sense of guilt and shame that I will never forget.

Their work done, the panther men stood, argued amongst themselves about how angry the Grigori would be at the loss of slaves, and whose fault it was for not seeing the tyrannosaur in time, then moved away to check the rest of their captives, and deal with any additional damage.

Nova and I lie on our backs, breathing heavily, the weight of what had just happened hitting us both extremely hard. We'd nearly died, survived, saved one another, nearly died again, then been given a gift—a golden opportunity to take back our freedom. But now we were—once again, possibly forever more—slaves.

Suddenly she rolled over on top of me, staring deeply into my eyes, studying me with a fearful intensity—as if she expected me to vanish, terrified that I'd never really been there, at all. Without waiting for invitation she kissed me, fierce and hot. Lust and longing, joy and fear, hope and love and concern all pulsed powerfully through her and into me. She pulled her mouth off mine, and began to move her hips and furry bottom back and forth against my already swelling member.

I saw that we were being watched with interest, though not by Milton, whose face was hidden in his hands as he most likely prayed. Nova grasped my face in her hands and moved my eyes back to hers, the insistent message coming through powerfully: don't remove them from her again.

Her breathing deepened as she stared at me—into me—and I felt her opening grow slick, wet and hot against the underside of my shaft. With a slight shift of her hips she maneuvered my tip so it fit neatly against her moist channel, and with a sudden move, I was filling her tightness, and she was moaning, I was moaning, we were moving, savoring, hands reaching around to caress needful flesh, her back, my arms, her soft, round ass, my hair, her hair. She fought to keep her eyes open, and her concentration on me, as I fought to keep mine on her.

"No babies," she said, sensing my thoughts.

"No babies," I answered.

"Grigori eat babies."

For a moment my horror overcame my lust, but I shoved it—and all this world's monstrosities—away, and down, deep into the recesses of my mind, burying my face against her neck, nibbling and licking her with the same, restrained intensity she used to claw my back. Her hips were moving furiously, now, pressing her sensitive spot hard against me, her moans growing louder, and then she came, her head flinging back, her cries sending birds into the sky, and I—too—had reached my end. I shoved her up and thrust into her madly, rolling her onto her back as I drove deeper and deeper into her, pushing myself right to the limit, then yanking myself free to release any potential babies into the grass and roots and twigs that formed our bed.

We were smiling at one another, holding each other tightly, kissing in quick bursts of love and passion, breathing deeply, happy, satisfied, lost in the moment, when suddenly my neck was being jerked upward with a wrenching pain that had me on my feet in seconds. The Angara who'd manhandled me off of Nova laughed and moved on, as my lover lifted herself gently and sadly to her feet, and just like that, we were done, moving once more in a single file line toward a life of captivity and slavery.

Without looking, she reached a hand back, I took it in mine, and held it gratefully.

I said nothing for a long time, walking with my head down, lost in a million different competing thoughts. I could easily understand the lack of concern for privacy in a world where death might literally eat and digest you before you even knew it was there, where slavery was the norm, and where the time for love and tenderness was impossibly limited. How did people manage to survive in this world? They were clearly not the dominant species. In truth they were really nothing more than a part of the food chain. I considered that I really hadn't seen any older people, Milton being an anomaly. I had to believe that life expectancy was so severely limited that death by old age was a rarity—or even an impossibility—and that fact defined the culture.

In a land with no time, there was no time to waste.

FOR A LONG WHILE the excitement of the dinosaur attack kept us all awake; but the tiresome monotony of the long march across that perpetually sun baked plain brought out the agonies of long-denied sleep. On and on we stumbled beneath that hateful, constant, scorching star. If anyone fell they were jabbed with the business end of a spear until they either caught up, or died from the 'incentive'. It had its intended effect. It became rarer and rarer that anyone ever stumbled.

The people ahead of us strode proudly, and tall; a noble collection of men and women despite their situation, lean and tan with perfect physiques. There wasn't a face among them that could be called unattractive. The men were all heavily bearded, lean, and muscular; the women lithe, strong and graceful, with great masses of raven hair tied loosely in tails, or piled carelessly up on their heads. Even as exhausted as they were, all of them seemed regal and proud, with a confidence born of survival in the toughest of circumstances. They wore no clothing, no jewelry, mostly because they had been stripped of everything valuable, just as we had. A few still wore strapped sandals, but nothing more.

In spite of their situation, they remained happy, and upbeat, which surprised me.

Angara were—as I've said—panther-like, though thinner and more human in build. Their hands were clawed, but more human than animal, their legs back turned like the cat they had descended from. For clothing they wore a simple loincloth of white, their feet minimally protected by the same basic, crude, rope sandals some of their captives wore, and their arms and necks were wrapped in layers and layers of chains and bulky medallions of varying colors and metals— predominantly silver.

They talked amongst themselves as they marched or rode along on either side of us, but in a language slightly different than the one we used. When they addressed us it was as though they were speaking down, using smaller words and oversimplified sentences. Their foreheads may have appeared to slope lower than ours, but they were obviously no less intelligent.

How far they marched us I have no idea, nor had Milton, or Nova. All I know is that it exhausted us, none of us had the energy for anything other than sleep during rest breaks, and I had begun to wonder if our journey would ever end.

OUR GUARDS WOKE US ROUGHLY from our most recent sleep, and we were all surprised to find that we felt considerably better. I'm not sure how long we slept—I'm not sure how long anything is in Pangea—but mine and Milton's beards were beginning to look more and more like the locals. Nova laughingly played with my ever-developing face-fuzz, one thing led quickly to another, and before long Milton was again turning away to pray.

Afterward, as Nova and I lie as contended as any two chained slaves can, side-by-side on the flattened grasses, an Angara came by and gave us food; strips of dried fish and a few pieces of fruit. It wasn't much, but it helped. Then they detoured us down to a river where we were all commanded to bathe quickly, and drink our fill. Apparently offended by the smell many of us were giving off, most of us still covered in blood from the dinosaur attack, they let us enjoy the cooling waters for quite a while. I watched Nova lecherously as she leaned over in front of me to bathe, bending down to wash the caked red, dried dirt and tree sap from her chest and arms. I marveled at her beauty, her indescribable sexiness, and found myself hardening again.

"Milton," I whispered, "Now might be a good time to pray."

He rolled his eyes, and turned away. I don't know if he actually prayed, or not, but it didn't matter. I slid up behind the woman I was falling in love with, aimed myself carefully, and entered her from behind. She squealed rather loudly, then laughed when every eye turned toward us. Most of them just shook their heads, and I could almost hear them thinking, 'not *those* two again.'

69

We moved together easily, almost musically for a few moments, my river soaked hands gliding easily across her wet, smooth, brown skin with sensual ease, her hips rolling in rhythm with mine. I slid my hands up along the curves of her rounded belly, her sloping ribs, her soft, pliant breasts and erect nipples, massaging deeply with heat and pressure. I was just about to pull myself free and climax when my neck was jerked by an Angara with the worst possible timing.

I fell backward into the water, and arose quickly to panther man laughter. Gripping the chain I glared at the Angara still pulling his end taut.

"I'm getting a little tired of that," I said, angrily.

His only response was to chuckle, darkly, then jerk harder, pulling me face first into the river. Leaping free of the gently flowing waters, I heard the Angara, and a captive further up the chain from Nova, both laughing hysterically.

"Hajah!" said another man, next in line to the laughing captive, a large, hairy gentleman I hadn't yet bothered to speak to.

He seemed to be warning the other man off, but it didn't have any effect. The asshole just kept on.

As I slowly stood, water streaming over my naked skin, something about it all made me furious to the point of blindness, I set myself, gripped the links dangling from my neck, and pulled with all my might.

The surprised Angara was immediately yanked off balance, and though he let go of the chain, he still stumbled forward, landing in the river near my feet—just as I had—face-first. And that's when I went a little nuts. Instead of letting my moment of revenge end there, I dropped on all fours and held the Angara under the surface, pressing his face into the sand. He struggled and fought, the waters roiling and seething around me, until his movements slowed, his effort weakened, and he began to let go of his life. At that point I realized that whatever this world had made me, whatever my actions with Jessica's boyfriend, I was not a conscious murderer.

I lifted the panther man up by the shoulders, and held him above the rippling waters until he finally, urgently, sucked air back into his lungs. Then I grabbed him by some of the many dangling chains around his neck and dragged him back to shore, tossing his limp body onto the rocky sand.

Leaving him where he lie, I walked over to 'Hajah' and stood staring into his unctuous, faux-charming face. He had one of those smiles that appeared bright and sincere, but from underneath peered a hint of loathsome contempt for you and everything you cared for. He'd stopped laughing, finally, and I saw his muscles tensing to escape if I made any sudden moves.

Without a word, I walked past him toward the hairy man who had tried to control him, and opened my hand in what I'd learned was the Pangean gesture of friendly greeting.

"I'm Brandon Mack," I said.

"Bruk, the Hairy," he said, returning my gesture, with a smile. "You're not from around here."

"No. I'm not from around anywhere."

"Only the bravest man alive, or a complete idiot picks a fight with people who have him chained and can kill him in his sleep."

"I'm not all that brave," I said, smiling, and watched him slowly roll into one of the most joyous laughs I've ever seen.

"I'm not sure I believe you." He said, then gestured to the other man, the one who had enjoyed my face-plant into the river just a little too much. "This is Hajah, the Wily. We're from the same tribe. But we are not friends."

I laughed, looked at Hajah, and didn't offer him the same gesture I'd made to Bruk. The panther man I'd nearly drowned suddenly stood, grabbed a spear, and charged my way. He stood at my toes, his face only inches from mine, his tiny, dark eyes boring into mine. I didn't move, didn't flinch. I simply returned his gaze, unblinking eye to unblinking eye.

"We're both slaves," I said, not knowing exactly why, and his expression changed very slightly, "which makes *us* more alike than *you* are to your *masters*. And that's why I let you live."

He said nothing, but after a few more seconds of silent staring, he backed away a pace or two, then turned and walked toward the front of the line without looking back.

"You've shamed him," Bruk said. "The others will make fun of him, and he will one day repay your... 'kindness' in 'letting' him live."

"I guess I'd better be ready, then."

"A man can build a fortress, and still die."

"Is that a local saying?" I asked, and he only smiled. "Upbeat. Positive. I'll have to remember it."

The chains tightened, and as one, we all began to move again along the trail.

MILTON WAS FAR FROM ATHLETIC. I'd teased him once for wanting to take my car to go the five blocks downtown for pizza—and he was paying for it now, though he held up much better than I would have expected. He couldn't talk much due to heavy breathing, but since we'd begun our march he'd become fit enough to stay with us easily, and that was something.

The country began to change at last. We finally left the level plain and threaded our way up through mighty mountains of virgin granite. The tropical abundance of the lowlands was quickly replaced by hardier shrubs and bushes, as well as sparser, coarser grasses; but even here the effects of the constant heat, frequent, short cloudbursts, and unceasing light were obvious in the immensity of the trees, the constant greenery, and the explosion of flowers and blossoms.

Crystalline streams roared through rocky channels, fed by perpetual snows far above. Beyond the snowcapped heights hung a mass of heavy clouds that spread out at least once a day to dump heavy rain over us and the rest of the land, which kept the vast majority of Pangea looking like a very large, tropical island.

"So the world is divided into tribes," I asked our little group.

"Yes," Nova said. "I'm from the Nyala. In Sa Fasi."

Bruk reacted strangely, though no one saw it but me.

"It's mostly a village built into the cliffs above the Usayasa Um," Nova continued, "the shallow sea beyond the Land of Endless Dark."

"How did you wind up here?" I asked her.

She sighed, and looked around at the others as if preferring not to speak in front of them.

"I was running away from Gudra, The Ugly," she answered, as though that was explanation aplenty.

"Who's Gudra, The Ugly?" I asked, " And why did you run away from him?"

She looked at me in surprise, then spoke to me as if I were an infant.

"He's called 'Gudra, The UGLY! Do I really need to say more than that?"

I laughed. "I suppose not. But why is he 'The Ugly'?"

"He was in a fight with a bear. Gudra lived, the bear died, but the bear won, if you know what I mean."

"Yeah. I think I do."

"Gudra placed his trophy before my father's house," she said, continuing to explain. "The head of a very large Endevak."

"The head of a … what's an Endevak?"

"An Endevak? Big, hairy… long, curving tusks." She looked at me very strangely. "You must be from *very* far away. Everyone knows what an Endevak is. Anyway, it sat there in front of our door, stinking terribly, collecting flies, for a long, *long* time. No one placed a bigger trophy beside it, so… Gudra, The Ugly was going to have me as his mate, and I didn't want to *be* his mate."

I stared blankly, waiting for more.

"So I left Sa Fasi," she said, simply.

"I would have put a… what's bigger than an Endevak?"

"Just a bigger Endevak. Maybe a Hakchata." She saw my confused expression. "Like what you saved me from many sleeps back?"

"I would have put the head of a Hakchata at your father's door. *Two* Hakchatas. Maybe a baby Hakchata as a bonus."

Bruk laughed, and I smiled at him. Nova leaned in against me and squeezed my upper arm, as if finding it wanting.

"Oh, would you, now? Well, then. Go ahead and get me one."

I grabbed the links of chain connecting us.

"Sadly," I said, not really sad at all, "I am unable to, at present."

"Well, then you'd better hope Gudra doesn't find me, because he has rightful claim."

"I can take him."

She laughed. A little too hard.

"I would fight for you," I said, wounded.

"I would rather you *lived* for me. You haven't seen Gudra."

"Well," I said, not liking her lack of faith in me, "no point in dying needlessly. It *is* a very weird kind of custom."

"It's the only custom we know," Nova said, looking at Bruk. "Do your people have a similar custom?"

"Doesn't everybody?" he shrugged.

"Not my people," I admitted. "We have to actually *ask* the girl. Usually with an offer of a ring for her finger."

Bruk laughed so hard I thought he might choke. When he saw I wasn't kidding, he stopped, and looked embarrassed.

"Oh," he said. "You were serious."

"Yes, I was serious."

"And what if the girl says 'no'," Nova asked, playfully.

"You have to find another girl."

"I like that custom," she said, leaning against me, again. "But you would not have to find another girl. I would not say 'no'."

Bruk and Milton smiled along with me, but I noticed that Hajah—who apparently had a thing for Nova—was not so pleased with her obvious devotion to me.

"When Gudra made his offer to my father," Nova said, "no one as powerful wanted me. My name... is from a hopeful parent, an old man who is no longer much of a hunter. He was once, but a Durik threw him, and he lost the use of his right arm and one side of his head. My brother, Naga, The Mighty, had gone to the land of the Hilleya to steal a mate for himself. So there was no one—no father, no brother, no lover—to fight Gudra for me, so I ran. After a few adventures and a lot of sleeping alone, I ended up down near the sea watching some idiot do a strange, circular dance with a young Hakchata and a Nyame. I foolishly speared the Hakchata and now look at me."

"Well, I'm sure he meant well... hey! Who you calling an 'idiot'?"

She and Bruk laughed. Even Milton was amused.

"So now you and this idiot are chained together," Bruk said, playfully. "Who's the *bigger* idiot?"

"That would be me," she said, leaning lovingly against my chest.

"Slaves of the 'Grigori'," I said. "So what are the Grigori, exactly?"

Again their faces gave away their obvious shock.

"I can almost believe you *are* from another world," she said, "because the alternative is that there's something wrong with your brain. Are you serious, Brandon, the Mack? Do you really mean to tell me that you don't know what a Grigori is—the mighty Grigori who think they own all of Pangea and everything that walks or grows, or creeps, or burrows, or swims, or flies within it—you and me included?"

"I really mean to tell you."

She shook her head, sadly. After a confused glance toward Bruk, who again, only shrugged, she tried valiantly to explain to me what a Grigori was. Unfortunately she could only use comparisons to other things I didn't know about or understand, and so I was lost. In this way they were like Ingonghus, in that way they were like the hairless Peeli.

73

They were smart, but couldn't speak. They were old, but their skin was sleek and smooth.

About all I learned was that they were hideous, had wings, and webbed feet; they lived in cities built underground; could swim beneath the water for long distances, and were very, very intelligent—much more than most Pangeans.

The Angara were their soldiers and slavers, weapons of offense and defense, while the weaker races like Nova's and Bruk's were their hands and feet—subservients who performed all their manual labor. The Grigori were the dominant species of the inner world... the supreme masters of Pangea.

And the only way to stop being their slaves... was to die.

HAJAH, PRETENDING TO TRY and help with Nova's explanations, occasionally forced his way into the conversation. Most of his remarks were directed toward her as he offered words that might—supposedly—help me better understand. It didn't take half an eye to see that he had it bad for the girl, and not knowing the customs of this world, I had no idea if it was as clear to everyone else as it was to me that it was a pointless thing—Nova was mine, and I was hers.

For her part, she appeared completely oblivious to Hajah's thinly veiled advances. Wait. Did I say thinly veiled? Supposedly there was a time when cavemen used to show interest in a mate by hitting her over the head with a club. By comparison to *that* Hajah's interest might be considered thinly veiled.

I had been making assumptions about the customs of this place because of Nova's sexual freedom, and ease with admitting her feelings for me. But I could clearly no longer afford to do that. At the next opportunity for privacy I had to ask her what it would take to make everyone else understand that I loved her, and would stand against anyone, Gudra, Hajah, the entire population of Grigori—if necessary—to keep her beside me forever.

I wanted her to understand that she would be protected from the Nyames and the Hakchatas, and the whatever elses. I wanted to grow old with her, have many beautiful children with her, and though back on the more prudish outer Earth, still somehow continue the practice of having sex with her anywhere and whenever the urge arose. I didn't know how I was going to work that one out, but I was motivated.

She spoke easily with me, with Milton, and with the taciturn Bruk because we were respectful, and kind, and friendly; but she couldn't even see Hajah the Wily, much less hear him, and by ignoring his interest and obvious attraction to her, she only made him furious. On the outer world he would have qualified as a stalker, and I had to make certain I never left Nova alone and unprotected with him. At one point, he tried to get one of the Angara—the one I'd nearly drowned—to switch her place in the chain with Bruk, moving her further from me and closer to him, but the panther man only jabbed him with his spear and warned him off.

"I will buy the girl from the Grigori," The Angara said, arrogantly. "She is ugly, but she has good hips for children, and likes sex. When we get to Emibi, she is mine," he said, glaring at me. "And no one else's."

Bruk glanced at me with an 'I told you so,' expression, and shook his head sadly.

Nova pretended she was unfazed by the comment, but the way she clung tightly to me told a different story. At the next rest stop our lovemaking was quiet and sad, and at the end Nova curled her face into my chest and cried, softly.

"Nova," I said, gently, "No, sweetie, don't cry. Look. You know I'm… that I'm not from around here… that my customs are different from yours. So, I want to know… can you… what exactly do I need to do…" I paused and realized I was confusing *myself*, so *she* must be hopelessly lost. "I want to marry you, Nova. How would I do that? How I would take you as my… whatever… my mate."

Her face turned quickly up to mine, her eyes sparkling in the constant noon of the sun.

"You would… really *want* me?" she asked as if it were the craziest thing she'd ever heard, and so unexpected that it was breaking her heart.

"More than you can possibly know," I said, kissing her.

When our lips separated, she again buried her head in my chest, and held me tight. I felt tears on my skin.

"You cannot have me. The only way is to fight Gudra, and he would kill you. I would rather lie under Gudra the rest of my days than watch him kill you."

"I might beat him. I'm tougher than I look."

"He is twice your size, and well-trained in all the weapons of war."

"Well, then," I said, sighing, and deciding I should give up trying to convince her, "maybe we'll just avoid him entirely. Would you mind if it meant you would never see your village—never see your father or brother, again. Would you be okay with that?"

She shook the chain that bound us.

"I *will* never see my village, or father, or brother again. I'm on my way to become a slave to the Grigori. And they decide who will have me."

"What if we could escape—be together, and not as slaves. Would that be enough to make you happy?"

She lie down and curled up close to me.

"We have a saying in Pangea," she said, trying to force a smile. "'Death takes you whether you laugh or cry. So you may as well die laughing.' I will be happy with you wherever we are, Brandon the Mack. For however long that will be, and be happy with the memories when we are finally pulled apart."

AFTER PASSING OVER the first string of mountains we skirted a flat, salty sea, whose surface churned with immense life, and fantastic underwater battles. We watched a fight between plesiosaurs with long necks stretching ten or more feet above their enormous bodies, snake-like heads splitting wide with gaping, fang-filled mouths whose sole purpose seemed to be shredding another plesiosaur's dark skin, lining it with rips and tears of red blood and dead, white flesh. Milton waxed poetically on all the astounding discoveries, the world-altering possibilities that would shock the scientific community if we ever made it back home.

None of it mattered to me. Only Nova mattered. I needed to find a way to get us out of this, and keep her with me.

Perhaps in an effort to distract me Nova explained that we were watching Endevakuum, or Endevaks of the sea, and that the other, more fearsome reptiles that occasionally rose from the deeper waters to battle them were called Umnyames, or sea-Nyames—what Milton called Ichthyosaurs. They looked like a cross between a whale and an alligator to me. I wondered absently if they were better, or worse looking than Gudra, The Ugly.

"Brandon," Milton called, after we had marched for too damn long beside that wild, insane sea. "Brandon, I used to study paleontology, and I believed what I learned—I really did; but now I can see that I didn't believe it—couldn't really; that it's impossible for people to believe anything like this until they experience it with their own eyes, and all their senses. We take things for granted, I suppose, because people tell us about them over and over again, with no real means of proving or disproving them—like religion, for example; but we don't really buy into these ideas, we only *think* we do. If I were faced with the living God right now I don't think I would be any more stunned than I have been seeing these living, breathing creatures from a child's pop-up book!"

At the next rest, as Milton and I discussed an idea for escape, Hajah the Wily managed to find enough slack in his chain to allow him to worm his way back, very close to Nova, who was sitting in the shade of a tree. The rest of us were all standing, and as he edged nearer to the girl I wanted to protect more than anything, she turned away from him in way calculated to make it clear that she didn't even want to acknowledge his existence, let alone his interest, and the gesture made me smile.

But in the next instant he grabbed her roughly by the hair, and forced her down with one hand while pressing her legs apart with the other, kneeling hard on her opposite inner thigh to give himself force and leverage. His pulsing erection sprang up, clearly visible to me and everyone around us. I nearly screamed as he maneuvered the thing between her legs.

Nova struggled, shot a pleading look in my direction, and it was done.

I moved explosively, my right fist denting the side of his head, my left breaking his ribs. He dropped like a bolted steer. The instant he hit the ground I was on top of him, pounding his face viciously as he tried desperately to block me. I never meant to kill Jessica's boyfriend, but in that moment, I would gladly have ended Hajah.

A roar of approval went up from the other prisoners and a few Angara who had absently watched the little drama unfold; not, apparently, because I had defended Nova, but simply for the neat and—to them—astounding method I'd used to fell my opponent.

Forcing myself to be done bloodying Hajah, I backed away from him, and carefully lifted Nova to my side, looking around at the others as if saying, 'she's mine. Touch her, and you'll get the same.'

Warning sent, I turned to her as she looked at me with wide, wondering, hopeful eyes. But after a few seconds of tense waiting during which I could feel every eye digging into me, her own eyes moistened with tears, and she slowly dropped her head, a delicate flush coloring her cheek. I looked around at the others, some smiling, some embarrassed, and many—mostly the women—furious with anger. What had happened? What had I done?

For a moment Nova stood completely still, in absolute silence. Then she lifted her head high, tears streaming down her face, and turned her back on me the same way she had on Hajah. Some of the prisoners laughed, a few made embarrassed sounds, and I watched the face of Bruk, the Hairy, turn dark with anger, bitterness and confusion.

"What?" I asked. "What did I do?"

But no one answered. Shortly we were resuming our march, and though I realized I had—in some way—offended my beautiful Nova I could not get her to talk to me. Sometimes she cried, sometimes she was angry, but all the time she was silent.

"I want to fix it," I said. "Let me fix it. Nova, *please!*"

Eventually my anger and pride took over, and I stopped any further attempts to communicate. What had felt like the love of my life had ended as abruptly as it had started. From that point on I confined my conversation to Milton. Hajah—face bruised, eyes swollen shut—avoided me, and because he tightened the chain to stay as far from me as possible, Bruk could not get near me to answer my questions. So it was Milton and I, alone again, at the center of this mad, mad world.

The endless marching now became a perfect nightmare for me. Though Nova and I were never more than five feet from one another, we were never closer than two worlds apart; the more she avoided me, the more I resisted talking to her; two disparate cultures, one similar kind of pride. I longed desperately to get close enough to Bruk to beg for the explanation I was sure he'd give, the simple thing I could do that would make everything right between Nova and I. But Hajah kept us too far apart for any reasonable conversation.

Eventually I became desperate, determined to swallow my anger, and once more beg her to please explain how I had offended her, what stupid thing I had done, and how I might make it all better. I decided to *insist* at the next rest stop. Force her to talk to me. Ahead, I could see us approaching another range of mountains, but when we reached it, instead of winding around and through the slopes over some windy and difficult path, we entered the mouth of a huge, natural tunnel—a series of twisting caverns as dark as a pit.

Just before we descended away from all visible light, Hajah turned and looked back at me, glanced once meaningfully at Nova, then returned his attention to me, grinning that shit-eating grin of his. He stopped just short of winking at me.

My heart collapsed.

"Nova," I said, trying to take her hand as darkness enveloped us. "Nova, stay close to me."

"Get away from me!" she said, yanking her hand free of my grasping fingertips.

"Nova, you don't understand…"

"Get off of me!"

"Nova! Take my damn hand!"

"I am not your slave, your servant, or even your friend! Leave me ALONE!"

"Nova!"

Silence. In the darkness I could feel her moving, but couldn't see her, or find her.

"Nova! Pease! If you won't take my hand, watch out for Hajah! Please, Nova!"

Silence.

"Nova, answer me!"

Still nothing. Now I was becoming frantic. I pulled the chain dangling from my neck, working my way forward.

"Nova, please listen to me!"

I pulled myself along, stopping only when Milton lagged behind and the chain tightened, stopping my momentum.

"Milton, hurry up!"

The chain quickly went slack, and I again moved forward. Before long I felt an arm, covered in hair.

"Who's touching me?" I heard Bruk ask.

Ice froze my veins. My heart stopped, my soul shattered. Nova was no longer between me and Bruk. And Hajah was gone.

"NOOOOOOOOOVVVAAAAAAAAA!"

MY MISTAKE

Nova was gone, and with her the vile Hajah and half a dozen other prisoners. The guards, racing back with torches held high saw it too, their rage ferocious and violent. One woman smiled and laughed briefly when she saw how many had escaped and a panther man punched her full in the face. This started a small explosion of activity as others came to her defense, and additional panther-men had to be summoned to quell the outburst.

Eventually the tiny uprising was put down, and the Angara turned their anger on one another, their fearsome, bestial faces twisted with heated embarrassment as they accused one another of being irresponsible. Eventually they stopped being angry at themselves and fell on us, beating mercilessly with spear shafts, and axe heads. They killed two near the head of the line before one of them realized they were making things worse, not better, by eliminating even more of their catch of slaves in a way that would only make their masters angrier.

As quickly as it had begun their leader put a stop to the brutal slaughter. Never in all my life had I seen anything more primitive or horrifying than that outburst of bestial rage—and I thanked God that Nova had not been here to be any part of it.

Bodies hung at weird, twisted angles along the tightened chains, blood leaked everywhere, and the stench of death and vacated bowels was revolting and horrifying. I admit I was scared, and saddened by the events, once more facing the way these people viewed their short lives. I no longer judged their need to take whatever pleasure their brief and tragic existences offered—the instant any such pleasure was offered. For the first time since arriving in Pangea, I wished I was back cleaning floors in my boring, old night job.

Of the twelve prisoners who had been chained ahead of me each alternate one had been freed. How had he done it? Or had he? Was he even capable of something so clever, of stealing the woman I loved? Or had it been another in the string of captives who'd masterminded the escape? And why only every *other* person?

The commander of the Angara was investigating, searching the area, inspecting the abandoned collars and links. He quickly discovered that the rude locks, which held the neckbands in place, had not been forced. They'd either been deftly picked, or simply unlocked.

"Hajah the Wily," grumbled Bruk, who had been moved to be next in line with me. "He took Nova as vengeance, and she went because you would not have her."

"Because I... because what?" I asked, amazed. "What do you mean 'I would not have her'? I wanted Nova more than anything!"

He looked at me closely for a moment.

"I doubted your story that you came from someplace so far away; that you didn't know our customs," he said slowly, still studying me carefully, "but I can't really imagine any other reason why you would be so cruel to that poor girl. You honestly don't know how you've offended her, do you?"

"I honestly don't, Bruk," I answered, precisely. "Please explain it to me."

"It's understandable," Bruk said, shrugging. "We have all made love to girls we don't really want to mate, as girls who don't want to mate with us, have done, as well. And when faced with having to either admit our love, or let go, we... well..." he shrugged again, "... we are men, after all."

"Believe me, Bruk, I have no *fucking* clue what you're talking about."

He sighed, heavily, and explained.

"An ugly girl like Nova..."

"What are you talking about? Nova's not ugly."

"That's very noble of you to say, but..."

"It's not noble. It's honest. Where I come from, Nova would be seen exactly as she is named, 'Nova, The Beautiful'. She's the most attractive woman I've ever seen."

Bruk again studied me silently, eyes moving back and forth across my face, searching, until a slow grin spread over his.

"You truly believe that," he said.

"*YES!*" I yelled.

"You do, don't you?" asked the woman who had been linked beside me in Nova's place, the woman we'd been captured with in the monkey-man arena.

She was very pretty, though older, and a bit heavy, and she smiled at me with a radiant hopefulness I didn't really understand.

"Yes, I do," I said firmly, thoroughly confused, turning back to Bruk. "How is it that you don't?"

He winced.

82

"Her nose is small," he said, "her eyes too large, her lips puffy like she was beaten too much as a child; she is thin, her breasts are too large, like a pregnant woman…"

I laughed.

"And that's *un*attractive to you?" I asked.

"Yes!" he insisted.

"And everyone in Pangea would think this way?"

"Everyone but *you*, apparently."

"Do all men where you're from," asked the woman beside me, "do they see beauty where others see… someone *not* attractive?"

"Are you asking…" I said, starting to understand, "are you wondering if men where I come from would find *you* pretty?"

She lowered her eyes shyly, and smiled, nodding just a bit.

"Yes," I said gently. "You would be considered *extremely* lovely where I come from. Any man would be proud to have you beside him."

She flushed and her eyes lit up the way Nova's had when I'd told her how beautiful she was to me.

"Isn't that right, Milton?" I said, noting that my friend was staring at her nervously.

"Oh, yes," he said, shaking himself out of his daze. "Quite lovely. Very, very attractive to… well… anyone where we come from. Understandable, really. You *are* rather beautiful. Striking, really. Hard to imagine anyone prettier."

She turned to Milton, and assessed him, apparently liking what she saw. The older man was not unattractive for someone his age, and though he hadn't seen a gym since his teenage years, his time in Pangea was toning him up, and making him—well—certainly a whole lot more attractive to this woman who had probably been ignored her whole life.

I turned my attention back to Bruk.

"Please tell me what happened between Nova and I," I begged.

"Well," Bruk began, scratching his thick beard and grimacing as he tried to sort his thoughts. "Nova the Beautiful is legendary among the Nyala—we are in the same extended tribe, she and I, on the plains of the Sa Fasi. Our clans are close together, though I'd never met her. From the moment she was born, so the story goes, her father loved her dearly, and when some men in his tribe called her ugly and made jokes about her as a child, he named her 'beautiful' because—as a father will—he truly believed it. Gudra, The Ugly only claimed her because he wanted to be king of the Nyala, and maybe because other women wouldn't have him, but mostly to be king. No man or lover would challenge Gudra because—and Nova knew this—because unless a man wanted to rule Sa Fasi, and not many did, she was not considered worth fighting for."

My chest tightened. I felt an unbearable pain in my stomach as I remembered some of the things she'd said to me. If I'd not only hurt her in some way, but played into her belief that she was ugly…

"So when you wouldn't claim her as yours," Bruk continued, "Hajah… obviously…"

"What do you mean; 'when I wouldn't claim her as mine'?"

"You really are from *very* far away," Bruk said, amazed. "Sex on Pangea—or at least my part of Pangea—is consensual, most of the time. Obviously not always. Sometimes you just don't want to. We have ways of asking—simple signals—and usually a rejection means you simply go away and ask someone else. Nova sent you those signals many times, but you never responded. We assumed because you thought as we did—that she was too ugly.

"I... no," I said, saddened. "I just... I didn't know, Bruk. I didn't understand... and I... I was afraid. We don't have sex in front of people where I come from."

"Well, she took it as you not liking her enough to see past her looks." Bruk said, equal sadness in his voice. "Until after the Hakchata attack, when she just couldn't leave you alone any longer. You see, *forcing* someone to have sex with you means you are *claiming* them. They are yours, and yours alone for sex, and children, and whatever else you may want—but not for love."

I remembered Nova rolling on top of me with such intensity and desire, and wondered if that's what had happened between the two of us. She had claimed me.

"What if you don't want to be claimed?" I asked.

"It doesn't matter. If no other person is interested in intervening, then the coupling means the one you have joined with is yours—as you became Nova's."

She *had* taken me. Again, my head felt light, and my heart hurt. I was hers. I *was* hers.

"So what does that mean?" I asked. "Nova is my mate?"

"Not exactly," Bruk said, cautiously, "though it often works out that way. I think she just did it because other women were looking at you, and considering doing what *she* did, and so—in the heat of the moment... and because *she* loved *you...*"

"She *did* love me."

He shrugged.

"What did it mean?" I asked. "What did she do... when she... when we...?"

"She made you her property. No request was made, no acceptance given, so in the eyes of the other women here..."

"You are a desirable man, Brandon the Mack," the new woman told me. "Bruk is right. Others were considering you as a partner. It is not entirely as Bruk says—custom means less when you are far from home and not likely to be seen, or caught—but in front of us, Nova was staking a claim. And we respected that."

I looked at her, then at some of the other women in the chain, and wondered about my desirability. A woman I'd heard called by the name 'Shalla' on the other side of Bruk had been eavesdropping on the conversation, saw me looking at her, flushed red, averted her eyes shyly, and nodded in agreement.

"It's true," she said, quietly.

"But…" I said, surprised at my desirability, "we're not married, Nova and I? Or 'mated', or whatever you call it?"

The woman and Bruk both shook their heads. Shalla flushed even redder, and continued smiling.

"Being officially mated involves ritual," Bruk said, "formal requests of the parents and…"

"Gudra's Endevak head."

"Yes. But often the parents die before the children are ready for marriage, and so this other method has come to be. It gets complicated because Gudra has made a *formal* request, Nova's father still lives, and you are *technically* Nova's sex slave…"

I laughed, when I wanted to cry.

"…and it gets *more* complicated when someone tries to force a coupling," the new woman said, "and another person—man or woman—steps in."

"The way Hajah tried to take Nova, and I punched him."

"It was very exciting," she said.

"I'm sorry," I said, turning to face her, "What is your name?"

"Elia," she said. "Elia, the Unfortunate."

I studied her, and knitted my brows in confusion. I was going to have to ask about this naming thing in Pangea. But later. Not now.

"When a man of Pangea intervenes where another man is trying to take a woman," Bruk said. "the woman belongs to the victor. All the rituals of marriage go out the window."

"Well…" said Elia, staring at Bruk with obvious disapproval. "Who the woman belongs to—or doesn't belong to— has more meaning to some than others…"

"Well, where *I* come from," Bruk said, becoming annoyed with Elia's persistent interruptions, "when a man has tried to *hurt* a woman, or take her against her will—as Hajah was intending to do—and another man—you, Brandon—steps in and makes clear that this woman is *not* to be mistreated, you are announcing to the world that you wish to protect this woman, whether for the moment, or for life depending on what you do next."

"It's gallant, and all," Elia said, once more irritating Bruk, "but sometimes it's staged so people can work around parents, and it's far from binding, unless it happens in your village, or near people you know, who are aware of what's happened, and even then…"

"Nova the Beautiful belongs to you," Bruk interrupted, then directed his next comment directly at Elia. "It is what *she* believes, *which is all that matters here!"*

Elia recoiled from his obvious anger, not out of fear so much as to avoid being spat on. Bruk's yelling had gotten a little moist. Her eye roll said plainly that she hadn't changed her opinion just because she'd been scolded.

Bruk struggled to regain his composure, turning back to me.

"You fought to protect her," he said, "and this takes precedence over Gudra's gift. You had beaten Gudra without having to face him."

"Which would have been ideal in her eyes," I said, realizing.

"Yes. He could have her, but he would have to make a formal demand to fight you for her; her father would never approve, and anyway he's on the other side of the sea. With one, quick action, you could have made Nova your mate for life."

"But I didn't. I fucked it up because I didn't do something. What Bruk? What did I do wrong? I need to fix this."

"You would have to find her, first."

"I will scour all of Pangea to make this right, Bruk," I said, and Elia gasped in delight. "What do I have to do?"

"You have to do what you should have done when you punched Hajah. You have to claim her, or release her. Had you taken her hand and held it up for all to see, then placed it over your heart, it would have shown your desire to make her your mate."

"It *is* kind of romantic," Elia said.

"Or if you'd raised her hand above her head and dropped it," Bruk continued, "it would have meant you didn't want her for yourself, and she was now free of any obligation to you. You were simply protecting her, and she owed you nothing for the act. By doing neither you have insulted her in the most degrading way a man can insult a woman."

I glanced at Elia, who looked pained.

"It's a bit old fashioned," she admitted. "But it *is* very insulting,"

"She is now your property," Bruk said.

"Well..." Elia said, dismissing Bruk.

"*She is now your property,*" Bruk repeated, angrily, more to her than me. "But not as someone you would want for your own, not even to have sex with, but only as a servant, or a toy for any *other* men or women who visited you that might wish to entertain themselves with her in some way. No one will ever want her as *their* mate after she's been so insulted..."

"Unless she escapes, and runs away from the insult, and you." Elia said.

"Which is what she did," I said, sadly. "Why did she have to escape? Why not just tell me what I needed to know to fix it?"

"She is ugly," Elia admitted. "I am ugly, but not as ugly as her. She probably took what you did as an inability to admit your love, publicly."

"She knows I don't understand your ways."

"In the theater of public opinion," Bruk said, "it is not what *we know* that matters, it is what others *think*."

He was right. It was the same on the outer world. I guess this is a universally human trait. I stared at him, furious with myself, and utterly humiliated over what I'd done.

"No other man," Bruk said, then rethought what he was going to say off Elia's expression, "no other man *who had witnessed* what you did could even take her honorably if he wanted, unless he believed he could kill you in combat. And because she is not pretty, no one will ever want to risk their life for her."

I stood silent, my expression saying it all, and Bruk put a hand on my shoulder, though it offered me no comfort.

"The rest of us thought you cared for her," Bruk said, "but couldn't get past her ugliness to take her as a wife."

"And she thought the same," I said, heartbroken. "My, poor, perfect Nova. Nothing could be further from the truth. I didn't know, Bruk! Elia! I honestly didn't know!"

"I believe you," Elia said, smiling, sadly.

"And I question your taste," Bruk said, "but I also believe you."

"Not for anything in this world would I have hurt Nova, ever, in any way. I don't want her as my slave. I want her—I want her as my—" I stopped. An image of that sweet, funny, smiling, beautiful, innocent face floated through my mind on the soft mists of imagination. "My wife. My mate. My friend. My companion. My lover. If I'd known I would have held up *both* her hands, placed them both against my heart and never let them go."

Elia sighed, happily, and put her hands to her mouth, moved. Bruk smiled.

"Lips can lie," he said, "but when the heart speaks through the eyes it tells nothing less than the truth. I know you meant no offense to Nova, the Beautiful. I can see that, now. But it's not *me* that you have to convince. The shame will stay with her for a long time. Maybe the rest of her short life."

"Her short life?" I said, dying inside.

"Life is short, then you die," Bruk said.

"Do all of your sayings end in some form of: 'and then you die'?" I asked.

"Most of them. This is Pangea, after all."

I felt drained, trampled, horrified and emotionally destroyed by what I'd inadvertently done to her. And now she might die, eaten alive by some horrible creature and never know I really loved her. To hurt someone who meant nothing less than the world to me—two worlds to me—was a pain that was difficult to bear.

"How can I fix this?" I asked Bruk.

"You'll never be able to," he answered matter-of-factly. "You are doomed to end your life a slave of the Grigori."

"There's no way to escape?" I asked.

"If you're wily," he said, smiling sinisterly. "Hajah escaped and took the others with him—Nova included. The Angara think he picked the locks, but he actually stole a key when you pulled that Angara into the river. He only pretended to fall in himself. Being wily means waiting for opportunities, and seizing them when they present themselves. If *you* are presented with an opportunity, perhaps you might escape. But perhaps the sun will go out and the whole world will go dark."

"Is it possible," I asked, considering an odd thought, "that Hajah might have forced himself on Nova *knowing* I would protect her, and also knowing that I wouldn't know what to do?"

"I wouldn't put anything past him," Bruk said. "He is legendarily devious, that one. His name is well earned. Perhaps—like Gudra—he desires kingship of the Nyala."

"How do I escape," I asked. "How do I find that son of a bitch and get Nova back?"

"I don't see how you can."

"There has to be a way!"

"We all want one, Brandon, the Mack. Believe me. But Hajah may have seized the only opportunity any of us ever gets. If there are no more dark tunnels or passageways between here and Emibi we'll have no chance, and once in the city of the Grigori it will only be more difficult; the Grigori are very smart. Even if you managed to escape from Emibi they have ways of tracking you, and then there are the Ingonghus—they would find you, and—" the Hairy One shuddered and made a weird motion in front of his face, like the sign of the cross, combined with a slicing motion across his neck. "No, you'll never escape the Grigori."

I felt depression drop on me like a stone.

"Have you been hearing any of this, Milton?" I asked, turning toward the older man.

To refill the gaps in line they had moved prisoners around, and he was now just beyond Elia.

"I've heard it all," Milton said. "It's a genuinely fascinating cultural study. So much of the Pangean customs are borne out of quick needs, and short life expectancy. Given Nova's history and probable unattractiveness to the locals, her unlikely attraction to you now makes much more sense."

"Thanks," I said, sarcastically.

"You're welcome," he answered, confused by my answer and not hearing the edge in my voice.

"Do you have any thoughts for how we might be able to escape, or how I can find Nova?"

"Are you asking me if there's a way for you to find one woman who could be anywhere in this world—including digesting inside a dinosaur—a woman who doesn't want to be found, on a continent the size of the Atlantic ocean, with only stone age tools and implements to help me search? Is that what you're asking me?"

The ridiculousness of my request hit me like a brick to the forehead. I lowered my eyes, and inhaled, deeply, trying to fight back the agony I was feeling.

"I'm sorry, Brandon," Milton said. "I had no idea you felt such genuine affection for this girl. I feel almost ashamed of myself for judging you poorly because you willingly engaged in public acts of sex…"

"You don't do that where you come from?" Bruk asked.

"Generally speaking, no," Milton said. "Most higher cultures in our… em, homeland… consider it improper to expose our bodies in any way, but especially during coitus."

"But... it's a part of life," said Elia, again interrupting. "And enjoyable."

"Perhaps," Milton said, "But nonetheless..."

"So, you've never done it with another, simply for fun?"

Milton blushed bright red, and shook his head, nervously.

"You should!" she said to Milton, happily. "I would be willing."

He looked as if she'd slapped him with a dead fish.

"I'm sorry?" he said.

"You are a handsome, if older man, and I would be willing to have sex with you if you do not tease me for being unattractive. Then maybe you'll see why it's enjoyable to make love whenever the desire arises."

"Yes, Milton," I said, brightly. "Consider it a scientific and cultural experiment for better understanding the local population. You can't write about it knowledgably for a journal when we get back if you haven't actually experienced it firsthand, now, can you?"

"I..." Milton said, then his eyes shifted to the smiling face of the amazingly attractive older woman. If she was considered ugly, then this place really *was* upside down. "I..."

Elia gently took hold of Milton's hand and walked him over to a flat spot, where she lay casually on her back, waving her fingertips for him to come down and join her. From where I stood I saw his lil Alvarado pop up and point sunward. He abruptly turned and looked shyly at me before making up his mind.

"Don't watch," he said to Bruk and I.

"It really matters to you?" Bruk asked.

Milton could only manage a jerky, stilted nod.

Bruk shrugged, turned away, and I did likewise. We both had to fight to keep from laughing as poor Milton went about his business, all the while making statements and asking questions.

"Ah. Ah, yes, I see. You want me to just—straight to it, eh? Right in there? Fine, fine, I... *Oh!* Oh, yes. My, that feels *quite* good, actually. Is it enjoyable for you? No? A little bit? What should I do differently? Just pinch there? Like so?"

There were two more marches broken up by two more rests for Bruk and I, while Milton and his new girlfriend continued to use any and all available time in the mutually satisfying pursuit of public fornication. Milton never stopped talking during the fun, but Elia didn't seem to mind.

EVENTUALLY WE REACHED the end of our unending journey, the fabled city of Emibi.

The entrance was framed by two massive, carved towers of granite, which housed Angara guards overlooking an immense flight of stone steps that led downward, deeply downward, into the dark, and cavernous city. Milton and I looked at one another as the massive structure came more fully into view. It was like a city of the future gone bad. Beautifully designed spires and structures nearly obscured beneath layers of grasses, vines, weeds, shrubs, trees, and stone. Very few windows contained unbroken glass. Nothing looked recent or well maintained.

"It's either a society in decline," Milton mused, "or a squatter civilization inhabiting the remains of some other, long dead culture."

"Does it matter which?" I asked.

"Ultimately… I suppose not."

We descended the ruined steps into the worn city. We had arrived at the home of the legendary and mysterious Grigori, our new masters, and if I were to believe my companions, I wouldn't leave again until I died.

THE LIFE OF A SLAVE

AS WE DESCENDED THE BROAD, stone steps into the main avenue of Emibi I finally got my first look at the dominant race of this inner world. We were moving along a surprisingly large main street of broken asphalt dotted with grasses and weeds; there were naked humans everywhere, along with sparsely clothed Angara, all drifting slowly and unenthusiastically from place to place. Buildings had crumbled and collapsed on either side of the lane, and through deglassed windows I could see movement, though not many clear images of anyone, or anything.

Until I noticed a large, rough, leathery, reptile bob past one of the obscured windows, and move through an open door, Angara and human alike stepping aside to avoid blocking its way. It stood over seven feet tall, with a tail at least as long as its body trailing behind to provide balance. Its head was stunted like a lizard, and narrow, with rows of spiky teeth that protruded up and down on either side of its top and bottom jaws. It had large, black, round eyes that reflected the dim, spotty light filtering in through a canopy of overlarge trees that had sprouted up randomly throughout the city. The thing's weird feet and hands were—like the head—evolved lizard; long, jointed and clawed, with webbing between the toes, just as Nova had said. Membranous, translucent wings sprouted from the ribs alongside, and flowed out behind it, folding carefully against the side and back of its muscled trunk.

As the thing passed I glanced over at Milton to catch his reaction. The old man's mouth hung open, his eyes goggling with amazement.

"Troodon!" he said, excitedly.

"What?" I asked.

He turned as if only just remembering I was there.

"Brandon, do you know of a man named Dale Russell?"

"No."

"He was a vertebrate fossil curator in Canada who hypothesized on the idea of a humanoid—called Troodon—evolving from Stenonychosaurus—a theropod from—well, what we was the Cretaceous period a hundred or so million years ago. His idea looked—or so I and others thought—too much like a man in a rubber suit. *But this! This* looks something more like an honest-to-god evolved Troodon! More muscled and dense, with a good deal of the bird-like posture and movement of the ancestor remaining in evidence. Holy heavens, that thing is *INCREDIBLE!*"

As we continued on down the main avenue of Emibi we eventually passed dozens of the things coming and going to whatever it was they did here. They traveled both alone, and in groups, but never seemed to speak, or communicate with the 'lower' races. In fact, they paid very little attention to any human unless one of us was in their way, and then only to shove them aside.

Having taken in my fill of the Grigori, I turned my attentions upward to the canopy above us, an interwoven tent of branches and leaves, marveling at how dense it was, and how effective at softening the power and perpetual heat of the unmoving sun. It also kept the light fairly even throughout the city, with only occasional pools of brightness here and there where the natural awning broke open a bit. Speckled sunlight filtered in through the leaves at fairly consistent, seemingly manufactured intervals, soft and diffuse. It gave the place a cool, almost comfortable feel. I was trying to see if the overhang was tended and groomed, or simply natural when I slammed into something hard, and leathery.

That something whooshed instantly through the air toward my face. I recoiled, instinctively, and felt more than heard the two massive jaws as they snapped in the empty space my head had just occupied.

The Grigori I'd bumped into had missed, but still drawn blood. I touched the wound on my cheek, realizing with expanding horror that if I hadn't moved in time, my head would be gone. The thing was surprisingly fast, and surprisingly pissed.

I jumped aside as it came at me again barely in time to avoid a second strike that was faster than the first. More blood flowed from a hot, new rip in my arm. The crowd around us flowed quickly away, forming a ring a safe distance from the action. Only Milton, Bruk, and Elia stayed close, but not by choice, as they clustered behind me in our chain of fools, all eyes locked on the furious spectacle playing out before them. Fellow slaves watched horrified, and one or two Angara smiled in anticipation of my imminent demise.

The Grigori continued to snap at me, recoil, then snap again, circling and striking with terrific speed and accuracy. I danced madly to avoid being struck, and my friends maneuvered clumsily in an equally desperate effort to avoid coming between me and my attacker. I had to move fast enough and far enough to avoid being killed, but not so far that I yanked one of my friends into becoming an alternate meal. It was a delicate balancing act, and failure meant I or one of my friends would be nothing more than stains and pieces on the concrete floor.

Diving to avoid another gnashing Grigori attack that startled me with how close it had been to my eyes, I stumbled backward, collided with Milton, and the two of us went sprawling on the floor, yanking Bruk over in the process. He tried to avoid falling toward the angry Grigori, dove too far to the right, and the sudden tightening in the chain yanked everyone behind him in exactly the wrong direction. In the resulting game of Slinky, Shalla—the girl just beyond Bruk who had shown red-faced interest in me—stumbled and collided with the evil Grigori.

Sadly, she wasn't as quick as I had been.

With one, fierce snap, the poor woman's head and one shoulder were gone, her lifeless remains collapsing out of the chains that tied her to us, dropping to the floor like a wet sack.

But the Grigori wasn't finished. As the humans surrounding us all cried out in horror and fear, the Ugly Master of Pangea leapt on what remained of poor Shalla's body, ripping it to bits, blood and gore spraying wetly in all directions. Once it had shredded the poor lady thoroughly, it savagely gobbled the remaining bits of flesh and bone like a ravenous beast, tossing pieces into the air and catching them in its open craw.

Human and Angara alike scattered in fear of being next, but for some reason I stood frozen in horror and anger, wanting to kill the fucking Grigori where it stood, knowing that would be impossible, but still unable to stop considering it and move away.

Fortunately for me, Bruk wrapped an arm around my throat and *insisted* I move away. We were a hundred yards from the still frenzied Grigori before my friend stopped garroting me. Pulling me around, he gripped me by the shoulders and stared at me the way an impatient parent stares at a child.

"My friend," Bruk said smiling, though his eyes were warning. "Life in Pangea is short enough without you trying to make it *shorter.*"

"That thing shredded Shalla like she was nothing! And ATE her!"

"As it would have shredded us all, my friend. *Move and Live. Stand and die.* It's a simple philosophy, really, and one I always try to keep foremost in my mind, *especially* when things are trying to eat *me.*"

"You're making jokes after what just happened?"

"You can laugh until you die, or cry until you die. But either way, you die."

Our Angara guards eventually overcame their fears, tracked us down, and angrily shoved us back in line. We were hurried along the still crowded central avenue and into a large public building, then taken through some darkened corridors and into an immense chamber. The room was huge, and filled with the reptilian Grigori, all scattered about, perching atop darkened, dirty stones, or standing around a central open-area on the floor.

The panther man who had been our most obnoxious guard, the one I'd dunked in the river, led us down an aisle to the central 'stage' and began to speak to one of the Grigori about my capture. The method of communication between the two was remarkable in that the Grigori spoke nothing, and it seemed entirely unable to hear.

"Have you noticed how the thing has to be facing the Angara to know what he's saying?" I asked Milton.

"Yes," Milton said, studying even more intently than I. "The Angara has to repeat himself when the Grigori looks away. Interesting. No auditory organs? Is it deaf, or does it simply have a vocal range that doesn't pick up the Angara's voice?"

"Are you asking me?"

"No. Rhetorical."

As we stood with nothing to do while the Grigori and our guard 'discussed' whatever it was that seemed so important, my mind slowly filled once more with images of Nova. I had to escape. I had to find her. The thought of her out there, alone, possibly being raped repeatedly by Hajah was too much for me to live with. The fear and rage of being trapped and unable to act were nearly crippling.

"You will be taken to one of the libraries," the Angara said to us. "You," he said pointing to Milton, "will catalogue, while you," he pointed to Bruk and I, "will dry and move the books to a new location."

"Thank you," I said, "for relaying that incredibly heavy and difficult message from your master and superior. It's nice to know they can find someone with your skills, courage and intelligence to relay those few, important words from all the way over there, back to us, over here. You should rest now. You're probably tired."

The Angara scowled, and didn't answer—simply annoyed that I'd even spoken—staring for a very long time. Then his fist slammed through my stomach, shoving it and my other internal organs against my spine, doubling me over, as his other fist pounded against the base of my skull. My vision clouded and I fell to my knees.

"You know, having given it some thought," I heard Bruk say. "I'm coming down on the side of stupid."

THE BOOKS WERE HEAVY, large, and covered in slime. Designed for larger, stronger hands than mine, they'd apparently been stored for quite a while in damp conditions, and for whatever reason the Grigori hadn't noticed they needed caring for. Or perhaps they had, but avoided doing it because the damn things were probably toxic.

There was fungus or mold in quite a few of them, enough that my lungs began aching, and my eyes burning from whatever fumes they'd been releasing almost as soon as I walked into the room. Several were so soaked through that any physical contact made them turn nearly to mush. I wasn't sure what I was supposed to do to save them, but everything I tried seemed to upset the Angara if my methods damaged the things in the slightest way. Bruising a book was a crime punishable by beatings with heavy leather clubs.

Bruk and I quickly devised a way to soak out most of the liquid so we could eventually move the damn things without completely destroying them. It didn't always save the books, but covering them for the 'drying' process also concealed any damage we'd inflicted on them while moving them, and spared us additional beatings.

As we moved and hauled Milton scoured the pages inside, trying to catalogue and organize them in their new home, a large, recently cleared out building whose moisture ridden walls seemed likely to recreate the same conditions as the previous library in very short order.

Because the work was hard on the lungs, conversation was kept to a minimum, which only meant more time for my agonizing thoughts about Nova, Hajah, and every horrible thing an imaginative mind can conjure to torture itself. The thought that he might be—repeatedly—finishing what he had attempted when I'd attacked him made my stomach feel as though large animals were trying to chew their way out of it. I couldn't eat, never slept, and before long the inner turmoil raging through me left me half the man I'd been when we'd arrived. The only positive thoughts that came to me in that time were that Nova had at least escaped captivity, avoided the Angara who had threatened to buy her, and was probably self-sufficient enough to defend herself against Hajah.

I hoped.

Sometimes I felt guilty that I would have preferred to have Nova here in Emibi, a slave of the Grigori, than somewhere out there at the mercy of savage Pangea, and that piece of shit Hajah. Bruk, Milton, and I often talked of escape, but our hairy friend was so convinced *no one* could escape the Grigori that he wasn't much help—sadly content to wait for the miracle to come to him. Which made me all the more determined to conjure one.

"What are these?" I asked Milton, who was poring through one of the moldy books.

"What?" he asked, looking over at me, then down to where I pointed. "Oh. Scraps of metal. Some Angara threw them there. I don't know why."

95

"They didn't say?"

"No. I think they were just looking for a place to dump them."

"Weirder and weirder. This place is mostly stone age, but right there are scraps of metal—common enough, apparently, to be garbage. Aren't they afraid we'll take them and use them?"

"The Pangean humans are quite fatalistic," Milton said, dismissively. "Bruk is not unique. They accept the fact that you cannot escape the Grigori."

"Why would they accept that?"

"Because it's true."

"What?" I said, stunned." Milton, what are you saying? Are you giving up, too?"

"No, I've just been reading. A side effect of the language implants appears to be an ability to comprehend the Grigori written language, as well."

"Language *implants*?"

"Yes. When the Angara placed those metallic things to our heads, they were implanting a device inside our skulls. Rather efficiently, too. No blood, no visible wound. The salient point here is that the device is more than a language translator; it's also a tracking device among other things. Once you have been 'tagged' by the Grigori as their property you truly cannot escape them."

I sat, deflated.

"Damn," was all I could manage to say.

"Yes. Indeed. So you needn't worry about Nova any longer, as I know you have been. She will be found."

"And she'll be brought here?"

Milton stared a moment, then shrugged.

"There are other Grigori cities," he said, sadly. "She might be taken to one of them."

"So Bruk was right. No one escapes the Grigori."

"It appears so. We put it off to superstition, but as is often the case with many superstitions, there is an underlying element of science. To Bruk, it is magic. To us, it's simple technology."

"Technology, metal, dinosaurs, reptilian masters, naked savages, slavery" I said, dejected. "This place is crazy." After a moment of silence, I asked the obvious; "Can we remove the device?"

"Yes," Milton said, also sounding a bit depressed. "But I have to assume it's impossible given the primitive tools available, and our general lack of surgical skill."

I dropped into a nearby chair and sulked. Milton seemed to be enjoying his stay here. He had Elia, and his research, and I was losing my mind.

"Brandon," Milton asked, "have you seen a book in any of your wanderings? Larger than most of these. Bound with metal. Possibly in a room like a laboratory?"

"No," I answered, reaching down into the discarded metal pile, I picked up a length of steel that seemed to be a remnant of an old sword. "Why?"

"It's mentioned often in some of these texts. I think it might be useful to us."

"I'll keep an eye out for it. And a lab."

"Not just an eye. Both eyes. In fact, I would appreciate it if you actively look for it, when you have time."

"It's that important?"

"I think it might be."

"What is it?"

"A cookbook, of sorts," he said.

"For cooking humans?"

"No. I'll tell you more when you find it, and I can read it."

"Okay."

I turned the broken sword piece over in my hands and watched the light from a nearby lantern play over it.

"Milton," I said, curious about the glittering flashes. "This metal looks like steel, which is harder to make than bronze, isn't it? Or even just stone tools?"

"It is, indeed."

"And the Grigori have implanted us with what would have to be a very sophisticated little piece of hardware. More sophisticated than anything we have up on the surface. How is all this weirdness possible?"

"I've been wondering the same thing. It's why I'm doing so much reading. I feel like I'm missing something about this place. Something which should be obvious."

"The books aren't helping?"

"They are, but like any book, they're about specific subjects of interest, rather than general knowledge—like this one which is about Grigori reproduction..."

"Ew."

"Actually it's quite fascinating..."

"To you."

Milton laughed.

"Okay," he said, " to me. But listen to this and tell me if it doesn't captivate you." he said it with a tone that told me he was about to lecture me at length about something boring. "This book explains how the Grigori are all female. That years and years ago they eliminated the need for males in the reproductive process."

"You're *kidding*," I said, astounded.

I was wrong. It wasn't boring.

"Not at all. Long ago, using a standard of time I don't understand, the various tribes of Grigori went to war. Some began mass-producing males who were apparently larger and more vicious then was normal in order to use them as soldiers. Eventually all the books containing the secret of reproduction were destroyed except the one they keep here. To control the other, more ambitious Grigori tribes, apparently."

"That's the book you're looking for? The one that tells how to make soldiers?"

"Or simply how to reproduce Grigori, in general. I'd love to get hold of that book."

"I bet you would."

"The unfortunate reality," he continued, "is that these books are filling in a bit of the picture, but not the whole thing. Grigori are highly intelligent, and technologically sophisticated. They can control reproduction. But all the tools are old, and often in disrepair. The possibilities are—as this city itself has indicated—that they're either a society in decline, or are borrowing technology from some other, long dead civilization. Or perhaps some third, or fourth possibility that I'm not yet seeing."

"What does that mean to us, and our hopes for escaping?"

Milton shrugged.

"Give me something, Milton," I said. "I can't stop worrying about Nova, and I need a little hope, here."

"I don't know," he said. "Hopefully I'll find a more detailed book that gives me some ideas and options. Maybe a history of Pangea, or the Grigori, or..."

He shrugged again.

I considered all of what Milton had said, and what it might mean. Would Nova eventually be found? Would she be brought back here? Or to some other Grigori city? Was escape *truly* impossible? Could the implanted devices ever be removed? Or at least deactivated? If they had such sophisticated technology for putting them into our heads, shouldn't they also have something similar for taking them out?

With no answers readily available, I went back to studying the reflections of light in my piece of metal, analyzing the sharpness of the edge, and began to consider other, less *intellectual* possibilities for escape.

THE WILY ONE RETURNS

GIVEN THAT WHATEVER PLAN we might concoct would require weapons, Milton and I began to take the scraps of metal the Angara left behind and shape them back into swords and knives.

Due—I supposed—to the fatalistic attitudes of the Pangeans, we were given almost unrestrained freedom within the confines of the buildings to which we'd been assigned, and no one seemed concerned if they saw us with tools, or sharpened steel. There were so many slaves that no one had more work than he or she could handle, and this gave us ample free time to do things they really wouldn't have wanted us doing had they been paying attention.

We hid our new weapons under the furs and skins that made up our beds, and then Milton came up with the idea of making bows and arrows—weapons apparently unheard of anywhere within Pangea. We decided we would also need shields; but these were easier to steal from the walls of the outer guardroom than they were to create ourselves.

To make a serious attempt at escape we needed a plan, and we needed to hide our getaway. Nothing seemed to click until I made a rather odd discovery in the basements beneath one of the buildings while searching for Milton's book.

I had been exploring deep inside the city, down twisted streets filled with empty shops and apartments, far beyond the normal routes we slaves were supposed to go—when I suddenly came upon four Grigori curled up on beds of fur. At first I thought they were dead, but then I noticed a slow, infrequent, but regular breathing and realized they were simply out cold. I backed away slowly so as not to disturb them and create a potential nest of problems for myself, planning to get away

99

and never give them another thought. But something about them kept obsessing me—though for some reason my conscious mind couldn't seem to connect with whatever my subconscious was trying to tell me.

We had enough weapons ready to make a serious attempt at escape when word trickled in to us from along the slave gossip lines that a hunting party of Angara had returned with a cache of recaptured prisoners. This had happened a few times before, and each time I'd been disappointed that none of the returnees had been anyone we knew—a certain cave girl in particular.

This time was different.

I raced out into the main avenue between buildings and stood on a bench to see over the gathered crowd, shoving people aside to get a clear view. From the direction of the massive stone stairs that descended into the city a group of angry Angara were beating forward several bruised and bloody men and women. Again, they were all people I didn't recognize, and certainly Nova wasn't among them. But suddenly one of the captives in front stepped forward to reveal a man behind him, and I saw a face that filled me with instant fury.

Hajah.

I leapt down and shoved my way through the crowd, racing over to the chained prisoners. Hajah saw me, his eyes widening with fear, his head pinioning back and forth looking for—I don't know—an escape? Assistance? It didn't matter, because there was neither and I was on him. I slammed a fist into his jaw and he practically flipped backwards into another prisoner who shoved him off, and onto the ground.

Hajah's head hit the stone floor hard, with me right on top of him.

"WHERE IS SHE?" I demanded. *"WHERE'S NOVA?"*
"GET OFF ME!"

I punched him hard in the nose, and he stopped struggling, his body going limp, but not unconscious. Blood began to seep from each nostril.

"I don't know!" he shrieked. "I never saw her after I unchained her! I didn't want her anyway, The ugly bitch!"

I slugged him again, and blood spurted from his tongue as he unintentionally bit it. Then I pounded him again, and again. He struggled weakly a while longer, maybe assuming I was going to continue beating him—which I wanted to—but instead I held myself back and asked him again.

"WHERE IS SHE?"

"She went a different way! I don't know! I swear it! Maybe she got lost in the tunnels!"

The thought horrified me. Nova, trapped in those caves, no torch, no way to get free. I raised my hand to hit him again, but several Angara pulled me off, pelting me in the side of the head for causing a disturbance. Once he saw he was free of me, Hajah smiled, his arrogance quickly returning when he knew I couldn't retaliate.

"I only freed her so *you* couldn't have her," he snarled. "I really don't give a fuck *what* happens to her, as long as she dies alone someplace where *you'll* never find her."

I went for him again, but the Angara held me fast, and though it took all of them to stop me, they did manage to keep me from cracking Hajah's skull open on the rock floor. The traitorous one got to his feet and shuffled off with the others in his chain, staring back and smiling at me the whole way.

"Oh," he said, now almost out of speaking distance, "but as a goodbye, I finished what I started. I took her. Twice. And the whole time I rode her, she just cried like a *baby*."

I nearly exploded, fighting like an insane animal, and had to be thrown to the ground and held down by—now—four Angara.

It took a while, but I eventually calmed down, and the Angara let me go.

"I don't mind you beating on that piece of shit," one of the panther-men said to me, his face gouged with a massive scar, "but the Grigori feel he has value as a slave, and so they would not be happy if I let you kill him."

"Only because they don't know him."

The Angara laughed, nodding agreement, his scarred face becoming far less frightening, and suddenly I recognized him.

"I know you," I said.

"And I know *you*," he said, smiling. "You're the fool who punched one of my men. Still making friends wherever you go, I see."

He laughed, and waved his hands as if to tell me to go away, and so I did, turning and heading back toward Milton and the library.

I'd been worried before, terrified, actually, of exactly what Hajah had claimed to have done—or worse. I also knew he was crafty enough to lie about it just to goad me. But now I was somehow *more* terrified to think of her out there in that savage world alone. Even though she'd managed just fine in this death trap of a world for some twenty years or so before I came along, I still wanted to find her, to protect her—a thought that made me laugh. The girl was incredible, had saved my life repeatedly and could obviously take care of herself. But somehow her self-sufficiency made me want to shield her all the more.

While awake, she was the constant center of my thoughts, and as I slept her beautiful face haunted my every dream—or nightmare. I loved her. I knew I loved her, and I wanted to find her more than I'd ever wanted anything in my life. I felt more for her than I'd ever thought it possible to feel for anyone. Jessica was a joke. Le… Any of them. All of them. They were nothing, compared to her.

I was terrified for Nova, and almost worse, I missed her. I missed laughing with her, talking to her, holding her, making love with her—missed everything I'd ever done with her, and it was killing me to think that our last moments together had been filled with anger and misunderstanding.

"There is no one more beautiful than you, Nova," I said aloud, wishing she could hear, pretending to hold her hand high, and then to my heart. "You can't imagine how sorry I am that I hurt you."

My words sounded hollow and pointless, not adequately conveying my sense of stupidity and loss. I wanted to think of something better to say when I saw her again, but hoped I would find her so quickly that I wouldn't have enough time to figure it out.

"MILTON," I SAID QUIETLY to the old man one evening as he read, "I have to get out of here. I have to find Nova. If it means searching every inch of this crazy, little, inside-out world I'm going to find that girl and spend the rest of my days making her know how much I love her."

"*Little* inside-out world!" he scoffed. "You don't know what you're talking about, Brandon."

He showed me a map of Pangea he had recently discovered among the latest, salvaged manuscript.

"Look," he said, pointing to it, "this is evidently water, and all this here… land. Do you notice the general configuration of the two areas? Where the oceans are on the outer crust, is land here. These relatively small areas of ocean seem to follow the general lines of the continents of the outer world. A bit smaller, perhaps, and not exactly, but more or less. I estimate the ratio of land to water is about fifty-fifty."

I sighed in frustration.

"So there's less water than on the outer surface," I snarled. "So what? You're not hearing me. I'm in agony!"

"Brandon," Milton said patiently, as if he were about to school a small boy, "given that the crust of the globe is about 500 miles in thickness; then the inside diameter of Pangea must be 7,000 miles, and the land mass area about a hundred and fifty *million* square miles! *Nova could be anywhere!* Granted this world is smaller than the outer surface, but it's still immense! Think about it! You're talking about finding her somewhere within an entire planet!"

He was right. I hadn't thought about it. It was worse than a needle in a haystack. It was a needle dropped from an airplane over the equator. I fought down a growing sense of hopelessness.

"But it must be possible," I said. "The Angara found Hajah—and some of the others. How?"

"I have no idea," he said, exasperated. "You'd have to ask one of them."

I thought about it a minute, and decided he was right. It was the obvious answer.

TAKING A BREAK from my book lugging, which never seemed to bother the guards, I wandered out onto the street to find the Angara with the scarred face. He had been more friendly to me than any of the others, even laughing at my joke. If I was going to get any information out of these irritable panther men, he was the most obvious candidate. But how to find him in this vast, overgrown city?

I searched the crowd, hoping—knowing—it would be pretty unlikely I'd find him easily. Maybe if I saw one of the prisoners who'd been captured with Hajah.

An idea occurred to me and I walked up to a different Angara and kept my head low the way they expected humans to approach them.

"Excuse me, sir," I said, in a quiet, respectful voice. "I have been sent to find a specific Angara. Can you help me?"

"Sent by who?" The panther man said, glaring down at me and not waiting for an answer. "What Angara?"

"I don't know his name," I responded, ignoring the first part of his question. "I couldn't pronounce it. I was told he has a large scar across one side of his face that cuts into his lip."

"Kiga-wok-naron," the other said as if annoyed. Maybe he didn't like the other Angara. "You can't pronounce that?"

"Not well," I said, continuing to keep my eyes down. "I'm not smart."

"None of you is," the Angara said, disdainfully. "He's in building three eleven. Usually on the ground floor, near the heating vent."

"Thank you," I said, turning to walk that way, grateful that he hadn't remembered to ask again about why I wanted to find the Angara. I suppose it was fairly rare for a human to be seeking out one of their kind.

I found building three-eleven and entered to find the Angara I wanted—as promised—seated in a chair near a heating vent. He was laughing with another guard, and—surprisingly—a human man.

The man made a comment that caused the guards to howl delightedly, then moved away to carry whatever was in his boxes up some nearby stairs.

The laughter stopped as soon as I approached.

"What do you want?" The non-scarred Angara asked, with annoyance.

"I have been sent to ask a question," I said, my eyes again lowered, "of Kiga..."

I struggled, but could not remember the remainder of his name.

"Humans," The non-scarred Angara said, then moved away, going up the same stairs the human had just risen. "He's Kiga... *wok... naron.*"

"Kiga, the Scarred might be easier for you to remember," Kiga said. "Or just Kiga. You're the one who jumped Hajah, the Wily."

"I am," I said, humbly.

"Nearly severed his tongue—which would have been a blessing. So cut the shit," he said, laughingly. "You also punched *my* man. You're about as humble as I am."

I laughed a little, and so did Kiga.

"I'm working with a man who's cleaning and restoring books in the library," I said, reciting the lie I'd practiced on the way over. "He has a question about a damaged passage he wants to repair. It has to do with tracking Grigori slaves."

"Yes, that's important work for the Grigori—for whatever reason. They're very pleased with what the old man is doing. What does he need to know?"

"I didn't... understand it completely," I lied again, thinking it might make telling me more acceptable. "There's something about... things... that are stuck inside our brains when you first capture us. He's missing some pages about how it works, and how you use it to find escaped slaves."

"That's in a book?" Kiga asked, then seemed to rethink it. "I guess everything is. The Grigori write it all down. It's very annoying, especially because the books keep getting wet, and they stink like an old woman's underwear."

I laughed, and he did, too. Then he looked at me carefully, studying me up and down.

"If I tell you, will you even be able to remember?" he asked.

"I... think so," I said, not prepared for the question.

"No," Kiga said after giving it some thought. "You'd never get it right. I'll come by later and explain it to the old man. It's too complicated for you."

I felt insulted, but had to calm myself, realizing I was actually going to get what I wanted. It was just going to take a little longer than I'd hoped. So I nodded, lowered my eyes, and exited the building, heading back to meet with Milton.

"I hope the old man can tell a convincing lie," I said to myself as I walked, smiling at the thought that—if all goes well—we would be free of this place, and I might even have a chance of finding Nova.

WHEN I ARRIVED BACK at the library, Elia and Milton were having sex on his desk.

I'd mostly gotten used to it, people going at it whenever and wherever the interest arose, as it were. But it was not always comfortable to be around—especially when it was Milton. The Grigori ignored it, and the Angara seemed amused by it, at times even aroused. We were treated essentially as pets, or cage animals that were expected to behave this way, and as long as we weren't interfering with something important—anything goes, as the song says.

I, myself, hadn't partaken in the fun of 'free-love', not since Nova had left. Monogamy didn't seem to be an issue with most Pangeans, and I'd had several offers, but I wanted Nova, and only Nova, and so I abstained. The women who expressed interest never seemed offended by my rejections, and after one or two attempts, eventually gave up for other, more willing partners.

After a few minutes of emotionless groaning, Milton and Elia finished, she kissed him goodbye, and walked past me toward the main door of the library office.

"Hello, Brandon," she said, smiling, then giggled to herself as she hurried down the corridor, and out the building.

"Having fun?" I asked Milton, playfully.

"I am," he answered, smiling. "Who thought being a slave could be so... amusing?"

"You act like a man who's never done it before."

Milton actually blushed, and—surprisingly—looked embarrassed. He'd just fucked a woman in front of me, and *now* he was embarrassed?

"Milton," I said, as it slowly sunk in. "You... before Elia... you *never*...?"

Milton turned away and shuffled some papers, straightened them into a pile, then reshuffled them and moved them back to where they were. Finally he sighed, and turned part way back to me.

"I am not a very *handsome* man..." he said, as if trying to understand it himself. "Nor am I especially adept at inter gender communication."

"Well," I said, smiling, "it's a good thing for you Elia doesn't seem much interested in talking."

Milton laughed and looked at me with brightening eyes.

"We do have nice conversations though," he said. "Sometimes. After. When you're not here."

"I'm sure you do. And I'm happy for you. But listen, Milton. I need your help with something."

I told him about the Angara coming over to see the fictional book, and he grew pale, flushed again, nervously, and became fidgety with the papers on his desk once more.

"But I don't have any such book," Milton complained.

"So just act as though you can't find it when he gets here," I said.

"I won't have to act," he said, his voice trembling. *"There is no such book!"*

"Milton," I said, trying to calm him down. "I know that. There doesn't need to be. I just want the information from him, and he seems perfectly happy to give it. So just write down whatever he tells you, pretending you'll insert it into the book later."

"But what if he doesn't believe me?" Milton fairly shrieked.

I saw now that Milton was actually afraid of potential repercussions from an angry Angara.

"Milton, relax," I said. "Don't worry. It will all go fine. You said it yourself. Everyone is fatalistic about life in Pangea. There is no reason for the Angara to feel suspicious."

He stared at me without believing.

"If you say so," he said, finally.

But I began to worry that his inability to remain calm might ruin the whole business.

A WAY TO FIND HER

THE ANGARA ARRIVED, and Milton looked as though he was going to pee his pants.

"What is it you need to know?" Kiga asked.

"I… uh…" Milton stammered, instantly forgetting everything we'd rehearsed. "Well…"

"It was just something about how you track escaped slaves, wasn't it?" I asked, sitting in a corner and trying to seem like I couldn't really care less. "How you find one specifically, if there's an individual identifier to help locate her." I caught myself. "Or him. Her or him."

Kiga stared at me, apparently angry. Then he glanced at Milton. Milton began to mumble, and shake, and I became genuinely afraid he was going to confess everything.

"That's all?" Kiga demanded, his anger stemming more from being interrupted for something so minor than for us asking the question at all.

He rolled his eyes, and smiled.

"Well," he said, falling back into his more carefree attitude, taking a seat near a heater vent. "At least it will be easy enough to answer. Do you want to write it down?" he asked Milton.

Milton, who was startled by the lack of ferocity in this particular Angara, stood silently for a moment, then suddenly jerked alert.

"Oh!" he said. "Yes! I… let me find something to write with."

I stood and helped the old man find a pencil and some blank paper.

Milton sat and looked across his cluttered desk at the comfortable Angara, who gestured absently with his hands, indicating a small device.

"There's this shiny little box," Kiga said, pleasantly. "About this big. Has things on it, and a small, flat area that glows like a tiny fire. It can even be seen in the dark. It has green lines of light on it, and dots, like stars. When one turns red, you know a slave has escaped. Or attempted to."

"When the slave crosses some kind of barrier?" Milton asked. "Or goes outside a Grigori city?"

Kiga looked at him blankly and answered as if Milton hadn't heard him correctly. "When a slave tries to *escape*... it turns *red*."

Milton stared at Kiga a moment, as we both realized Kiga was explaining a technology he plainly did not understand himself, and then wrote something on the paper.

"Right," Milton said. "When it turns red."

"Then you push a thing on the silver box," Kiga continued. "And a blue light appears. That is you. Whoever holds the box. You then move toward the red light until the blue light is on top of it. It becomes purple. And boom. You have found your slave."

"Sort of a simplistic G. P. S." I said, quietly.

"Apparently," Milton agreed.

"No," Kiga said, not understanding. "It's a silver box."

"Right," I said. "And who has these silver boxes?"

"The Grigori have them. They give them to certain Angara." His eyes darkened, and his voice seemed tinged with a bit of sadness. "Hunters."

"The Grigori have them," Milton repeated. "And where are they stored?"

"Some room," Kiga said waving dismissively. "Grigori give them to us." Then he corrected sadly. "To hunters. Does that need to go in the book?"

"More information is always better," Milton said slyly, beginning to enjoy the clandestine nature of the questioning.

"Hmm." Kiga said. "Grigori always want to know more than anyone really needs to. Well, I never cared when I was a... a full-time hunter. But I could ask one."

"I would appreciate it," Milton said.

"And how long does it usually take," I asked, "for the blue light to meet up with the red light."

The Angara scowled and looked at me curiously.

"How long? What do you mean?"

I frowned back at him, amazed that my question had confused him, then remembered I was in a world where time was far less specific without a rising and setting sun.

"When does..." I began, then reconsidered. "How much time... when you travel over a distance..."

I stopped, and really thought through my question. All I wanted to know was how long it would be before a blue dot overcame Nova.

Could I get to her first? But how to find out? How was I to know how much time she had left before an Angara hunter found her?

"Never mind," I said, dismissing it.

Kiga chuckled.

"You should let the smart ones ask the questions," he said to me. "Accept your lot in life as a fighter, and one who helps those who are intelligent."

I bristled, but slowly realized that he was smiling at me with understanding, and perhaps even a little sympathy. He was including himself in that statement. *He* was a less intelligent helper of the Grigori.

"You're right," I admitted, chuckling in return. "It's usually best when I just keep my mouth shut."

Kiga returned my laugh, then returned his attentions to Milton. "Anything else?"

Milton stared silently a moment, perhaps trying to find a way to ask the question I couldn't, but then only shook his head.

"Thank you," Milton said, scribbling something on the paper. "You have been very helpful."

"Helping the Grigori helps us all," Kiga said, standing. I noticed a slight shake in one leg, the twisted way it landed when he walked, and wondered if the scar, and some other less obvious wounds had made him someone who could no longer be a full-time hunter.

He politely said goodbye, and moved toward the door.

"Kiga?" I asked.

He stopped just inside the room and turned back to me.

"May I ask…" I began, hesitantly, "… how you got that scar?"

He stood there a moment, and I thought perhaps I'd crossed a line—that maybe he considered it a serious offense for a human slave to even ask. But then he smiled, slightly, his eyes clouded with memory, and he spoke through distant pain.

"An Ingonghu was eating me. Had me in its mouth. Broke my spine."

"And you survived?" I said, amazed.

"I did," Kiga said, brightening, but just as quickly his face darkened again. "A human saved me. Stabbed the Ingonghu in the eye until it released me, then nursed me back to health."

"That's incredible," Milton said.

"Yes," Kiga agreed.

"And how did you get back here?" I asked.

"The human brought me. He was a slave who had been my companion on…" he paused as if remembering was painful, "… when we would hunt."

"But you don't hunt anymore?"

"Only when we are short handed. I did not heal well enough."

"What happened to the human who saved you?" Milton asked.

"The Grigori ate him," Kiga said, his voice barely betraying his inner turmoil.

Milton and I stared, silently. Kiga nodded a curt goodbye, and left.

"IF BRUK WILL GO with us, we might be able to do it," I suggested.

Milton nodded.

"I would not wish to leave Elia," he said, sweetly.

"Of course not," I said. "Any plan we make will have to involve all of us getting out safely. I'm thinking we should probably have Bruk take you and Elia back to his home, while I go off to find Nova on my own."

"Brandon, no..."

"It would be better, Milton. You can start on some method for neutralizing the devices implanted in our heads so no hunters come looking for us, and I can find Nova without you and Elia slowing me down. Not to be blunt."

"No," Milton said, obviously wounded. "Not to be blunt."

"The bigger question is:" I said, pointing to my head, "can *any of us* outrun the Angara if we can't find a way to block these trackers, first?"

Milton sighed. "I doubt it. They will always be traveling in the straightest line, while we will be relying on terrain, and I'm supposing some kind of complicated form of tracking to get from here to Bruk's home."

"How *do* the people of Pangea—without the silver things Kiga spoke of—find their way around without stars, or the motion of the sun to guide them?" I asked.

"I have no idea. I'm assuming landmarks, and distant sighting of geography along the inner curve of the world. Or maybe they have nothing to guide them. Maybe that's part of the reason why once they are taken captive by Grigori they never see home again."

"I suppose we'll have to ask Bruk."

"Whatever the case, the Angara will certainly have the advantage over us. And above that—as you 'not bluntly' pointed out—Elia and I will hardly be the speediest of fugitives."

"But at least we know how they'll be tracking you—us," I said. "Maybe we can figure out a way to shield the signal—even temporarily. Maybe some kind of metal cap, or something, might block the signal?"

"Perhaps. Whatever—we won't be able to test anything until we get one of those silver boxes Kiga told us about."

"Then that has to be my priority."

"Can you do it without killing?" Milton asked with genuine concern.

"Killing... a Grigori?" I asked, my tone saying clearly how ludicrous it was for him to even ask.

"They are sentient beings, Brandon. Intelligent life."

"They force people into slavery, and eat them on the streets as punishment."

"A crime for which the individual should be held accountable, not the entire race..."

"I'm not having this conversation with you," I snapped, and headed for the exit.

ELIA'S LOVE

BRUK ENTERED, WALKING INTO ME, and because of my mood, I spoke rather bluntly to the Hairy One.

"We're planning to escape," I said quickly. "Or, I am. Are you with me?"

"Why?" He asked, sincerely. "They'll set Ingonghus on us, and we'll be killed, or recaptured. There is no escape from the Grigori. I've told you."

"And you were right," Milton said. "And we've discovered why."

As best and simply as he could Milton explained about the implants that allowed us to be tracked anywhere on the surface of the inner world.

"And this is inside my head?" Bruk asked, growing angry. *"Now?"*

"Yes," I said.

He stood and moved uncomfortably close to me, his face very near mine.

"Can you take it out?"

"I don't know," I said, trying to speak calmly.

"We're certainly going to try," Milton said, helpfully. "Have you seen—anywhere inside this compound—a small, hand sized silver box with a glowing window on it?"

Bruk looked at him with barely concealed rage.

"Will it take this thing out of my head?"

"It might, if we can find one," Milton said, calmly. "Or better yet, the place where they're stored so we can find other such devices. Perhaps those silver, octopus-like machines they used to put the things inside us in the first place. I have to believe there exists something that *will* remove the thing in your head in case of malfunction or... I don't know... battery replacement."

"Why?" I asked. "They don't seem to care about our lives so much as our usefulness. If the thing malfunctions, just get another slave."

Milton looked momentarily horrified, then his eyes lowered and he nodded as he accepted the truth of it.

"Angara who come back from tracking escaped slaves sometimes have the things you talk about," Bruk said, slowly relaxing. "I don't know where they keep them, but I will make a point of watching to find out."

"Do that," I said. "The sooner we find one, the sooner we'll be able to leave—without being followed by Angara."

Bruk looked at me, the fury still roiling under the surface, but slowly—very slowly—his eyes began to sparkle, and the almost perpetual smile that he usually wore returned to his bearded lips.

"Without being followed," he said, hopefully. "We can return to my home without fear of being tracked again. Really and truly."

"Yes," I said, smiling.

"Could you find your way back to your own land?" asked Milton. "Could you take us—take Elia and I—to where you and your people live?"

"I can!" Bruk said, sudden life coursing through him. I suppose he really had been fairly fatalistic about being trapped here forever, such that the prospect of returning home, and not being taken away again at some point in the future, had become an exhilarating one.

"But how," persisted Milton, "how could you travel through this hostile country without stars or a compass to guide you?"

Bruk didn't know what my old friend meant by 'stars' or 'compass', but he assured us that you could blindfold any man in Pangea, carry him to the farthest corner of the world, and he would still be able to come directly home again by the shortest route. He seemed surprised to think that we found anything amazing about it.

"Sounds like a homing pigeon," I said.

"My thoughts exactly," said Milton.

Then something occurred to me.

"So... Nova could have found her way straight to her own people?" I asked.

"Of course," Bruk replied, "unless something killed her."

"Uh... yeah," I said, stunned. "Unless... you know... that," I chewed a lip and pondered, coming quickly to a decision. "We have to get going. Now. We have to find one of these tracking devices, and..."

"No, no, no..." said Bruk, cutting me off.

Both he and Milton advised waiting for some 'happy accident' that would allow us a little cover and a better chance of success. I didn't see what accident could be big enough to affect an entire community, and why I should wait for that while Nova was out in the world potentially fighting for her life, but then the wheels in my brain began to turn and I wondered if such a thing might possibly be arranged.

While I'm sure that some of the Grigori never sleep, others did, for long intervals, crawl into the dark recesses beneath the city and curl up for a substantial slumber. Milton seemed to think that if a Grigori stayed awake for three straight years the thing could make up all its lost sleep with one, long, seemingly endless snooze. Maybe that was true, but I'd never seen more than four of them sleeping at a time, and it was with a sudden rush that thoughts of those four suddenly coalesced with exactly what my subconscious had been trying to tell me.

Barely able to contain my excitement, I explained my plan to Milton.

"We kill those Grigori, skin them, and walk out wearing those skins as suits. No one will even challenge us. In fact, most people—Angara included—will just back the hell away. It's foolproof."

To my surprise he was horrified.

"It would be *murder*, Brandon," he said.

"Murder to kill a slaving lizard monster?" I asked in astonishment.

"They're not *monsters*, Brandon," he replied. "They're the dominant race—*we* are the 'monsters'—the lower orders. In Pangea evolution has progressed along different lines than on the outer world. It's just evolutionary luck that some, quote, 'monster' of the Saurozoic epoch didn't grow into a sentient race to eventually rule our outer Earth. We see here in Pangea what might well have occurred in our own history had conditions been just a little different.

"Life down here is far younger than upon the outer surface. Here man has only reached a level that would be analogous to the Stone Age of our own Earth's history, while for countless millions of years these Grigori have been progressing and moving forward—ahead of humans. Maybe it's simply their advanced intelligence, or perhaps it's this sixth sense I believe they possess and use to communicate that has given them an advantage over the rest of the scary creatures that inhabit this concave world; we may never know.

"Whatever caused it to happen, they look upon us as we look upon insects, or beasts of the field. I've even discovered in some of the forbidden readings in these old books that some of the Grigori regularly and routinely feed on humans, not just the occasional angry rage slaughter we've witnessed, but actually keeping them in enormous herds, much as we keep cattle. They breed them very carefully for flavor and delicacy, and when they've reached Grigori perfection, they slaughter and eat them."

It was something I'd assumed based on what we'd seen, but nonetheless I still shuddered.

"Oooh, don't be so squeamish," the old man said. "What is there that's so horrible about it, Brandon? You eat beef! Do you ever stop to think about the poor cow? No. Well, they understand us no better than we understand the lower animals *we* raise and eat. Although I *have* come across some very learned discussions on the question of whether Nguni—that's us, *men*, or *humans*—should *not* be eaten because they might possess sentience. One writer claims that we can't even reason—that our every action is simply mechanical, and instinctive. Others believe we are nearly as smart as the Angara. The dominant race of Pangea, Brandon, has not yet learned that humans are... well... *human*."

"Then they're not paying attention," I said, angrily. "I feel no sympathy for that kind of willful stupidity."

"They are an intelligent, reasoning species, Brandon. It would most definitely be murder to carry out your plan."

"But simply because they don't understand us, is it any less murder when *they* kill humans... *eat* humans?"

"Is it murder to eat a cow? A chicken?"

"I spent a lot of summers on my grandfather's farm," I told him. "Chickens deserve to be eaten."

"Which you can justify because you do not recognize their right to independent life. As Grigori do not recognize ours. Their crime is forgivable because they are not fully aware."

"Tell me that when they're eating Elia."

Milton looked momentarily horrified, but recovered somewhat before saying:

"They wouldn't."

But he was plainly *very* far from certain.

I cocked an eye at him as if saying, *'don't bet on it.'*

"I'm getting out, Milton." I replied. "And if it means murder, then I'll be a murderer. Won't be the first time. At least this time it'll be for something important."

He got me to go over the plan again very carefully and in great detail, backing me up to make me explain things that either weren't clear to him, or I hadn't thought through completely enough. For some reason I didn't understand he insisted on a very careful description of the apartments and corridors all around the sleeping Grigori.

"Have you ever seen a laboratory..." he asked, "perhaps with gestating Grigori?"

"Um... no. You've asked me that before."

"Hmm," Milton said. "You're right. I'd forgotten. And they're still down there? These four Grigori?"

"I checked on them again just before I came in."

"So, we carry out your plan—after, I presume, we've found the tracking devices."

"Of course," I said. "But…"

"Which we might *never* actually find," he reminded me.

"I've got some thoughts about how to expedite that process."

"But if you can't…"

"I can."

"But if you *can't*…" Milton repeated, firmly, assuring me he thought it improbable. "Then we might never actually have to kill those Grigori. It might not be necessary."

"It *might* not be. But it *will* be."

"I can live with that," Milton said, flatly. "If it comes to us escaping I might be able to justify taking one of their lives."

"*Four of their lives!* And there's no 'might' about it, Milton!" I snapped. "I can't carry you, but I'm not leaving without you. You *have* to do this!"

"I can't promise you anything, Brandon. I'm not anywhere near as certain as you that I can kill a sentient creature with no provocation!"

"Then I'll kill one for you! Milton, don't be stupid! We've been captured! Enslaved! I've witnessed these creatures savagely ripping apart human beings like they were bobbing for apples!"

"None of which motivates me to…!"

"*MILTON!*"

"*BRANDON!*"

"Milton?"

The last voice was quiet, and feminine, and shockingly sad. Milton and I both turned from our argument and faced the newly arrived Elia, who stood shyly in the doorway, looking at Milton with eyes as dark as the night that never came to Pangea.

"Please don't argue, you two," she said. "Your friendship is too special."

"We're done arguing, anyway," I said angrily.

"Brandon," she said, quietly. "Would you give Milton and I a moment alone?"

I sighed heavily, and glanced at Milton.

"Of course," I said, curtly.

Elia began to cry.

"Dearest," Milton said, going to her. "What's wrong?"

She glanced at me nervously, then back to Milton, more tears streaming down her cheeks.

"I'm sorry. I'll go," I said.

"It's all right," Elia said. "I just wanted to tell Milton… that I'm pregnant."

A shock went through the room, and when Milton eventually recovered a smile danced on, then off his face, then back on again. He looked at Elia, saw nothing but sadness and fear, and put gentle hands around her shoulders.

"My dear," he said in a near whisper, "oh my dearest, darling…"

He looked at me, and I saw the tears in *his* eyes.

"Brandon," he said, choking a bit. "Did you hear?"

"I heard," I said, smiling.

"I never expected… to become a father," he said, emotion nearly overtaking him. "Ever."

I stared at him, wordlessly, forcing the small, hopeful smile to remain on my face because I knew this would change everything. He would never leave what he considered the safe confines of Emibi now, Grigori enslavement or no, and I could never force him.

MILTON SAT ON THE floor with an arm around Elia, smiling broadly, his eyes anchored onto hers.

"I never thought I would find love," she said to him sweetly. "I am so ugly…"

"Ssshhh…" Milton cooed. "You are nothing of the kind. To me, there was never any woman more beautiful." He touched her belly gently. "Especially now."

Milton looked over at me, and finally faced the elephant in the room.

"I can see by your face that you know what this means," he said to me.

"Of course," I said, quietly, still holding onto my smile, as empty as it might have been.

"This place is the safest—probably in all of Pangea—for a new child."

"What?" I said, stunned. "Milton, no! I've watched the Grigori devour slaves on the street! We both have! Nova used to say that the Grigori eat babies…!"

"I've found no such stories in any of these books. And I have seen plenty of evidence of what happens to the vulnerable beyond these walls."

"Milton…!"

"It's a children's story," Elia said. "Something people say, but no one's ever seen it."

Milton smiled at her, then looked at me with an 'I told you so' expression.

"No one has ever seen a Grigori eat a baby," Elia said.

"But there are no children here in Emibi," I warned. "That's…"

"Because most women don't want to get pregnant, so babies are rare, and even if they somehow do—as I have—they are removed from slave work, and sent to another Grigori city to raise infant Grigori."

"Which is what the books all say," Milton confirmed.

"But… Nova was so serious…" I said, unable to be convinced.

"A belief can be more real than reality, Brandon," Milton offered.

"I know, Milton, but…"

"I'm sorry, Brandon."

I shook my head, sincerely, finally getting past my own needs and jealousy to see that this was what was truly best for Milton. Pangea was a massive gamble for anyone. Even if Grigori *did* eat babies, the child's chances were as good here as anywhere, and probably better for Milton.

For an older, less athletic man like him, Pangea was inevitable death. Here was where he belonged, looking through books, studying and reading and learning about the Grigori, the Angara, and this fascinating world we all inhabited from a safe distance, behind walls, and guards, and protective barriers where he could be with Elia, and their eventual child. I looked at Elia's hopeful face. Eventual *children*. She wanted this child as much as he did—and more. I couldn't take that from either of them.

"You won't leave, no matter what I say," I said aloud to my friend, "and I can't stay. I have to go to Nova. I have to find her, if I can."

Milton's face took on a haunted sadness that brought tears to both our eyes.

"I'm sorry, Brandon," he said, the water streaming down his cheeks.

"No, no, no," I reassured him, backing off my fears that Nova was right. "You have a family, now. You need to stay. And I need to go." I forced another smile. "Nothing lasts forever."

"An old Pangean cliché," Elia threw in with a sad smile of her own.

"It's a cliché everywhere, I suppose. For good reason."

WITHIN THE HOLLOW WORLD of Pangea one time is as good as any other. There was no night to hide our escape. Everything had to be done in broad daylight. So I decided to move on my plan immediately—without Milton's help—to make sure the sleeping Grigori that made it possible remained asleep. I grabbed some small weapons that wouldn't draw any attention, found Bruk in the next building and gave him one, then the two of us headed off together into the depths of the city of Emibi.

"Do you remember which room they were in," Bruk asked.

"I hope so," I said.

"That is not a very encouraging answer, my friend," he said, laughing.

We moved quickly and carefully down a familiar tunnel, ran into a fork that branched in three directions, and I realized Bruk had been right to be concerned. I had no idea where I was.

"Dammit," I said.

"Never trust a confident man," Bruk said.

"You and your sayings."

"A man with too many sayings, is usually saying nothing."

I laughed, and chose a tunnel at random.

"This one," I said, pointing.

"Are you sure?"

"Perfectly confident," I said, moving the way I'd indicated, as—chuckling—he followed.

I was running fast, now, and realized I had increased speed with my desperation. We probably only had one chance at this, and not being able to find the sleeping chamber was scaring the shit out of me. But did I really need to run?

The buildings of Emibi were basic and bland. There was nothing at all remarkable about the architecture. The rooms were sometimes rectangular, sometimes circular, occasionally oval. The corridors, which connected them, were narrow and not always straight. The chambers were lit by either diffuse sunlight reflected through windows on the higher levels, or artificial, bluish light further down coming from old boxes and unreadable signs that seemed more like emergency exit markers than serious illumination. The lower you went the darker the rooms became. Most of the corridors remained unlit because few humans ever came down here, and the Grigori could apparently see quite well in the dark.

Hearing noises I reduced my speed to a brisk walk. After a while we came to a passage that seemed familiar, and I chanced a glance inside a chamber that branched off to our right. Inside I saw four Grigori curled up in lumps and leathery folds on their simple beds. I nearly screamed with relief. All four of the hideous reptiles were still here, and still asleep.

I entered their chamber silently, forgetting that the damned things couldn't hear. When I did remember, I raised a knife and spoke to the Grigori I was about to kill.

"Fuck you, and your superior intelligence," I whispered. "This is for Shalla." And with a quick thrust through the heart, the thing died almost without a twitch.

Bruk had silently done the same with one of the others, but the third and fourth were a different matter. We'd made almost no noise, and the things were completely deaf, but somehow the other two became aware of what was happening and before either of us could approach our next victims they sprang quickly up and faced us with wide, hissing mouths, and saber filled jaws, apparently ready to battle.

But when they saw what Bruk and I had already done to the other two, our blades dripping red with Grigori blood, the remaining pair changed their minds and made for the doorway in a mad rush to escape. But we were built for running, and they really weren't. So as the things went off, half hopping, half flying, scurrying and stumbling back up the corridor the way we'd come, we were right behind them, hot on their weird little asses.

If either of them escaped our plan was ruined, our deaths guaranteed. Knowing this made both Bruk and I move like the wind, he a little ahead of me; but even at my best I could do no more than keep pace. A sprinter I'm not.

Probably recognizing his inability to escape, one of them suddenly turned into a compartment on the left side of the corridor, and assuming my friend to be the faster of us, I waved Bruk on.

"I'll take this one!" I said, turning in through the open doorway.

I rushed in, and found myself facing *two* of the damn things, both facing me with stunned expressions.

"Shit," I said.

The one who was in the room when we entered had been working at a lab bench with a bunch of glass containers filled with powders and liquids. Beside it was an open, leather volume filled with text and images.

All around us hung tubes and hoses and jars and containers of various sizes filled with thick, viscous, slowly bubbling liquid, flowing slowly into larger, glass vessels—each of which held a developing Grigori.

I realized instantly what I'd stumbled upon. This was the room Milton had been quizzing me so hard for, hoping to find; the sacred chamber, which held the Great Secret of the Grigori race, and the book on the table was the thing he most wanted to find. If it really controlled the reproduction of the Grigori, I could understand its incredible value, not only to the flying reptiles, but to anyone who hoped to wipe them off the face of Pangea.

I looked around and saw that there was no exit from the room other than the doorway I stood in. I set myself and knew that any escape plan was now secondary. That book could put an end to Grigori dominance forever. I raised my blade and smiled.

It would be mine.

Cornered, and probably fearful of my damaging anything in this room, I knew that these two would fight like demons, and they were well equipped for it—slicing teeth, jagged claws on both hands and feet. Fear for personal survival was one thing. Fear for the survival of their entire race was something else entirely.

Each of them glanced nervously at the book, as did I, and as one they flew at me. I ducked and thrust upward impaling one through the heart, killing her instantly, as the other fastened its foot-long fangs onto my left arm above the elbow. Clamped on tightly, she immediately ripped into my abdomen with her sharp talons and raked downward into my thighs, probably trying to open my guts to the air. I couldn't free my arm from the powerful, viselike grip of her jaws, and felt her twist her head in an effort to rip my arm from my body. The pain was intense, but rather than slow me down it only motivated me. She was desperate. She was afraid. I wasn't.

Rolling backward to throw myself off balance, we fell across a table, glass beakers shattering all around us, metal instruments flying in all directions, liquids and powders exploding everywhere as we somersaulted across the surface of the desk and onto the opposite floor.

Back and forth across the room we struggled—the Grigori digging in deeply, shredding my torso with her feet, while I fought like hell to protect my body with my free hand. Feeling the blood leak from my abdomen, I stopped being defensive, and went offensive, jabbing my free fingers deep into one of the thing's eyes until it popped.

Horrifying and disgusting, but effective as hell.

She shrieked loudly enough to be heard back on the outer surface of the planet. She also stopped digging her fucking talons into my entrails. She rolled off me and thrashed madly about the room. Her pain must have been agonizing, but I didn't care. We saw each other the same way—as lesser animals in a kill-or-be-killed world.

She flopped wildly about, blood pulsing out of her own body with each thudding heartbeat from places I hadn't even realized I'd cut. I got to my feet holding my insides in place with my shredded left hand while readying my blade in my right. I walked over to her as she twitched across the floor, smears of blood staining the concrete surface in a path behind her—trying to crawl to where, I have no idea. Her movements slowing even as I watched, I realized I probably needed to do something first, before killing her.

I stepped over the Grigori's jerking, dying corpse to triumphantly, and with great flourish, snatch up the most powerful secret of this inner world.

I held the book out in front of me, showing her one, good eye that I knew what—and how important—it was, and she stopped twitching long enough to focus her remaining good eye—first on it, then on me.

Knowing that she'd gotten a good long look at both the book and its thief, I raised my right hand, and jammed my blade down into her heart, twisting until she lay absolutely still.

With a last, hissing expulsion of breath she died.

As I let go and stood, breathing heavily over the Grigori's lifeless body, I thought how this book, and this book alone, could make Nova, and Milton, and I—and all our children, and all our children's children—safe from the fear of the Grigori forever and ever, for the rest of our lives.

My beautiful Nova. Safe from slavery. Safe from being eaten. Safe from the dominant race. I pictured her beautiful, tanned face, gazing up at me with crystalline, blue eyes, surrounded be a waving mass of jet-black hair. I thought of those dark, red, lips, and remembered the feel of them against mine—and how she would thank me with them for making her safe from the Grigori.

It was at that moment that I realized how much I genuinely and deeply loved Nova the Beautiful, and how that love meant I never again wanted to leave her side, never spend a moment without her, never return to my home on the outer world so I could forever and always be by her side.

I also understood deeply and profoundly how what I had just done meant that as much as I wanted a life with her, it could never happen, and I would never live to see her again.

THE EVIL QUEEN

FOR AN INSTANT I STOOD there thinking of Nova—and only of Nova—until, with a sigh, I found some skins and rags and wrapped them around the book until it looked like a lumpy, fur pillow. Then I turned to leave the weird little lab.

In the doorway I took a brief look around the room, and felt revulsion at the sight of the tiny, twitching Grigori bodies in their bizarre, artificial uteruses. I considered for a moment running through the large space and smashing the glass surrounding every unborn monster in the room. But I knew that what had just happened in this room was going to make me enough of a target for the Grigori that our simple plans of escape were now a thing of the past. No need to make it worse.

Five dead Grigori, the sacred lab ruined, the greatest secret of a race stolen and missing—possibly forever. If there was a way to make this situation any worse, killing these unborns was likely the only way.

Bruk returned from down the hallway, smiling at me.

"It took longer than it should have. I was trying not to ruin the skins for our escape."

He reached me in the doorway of the lab, looked inside and smiled at my accomplishment, then scowled at my wounds.

"Those are bad," he said, and I looked down at them for the first time.

"Yes," I agreed. "We have to change our plans," I told him, ignoring the blood and muck. "Those Grigori in the sleeping chamber knew we were there as we were slaughtering the first two."

"I noticed that," Bruk nodded.

"They were communicating soundlessly."

"As Milton has often said."

"And I don't know how far a distance that communication can cover," I told him.

"I..." he began, but only shook his head, "I don't understand what you mean."

"I'm saying that as we killed these Grigori they may have been speaking to *other* Grigori here in Emibi, not necessarily in this room. Warning them. Calling for help. Sending images of our faces."

"Is that possible?"

"It *is* possible... in my... land," I said. "Where I come from images can be sent many, many miles."

Bruk turned a little pale. But then he scowled and looked determined.

"So more Grigori are coming," he snarled. "We should escape now."

"No," I said. "*You* go. And avoid Milton. At least for a while. With your beard and clothing you look about the same as most slave men in Emibi. I'm hoping the Grigori won't know you from any other slave. Me, however..."

"You are quite distinct," he said, looking me over.

"And I made them remember me."

"What do you mean?"

"It's a long story," I said, looking back into the room at the dead, one-eyed Grigori.

I turned back to Bruk and handed him the pillow.

"Take this and hide it," I said. "Somewhere safe. Somewhere Grigori will never look. When the craziness I think is about to come has finally ended, and the Grigori have settled down, give it to Milton. He'll know what to do with it."

"What is it?"

"The end of the Grigori."

Bruk looked at me with wide eyes, his mouth hanging slack. *Are you serious*, I could hear him thinking, and then his face stiffened as the bloody, exhausted expression on my face gave him the answer.

"Can't you hide it yourself?" he asked.

"I don't have time," I said. "I have to clean up this mess before the army arrives—and I think it might be better if when they get here, I don't actually know where it is."

"But Brandon..." he objected.

"Hurry, Bruk. There's no time. It's crucial that the Grigori focus on me and not you. You *have* to hurry. For Milton, for Elia, for you... for all of Pangea."

Bruk stood a moment, holding the precious cargo, and just stared at me. I watched a great sadness creep across his face as he realized what I was saying.

"You are a good man, Brandon."

"Tell that to Nova, if you ever see her, again. And tell her that I really, truly loved her," tears surprised me by squeezing free of my eyes. "With all my heart."

Bruk touched my shoulder, nodded, I told him to go, and after watching me as he backed away for a few steps, he finally turned and ran away from me down the limestone corridor with all the speed he could manage, disappearing around a corner.

I turned and surveyed the carnage behind me.

"Now," I said to no one in particular. "Think fast, Brandon. What are you going to make out of this mess?

I HAD MORE TIME than I'd expected, but my guess was right; the Grigori *could* speak to one another over great distances, and the cavalry arrived just as I was cleaning up the last of the blood trails.

The corridors flooded with armed Angara and anxious Grigori, all looking around to confirm what they'd probably received in some form of telepathic communication. But things didn't match up. There were no bodies, and very little blood—and what blood there was seemed to be mine. The lead Angara stepped forward and placed a hand around my throat, but only to hold me in place while he inspected the lab. He dragged me around like a rag doll, and I had to struggle to stay on my feet with his nervous, searching tour of the place.

Eventually he stopped and seemed about to ask me something when the crowd parted and what I have to assume was the queen Grigori strode regally in, head swinging slowly back and forth to survey the room. She froze a moment with her eyes on the table where the book had once lain, then turned to stare directly at me. After a few moments of silently boring her eyes into mine, she purposefully stepped right up to me. She was very tall—a good two feet taller than any other Grigori I'd seen—and the rough skin around her eyes was colored differently than that of her sisters.

She stopped very close to me, my Angara guard taking a nervous step back, the queen's head ratcheting around for one, final scan of the premises. Then she aimed her eyes directly at me and fixed her intense, unblinking gaze on mine.

Suddenly a searing pain split my skull, and a voice rose up from the depths of hell to fill the inside of my head.

Where is it?

I looked around, trying to figure out where the voice was coming from, not yet getting that it was coming from the mind of the queen. Eventually it sunk in, and I tried to re-affix my eyes to hers, but the pain was incredible.

"What are you talking about?" I asked, trying to sound coy.

Faster than I could even see, her mouth was open and her jaws clamped around my skull. She had grabbed me with a precision that prevented her teeth from doing more than lightly breaking the skin. The effect was terrifying.

Do not play with me, the voice said.

"I'm not playing," I said, trying to prevent my head from being crushed, and probably swallowed. "There were several things in here, and all of them are gone. Which thing are you referring to specifically?"

The book. An image of the book blasted in my mind's eye.

"Someone came and took that from me," I said.

I felt the teeth press inward, penetrating further into my skin. Against my will I screamed. I didn't want to give her the satisfaction, but she knew what she was doing. It hurt like fuck.

"*I'm telling the truth!*" I said. "*Some caveman I've never seen! He and his friends took that thing and the Grigori bodies and ran off!*"

Why do you say caveman?

"What?" I said, surprised.

The Grigori queen suddenly released me, and focused her eyes on me once more. After an intense, fear-filled moment, she turned to the Angara still holding my neck.

Who is this human?

"Just a human," the Angara said, looking at me as if trying to understands the question. "No different than the others, though he claims to be from another world. A world outside this world. He works with the smart one who does the work in the library."

The Grigori queen snapped her gaze back to mine.

Bring in the other, I heard in my skull.

Again the crowd parted and a human slave stepped forward. He raised his head as if listening to the queen, then turned and smiled at me.

It was Hajah.

What do you know of this? The queen's voice demanded. *Is this one truly from a world outside ours?*

"That's what he claims," the betrayer said. "He knows nothing about Pangean culture or lands. Does it matter? He's tricky, and a troublemaker. Do away with him. It's best for us all."

He claims another human took something of value from this room. Would that be the one you told us about?

"I doubt it," Hajah said, and I wondered how long we should have been watching our backs with this asshole. "It would mean nothing to Bruk. But they could be working together, this one and that."

The queen seemed to consider this, and as she did, I glared at Hajah wishing I could take the knife that was still in my hand and embed it in his smarmy fucking face. The prick saw me glaring at him, and just smiled with that arrogant, shit-eating grin of his. I wanted nothing more than to beat the smile off his face. Preferably with a torn off body part of the queen.

As if sensing my thoughts, the evil leader of the Grigori turned back to me.

125

Where is the book? she repeated.

"I told you..." I began, then stopped as a razor of pain shot through me. I felt images and memories bubbling up from somewhere deep inside me, unbidden, and realized she was trying to read my mind. I fought her, thinking of Nova, her beauty, how much I loved her, and how desperately I wanted to see her again. Underneath the occasional image of Bruk, blurry and unfocused, came forward holding the 'pillow' but I fought it down before it could clarify, overlaying it with pictures of Nova and I making love, her naked body, her holding me, her breathtaking smile. The thoughts were pleasant and powerful, the best I could come up with for keeping my mind off of Bruk, but even as much as they meant to me, and as powerful as they were, those thoughts were nearly impossible to hold onto. The queen's brain was ripping mine in two.

We struggled like that for what seemed like hours, but was more likely only seconds. Just as my skull was about to crack apart to reveal Bruk full blown between us, the queen abandoned her search, the pain vanished, and my head cleared.

I fell forward into the Angara's grip, breathing deeply, exhausted and spent.

Chain him, the queen said, angrily, but weakly, my mind flinching at her slight re-entry. *Then... take him... to the... arena.* She was apparently as depleted as I. *Gather... all the slaves.*

I felt her mind drift out of mine, and sighed with appreciation. Hers was an ugly presence, and my head felt cleaner having her vacated. Obviously a little unbalanced, she strode out through the parting crowd, and vanished into the hall. Hajah gave me a last, evil smirk, a tiny salute of goodbye, and followed her.

"So, what now?" I asked the Angara still holding me by the throat.

"Now, they're going to throw you into the pit," he said, smiling, "and we'll see how well a man from this *'other world'* you claim to come from can do in a fight for his life."

"Trust me," I said, smiling. "We fight the same as you. And if we lose, we die... the same as you."

The Angara laughed loudly, and shoved me toward the open doorway.

WE REACHED THE main floor and headed immediately out into the street where an enormous crowd of slaves was being forced toward the amphitheater that adjoined the building where I'd met with Kiga. As the Angara shoved me down the steps and into the flow of the nervous throng I saw Milton, Elia, and Bruk far to my left shuffling along with the chaotic crowd. They couldn't see me.

"MILTON!" I yelled, trying to be heard above the noise of mob chatter. *"MILTON! BRUK!"*

An Angara took exception to my shouts, and slammed me in the back of the head. But before I was bent forward I caught a glimpse of Bruk looking my way. By the time I'd recovered from the shot I'd taken to my skull, we were at street level with the others and I could no longer see my friends.

As we trudged forward, a rumor began to filter back through the mass of captives that there had been another pair of returned escapees—a man and a woman—apparently the woman had killed an Angara who'd been trying to retake her, and so we were on our way to witness her punishment, and probable execution.

My heart stopped beating. It had to be Nova.

Lost in my own head, and deeply distressed, I finally noticed someone on the periphery of my vision trying to get my attention. It was

Bruk and Milton and by their faces I could see that the two of them were thinking the same thing I was.

"Is it Nova?" Bruk asked.

"No idea," I said looking straight ahead. "Don't look right at me. Pretend you don't even see me. They're looking for you."

"Because of that book?"

"Don't even think about it. They can get inside your head."

We walked a bit, pretending to ignore one another.

"What can we do?" I asked Bruk. "How can we save Nova, if it is her?"

"We can't," he replied, looking around at the Angara on all sides, heavily armed and already enraged at the murder of one of their own. "Unless we're in the pits with them."

"Well, then maybe *I'll* have a chance to help her."

"What do you mean? They're taking *you* to the arena?"

"Listen, Bruk," I said, ignoring his question. "Two doors down and to the left from where we were, there's a storage room…"

My Angara guard finally caught on that I was speaking and clubbed me again in the back of the head. I nearly fell over, but caught myself. I was going to be lucky if I didn't pass out from a concussion.

"Two doors down, Bruk," I continued, "and…" BAM! I literally saw stars.

I fell to my knees, momentarily unaware of where I was. When I shook it off it surprised me to see a seven-foot tall panther man standing over me holding a mace that had a clump of my blood and hair on it.

"Keep it up," I told my guard with a smile, "and there won't be anything left for the arena."

He booted me in the face, and I slammed over backward onto the dirty ground.

"Like I care," he said, snatching my cuffed hands, and yanking me back to my feet.

Mercilessly, he shoved me toward the arena away from Bruk, slamming into a few people, which knocked them aside. The other slaves looked momentarily angered, then saw my chains, and my escort, and backed away quickly and nervously. Word spread rapidly, and as if I were Moses parting the water the crowd opened up before me until I had a clear path into the arena. My tormentors jabbed me with their spears and batted back the others with the flats of their axes for any reason and no reason.

It was a miserable journey until I was finally forced through a low, dank entrance into a huge building that turned out to contain a rather surprisingly expansive recessed stage. The crowd around me drifted out and around into the rows and rows of wooden benches set along three sides of the open space, and quickly sat facing the opposite wall and piles of immense, rounded boulders rising in uneven tiers nearly to the ceiling.

Grigori luxury boxes.

I was shoved and jabbed toward a thick, stone pylon in the center of the arena that had heavy bolts and anchors set deeply into its four sides; enough to hold as many as a dozen captives. My chains were attached to one of the anchor clamps and my Angara tormenter gave me one last, joyful smile before tousling my hair and walking away with his companions.

I tested my shackles and found them as secure as I'd expected. Dejected, knowing this would be my end, I turned to face the crowd with a confident smile. As I stood there, tall, defiant, patient, I scanned the crowd for my friends, but there were too many faces, and Bruk really did look like every other caveman in the place.

Once the wooden benches before me had been fairly well filled with slaves and Angara, our winged masters slowly descended into the enclosure, to take their seats at varying intervals along the fourth wall.

I imagined that the rough, gray rocks were as plush to them as cushions and upholstery would be to us. They lolled, and hunched, blinking their hideous eyes, probably chatting idly with one another in their sixth-sense-telepathic-fourth-dimensional-bullshit language.

Then the queen—that arrogant, heartless bitch, so much larger than the rest, and I could see now textured all over with a subtly different coloration—strode with superior confidence through a special door followed closely by two pet pterosaurs, and a guard of more Angara than I'd ever seen together in one place. She waddled up to a central area before the stone benches, and with a quick leap, and tiny flick of her massive wings, launched herself over the heads of the others to drop gently and precisely onto a high, central stone set slightly forward from the others. Her little, lizard-like flying rats followed, taking up deferential positions beside her, waiting impatiently for little treats an Angara guardsman quickly and nervously provided.

And then the 'band' began to 'play'.

Since Grigori cannot hear, whatever they call musical entertainment is something completely beyond us, and weird beyond words. The 'band' consisted of more than a dozen Grigori that filed out into the center of the arena where they crawled up on a small island of rocks not far from me, and after a moment of silent immobility—queuing up the orchestra, I suppose—they began to bob and weave, their mouths opening and closing in unison like mutes pretending to sing.

"What…" I said, "the fuck?"

The entire group twisted and gyrated like that, 'performing' for a good fifteen to twenty minutes. I just laughed my ass off.

Their entire technique consisted of waving their tails and moving their heads in a regular succession of measured movements that created a kind of cadence which—I don't know—maybe pleased the eye of the audience of Grigori the way 'music' would please our ears. Sometimes the band took precise steps in unison to one side or the other, or backward and forward again like some lizard-bird Motown group—it all seemed very silly and bizarre to me.

At the end of the first piece the gathered Grigori on the rocks showed their enthusiasm by rising up on their hind quarters, slapping their chests, beating their wings and opening and closing their mouths in a kind of appreciation that was almost as silent as the performance had been. They flapped their huge arms up and down, and smacked their rocky perches until the ground fairly shook. Then the band began another piece, the audience settled, and the arena became once again as silent as a grave.

The best thing about Grigori music? If you didn't like it, all you had to do was close your eyes.

When the band had exhausted its play-list it took wing and settled on various rocks above and behind the queen. And so, the business of the day was begun; I being the business of the day.

An Angara guard came through a door to my left, and limped my way. I recognized him almost instantly as Kiga. He closed the distance between us, the silence becoming more deafening. No one in the crowd had made a sound since shortly before the Grigori had begun 'performing', and now they were on the edge of their seats as the announcement approached for exactly what this was all about.

Kiga reached me, and stood quietly, studying my face. Then he shook his head.

"I knew you weren't very smart," he said, grinning, and lowering his eyes, slightly.

"Smart enough to have just killed the entire Grigori race," I said, with a shit-eating smile that would have made Hajah proud.

He gave no indication that he'd even heard me. His face didn't move, and his eyes never left mine. I think he was wondering if I was crazy. After a minute he looked around at the crowd, the amphitheater, and the attendant Grigori. Something in his mind seemed to be grinding into place about the lengths to which the Grigori had gone to execute *one* slave, and how there might be some very serious reason behind it.

"What are you talking about?" he asked, finally, cocking his head, and becoming intrigued.

"Grigori are all females," I said, simply. "And I took the book that helps them make babies."

"You can't have babies with a book," he said, not having grasped the rest of my sentence.

"You *can*. The book doesn't *make* the babies, but it tells you *how*— tells the Grigori how to make them—without males. And I stole their book."

"So… no more baby Grigori," he said, simply.

"No more baby Grigori."

"And when the adults die…"

"No more Grigori, ever again."

He considered those words, and smiled very slightly.

"And if someone kills all the adults…" he said, tasting it and liking it.

"We can fight over who will be the dominant race of Pangea, Angara or human," I finished for him.

"Or *not* fight," he said.

I shrugged.

"What's your name?" he asked.

"Brandon Mack."

"I will tell my children, Brandon the Mack, of how you liberated Pangea before you died."

"I... wait. What?"

"I cannot help you, Brandon the Mack. I will need time to convince the others, and that will be difficult. But if what you say is true, you have earned the respect and admiration of your people, and mine, and will long be remembered."

"Yeah, that's not very comforting," I said. "I was hoping to *not* die, and then spend a long life savoring all that respect and admiration."

"We all die, Brandon the Mack. Some die better than others. You are about to die greater than most."

I stared at him disbelieving.

"Thanks," I said finally, sarcastically.

He nodded once, not getting my sarcasm, and with that he turned to the crowd, raising his arms.

"This man took something that belongs to the Grigori!" he shouted to the crowd. *"Another took it from him! It must be returned, or you will ALL be put to death! Once this man has been killed, the Grigori will bring down another slave and stake them here until THEY die, and then another, and another until the item is returned, or you are all DEAD!"*

A nervous murmur ran through the crowd. I finally spotted Bruk and saw him giving the worst acting performance I've ever seen, this world or mine. No one was talking to him, but he was speaking to the air, pretending *he* didn't know who had it, *he* wasn't the one who took it, *he* didn't even know what the damn thing was!

I just shook my head and was glad no Grigori or Angara was looking at him.

"Oh, and there are two escaped slaves who killed an Angara, and they will be sacrificed here, as well!" Kiga concluded.

INSANITY AND OPPORTUNITY

DONE PLAYING EMCEE, KIGA turned, stared at me a moment, reached out and took my hands briefly in his, then dipped his eyes in gratitude before hobbling slowly back toward the door. He was barely inside before a pair of Angara guardsmen shoved a man and woman violently into the arena.

I leaned forward and pulled on my chains to better see the girl—hoping against all possible hope that she would be someone other than my Nova. Her bare back was toward me, the man blocking my view, with only a pile of raven black hair, really, to judge her by. But my heart began to beat faster with the fear that it *could* be her. Goosebumps exploded onto my skin, and my heart and breathing both raced out of control.

Suddenly a door on the far side of the arena slammed aside, and a T-Rex looking thing leapt out into the arena, its back and haunches porcupined with spears in an obvious and successful attempt to enrage the monstrous beast. I'm sure Milton could have given the technical name for it, but all that mattered to me was that it was huge, and had razor sharp teeth—big ones and lots of them.

It was closer to the pair of captives than me, so they kept their faces to it, obviously, so all I could still see was the raven hair of a naked girl, my view of her mostly blocked. Even without seeing her face I thought because of her build that this probably wasn't Nova. She was slightly heavier, and seemed shorter, but it had been so long, and maybe she'd been eating more while in hiding. There was enough uncertainty that my heart stopped racing and stood still in horrified misery as the dinosaur moved slowly toward her.

I couldn't take the doubt or the fear any more. I reached up to yank on my chains in what I knew would be a futile attempt to rip myself free, and felt a small something bounce against the back of my hand.

Looking down I saw a leather cord wrapped around my wrist. It had a key attached.

"What the…" I said, confused as hell.

Suddenly it dawned on me that Kiga had taken my hands before he had left. He must have placed the leather cord, and key around my wrists, and I hadn't noticed because of my shackles.

Working furiously I grabbed the key and twisted my hands around so I could slip it into the lock, but my hands were so bound up it was difficult to get the length of it into the hole. Terrified beyond reason that the girl might be Nova and about to be eaten, I risked a glance her way, and the key fell from my fingertips into the dirt at my feet.

"NO!"

On the opposite side of the theater the other two had bigger problems. With the entrance of the dinosaur a pair of spears had been tossed into the arena at their feet, but they seemed more for drawing out the inevitable than to actually give the intended victims any kind of realistic chance. The man snagged the spears, handing one of them to the woman, and they both began to back away, keeping the points between them and the slowly approaching dinosaur. I shook my head. A water pistol would have been more use.

The prehistoric predator stalked towards the pair, slowly picking up speed until it was charging full on, howling and thundering across the ground with the sound and power of a goddam elephant. Without warning a second door slammed up, and the most horrific roar I've ever heard in my life exploded from within. I couldn't see what made the noise but it spun the two victims around with a start, and finally separated them a bit, and that's when I saw the girl's face…

It *wasn't* Nova! God, I could have cried!

But now, as the two stood frozen in absolute horror, the thing that had roared so incredibly strode confidently out of the tunnel from beneath the slave seating and revealed itself—a massive sabertooth tiger—an enormous monster of a beast easily as tall as a horse. The color and markings were similar to any tiger you've ever seen; but its size was colossal in comparison.

The sabertooth moved slowly out of the shadows and into the diffuse light—open mouth growling, Pavlovian fangs dripping—advancing not only on the frightened couple, but also on the dinosaur, which had stopped its own attack to reassess the situation.

At the approach of the confident tiger the dinosaur began hissing in a frenzy of rage and noise. Never in my life had I heard such a horrible set of sounds as those two monsters made, all ironically lost on the main audience, the Grigori behind me.

More than ever I had to get free. Moving quickly I bent to the ground and found—to my horror—that my chains kept me from reaching the key! As the circling creatures spat terrifying sounds at one another, I panicked and tried to get my foot under the narrow, leather strap, hoping I could kick the thing up into my hand. I got a toe under it, and flicked, but only managed to kick the damn thing further away.

"Mother fucking son of a..."

Glancing over at the warm-up act, I watched for a moment as the T-Rex thing circled the couple, keeping them between it and the sabertooth. The monstrous tiger, for its part, decided it was done waiting and suddenly charged at the man and woman. Not wanting to lose out on a meal, the dinosaur raced in from the opposite side. The puny people standing terrified between them already seemed lost, but at the instant the beasts came together the man shoved the woman aside and the ferocious creatures slammed into him like colliding trains. Blood exploded in all directions, body parts flew, and what remained together was quickly ripped apart by the frenzied beasts.

The woman, terrified, having dropped her spear, ran directly at me, screaming. As she got nearer I could see an all consuming fear in her eyes before, in an instant, she was past me, apparently believing the pylon I was chained to would provide her with a shield if she could manage to keep it between her and the things devouring the man who'd just saved her life.

I looked back at the mess not far enough away from me, and saw that the creatures were going to be done with their little morsel pretty quickly. I returned my attention to the key, extending my leg as far as it would go, and being much more careful this time, managed to wriggle my toes more fully under the leather strap.

Needing just another inch or two, I pulled my hands desperately through the chains, and felt blood trickle down my forearms from wounds I was apparently inflicting on my wrists. The additional cuts from my life-and-death battle with the Grigori in the lab had left my torso in ribbons, and those injuries had finally managed to stop bleeding. But now I was reopening them again in my agonizing stretch for that damned, tiny, too far away key.

I took a safety check of my surroundings and saw that the predators had finally finished off their victim's remains, and were now heading my way. The T-Rex thing tossed a last bit of arm into the air so it would fall into its mouth and down its gullet, then lowered its gaze directly onto me.

I'd managed to get my toes far enough under the strap that I was able to lift it onto my foot. Now it was a matter of pulling it up slowly enough not to drop it, but fast enough to not be eaten before it could help me.

The sabertooth and T-Rex were both slowly circling in my direction, and I had only seconds before they'd be on me, so I worked the key up to my greedy fingertips, and immediately dropped it. But in a moment of supreme luck it fell, and bounced right into the keyhole. I grabbed it and held fast before it could slip free, then cranked it around carefully but quickly, until it stopped moving. Saying a quick prayer, I pressed harder until I felt the key begin to bend, and twist.

Damn it. It wasn't opening.

I continued to turn, increasing pressure to force the tines, beginning to fear the key would snap before doing its job. A last glance toward my attackers told me it wouldn't matter; I had no time left to wait. I gave the key one last shove, and rather than continuing to give, and breaking, the little miracle did its job and the cuffs fell open.

Behind me I heard one of the howling animals growl, open a mouth and blow hot breath against the side of my head. Without looking, moving faster than I've ever moved, I leaped around and behind the pylon beside where the woman was cowering. She shot a look up at me, eyes filled with terror, cheeks soaked with tears, shaking violently, teeth chattering like castanets. Her expression changed to instant shock as the pylon we crouched behind suddenly jolted on its foundation, rocked, and fell over toward us both, nearly trapping her beneath it as it fell.

We both leaped back. So much for our shield. A second impact, a horrific snarl, and suddenly the ground was shaking. Behind the toppled pylon we saw flashing claws, flying fur, a blur of white fangs, and the whip of a leathery tail.

Apparently the two creatures had turned on one another.

A ferocious battle now raged between them; claws slashed fur, teeth ripped deeply into blood red flesh, and all in such an insane whirl of speed and hostility that it was impossible to tell which animal had the upper hand. Their bodies vibrated with ferocity, fanged mouths locked into one another, clawed feet raking away hair and meat and cartilage.

After one particularly savage twist of the head by the T-Rex, blood began to spurt in a small geyser from the neck of the shrieking cat. As the immense feline lost momentary advantage, the T-Rex jerked again and tossed the enormous tiger high into the air, but the massive beast, now soaked crimson, only seemed angrier, landed easily on all fours, and dove back into the battle with no apparent loss of strength or intensity.

The woman and I now spent most of our time keeping out of the way of the two rampaging monsters, but as the fight raged on with no end in sight, I saw her begin to move carefully forward—stepping slowly so as not to draw attention. I knew what she was doing. The spears had fallen near to where the monsters raged, and she hoped to get hold of one. Letting her take the lead, I crept forward just as cautiously toward the second lance.

The tiger was now upon the Rex's narrow back, clamping on to the huge neck with its powerful teeth, chewing and scissoring its blade-like fangs, sawing deeply into the screaming Rex's pulpy flesh. At the same time the cat's long, powerful talons tore the dinosaur's heavy hide into bloody ribbons.

For a moment the T-Rex thing stumbled about the arena howling and quivering with pain and fury, its splayed, bird-like feet spread wide, its tail lashing angrily side to side. Finally, in a mad orgy of bucking it went careening around the arena in a frantic effort to unseat its deadly rider, and nearly trampled the girl in the process.

All its efforts to rid itself of the tiger seemed futile, until in desperation the Rex threw itself to the ground, and rolled over. This caught the sabertooth completely by surprise. It slammed into the earth, was winded, and from the sound of things, cracked a few bones. With a hissing shriek it lost its hold and then, before the cat could right itself, something inside it apparently painfully damaged, the great Rex was up again. Bent in agony, furiously charging its enemy, jaws wide, the dinosaur dove onto its opponent. Its sword-like teeth dug deep into the sabertooth's neck, and inertia slid the two animals across the arena floor where they slammed into a wall, the tiger viciously pinned.

The great cat clawed fiercely at the already ragged head of its adversary until eyes and lips were all but gone, and nothing more than a few stringy, red lumps of ragged, bloody flesh were left dangling from its skull. But the dinosaur held. It wasn't done. Through all the agony of that excruciating, murderous punishment the Rex-thing stood nearly motionless, jamming down its adversary, its only movement to occasionally drive those teeth deeper and harder into the bleeding abdomen of the giant cat.

That's when the girl leaped in—apparently deciding that the blind Rex would now be the easiest to defeat—and jammed her spear into the monster's heart.

The Rex-thing withdrew its jaws from the cat and raised its gory, sightless head, crying out horribly. I guess the crazy girl missed everything vital, or the dinosaur had no heart, because with a shriek that chilled my spine the ruined beast turned to run blindly and crazily about the arena. Pounding and leaping, screaming and bellowing, the poor, dying thing eventually circled back toward us. As it did, I jammed the back end of the spear I'd picked up into the dirt, and aimed it so that the dinosaur would run straight into the sharp end.

Impaling itself, it screamed insanely, but still wouldn't die.

Stopping only momentarily the beast shot quickly to the side where it slammed into the gate that had earlier contained the sabertooth. The great wooden door dislodged, and fell to become a kind of ramp that allowed the maddened creature to scrabble up and out of the arena, practically into Bruk's lap. An Angara was crushed only inches in front of my hairy friend, the panther man's head exploding brains and blood in all directions. A male slave was impaled on a thrashing tooth and the crying, sightless Rex snapped his jaws mercilessly like a garbage disposal until the man's body became nothing more than silent flying bits of flesh scattering over several other slaves frenziedly trying to escape.

The girl took my hand and pulled me away, back toward the center of the arena. Fearful for my friends, I resisted her, madly scanning the insanity of the crowd for Milton and Elia—Bruk having apparently gotten away. The girl continued to yank me impatiently, and before long I saw the wisdom in her effort, turned and ran with her away from the enraged and flailing dinosaur.

The terrified crowd formed a wall of frightened flesh in all directions. More slaves were crushed as the lunatic Rex struggled to escape its pain. Its head swung back down, and around, tossing aside countless numbers of screaming slaves.

Back in the arena the sabertooth had gotten to its feet, and like the Rex had decided the best way to escape its own misery was through the stadium seating. Terror and panic ruled the day.

Seeing no other choice, our escape cut off on three sides, a wall blocking the fourth, bodies piling up in all directions, every exit packed with the dead and the dying, I leapt forward dragging the girl behind me, and pulled us atop the back of the gigantic prehistoric tiger. She resisted, of course, but I insisted, and before long we were atop the senselessly wandering, dying creature.

"HOLD ON!" I commanded.

She did, both of us gripping bloody fur and torn flesh like reigns, my mind racing with the question of how this could possibly be any better than where we'd been. I had convinced the girl, but I hadn't convinced myself. The thinking had been it had a better chance of clearing a path out of here than we did, and if we were on it, it couldn't hurt us. But I was no longer so sure.

As the thing staggered forward, I finally saw Milton and Elia, one pawed limb of the sabertooth stepping mindlessly toward them. Milton stared at me and froze in the worst possible place, his hand holding Elia motionless beside him. Cursing, I yanked on the bits of ragged meat clasped in my hands in an effort to redirect the thing, and I'll be damned if it didn't actually work. Rising up momentarily like a bucking bronco, the prehistoric beast arched its back toward the pain I was inflicting, and moved away from my two friends, just as I'd hoped.

Releasing my grip on the monster's back, it resumed clawing its way through the frantic crowd, around the arena seats and eventually headed back toward the Grigori area, which was now empty of the winged masters of Pangea. The raging sabertooth seemed to have no more of an idea how to escape than I did.

Crazed with pain, and nearly dead, the sabertooth suddenly lurched forward at top speed, going exactly nowhere as fast as it could. With quick jerks on its raw flesh I attempted to guide it at the queen's special doorway—now clotted with slave bodies, Angara, and a Grigori or two—hoping the wall might be thinner in that area.

My steed slammed into the wall, shattering the stone enclosure completely and exploding open a hole big enough for a truck.

A bit of debris hit me, no real harm done, and after a few more desperate steps across the rubble, and the bodies trapped beneath it, the tiger finally collapsed to the floor and died quickly with a final, gurgling breath. The once fearsome creature was now nothing more than a lifeless pile of colorful hair and wet, red meat.

From my perch on its back I turned to see what had happened to the others. Ignoring everyone, the guards had joined in the general rush for the exits, slaves were still screaming and scattering in all directions and no direction, some being chased by the bloody and frantic Rex, which continued to stumble about aimlessly. Milton, Elia and Bruk were nowhere to be seen, all hopefully doing their level best to stay alive.

I hopped down from the dead cat and ran along the arena's outer corridor, the girl following closely behind. We passed several exits choked with fear mad slaves and Angara, none apparently aware that they were now fairly safe on this side of the arena wall.

But—thankfully in this case—that's how panic affects a crowd.

Toward the back of the amphitheater we found a little used exit, and made our way outside the building. Once in the open my adrenaline began to subside, and I felt instead a surge of hope. This was the event we'd most needed. On the far side of the arena I could still hear the howls of the T-Rex, and the screams of the humans. No Angara would stand still long enough to recognize that I was an unescorted slave who might be doing something he shouldn't.

I discovered a mostly clear doorway leading from the arena to the outer stairs that would take us to the street, and still followed by the girl, stepped out into the open city. Near the top of the steps I once more sighted my friends. They were across the avenue, near the opposite end of a huge mass of milling, frightened humans and Angara. Milton, Elia and Bruk were all safe, all alive, standing with the others and listening to the dying cries of the blinded T-Rex. Everyone was nervously waiting for the last embers of horror to die away.

I considered running over to them and bringing them with me. The three of us could easily use this opportunity to escape. But Milton still might not *want* to leave, might not even be able to keep up with a frantic, running getaway—at the very least it would be an argument— and our chance might be lost. My sudden notoriety also changed things. The fact that I had made myself a target as the thief of the Grigori's most precious book would make it impossible for us all once the insanity of this moment settled down. They would come for me. Come for them.

I couldn't endanger them that way.

And just as importantly, Milton was right. He and Elia *were* both safer here than out there where what had just happened in the arena moments ago could happen at any time, and with no warning. Inside Emibi death was certainly a constant possibility. Out there, it was inevitable.

I took one, last, loving look at all of them, and felt deeply saddened, even more so as they turned to head back into the building where Milton worked.

The girl tugged at my hand.

"We should go," she said.

And she was right. We should.

Playing the part of terrified slaves, I motioned for her to follow me, and ran toward the entrance to the city. When I reached an Angara, I pointed frantically—as did others near me—back toward the arena, and yelled *"Creature! Loose!"* and as the Angara looked that way, deciding what to do, the girl and I exchanged smiles, and continued our race for the city's exit. Most of the Angara yelled for other, nearby guards, indicating that they should all head in the direction of the arena. Not necessarily to help, but more just to be near enough for a good view in case anything interesting happened. Before long, there were no Angara anywhere near the gates of Emibi.

The girl and I reached the base of the seemingly endless steps leading up and out of the city, and into the wilds of Pangea. I looked around at the streets that had—since my arrival—been almost perpetually crowded with humans, panther-men, or the occasional Grigori. They were now almost entirely deserted, only a single runner heading off in the direction of the now out of sight arena.

It was almost too easy.

With cautious, careful steps, the girl and I began to ascend the stairs, upward, upward, out of captivity toward the outside world, and the eternal noonday sun of Pangea.

With each step I became less cautious, and more excited, until—before long—I was laughing out loud along with my naked companion, and we were running with all our strength and heart toward...

FREEDOM

I STOOD STARING OUT ACROSS the broad plain that spread expansively before Emibi. The three lofty, granite towers that mark the entrances to the sunken city were behind us—ahead, the valley and meadow stretched level and serene all the way to the nearby foothills. We had reached the surface, beyond the city, and our chance at a life of liberty seemed certain.

My first impulse was to wait for darkness before attempting to cross the open flatland; but then I remembered the sun never sets in Pangea. I laughed at myself, the girl laughing along with me, not realizing that I wasn't amused because of our situation. Smiling together we stepped out of the shadows of the Grigori city and into the perpetual sunshine.

"What are you called?" she asked me.

"Brandon. Brandon Mack. And you?"

"I am Nala the Desirable. Nice to meet you Brandon, Brandon the Mack."

"No, uh…" but then I thought about it and decided to let it go. "Just Brandon. One Brandon."

She stared at me confused.

"Brandon," I said.

"Brandon," she answered simply.

"Yes. Nice to meet you, Nala… the Desirable. Was the man in the arena your mate?"

She laughed. Very hard. So hard she had a difficult time composing herself.

"Oh, my, no," she said, catching her breath. "Did you really think so? He was so *ugly*. Though he wanted me badly, at least to put his spear in. But he had nothing, and was not very brave."

"Oh?" I said, a little surprised by her coldness. "He seemed rather brave to me. He died saving your life."

She thought about it, then shrugged, not the least bit appreciative, or concerned.

"I'm glad he did," she said, and that seemed to be the best she would offer the man who had made the ultimate sacrifice for her. "But it was the only time he showed bravery."

"At least he showed it when it counted," I said.

"I suppose."

Nala and I moved down a pretty slope of grass and young trees that must have been cleared in the recent geologic past, perhaps by a passing glacier. It was more like a park hill than a naturally occurring phenomenon, and for a moment I wondered if the Grigori sent Angara out now and again to mow it, it was that neat and tidy.

We moved down the hill and into lush grasses that rose from barely to our ankles all the way up to thick, waist high fronds. The stalks dominated the meadowland—a gorgeous flowering savanna unique to the inner world. Every hundredth blade was tipped by tiny, five-pointed blossoms, brilliant little stars of purples and yellows that danced gently atop the green foliage like tiny stars, adding a deceptive charm to the weird, yet lovely, otherworldly landscape.

Nala bent and picked a few of the flowers, handing the bunch to me as we walked.

"A thank you for saving my life," she said, smiling up at me.

Apparently she found me more attractive than the last man who'd saved her life.

"I have a mate," I said.

"Not here," she said, smiling with even more warmth.

I ignored the flirt and continued on with a little more speed to make it clear I was avoiding the naked girl's sexual offer. To further close myself off I focused on the distant hills, and any areas that might hold a cave, or several of them. Bruk and I had worked out a plan with Milton that required one, and with luck that plan would take me straight to Nova.

Hurrying on, trampling the endless blossoms mercilessly beneath my rushing feet, I thought only of her beautiful face.

Milton had once said that the force of gravity was lower on the inner surface of the Earth than the outer. He explained it all to me in great detail, but it was all too much like those lectures back in school that I always had a hard time focusing on, and so most of whatever he said went over my head. Something to do with the counter-attraction of the opposite side of the earth's crust overhead, I think.

Whatever. I definitely felt much stronger, like I could move faster and with greater agility. As I ran across Emibi's flower-speckled lowland I seemed to fly, though how much of the sensation was due to Milton's suggestion, and how much to my excitement at potentially finding Nova, I really have no idea.

The more I thought of Milton—and Elia, and Bruk—the less I enjoyed my newfound freedom. I could never be completely happy in Pangea until I knew that the old man was completely safe and as free as I; he, Elia, *and* Bruk. I had learned to love them all, I supposed. They would be safe for now, but someday I would find a way to go back, and release them from Grigori captivity.

Just how I was going to accomplish all my many lofty goals, stripped naked and unarmed, surrounded by wild animals and dinosaurs, was the million-dollar question. I wasn't even sure I could retrace my steps to Emibi once I passed beyond the view of this grassland.

Fighting back my fears with a stubborn insistence I forged ahead toward the foothills.

"Slow *down!*" Nala insisted. I had forgotten she was even there. "What's the hurry?"

I didn't answer. No sign of pursuit had appeared from the direction of Emibi, and ahead of me I saw nothing moving. No dangers, no animals, no hungry beasts. It was as though we were moving through a long dead and completely forgotten world.

"OW!" Nala said. "Hold on. I cut myself on something."

We both stopped as she hopped on one foot, trying to get a look at what appeared to be a scratch on her shin. Like me, she wore strap sandals, but nothing else, and I suppose it was only a matter of time before one of us was ripped open by something out here.

She bounced over to a rock and sat down, making faces at the tiny wound.

"It hurts," she said, hissing. "Would you look at it?"

I stared a moment in amazement before moving. This woman lived in a prehistoric world filled with unheard of dangers, giant insects, and sudden death. I had watched her leap atop a T-Rex and stab the damn thing straight through the chest. How is it this scratch was bothering her in the least?

Kneeling before her I took the shin in hand and turned it gently, studying the wound. It was long, but not deep. I probably had five such scratches on various body parts of my own.

"Your touch is very gentle," she said.

"Thank you," I said absently.

She moved her leg to one side and leaned back a little, pressing fingertips into the dark bush of hair, between her legs.

"I have a deeper wound here," she said seductively, moving the hair aside to expose pink folds of flesh. "Perhaps you could fill it with something… and heal me."

I dropped her leg and started again toward the foothills.

"Do you prefer boys?" she asked, harshly.

"I prefer Nova," I said.

"Is that her name? The one who was your mate? 'Nova'?"

"Yes."

"Why is she not with you?"

"She escaped on our way here."

"Alone?" Nala asked.

"Yes," I lied.

"Well, it's unlikely she's even alive. It would be a miracle, you know? Pangea is brutally cruel to lone travelers."

"You managed to survive the last time you escaped."

"I had a man to help me."

"A lot of good it did him."

"*I* am still alive," she said.

I realized I had slowed for her, and had now stopped walking completely, so I could turn to face her, amazed. As I stared at her not hideous, but not to me particularly attractive face, I began to wonder if she was what Pangean men considered beautiful. Rounded face, large, arched nose, heavy hips and stomach.

"Did you offer the other man sex for his protection," I asked, snidely, "or slow him down when you were tired?"

She looked stung, but shook it off, and glared at me.

"Well, if you want *my* help staying alive," I said, returning to my journey, "you'd better keep up."

"I'm tired and want to rest. We've walked very far, and there are many more fun things to do than walk, you know."

"You're free to stop and enjoy those things by yourself, if you want. But I need to find Nova, so I'm continuing on."

I thought I heard her stamp a foot.

"Brandon!"

I stopped, sighed heavily, and reluctantly turned back toward her again. She had her hands on her hips, and was snarling at me in that petulant way my little sister used to do when she was five and had been told she couldn't have the doll she'd just seen on TV.

"I *said*," Nala snarled, "I am *tired*. And I would like to stop and rest."

"I'm not stopping you," I said, returning along the path.

"*BRANDON!*"

I sighed again... and turned back... *again.*

"I *said*," she repeated, "I am *tired.*"

"*And I have to find my mate!*" I snapped.

I wheeled around and walked away from her. I'd gone a good distance before I heard her sandals slapping the earthen trail we'd been following, heading right for me.

"*Brandon, wait!*"

She reached me, ran in front of me, and took hold of my arms, staring into my eyes.

"Please," she said, sounding sad, and pitiful, and if I hadn't already gotten a good sense of her, I would have thought she was actually sincere. "Please, Brandon, just a few minutes rest."

She let go of my arms and put her hands around my waist, pulling me to her, and pressing her cheek to my chest.

"You're just so much stronger and faster than I am," she said. "I've never known a man who was so… powerful."

One of her hands left my back and found its way to my bare ass, the fingers taking delicate hold. I pushed her away.

"If you want to rest, we'll rest. But none of that," I said, motioning toward her clutching fingers. "I love Nova."

"And you can love her *still*. But let's enjoy one another while you do."

"Is that how you do things here?" I said, thoughts of Nova with someone else tearing open my heart in a jealous fury. Nala must have picked up on it, because she smiled, and her seductive look returned.

"You're not from here?" she asked. "That explains everything. Most of the tribes in this part of Pangea… if you want to, you do. Spearing and being speared—it's fun. And there is so little fun in Pangea."

I fought away thoughts of Nova being speared by another. But Nala—probably sensing weakness—pounced.

"If your Nova is alive, and she meets a man, it will happen. It's like saying 'hello'. She will let men inside her whenever the opportunity arises. Or the spear arises, as it were."

I sat down on a nearby boulder and felt a mixture of rage, horror, and sadness slam through me. It made a kind of sense. This place was nothing like my world. But was it really *so* different? Men and women seemed very similar, for the most part. Physically. Emotionally. But sex *was* incredibly free, and perhaps necessarily so, if the species was to survive. It was almost Darwinian in its obviousness. There **could be** no possessiveness. No jealousy. Such notions would only interfere with reproduction and survival. I put my head in my hands and agonized about it.

"This hurts you," Nala said, kneeling before me and placing her hands gently on my arms. "Don't let it hurt you. This is just our way. She will still love you. Fucking is only for fun."

"It has great meaning where I come from," I said. "For lots of reasons. Not the least of which is knowing whose child you're raising."

"What does it matter whose child you raise? A child needs to be protected by the tribe. It belongs to all. But that has nothing to do with spearing."

I raised my head and looked at her carefully.

"Spearing is what makes babies," I said.

She looked at me, confused. She shook her head.

"No. Babies are placed inside us by the goddess of life," she said. "But if you pray before the shoranja, eat its root or drink its tea, the gods will be merciful and give you no babies."

"Merciful," I said, stunned.

"Life in Pangea is hard. It is not a place for babies, or being tied down to them."

144

"Grigori eat babies," I said, remembering what Nova had said.

"No they don't," Nala said, nearly laughing. "That's just a story mothers tell to scare their children so they won't wander off."

I thought about that. No, Nova had meant it. And she had known that having sex with me could lead to babies—babies she genuinely feared the Grigori would eat.

Just as she had feared other women would want me, and so had taken steps to prevent it, she also feared pregnancy because she knew it would be ours. Hers and mine. She *knew* it.

Nova wasn't like Nala, even if Nala was telling the truth. She wouldn't take just any 'spear' that came along.

I was fairly sure.

I shook my head to clear the thought, and stood up.

"Enough rest," I said, and began walking again.

Behind me I heard Nala sigh, heavily, but she didn't try to stop me anymore.

I HAVE NO IDEA, of course, how long it took us to reach the limit of the plain, but eventually we entered the foothills, and began following a pretty little canyon upward into the mountains. Nala hadn't spoken much since the stop so long ago, and I'd said almost nothing. What little she did say was usually complaint or criticism. The only sound as we climbed was her struggling, and moaning, or the trickling of a little brook, splashing pleasantly alongside us down toward some distant sea.

The tiny stream settled into larger pools along the way, and in one of its quieter ponds I found some small fish, four-or five-pounds each, I think. They looked more like tiny whales than trout, or salmon. As I climbed, I occasionally noticed that they not only suckled their young like mammals, but also came to the surface to breathe and feed on some of the tender grasses and a strange, scarlet lichen that grew on the rocks just above the water line.

This, of course, made it easier for me to snag one and make a meal of it. A good meal, at that. Nala cooked the things on a spit over a small fire she started with nearby rocks and scrub. It was plain, and unevenly cooked, but the meat was tasty. By now I'd gotten rather used to eating food in its raw, natural state, though I still cringed at the thought of eyes and entrails, much to Bruk's never ending amusement. He particularly loved those little treats. Having something roasted was a kind of delicacy for me, even if I knew Nala had done it primarily so we could stop moving for a while. She really was quite lazy.

After dining on a couple of the fish, I brought her water from a clear pool, and we drank the precious liquid together. Then I washed my hands and face and for the thousandth time checked behind us, in the direction of Emibi.

Off in the distance I thought I could make out a small group of figures moving our way.

I sighed. And then I smiled.

"Finally," I said to no one.

"Finally, what?" Nala asked.

"The Angara are coming."

She stood, instantly frightened, grabbed her spear and moved around behind me. I laughed a little.

"Far off," I said. "Back near Emibi."

She suddenly kicked over the fire, extinguishing it.

"Will they find us?" she asked.

"Absolutely," I said. "In fact, I'm counting on it."

Turning around, I continued my ascent. Nala, after taking a last look at the distant hunters, followed. Above us in the direction of the source of the brook there was a more rugged climb that led all the way to the summit of the mountain ridge. We reached it in no time, and beyond found a steep decline that sliced almost straight down, directly to the shore of a peaceful, little, inland sea. Out along the upwardly curving surface I could see several beautiful islands.

"What do we do?" Nala asked. "About the Angara?"

"Nothing," I said, topping the rise and heading down.

"But if they find us, they'll take us!"

"No, they won't."

"They will!" she screamed, panicked.

I stopped and faced her, smiling to show my calm.

"They *will* find us, Nala, yes," I said, patiently. "Because they have a thing that tells them where we are. There is no escaping them."

She started to interrupt with fearful sputtering, but I held my hands up and assured her it would be fine.

"I'll be ready for them when they get here. And then I'll take their little tracking device and use it to find Nova."

She looked momentarily stunned, but not much reassured, and I didn't care.

The view was beautiful, but I didn't spare any time to sightsee. As I had all during the hike up I searched during the descent for a suitable cave, but there didn't seem to be one. I stepped over the edge of a little bluff, and half sliding, half falling, dropped into the pretty, little valley that led out to the sea, marveling at the profound sense of peace and security I felt. Behind me Nala stumbled over a vine and fell on her face. She stood, spitting grass and twigs, and growled.

"Why did we have to come here?" she demanded.

"You have a better place for us to go?"

"Back to my village!"

"So go there!" I said, tired of her bitching and whining.

Turning up the coast, I began to search along its edge for any opening that might be big enough for my purposes. The gently sloping beach along which I walked was thickly matted with strangely shaped, brightly colored shells; some empty, others still housing some of the weirdest critters that ever slimed a trail. As I walked I couldn't help but think of myself as the first man on earth, so primal and untouched were these virgin wonders and ancient beauties, so completely devoid of people did this entire world seem. I felt like a second Adam wending his lonely way through a newborn Garden of Eden, desperately searching for my Eve.

"Brandon!" Nala called. "Brandon, wait!"

While being trailed by an obnoxious, high maintenance Pangean princess.

I stopped, sighed, and turned to find her struggling to get over some branches and ferns, attempting to protect her naked body from the shrubs, and the skittering little creatures on the sand.

"EW!" she said, flinching from something I couldn't see. "Brandon, wait for me!"

Nala was—as I said—not attractive to me, but she was far from hideous, her body quite a thing of beauty. A little heavy, but that only made it full, and soft, and appealing. Watching her walk toward me in the nude wasn't exactly unpleasant. But as she sneered at me out of disgust for the pretty little area surrounding us, an image bubbled up before my mind's eye of the exquisite outlines of a perfect face wrapped in the loose tangle of luxurious, raven hair that I knew would enjoy this place as much as I did. She wouldn't complain, or whine, or bitch me into distraction. She would laugh, and joke, and enjoy.

"God, Brandon," Nala said, irritated, "you don't make it easy to stay with you, you know."

I instantly tired of looking at her naked body, and searched the area again for a place to set up. That's when I saw a series of small caves cut into the ridge that lined the beach.

One of them seemed perfect from where I stood, but eager to be certain, I bounded over the thick weeds and matted undergrowth to reach its mouth.

"Dammit, Brandon!" Nala yelled. *"Slow down!"*

The cave seemed deep enough, creating both shadow and darkness to hide in. It was also quite damp and muddy owing to a small river whose steady flow still trickled quietly along its floor. But that gave me an idea for something lacking in my plan that had been bothering me—how to hide. The water had probably eroded the tunnel into existence over many, many centuries, and its constant moisture was going to be just what I needed.

I backed out and studied the mouth, noting a small overhang that seemed perfectly suited for my little plot.

"Yeah," I said to no one. "Yeah, this will do nicely."

"What will do nicely?" Nala asked, stepping carefully over to where I was.

"I need to set something up, here in this cave," I told her. "Will you help me?"

She stopped and looked at me like I was insane.

"What kind of help?" she asked.

"Moving boulders, and weaving some grass mats."

"Why should I do that?"

"So we'll be free of the Angara and the Grigori."

She continued to stare, and I thought she wasn't going to answer. But I was wrong.

"Fuck me first," she said.

I stared back at her, stunned.

"I'll do it myself," I said.

I headed off toward a small cluster of stones.

"Gods, Brandon, why don't you want to have sex? Most men would be *begging ME* for sex!"

"Go find one of *them*," I said.

And so, anticipating my visitors sometime soon, I began the preparations I hoped would free, Milton, Elia, Nova, and I from the ever-watchful eye of the Grigori.

THREE ANGARA WERE coming as if drawn to us by magnets. One of them held out a silvery device before him, checked his surroundings, then the device, and finally pointed in our direction, saying something I couldn't hear. The other Angara moved slightly ahead of him, coming much the same way we'd come, over roots and logs, across ditches and small streams until they all stood near the mouth of the cave, looking in.

The lead Angara checked the device in his hand, adjusted something, and looked into the cave.

"Slaves of the Grigori!" he yelled. "You have been found! Come out now and you won't be harmed. I really don't mind getting out of the city now and then, but only to a point. Searching through darkened caves goes beyond that point. So spare yourself a beating, and spare me the exertion that will only make that beating more painful."

I, of course, said nothing, and thankfully, neither did Nala.

I heard the lead Angara sigh, heavily, in exasperation.

"Go on," he told the others. "Drag them out."

The other two looked at one another, and one of them glanced inside, uncertain.

"What if it's a trick, and there's a beast in there, or something."

"Not my problem," said the lead Angara, who simply stared back at the questioning hunter with stern indifference.

The panther man who had spoken groaned, then trudged slowly forward, followed reluctantly by the nervous third. The two searchers stepped carefully through the mud, moving deeper into the cave, as far as they dared without light.

"We'll need torches," one hunter said.

The lead Angara outside the cave stared silently for a moment, then held his hands out as if beseeching some unseen god overhead.

"AAAAAH!" he growled. *"I'M GOING TO GUT THESE SLAVES AND EAT THEIR LUNGS!"*

After a moment of annoyed head shaking, he stepped forward toward his fellows, daintily trying to avoid the mud. He stopped about ten paces from the others, looking at the device in his hand, then slipped, and sunk into the mud up to his shins. He dropped his arms and turned his eyes skyward, again.

"Hasha be merciful," he said, and shook his head. *"I'M REALLY HATING YOU RIGHT NOW, SLAVES!"*

Then he looked again at the thing in his hands, and up, again, quickly, searching the cave.

"According to this, they're right here," he said.

The other two looked at one another confused.

"Are you on 'close'?" The other asked.

"Don't be stupid. Of course I'm on 'close'! *They should be standing right here!"*

Nala leaped out from under her grass mat before she was supposed to, screamed, and ran the third Angara through with her spear tip. He howled, grabbed the wooden shaft, jerked it from her hand, and charged after her. That's when she looked my way and cried out.

"BRANDON! HELP!"

The lead Angara followed her glance and finally noticed me, buried in the mud along the wall of the cave right beside him. As I'd hoped, he was startled enough to freeze for the moment it took me to wrench loose my spear and run it through his stomach. He spasmed back with my plunge, but his expression of shocked horror never changed. He tried futilely to raise his axe, but blood spurted from his mouth, and his body began to go limp.

Moving quickly, I snagged the device and the axe from his hands before he could drop them, placed a foot against his chest and tried to shove him off my spear. But his weight folded in on me, and I couldn't get the thing loose. So I kicked him away and raced for the Angara now menacing Nala, axe raised. The third Angara, partially rooted in the mud, saw me coming and raised his own weapon to deflect mine. The axes clanged, sparking in the dim light, and unfortunately for him my blade caromed directly into his face. He was dead before he realized what had happened.

Spear lodged in one Angara, axe lodged in the other, I had no remaining weapons so I just grabbed Nala's hand, and ran for the cave's exit. I heard the panther man gathering himself behind me, and terrifyingly found myself struggling through the wet muck floor of the cave. Nala screamed when she realized that she, too, was virtually trapped.

I turned to look over my shoulder, and saw the remaining Angara struggling our way, Nala's spear still impaling him. The wood of her weapon snagged on a sodden root, jerked his torso downward, and snapped. The Angara screamed, but shrugged it off and kept moving, straining in our direction, fury gouging his face into a mask of animalistic rage. If we didn't get free of this sticky, wet earth around our ankles and shins, he was going to reach us and, as promised, eat our lungs.

"Shit!" I snarled, trying to work myself loose. *"Shit, shit, shit!"*

"BRANDON!" Nala yelled.

Trying to think quickly, I leaned forward and pulled myself with my arms.

"Crawl, Nala!" I said.

Crawling turned out to be much faster than running, and as the Angara got closer, he, too, leaned forward and pulled himself with both hands and legs. The three of us struggled, digging toes and clawing fingers, and before long I'd yanked myself free, pulling Nala up beside me just ahead of the Angara's reach, and together we exploded from the mouth of the cave, just beyond the grasp of our unceasing pursuer.

Shoving Nala from the cave, I heard her shriek and fall from the force of my push, but I didn't care. I grabbed a vine that dangled near the opening, and pulled for all I was worth. From the overhang above, hundreds of pounds of loose stone dropped between me and the panther man hunter, crushing him in the process. The cave wasn't completely sealed, but the opening that remained was too small for any man, or Angara, to squirm through.

My little scheme had worked almost as well as I'd planned.

"Dammit, Brandon!" Nala yelled. "I was almost killed!"

"You jumped out too soon!" I said.

"They weren't going any further into the cave! I *had* to go!"

"I wanted to avoid killing them if possible!"

"I still don't understand why you wouldn't want to kill an Angara!" she said, shaking her head. We'd argued about it for quite a while before hiding ourselves.

I thought momentarily of Kiga, and shook my head.

"Never mind," I told her. "It's done."

I turned my attention to the device in my hand that would hopefully take me straight to Nova.

"I've got what we needed," I said.

"What *you* needed! It's not going to do *me* any damn good!"

Ignoring her, I turned and headed back the way we'd come, looking for a place to sit so I could figure out how to work my little, prehistoric GPS.

A fallen tree ahead and to my right formed a rather neat little bench, so I sat there and began studying the rounded, metallic, silver box. Nala situated herself behind me, leaning over for a good look, and perching her breasts awkwardly atop my shoulders.

The thing seemed pretty rudimentary. A small, radar-like screen showed a purple dot in the middle that I assumed was me. Two small knobs on either side of the screen, and a couple buttons were the only controls. Hoping I wouldn't break it in some way, I twisted one of the knobs. My purple dot moved quickly to one side. Not wanting to lose the only marker I could see, I turned the knob back, to re-center my light.

Twisting the second knob made my dot shrink, and I began to see outlines of the coastline before me, with indications of the mountains behind. Ah, okay. So this was how to get a wider perspective. But how to find Nova? There were other dots on the device, including a blue one not far from me. Could there be other hunters out searching for...

"What are those lights?" Nala asked, mesmerized, and covering the device with her hand to shade out the blinding noonday sun, her lips very close to my ear. "They glow like the spots on a vishanti fish."

Goosebumps rose on my flesh, and not from Nala's contact. The blue dot was moving fast toward my purple dot, and nearly on top of it.

A spear suddenly exploded through Nala's chest, between her breasts, clipping my shoulder. Startled, she looked down at the wooden shaft, the blood, and began to shake, staring at me, pleadingly.

"Brandon," she said, her voice trembling.

"Nala?"

"It hurts..."

She fell to the ground, and lay very still, her eyes staring emptily up at me.

DEATH AND THE SEA

I turned just in time to see the Angara from the cave, face split wide from the impact of the axe that was still lodged there, swinging a club down on a collision course with my skull. I dove and the thing splintered the redwood log I had been sitting on. If it had connected with my head, much of my upper torso would be nothing more than a moist spray of red. Leaping to my feet I backed away as the panther man expertly yanked his weapon from my former position, made a quick check down at Nala, deduced that she was no threat, and hurled his immense body right at me with shocking speed.

"Don't leave me..." Nala pleaded, her voice barely above a whisper.

The Angara swung, I ducked, cudgel once again impacting wood instead of my face, as another, only slightly smaller tree shattered and fell. I danced aside a third time as the weapon rushed back around, scraped my face and embedded itself on its downward arc in the soft, damp, moss covered earth. The stone club became tangled in the detritus, and was stuck just long enough to allow me to roll free and run.

I knew that once he'd loosened his weapon the Angara would be back on me, and wasn't likely to miss many more times. I searched frantically for a weapon, or a hole to dive into, but there was nothing.

Arcing back around to where he'd first attacked us, I dropped beside Nala, and turned her head gently to look up at me. Her eyes were still open, her mouth moving, but making no sound. Checking on my enemy, I saw the Angara pull his club-head free and turn back my way.

Lifting Nala, relieved that she was lighter than she looked, I ran—sprinting and leaping with a speed I never knew I had. I was nearly to the beach when I saw what at first glance seemed to be another downed tree, but after a second and third glance turned out to be an upturned canoe partially hidden in the thick foliage.

Hearing the Angara frighteningly close behind me, I angled toward the canoe, hoping to use it as a temporary shield. I thought I felt the panther man's weapon graze the back of my head, just as I leaped forward, beneath the handmade boat.

Nala screamed from the pain of the spear through her chest—the same one she'd shoved through the Angara in the cave—as it bent and twisted with my dive.

Not waiting for the Angara to smash through the canoe and pulp me, I stood up from underneath and lifted my cover, shoving the boat in his direction, apparently just as he was about to strike. The stunned Angara was caught off guard as I had shortened the arc of his swing enough that he had no strength in it, the blow bounced harmlessly off the canoe, and I could see his feet—very close to mine—stumble backwards.

His ankles tangled in some roots or vines, and he fell over into a thicket of low scrub with the now upright canoe on top of him. Not knowing what else to do, I jumped on the canoe, and him, pining the panther man atop his chest, then leaned over to punch him—repeatedly and hard—on either side of his split open face. He screamed, horribly. Then I grabbed the axe handle, pressed my foot onto his screaming mouth and yanked the blade free.

For a moment he seemed to go limp, so I took the moment to return to Nala, lift her, and lay her inside the little boat. Shoving with all I had I forced it and her in a line toward the sandy beach, hoping to escape on the water.

"Hey!" Someone yelled. But I didn't care enough to slow down and see who.

"HEY!" The voice repeated, as the little skiff hit ocean, skipped across some gentle waves, and I threw myself in. Grabbing hold of a crude paddle lodged under the rough-cut seat, I dragged it ferociously through the crystalline sea.

Finally I turned to see who was calling.

Further down the shore a huge, incredibly tall, brown-skinned man was running rapidly toward me, arms waving, anger etching his face.

"STOP!" He insisted, as he reached the edge of the sand where I had entered the sea. "STOP!"

I didn't.

But I did slow my rowing enough to point warningly behind him. Surprised, and confused, he did as I suggested, just in time to see the enormous Angara, flesh falling away from the center of his face, charging out of the trees and right for him.

The brown man screamed.

When he turned back to me his face had changed completely from angry to terrified, his eyes so wide he looked like a cartoon drawing of... well... a man in fear for his life.

He tossed aside the weapon and a string of small rodents he must have captured, and with a massive leap dove into the waters to swim after me. The Angara threw his club at one of us, but overthrew—at least I think he did—and the damn thing only grazed my shoulder as it clanked against the bow of the boat behind me, and bounced into the sea beyond.

"Bran... don," Nala said. "Are... you... there?"

"I'm here, Nala," I said.

Keeping an eye on the events behind us, I reached a hand down and rubbed her thigh, comfortingly. As I did, she grabbed my fingers tightly, desperately.

Behind us, weapon spent, the enormous panther man followed the brown man whose boat I was probably stealing into the transparent waves and began to swim awkwardly, frenziedly, but still very quickly in our direction. I didn't want to abandon the poor brown-skinned man, but I recognized that if he caught us Nala and I might both be in serious trouble, so I grasped the paddle again, intending to urge the awkward, wobbly little craft away from him, further out onto the surface of the bowl-shaped sea. But Nala refused to let go of my fingers, and given her state, I didn't want to force them free.

At best I was only able to make slow progress with one arm, especially in an unfamiliar little skiff that bobbed stubbornly in every direction but the one I wanted to go. A glance over my shoulder showed me that the brown man was rapidly closing the gap, his mighty strokes assuring he would overtake us in no time. Even with both hands free I could never outdistance him.

With Nala still clamped to my hand, I set the paddle aside and waited for the boat's owner. We were about a hundred yards from shore when it became clear that the poorly swimming but powerful Angara would reach my pursuer before he reached us, probably within a few dozen strokes. I debated rowing back to help him, knowing he'd probably just throw me out of his boat and into the angry arms of the still thrashing panther man.

"Aaah, damn my conscience," I said to no one.

I forced my fingers free of Nala's grasp, and bent to the grandfather of all paddles, forcing it to row me back in the direction of the brown giant, as the enormous panther man gained and gained.

I was close enough, now, that the brown giant's hand was reaching upward for the stern when suddenly a sleek, sinuous body burst from the depths in a violent surge. The brown man saw it too, and the look of horror and certain death that erupted across his face told me I wasn't going to have to worry about him, or the Angara for much longer.

The thing was probably a plesiosaur, but I barely remember most of the dinosaurs I loved as a kid, so I couldn't swear to it. Whatever it was, it had a long neck with a giant mouth at the end, filled with rows of glistening teeth.

The head arced and plunged down toward the brown giant and as it was about to engulf the poor man in its razor filled jaws I surprised even myself by slamming its head aside with the paddle. I knocked the thing just far enough off course that the head narrowly missed the brown giant, but still almost dragged him under with the force of its dive.

The man turned pleading eyes my way, and in them I saw surprise, fear, and... gratitude. I stunned us both by reaching out a hand to lift him aboard. He responded quickly, not questioning my motives, gripping my fingers tightly and pulling with everything he had. Obviously skilled at struggling in and out of boats on an unstable sea, the brown man was inside and beside me in seconds. But neither of us felt anything like safe. He glanced briefly at the still breathing Nala, then at me again, then over the edge of the boat at the prehistoric threat.

The plesiosaur circled the tiny canoe, under and around, the length of the monster easily fifteen or twenty feet. I saw no chance for us if it registered in that tiny, dinosaur brain how easy it would be to capsize us.

We both stood, now, the brown man and I, each carefully following the submerged, circling beast as it flew through the depths. I held out the paddle before me like a sword, keeping it between me and the hungry beast that should have died millions of years ago.

My companion's brown hand pointed, and I knew what he was indicating.

"It's picking up speed," he said, unnecessarily.

We watched as it moved faster and faster in a circle around us, then suddenly it dove, deep beneath the clear, blue-tinged waters. We could still see it, far below near the seabed, increasing velocity with each stroke of its massive flippers. Then—to our complete horror—it turned sharply and headed straight back up, directly at us.

"GET DOWN!" I shouted, and we both did, just moments before the thing exploded from the waters beside us, sailing inches above the boat, mouth open wide, right where we'd been standing.

Instinctively I swung the paddle and slammed it into something I didn't see because I was hunkered down beside Nala's body on the floor of our flimsy, hand carved, death trap. The boat jerked, and nearly capsized, water splashed on the opposite side of us, and I felt waves coming over the edge of the canoe. One of the plesiosaur's fins must have smacked against the canoe, nearly tipping us, and we took on several gallons of water before righting ourselves.

Nervously, the brown man and I raised our heads and peeked around in search of our attacker. Neither of us saw anything until its snake-like neck burst from under the surface again right beside us, and nearly snapped the brown man's head off his shoulders. As it was he'd been nipped, and I saw blood spread across his cheek. I took another swing and slammed my makeshift weapon into the monstrous thing's eye, it screeched and withdrew, but instead of dropping again beneath the waves, it simply arched its neck higher, one eye bleeding and glazed, mouth wide and hissing.

Recovering quickly, it shot its head down sharply, snapping at me. I swung again to deflect it, narrowly missing as it learned my game, and avoided my swings. Clear of my reach, it again arched its neck high and away, returning almost instantly after my weapon had past it. It arched in and out like that, striking repeatedly, tearing at my arms and shoulders; it could reach me easily, and I couldn't connect in any meaningful way.

Then suddenly, the head stopped hissing, and it turned its attention toward shore.

No, not toward shore, toward the Angara.

The massive panther man had long ago stopped swimming, and now tread water about ten yards behind us, just absorbing the insanity that had played out before him. But now the plesiosaur had him in its sights, and he knew it. His eyes widened, he looked around trying to gauge if he had time to reach the shore, realized he didn't, turned back to us and screamed.

And the plesiosaur dove. It's entire body snaked furiously beneath the roiling surface of the ocean, heading straight for the Angara.

"COME ON!" I yelled, not even realizing what I was doing.

"What are you saying?" the brown man asked. *"That's an Angara, the servants of the Grigori!"*

"I know. *COME ON!"* I repeated, waving my hands, and the Angara did.

Thrashing terribly, the panther man moved faster than I could have believed possible, just as the plesiosaur churned through the surface near where he'd just been. The Angara shot a horrified glance over his shoulder, then splashed frantically toward us once more. As he reached for the boat, I reached for him. All four of our hands locked before the plesiosaur returned, and hit him like a freight train.

It took us both straight up into the air, launching a good fifteen feet into the clear, blue sky. I hung there for what felt like minutes, in shock, in terror, and saw even greater fear on the face of the Angara. For several heartbeats there was no sound, no movement, and it was as if the universe had begun moving in slow motion, droplets of water hanging suspended all around us, drifting like beads of glass. The Angara stared straight into my eyes, what was left of his face shifting from fear, to horror, to the blank and emotionless expression of the dead, and that's when I saw the crystalline beads of red float by.

It felt like the moment would go on forever, but it ended abruptly, and I slammed back down onto the floor of the tiny canoe practically on top of Nala, almost capsizing the boat, nearly toppling the brown man over into the deadly waters surrounding us.

The Angara still gripped my hands, his blank eyes staring sightlessly into mine. I moved, but they didn't follow me. I knelt, and struggled to free my hands from his desperate grasp, barely noticing the flow of red that swirled around my legs, and filled the bottom of the canoe, surrounding Nala's body. Once upright I could see that the bottom half of the panther man was entirely gone.

"Quickly," the brown man ordered, leaning down and gripping the heavy half of an Angara along with me. "Into the water. It will keep the monster busy so we can escape."

Moving with all the speed I could manage, but a little woodenly, still in shock, I did as he suggested and helped him toss the lifeless piece of Angara hunter into the water alongside the canoe. I stared blankly as his body bobbed oddly, drifting and rolling over to reveal that lifeless, blank expression, and then something black ripped by, the Angara's torso jerked, and the sightless eyes stared at me no more as the head abruptly disappeared.

"Sit," the brown man commanded, and I did.

He rowed frantically, checking occasionally over his shoulder to make certain the plesiosaur wasn't following. I couldn't take my eyes off the scene as darkened lumps broke the now almost placid surface near the Angara, and another chunk of torso vanished beneath the waves. The process repeated itself over and over until I couldn't imagine there was anything left.

I turned to my new companion, who looked very sad, his eyes down on Nala.

I bent over to be closer to her, taking her hand in mine. She gripped my fingers again, but not with the strength she'd had before. I checked the spear. There were no bubbles around the wound. Maybe she hadn't pierced a lung. She was still alive so her heart must be beating. I shook my head. What did it mean? Could I do *anything* to help her? *Anything at all?*

"Bran... don?" she asked, only able to speak in syllables between gasping breaths, her eyes staring sightlessly at the inside of the canoe. Bloody water pooled in the bottom of the boat all around her, and she shivered from cold. "Bran... don?"

"Nala?" I said, lying beside her and wrapping my arms around her to warm her. "I'm here."

"Did... you... find... your... mate...? Did... you... find... your... mate...?"

"Not yet," I said.

"But... you... will. You... will. She... is... out... there. You... love... her... too... much."

"Don't talk, Nala."

"I... wan... ted... to... be... loved... that... much. I... wan... ted... to... be... loved... that..."

Her breathing slowed, and finally stopped. I kissed her cheek, and felt the tears in my eyes as I closed hers.

THE CHUTANGA

I SAT BACK ON THE bench of the boat, and stared down at Nala's now lifeless body, feeling strangely guilty for not being able to give her what she wanted. Her annoying personality seemed unimportant given her short life and violent end. As I'd been doing since I arrived in Pangea I began to question everything I believed about right and wrong, good and evil, social mores and social conventions. Based on what Nala and others had told me since I'd arrived here, Nova might not even have minded my sharing a little pleasure with her given the world she understood, especially knowing how brutal Nala's death had been. But I knew for certain that my love for Nova—as I knew and felt love—wouldn't allow me to be 'unfaithful' to her, and yet somehow that noble attitude made me feel strangely cruel at this particular moment.

Ironically, it was my restraint and devotion that had seemed to appeal to Nala most.

With these complicated and unpleasant thoughts came the startling, life-altering realization that our lives—our entire existences—were without meaning in the grand design of the world and the universe around it. Ultimately what difference did any tiny, inconsequential choice matter in the multi-billions of years journey the stars and planets took through the cosmos? The entirety of human existence was a pop, a blip, on an infinite timeline. Our individual lives even less.

We could be snuffed out without warning, and for a few brief days our friends would speak of us in quiet whispers with downturned faces. Within days, as the first worms were already testing the stability of our coffins, those same friends would be pleasantly watching television, only occasionally distracted by poignant memories of some minor way we'd touched their lives, while living even less impactful existences than the ones the dead had just left behind.

None of it mattered.

Not the worries, nor the doubts, nor the fears, nor the concerns about failure, or success, or money, or cars, or clothes, or houses, or colleges, or jobs, or plans for the future… what I got, what you didn't, did I look stupid, did I make a fool of myself, do they hate me, do you love me, was I right, were you wrong, should we wait before sex, should we fuck on the street, did you hurt me, did I hurt you, he said, she said, they said, nobody said.

All that mattered was what meant the most to me right now, right this endless Pangean second, and that was love. All I cared about were my friends. All that had meaning for me… was them. Milton. Elia. Bruk.

Nala. Yes. Even Nala. Right now—in this moment—I loved her for having given me this revelation.

But mostly I loved Nova. Loved, and cared, and worried for her… wanted to make her happy, make her safe, keep her with me to love for as long possible, and if not, then to treasure the few memories we'd had. These were the only things that gave my pitiful, inconsequential, meaningless life meaning.

"I'm sorry," the brown man said, simply.

I looked up at him, rowing, and realized I had forgotten he was there. I was now entirely within the power of the man whose boat I had stolen, and I had forgotten he was there. He stared into my eyes with sadness and sympathy, and I hoped it was sincere.

"Thank you," I said to him.

"She was very beautiful. She was your mate?"

"We barely knew each other."

"You did a lot for a dead woman you barely knew."

"Dead woman?"

"She was dead before you put her in this boat, and yet…"

"I didn't know she was definitely going to die. I guess I hoped…" I wiped another tear and thought about how irritating she'd been during our journey. Had it all been real? It seemed so distant, and stupid, now. I shook my head and tried not to think about how much I'd disliked her. It seemed wrong and disrespectful, but…

"We escaped…" I began.

"… from the Grigori. I know. You speak the slave language, as do I."

"You're an escaped slave, too?" I asked.

"No," he said, and looked past me, apparently not feeling inclined to explain further.

As he watched the waters behind me, I checked the inside of the boat, and saw spears wedged under the seat of the canoe near Nala's body, too tightly jammed in to have been much help in the fight with the plesiosaur, but given there was time to get them now, they could easily be used against me, if it was what this tall man wanted. After a moment of consideration, I looked at my companion, and saw him staring at me with an odd smile on his face.

"Curious about my spears?" he asked.

I said nothing.

"What interests you about them?"

"Just wondering if you might use one to run me through," I replied.

"Why would I do that?" he asked. "You just saved my life."

"But I also stole your boat."

He shrugged.

"My life is more valuable than my boat," he said.

He smiled again, and continued rowing. I returned his grin. We'd gone quite a way over the placid sea and I could see him studying me with questioning eyes.

"Who are you," he asked after a while, his brows furrowed. "What land do you come from?"

I stared a bit myself, then answered simply, "Pasadena."

He furrowed a brow, obviously never having heard of it before, I shook my head, and tried to explain about the outer world I'd come from.

"If you don't want to tell me, just say so," he said when I'd finished.

We floated along in silence a while longer before he spoke again.

"Why did you try to help that Angara?"

I thought about it a moment, then simply shrugged.

"I met an Angara recently who... he helped me. Made me think differently about things. I thought..." I considered what I was going to say next, and realized I had no idea. "I don't know," I said, finally.

More silence, and then:

"What about you?" I asked. "Who are you, and where are *you* from?"

He looked at me in surprise.

"I am a Chutanga, as you can see. My name is Zash."

"You say that like I should know what a Chutanga is."

"Because everyone does. I can't believe you don't. Maybe you *are* from outside Pangea."

I smiled.

"The Chutanga," he continued, "live on the islands of the central sea—the Usayasa Úm. I don't know about other islands on other seas, but this is the central sea, and one of the largest. We are well known. My people are legendary for their height and their color, as well as for being a fairly peaceful people who were once slaves to the Grigori, but are now free. Legendary among most Pangeans, anyway."

I looked him over more carefully for the first time, really. I saw that his skin wasn't so much brown, as a dark bronze color, like a gold dusted African. His hair had a tightly curled texture, like many black men I'd known back on Earth's surface, but it was lighter in color, an almost copper blonde. Overall, he was a damn fine looking human being.

"We're fishermen," Zash continued. "which is probably obvious— though we're known as excellent hunters as well. I'd just gone to the mainland for some Hajet, you know. They're not native to our islands, and my wife loves them."

I must have been staring at him blankly, because he felt the need to explain.

"Hajet," he said, as if no one could be as stupid as I obviously was. "Little furry creatures that are kind of a delicacy, and not easy to find. Their meat is very tender when cooked properly and tastes wonderful."

"Ill have to try it someday," I said.

"Well... not anytime soon. I tossed mine aside when I saw that Angara. It was tough catching that many, let me tell you." He paused, lamenting his loss, shaking his head.

"Everyone knows and fears the Angara, I take it."

"Not my people, so much. We're big—nearly as big as they are, and fierce. But that one back there was *really* big, and he looked angry. What did you do to him?"

"I split his face with an axe. Dropped a wall of rocks on his head. Killed two of his friends."

"Mmm. That would make anyone angry. And then you tried to help him. Strange."

Again, I just shrugged.

"You're an odd man. What is your name?"

"Brandon Mack."

"Well, Brandon the Mack..." he said, smiling, "thank the gods for your weird point of view. It led you to save me, as well. Our meeting may have been a little unusual, but it seems to have been destined. We're alive, and I will once again see my wife and family."

I suddenly remembered the whole reason for tricking and killing the Angara, and for dropping the wall of rocks. I turned around, frantically searching the bottom of the boat. I didn't see it! Not anywhere!

"Are you looking for this?" Zash asked.

I looked, and he held up the silver device I wanted so desperately. He handed it to me gently, and I took it as if it were the most valuable thing in the world. Which, to me, it was.

"You dropped it along with the oar when you went to save the Angara. What is it?"

"Something that tracks slaves of the Grigori. It's the whole reason I killed the other two in the first place. My whole reason for *being*, right now. I'm hoping it will lead me to my..." I stopped and considered it for a minute. "To the woman I love, and hope to make my wife."

Zash smiled.

"Ah," he said. "As good a reason as any for dropping rocks on Angara heads. Does it work? Will it lead you to your woman?"

I looked at the little screen, wiping blood off the face of it. I turned the knob that widened its view, saw the outline of the shore, the islands behind us, and continued adjusting until I saw nearly the entire sea. Finally another dot appeared on the curving edge of a peninsula to our right. A single red light, with two blue ones nearby.

162

"I don't know," I answered. "It shows an escaped slave, but I don't know if it's her or not."

"Well, you must go and be sure. Where is she?"

"That way." I pointed. "That peninsula, and a little in. Back on the mainland."

He looked in the direction I'd indicated, and nodded.

"Sa Fasi. Home of the Nyala."

"Yes!" I said, suddenly enthusiastic, remembering Sa Fasi had been Nova's home.

"It's not hard to reach," Zash said. "There are two islands between here and there. Mine is only a little further—right there. You can eat and rest with me, then begin your search, once refreshed."

"I'll go as soon as we land."

"You will drop from exhaustion as soon as we land," Zash said, grinning. "I know that look."

"If I sleep the Angara will come for me."

Zash shook his head.

"Not on the islands. Did you ever see one of my kind when you were a slave?"

I shook my head.

"No," Zash said. "You wouldn't. Long ago, when Pangea was young, the Angara would often attempt to make us slaves because we were big and strong and could do hard work. They had taken many of us, and preferred us over the other tribes of Pangea.

"The story goes that once, long ago, a massive raiding party landed on our shores. But this time, everyone united; friend, enemy, man, woman, child. We fought so fiercely, and so desperately, slew so many Angara that there were barely any left to take people prisoner, though they did manage to make off with a few. Those of my people that were taken back to the Grigori cities refused, this time, to bow down, and others of our people who were already slaves rose up with them. They killed even more Angara and so many Grigori right in their own cities that at last the flying beasts learned it was better to leave us alone than try to make us theirs. When they released the hundreds of other captured Chutanga, the slave language became one of our tongues.

"Eventually—with slaves doing all the work—the Grigori became too lazy to even catch their own fish, and so they realized they needed us as merchants to supply their needs. Soon a truce was made between the races. Now they give us certain things that we need, metal and other items, and we give them certain things, and the Chutanga and the Grigori live in peace."

"What things do you provide them?" I asked.

Zash considered an answer, then shrugged and looked away, apparently deciding it was better not to.

"Do you provide them with people?" I asked. "To eat?"

"We do not provide them. But the Grigori bring them."

"And you allow this?"

He shrugged again.

"They are not *our* people," he said. "It does disturb me, but it's better than the alternative of Grigori feeding on Chutanga."

"Do Grigori eat babies?"

He tried not to show it, but I could tell I'd hit on a truth, one that bothered him more than he was willing to admit. His 'admission' made me think of something. Something unsettling.

"I never saw any Chutanga, back in Emibi," I said, "but I also never saw any children."

Zash continued his silence.

"Or… pregnant women," I fairly whispered.

Still nothing.

"Do they eat the mothers, as well?" I asked.

Zash didn't speak. But his intense stare was answer enough.

"I'll need to return to Emibi," I said, realizing I could no longer leave Milton and Elia to the 'safety' of the Grigori city. "I have to rescue a friend of mine and his mate before their child is born, and the Grigori bring it here to…"

Zash continued to row, but his jaw had set and his eyes focused, not on the horizon in front of him, but at the stormy thoughts gathering in his head.

"I will, Zash," I said. "rescue them, I mean. I won't let them die."

"I believe you."

"And then I will kill every last one of those evil fucking Grigori," I continued with fury, "and wipe the entire race off the face of Pangea."

Zash was a tall, thin but well-muscled man, standing a good six foot six, or six foot seven. He had a full, rounded nose and that copper-blonde hair, loosely tied in a thick ponytail. His face was chiseled, with prominent cheekbones, a strong jaw, large, full lips, and gold-flecked, gentle, eyes. All in all, he was an impressive, good-looking man, and he spoke well and thoughtfully.

All during our conversation Zash had continued propelling the skiff with long, powerful strokes toward his home island. I admired the skill with which he handled his crude and awkward craft, particularly after I'd made such a mess of it during my escape. But now he stopped rowing, stared deeply into my eyes, searching into my soul for truth and honesty.

"How can you say that with such confidence?" he eventually asked me. "The Grigori have ruled this world harshly and cruelly since before my great, great grandfather was small. And yet, I believe you when you say you will kill them. What makes you so certain?"

"Because I'm smarter than they are," I said, confidently. "And they think I'm just another stupid human. They seriously underestimate me."

Zash kept staring at me, but slowly a smile spread over his lips, and infused his eyes with mirth.

"No one is as smart as the Grigori," he said, finally, continuing to stroke toward the island. "But I would be glad for you to prove me wrong."

THE ISLAND

WE FINALLY REACHED SHORE, a pretty, broad and level beach rimmed with thick leafed tropical foliage and tall, heavy palms. The canoe scraped its bottom on the sand, Zash leaped out and I followed him. Together we dragged the skiff far up into the bushes that grew beyond the strand and sparse sward at the shore, lifted Nala's lifeless body from inside and lay it gently on the grass. Then we overturned the canoe, and covered it carefully with palm fronds and leaves.

"We must hide our canoes," explained Zash, "better than I apparently did on the mainland."

I smiled, and he did, too.

"People steal them," he said. "Especially the Chutanga of Luana. They're a lazy bunch of fools who won't even put out the energy to make their own." He nodded toward an island farther out to sea, so far away it seemed more of a blur than an actual landmass, hanging in the distant sky.

The upward curve of the surface of Pangea was constantly revealing the impossible to my surprised eyes. To see land and water curving up in the distance *above* the horizon as though it stood on edge before melting into the distant sky, to feel that seas and mountains were suspended directly above my head required such a complete reversal of perception that it sometimes made me light-headed.

We then returned to Nala, and I looked at her lifeless face, once again overcome with stabs of guilt.

"What type of death ritual do her people observe?" Zash asked.

"I have no idea," I said. "I barely knew her."

"Well, most Pangeans believe in placing their dead in trees."

"My people bury theirs in the ground."

Zash looked at me strangely.

"That is very weird, Brandon," he said. "I'm beginning to believe you *are* from outside Pangea. Don't demons come and take the flesh of your dead down into the Um Hecha when you put your dead in the ground?"

"What's the Um Hecha?"

"Is that a joke? The sea of fire. Did you really not know?"

"We call it 'Hell' where I'm from. And no, as far as I know no one really goes to—to Um Hecha. Mostly they're eaten by worms, I think."

He again stared at me, aghast.

"And you prefer this to being eaten by birds?" he wondered.

"Do the dead really care?"

He thought about it, and shrugged, laughing. "I never asked."

Together we lifted Nala into a nearby tall tree as high as we could manage, and laid her carefully along a thick branch. Zash took some leather straps from a pouch attached to his loincloth and tied her securely to the limb. I kept looking at her face, dirty with dried blood, hair matted, and was overwhelmed by sadness. I should have been faster realizing the Angara was behind us. I should have this, I should have that. I was burdened with a sense of failure, and terrified that Nova had already suffered a similar fate all alone out there in this crazy dangerous world; that the dot on the tiny tracking device's screen wasn't even her.

"Should I say something?" I asked Zash.

"Say what?" he asked. "She's dead. She can't hear you."

"Not to her, to..." I looked at him, then up at the sky. I shook my head. "Never mind."

"If a god cared, they'd have protected her," he said, sagely.

We both dropped to the ground and he began to move across to where we'd left his canoe. I kept staring up at Nala.

"And now... the birds just come and... you know?"

"Or sometimes wild animals. But we put her high enough to deter most of those."

"What difference does it make, wild animals or birds?"

Zash gave me another of those 'are you serious' looks and shook his head involuntarily, as if shivering, as if he suddenly realized he was talking to someone who couldn't really be here.

"The birds and the fliers take the body up to the paradise beyond the sun," he said, patiently, as if speaking to a small child. "Wild animals just eat it."

Now it was my turn to look at him as if questioning that *he* was serious. Sometimes the people of Pangea could be so wise, and sometimes they could be so... not.

Apparently done talking, Zash motioned me to follow him, and plunged into the jungle, stepping through the overgrowth and into a narrow but well-defined trail. I took a last look at Nala before him, and very quickly nearly lost my guide along a path that seemed to wind all over hell and back.

It would run on, plain and clear and well defined, then suddenly end in a tangle of twisted jungle. Just stop. Most trails like this are made by animals, and then widened by man through extensive use, but these seemed not to have been accidentally formed by anyone or anything, as if made intentionally by the Chutanga as a way of confusing intruders.

As I watched carefully, Zash—facing the end of a trail—would turn directly back in his tracks for a short distance, spring into a tree, climb up and through it to the other side of the blockage, drop onto a fallen log, leap over a low bush and suddenly he was once more back on a clear and distinct trail, motioning for me to follow. We'd then go on for another short distance only to turn immediately back around and retrace our steps. After a mile or so this new pathway ended as suddenly and mysteriously as the previous one had. Then he would repeat the leaping, swinging and dropping business until he found the next section of our hidden road.

I couldn't help but admire the genius of whatever ancient Chutanga had figured out this screwball idea to throw enemies off the track. The process would at least delay, but more likely prevent them entirely from following a Chutanga to their home and loved ones. I'm sure there was a trick to finding each next path, but Zash wasn't telling, and I couldn't figure it out.

I suppose it might seem like a painfully slow way to get home, but the irony of Pangea is that there's nothing but time, and yet never enough, Nala's recent death being a rather painful example of the latter.

After proceeding through the jungle for what must have been at least five miles or more we suddenly emerged into a large clearing filled with the gardens, fields, homes and buildings of Zash's village.

Thick based trees had been chopped down fifteen or twenty feet above the ground, and spherical houses of woven twigs, and mud-packed bark had been built on their high, flat surfaces. Each ball-like apartment was topped by one kind of carven image or another, which Zash explained to me was a kind of 'coat-of-arms' for the family housed within.

Horizontal slits, six inches high, and two or three feet wide, allowed in light and ventilation. The entrance to each home was through a small opening in the base of the tree and once inside you worked your way up to the rooms above through the hollow trunks by way of crude, rope and bamboo ladders. The houses varied in size from a single studio apartment, to several rooms. The largest I entered was divided into two floors.

All around the village, between it and the jungle, lay beautifully cultivated fields where the Chutanga raised whatever food they required to supplement their occasional hunting—fruits, vegetables, grains. Several villagers and most of the children were working in those gardens as we crossed through them, heading toward a small bridge laid across a narrow river that would take us into the community center.

Most of the kids cheered at the sight of Zash and a few ran over to give him a hug as he passed, but to me they gave only wary stares and nervous scowls. As we landed on the other side of the bridge several men walked out to meet us, smiling as they recognized my companion, but eyeing me as warily as the children had. One made a kind of waving salute to Zash, and the two touched the points of their spears, then tapped the weapons to the ground between them.

Greetings and introductions aside, Zash conducted me to a large house in the center of the community—his—and after making sure I was comfortable offered me food and wine. There I met his wife, a sweet copper brown girl named Suri who was as naked as he, holding a sleeping baby in her arms. Zash kissed them both, playfully licked the nipples of his wife's full breasts, then told her how I'd saved his life. She looked momentarily horrified at the thought of almost losing her husband, and turned to me with something very close to love in her eyes. From that moment on she treated me like royalty, even allowing me to hold the tiny bundle of joy that her father assured me would one day rule all of Pangea.

As I held the baby, Zash's wife pressed her husband back onto some animal hide pillows, and settled herself onto his growing erection, slowly inserting him into her, eyes closing briefly with pleasure, sighing out a whisper of joy. I'd still not quite gotten used to this with Pangeans, but given my firsthand experience at how quickly life could end in this world, I certainly understood it.

"Perhaps you would like to meet Zash's sister?" his beautiful wife asked me as she rocked back and forth on the delighted Zash. "She is very pretty, and would not mind that you are small."

I nearly choked on my meal, glancing between my legs.

"She means your *height*," Zash said, laughing. "I'm sure you could manage to satisfy her enough to keep her. You're spear is not exactly tiny, though you're not as big as a Chutanga man."

I smiled in response, and shook my head.

"I'm afraid I'm taken," I told Suri gently. "In fact, once I've finished eating I intend to go right back out and find my... my mate."

"You should rest awhile, first," Zash said, kindly. "You look terrible."

I laughed. "Thanks for the compliment. But I'll be fine. Once I've finish your wife's brilliant food I'll have my strength back and be good to go."

They both looked doubtful. Even the baby looked doubtful.

"I will," I said, laughing. "I'll be fine."

"HOW LONG WAS I asleep?" I asked.

Suri's brows crinkled.

"How... *long*?" she asked, plainly confused by my use of a measurement of length to describe a concept of 'time' that meant nothing to her. "You did not grow while you slept."

"I meant... no. I was trying to ask... never mind."

I stood and stretched, feeling some of the aches and pains of the last few... I don't know... 'days' of athletic activity. After a few pops and cracks that felt better than they sounded, I scanned around the little apartment for my GPS device.

"Are you looking for this?" Suri asked, holding out the little box.

"Yes," I said, taking it. "Thanks."

"It was making sounds. Is it supposed to do that?"

"I have no idea. It's a Grigori device and it didn't come with instructions."

As she watched, I held the thing close to my face and adjusted knobs. The lone red dot I'd seen before was gone, and there were only three motionless blue dots. Where had the red dot gone? Where was Nova? Was her dot under one of theirs? Had they captured her already? Or worse, killed her?

"I have to go," I told Suri. "Tell Zash ..."

"No," she said, gently, but firmly. "Zash wanted to see you before you go. He said it was important that he tell you something about your friend."

"Which friend? Nova?"

She shrugged.

"Milton?"

She shrugged again and gestured for me to sit down. But I was too nervous to stay still, so I excused myself, promising not to leave the village, went down the inner stairs that had been carved out of the tree stump, and left the hut, heading out into the common area of the town square in search of Zash.

Several of the copper brown Chutanga were there, a few chatting and laughing, while another drew water from a community well, and another carefully carved a block of wood into a small sculpture, or talisman of some kind. Everyone stopped what they were doing and looked at me with that same edgy wariness as before, though when I nodded and smiled, they returned the gesture. I suppose word had gotten around about who I was, and what I'd done for Zash.

I wandered a bit with no specific direction in mind passing huts both empty and full, watching small children run and play, absorbing the daily life of the island tribe. I was just becoming concerned about getting lost, and considered turning around when I came out into a second small clearing on the back-side of the main circle of houses.

Zash was there, arguing with someone, likely the community leader or chief by his age and dress. As I stepped closer the argument became more heated, and Zash looked as if he were going to spit blood, he became so enraged. In the middle of yelling he noticed me, and held up a hand for me to keep my distance. The king—or whoever he was—turned his eyes my way and stared with an intensity that told me I had something to do with this particular disagreement. As they fought, snippets of words floated over to me.

"I don't care... not of our tribe!" from the king, then from Zash, "...horror... no one should... we *must!*"

The chief argued something about the good of his tribe, and others not being his concern when Zash stepped back, and for a moment I feared might step forward again and strike the older man. Instead he vibrated as if struggling with that very thought, until he turned and walked straight toward me. He didn't ask me to, but I assumed I was supposed to follow him.

"You all right?" I asked.

"No," he said, flatly, then after we'd gotten far enough from the tribal leaders to not be heard, Zash stopped—checked to make sure we weren't followed—then stared at me with a nervous intensity. He was struggling with whether or not to tell me something, and I waited out the decision.

"Come with me," he said simply, then headed straight out of the village as I hurried to keep up with his much longer legs.

THE TEMPLE OF HORROR

WHEN WE'D GOTTEN SAFELY into the forest he spoke in short bursts without turning to look at me.

"When you tried to save that Angara, Brandon the Mack, you impressed me. You'd done it at the expense of potentially losing the silver device that could take you to your mate. You'd done it without concern for your own life. You'd done it just after having saved *my* life."

"Well, I'm glad you were so impressed by my stupidity."

Zash laughed.

"No," he said. "With your *compassion*. It did not make you weak. You fought the Indovu Um bravely. But you saw life with an understanding that we are all united... all essentially the same, in spite of our differences." He stopped and turned to face me with a smile. "*That* impressed me."

"Why?" I asked, sincerely. "It's hardly a smart way to look at the world. Especially *this* world. I could have died... could have lost that device, and Nova. That thought haunts me."

"And you reached for the Angara anyway. Because you saw his fear—his 'humanity'. I like that, Brandon the Mack, because I myself feel the same way, that the only way to truly make our lives better in this world is to see our similarities over our differences," he turned to continue on his path, "to unite against our common enemies—the beasts, the dinosaurs—the Grigori."

"Is that what your argument was about back there?"

"In essence, yes. We have a pact with the Grigori—we leave them alone and they do the same for us. We trade, we exchange goods and necessities, and we also allow the Grigori to come here to perform a private ritual—a ritual that even the Angara are not aware of. I don't understand it, or know what it's for, or why it's done, but I *do* know that it sickens me. It sickens many of the Chutanga."

"Do you expect me to stop it, somehow?"

"No, but you need to know of it, because it concerns your friend and his unborn child, I think. Or it will."

"They eat babies during this ritual?"

"I can't begin to explain. I... you have to see."

"You're confusing me, Zash."

"Welcome to the tribe," he said simply.

"Where are we going?"

We stepped into a large clearing and he just pointed.

Before us sat a large, beetle-shaped building with a rounded roof that had several large openings in the top. Grigori were fluttering low, and dropping through these openings, disappearing inside the building. There were no doors or windows visible anywhere else on the structure other than those, except a single, ground-level entrance that was apparently for slaves, a line of which I saw were being brought in by other Chutanga. I almost hadn't seen any of that because the height of the grasses and plants surrounding the bottom of the building rose to almost neck level.

Zash and I had hunkered low in that cover, and watched as the last of the heads and shoulders of several slaves were escorted into the building.

"This is my shame," Zash said. "I have never helped herd slaves as these off-Islanders are doing, but I have also done nothing to stop it."

"Stop what?" I asked.

"You have to see." He pointed. "There's an entrance near the base on the opposite side no one seems to know about. We used to sneak there as children to watch. Come on."

The other Chutanga had led the slaves in through the small opening, then moved a large stone over the hole, and left the way they had come, through the forest behind the building. No one was left to see us, other than an occasional Grigori arriving overhead.

"Stay under the trees as long as possible," Zash told me, leading me across the clearing and around the end of the structure to a loose pile of rocks against the foot of the wall.

He moved aside a couple of large boulders to reveal a small crack that created an opening into the building. Checking overhead for Grigori, he dove quickly into the hole and I followed. The space beyond was nearly completely black with darkness.

"We're between an inner and outer wall," said Zash. "It's a hollow space between the main structure and the pool and theater within. Stay close."

The dark, bronze man groped ahead a few paces and then began to ascend a rough tied ladder. We went up about some forty feet and the space between the walls began to grow brighter. Fairly quickly we came to an opening in the inner wall that provided an unobstructed view of the entire interior of the temple's amphitheater.

The lower third of the room was an enormous tank of clear water in which five or six of the hideous Grigori swam lazily around artificial islands of stone. Clusters of slaves were being forced by other Grigori out onto the tiny atolls. The humans were of various colors; red, black, brown—only the dark brown, bronze color of the Chutanga was missing.

I was most surprised to see an Angara female—something I'd never come across even back in the Grigori city of Emibi—cowering on an edge of one of the rocky islets.

"What are the slaves here for?" I asked. "Or are they slaves? Is that an Angara woman?"

"Not slaves," Zash said. "And women only. Well... not *just* women..."

I looked again and noticed something that hadn't registered before. The women were all heavy, and full-bodied, with protruding stomachs.

"Are..." I said, as realization dawned, "are they *all* pregnant?"

Zash looked at me with intense eyes, and was silent for quite a while.

"Zash," I asked, desperate to break the tension. "What the hell is going on here?"

"I can't explain," he replied. "Wait and you'll see. These women—and their children—the unborn babies they carry—are a part of some ceremony that the Grigori perform here. You will be thankful to be a male slave when you see what happens."

"Zash ..." I began, about to insist that he tell me now, his tone and suggestive wording making my skin crawl. But I'd barely spoken when we heard a fluttering cacophony of wings from above as a long procession of the evil master race of Pangea slowly and majestically descended through the large, central opening in the roof.

Fifteen or twenty Grigori swooped in, followed by at least as many of their awe-inspiring pterodactyl pets. Behind the flocking procession came what had to be the queen, flanked by her personal pterodactyls much as she had been when she'd entered the amphitheater at Emibi. She looked similar in coloration and size to the queen I'd encountered in Emibi, but it wasn't her. She must be from another city, or tribe, and I wondered idly how many more Grigori cities there might be—how many groups of Grigori the Pangeans would have to fight in order to actually be rid of them.

Three times the great black swarm swirled around the upper interior of the oval chamber until they finally settled down on the damp, cold boulders fringing the outer edge of the pool. A larger, center rock had again been reserved for the queen, and she took her place on the slightly protruding perch, shaking out her wings and pulling them against her body, regally.

Everything fell silent for several minutes after she and her entourage had come to rest in their places, almost as if in silent prayer. The poor women upon the tiny islands watched the horrid creatures with wide eyes and fearful expressions. One woman wept openly, as another offered useless comfort.

Suddenly the queen flinched, and all other movement in the temple ceased. She raised her ugly head sharply, and some of the women gasped. Instinctively, Zash and I both moved lower, behind the stones shielding us, getting deeper into the shadows.

After another moment of silent stillness, the lizard monarch began looking slowly around, her long, hideous head bobbing back and forth in a rhythmic dance. At one point I thought we made eye-contact, but it was only my nerves and imagination. Slowly, very, very slowly she crawled to the edge of her throne and slipped noiselessly into the water, her body nearly submerging, but not completely, pushing off into the artificial lake, and drifting through the crystalline waters like a crocodile. Slowly, so eerily slowly, she swam up and down the long tank, turning fluidly at the ends and arcing back along a slightly different path than the one she'd just taken.

Her motion took her in front of each island, her eyes obviously focusing—first on one, then on another of the various different women. She seemed to be choosing; deciding which one she wanted, for whatever purpose. All eyes followed that glistening, black head, each woman waiting patiently for whatever was to come next, knowing it would come from this lone, swimming Grigori.

Finally, the queen seemed to decide.

Nearer and nearer to one specific island she circled, as the women on it began to realize that one or more of them had been 'chosen'. Each of them began to back quickly away from the center toward the edges of their little precipice, one or two actually diving in and swimming away to another rock. Still the Grigori circled, ignoring those other women, its eyes intently focused on one or more of the remaining females.

Suddenly, the hideous queen-mother of the intelligent flying reptiles stopped, and raised her misshapen head from the water to fix her great, round eyes upon the center of the remaining girls. The females were heavy and soft, and I began to realize that they'd probably been intentionally bred and fattened, the way we breed and fatten cows, sheep and pigs.

It suddenly hit me that I had been brought to witness a feast.

"Zash," I said, but he held up a stern hand to silence me. Why, I'm not sure. The Grigori can't hear, and there were no Angara to do their listening for them.

"We have to stop this," I whispered, and he finally turned to look at me.

"Only if you want to die," Zash snapped, "and me, my wife, my child, and all the rest of my tribe along with you. I brought you here to *see*, not to *act*."

I turned back to the theater, realizing that this is what the argument in the village had been about. To intervene and stop what I was about to witness, or to let sleeping lizards lie.

As I stared, helplessly, the queen fixed her gaze on a nude, plump, dark-haired young girl, her belly full to bursting. The victim tried to turn away, hiding her face in her hands, kneeling behind an older woman; but the reptile, with unblinking eyes, stared on with such furious focus that I would have thought her vision penetrated the woman in front, all the way through both her, and the selected victim's arms, directly into the very center of the poor girl's brain.

Slowly the Grigori's head began to move to and fro, to and fro, her eyes never leaving their lock on the frightened young girl, until finally, surprisingly, the victim responded. She moved her arms away from her face, and turned wide, fear-haunted eyes toward the Grigori queen. Slowly, very slowly, as though dragged by some unseen power the victim rose to her feet, then moved as though in a trance straight toward the unblinking queen, glassy eyes unblinkingly fixed upon those of her captor.

To the water's edge the naked girl came without pause, bare feet docilely stepping into the shallows before the little island and moving unhesitatingly toward the Grigori, who now slowly retreated as though leading her victim like a stage magician leads a guest from the audience. The girl's knees slipped below the surface, and still she advanced, her mind chained by those glistening, black eyes. Now the water was above her distended belly; now at her armpits; now at her neck. The other women on the various islands stared on in rapt horror, unable to prevent the poor girl's doom, horribly aware that this would be their fate as well.

The Grigori had moved backward until only the long, bony upper bill and unblinking eyes were exposed above the surface of the water, and the girl had followed helplessly until the end of that repulsive beak was only an inch or two from her face, her horror-filled eyes riveted upon those of the commanding reptile.

The water passed above the girl's mouth and nose—her eyes and forehead now all that could be seen above the surface—yet she did not drown, nor panic, and continued to walk on after the retreating Grigori. The queen's head gradually disappeared beneath the surface and after it went the eyes of her victim—only a slight ripple widened toward the shores to mark where the two had vanished. They were in the far end of the pool, which was dark and hard to see into clearly, but the rippling shadows of Grigori and its victim were still visible. Suddenly the surface of the water roiled, very slightly, blood swirled outward and clouded the clarity of the false lake.

I assumed it was all over. Probably near the end of the poor girl's breath the queen had struck, the horror of the mother-to-be was finally— mercifully—at an end, killed, and perhaps eaten by the vicious queen.

I could not have been more wrong.

For a while there was only silence within the temple. The other women were motionless with gut wrenching fear, all eyes fixed on the far end of that pool, the drifting shadows barely visible beneath the red, clouded surface. Even the Grigori watched the stillness of the water for the reappearance of their queen—until there she was. Not far from the spot where she had gone under, her head rose slowly out of the now murky waters and backed once more into view. She was moving toward the little island as if retracing her steps, her eyes fixed before her as they had been when she'd dragged the helpless girl to her doom.

And then I saw her. My skin bubbled with goose-flesh, and I gasped out loud. The forehead and eyes of the young girl rose slowly out of the depths, following the gaze of the reptile just as she had when she'd vanished beneath the surface. On and on came the girl until she stood in water that reached barely below her breasts, and that's when the horror began.

Her stomach had been ripped open and was now empty of any child, and many of her internal organs. I felt sick—wanted to throw up. I turned away, and saw Zash had done the same. We both breathed hard, our wide-eyes avoiding one another for quite a while, until I finally stared at him, and waited.

"What the fuck, Zash?" I snarled. "Your people let *this* go on? *Under their noses?* Even helping to bring these poor women into this arena for *that?"*

"I want to change it, Brandon the Mack," he said. "But I—we—can't do it alone. You're a smart man. A brave man. *Help me find a way!"*

I looked around and saw a pile of bones we'd moved through, dropped down and grabbed what must have once been the femur and shin bone of a large woman. I held up the weapons to my new friend and gave him a look that said: like *this!*

"How can that work," he responded, angrily, though quietly. The Grigori couldn't hear, but the women would. "Look what they can do! That woman should have drowned! Three times by now! She's a walking dead woman with her guts ripped out and the Grigori is *still* controlling her!"

I turned and forced myself to look at the scene again. Up and out the girl came until she stood in water that reached barely to her knees. Zash was right. She'd been under the surface for what could have been half an hour, but other than her dripping hair and glistening body you couldn't tell she'd been under at all. She was oblivious to everything, including the fact that her stomach was a hole, and she should be dead.

The Grigori curved around the tank drawing its victim along behind, eyes still boring into the dead girl's mind, and began moving back once more into the deeper part of the pool. Blood trailed through the waters, entrails hanging from the girl's stomach all the way to the water's placid surface. As they began to submerge once more my imagination raced with what might be next.

"Zash, we *have* to…" I looked at him, and saw the helplessness in his eyes, the sadness in his now pale features.

Against all orders, against Grigori wishes, he'd shown me this to warn me so I could warn Milton. The only way to protect my friend's wife and child suffering this same fate was to stop them ever coming here, because he had no idea how to end this horror any more than I did.

As the poor girl's head vanished once more under the bloodying waters I turned my eyes to the ceiling and thought about blocking the hole. Filling the place with smoke; fire. Trapping the Grigori. But what then? Could we kill them? Save these women? Would Grigori mind control work on us? Stopping us before we began? And would it stop the carnage, or just delay it a bit until some *other* group of Grigori came for *their* turn in this killing pool? Would anything we tried be wasted heroics as more Grigori arrived?

I looked again at Zash, saw the anger in his eyes, and knew. Knew he'd thought of all these things. Wanted to do them himself. *This* had been the argument with the village elder. He had been asking for an end to this. Asking for help, an attack, support—anything—and had been given nothing.

The Grigori had once more returned to the surface, followed by the robotic girl. Her head reappeared, ruby waters flowing down her forehead, her cheeks, her neck, until we were sickened to see that one of her arms had gone—ripped off completely at the shoulder, a fragment of bone visible in the washed out flesh—and still the poor thing showed no indication of pain, only the focus of her eyes seemed intensified.

My mind raced. There had to be a way. This theater, this tomb, this crypt was filled with pregnant women. I couldn't live with the thought that they were all about to die in this most horrifying of ways while I did nothing. No more Nalas. I *had* to intervene.

"What is the ritual?" I asked, swallowing hard, hoping for some clue about how to deal with this; change it; end it. "Why this way? Why not just eat them?"

"I've asked myself that many times," Zash said, sadly. "I don't know."

"How does it all play out?"

"The Grigori will all feast like this in turn—by some sort of hierarchy, I believe—until full," Zash said, quietly, "and the Ingonghus will finish the remains. Nothing will be left but some bones coughed up afterward. And then they will all sleep. For a long time."

"I've only ever seen four Grigori sleeping the whole time I was in Emibi. It doesn't seem like something they do very often."

"They do a lot of things in this temple they don't do elsewhere," he replied. "The Grigori are not supposed to eat women or babies, for obvious reasons."

"Because the humans would rise up against them," I said, flatly. "Men are very protective of their mates, and heirs."

"Humans, Angara, Chutanga," Zash admitted, not looking at me, "all the higher creatures of Pangea—if they knew this was happening to their wives and unborn... having others you don't know or care about being enslaved to a superior race is one thing. What goes on here is something else entirely, and would obviously bring the wrath of the entire world down upon—not only the Grigori—but the Chutanga as well."

177

"So your tribe, even other Chutanga tribes, worked out a deal with the Grigori to save themselves..."

"I can't believe the elders who worked out this deal ever imagined that *this* would be the result!" Zash said defensively; even angrily. "We are an honorable race, Brandon! Many *still* don't know! Chutanga are not allowed to see inside this building. The break in the wall has given access the Grigori would never permit, and while some of us snuck in here as children, and the secret is slowly getting out, it's not enough to force trouble with the Grigori."

"*Trouble with the Grigori is the least of your worries!*" I snapped! "A war with all of *Pangea* should be your worry! Those Chutanga men brought these women and *guided them in here!* And they don't come back again to guide them *out! What do they THINK is going on in here?*"

He glared at me, silently, and gave no answer.

"You can pretend all you want that no one knew..." I snapped. "But on some level you all did. I don't even want to think about how many women and their unborn babies have died here—how many ages this has gone on."

Zash's shoulders slumped. His eyes filled with self-loathing.

"Many of us want it to end, Brandon," he said, gently. "You can see how it affects me. Others in our tribe feel the same way. Those that don't feel as we do have never seen, and choose not to."

"Out of sight, out of mind."

"If a Nyame dies in the forest and no one is there to see, who is to say it's actually dead?"

"And now Milton's—my friend's... I don't know what to call her... woman? Is going to be fattened up for *this*." I paused and thought about what Zash had done, and realized he had probably endangered himself and even his family by showing me this. "Thank you for bringing me, Zash. You're a good man. I *will* need to warn my friend—at the very least."

I looked again at the device in my hand. The little red dot had returned! The two blues were moving quickly and narrowing the distance between themselves and the lone runner—whoever it was. Probably only ten or so miles separated them. There was no way I could cross the distance between us before the dots connected. But I could intercept those dots after the red had been recaptured. They might not harm her, if it was indeed Nova, and I could rescue her on the way back to Emibi.

If I lived that long. Which didn't seem likely based on the decision I'd just come to.

"I have to act now," I told Zash. "I'm sorry. I know it means I'll force your tribe to change their minds on this, by taking the decision from them, but I can't sit by."

Zash looked hopeful. "How?" he asked.

"Do you want to help?"

"Yes," he said, reluctantly, and I know his reluctance was only because of Suri and his child.

"Gather anything large and flammable; flat, broad, dry leaves, grass, wood, whatever fits and cover the holes in the ceiling."

"And what will you do?"

"I'm going to do the stupid part."

"Do you think this will work?" Zash asked, nervously after I'd told him my plan.

"Even if we fail, it's going to get someone's attention. And maybe generate change. If it comes to that, I'll be the dead one, and you can go back to your family and pretend it never happened, or finish what we start. Your choice"

"Brandon, no. I am bound to you since you saved my life…"

"If you're bound to me then you have to do what I say and I order you to start a fire in that hole in the ceiling, keep it burning and stay long enough to jab the Grigori and Ingonghus back if they try escaping. No matter what you hear happening down here, stay up there and keep these assholes penned inside this chamber. And then—when it's all over—go back to Suri and your child. You're bound to them more than you are to me."

Zash looked reluctant, then shook his head in frustration.

"But *your* mate… your Nova. And whatever family the two of you might have…"

"Nova would understand. In fact, she would probably think less of me if I *didn't* do this. I know I would."

Zash nodded, understanding, and said, "be safe, my friend," then moved quickly away, down the ladder and out the hole we'd come through. I turned back to the ghastly scene still playing out at the center of the pool.

There had been another circle through the depths and the other arm was gone, and as I watched there was still another, and the breasts disappeared, another and a part of her face—I felt the agony the victim apparently couldn't. But I wouldn't intervene. Not yet. The poor girl was dead already, and stopping the ritual might wake her from her trance, and in doing so be more cruel and horrible than letting the Grigori finish her off.

The other terrified women on the little rock islands sat trembling, awaiting their fates with covered eyes. A few shrieked at each horrifying reveal, but too many of them seemed sadly accepting of their own inevitable fates.

Feeling incredibly frustrated I circled around the edge of the inner wall of the amphitheater and considered my next move, and where best to make it. After some careful consideration I decided that there was no *good* plan, just a plan that was likely to be less disastrous than the others. Making my decision, I got into position and waited.

Finally the queen submerged longer than she ever had before, and when she arose she came alone, swimming sleepily toward her boulder. She moved as if completely exhausted, and lay out on the rock preparing for a long nap in the thin shaft of sun that glowed through the opening above. As she settled herself, I noticed that shaft narrowing, the room growing gradually darker, and I knew it was time. I leaped from behind my wall, having decided to start at a point nearest the queen's 'royal throne'.

Coming down fast and hard I smashed a foot onto the lolling head of one of the queen's pet flying lizards, crushing it into the stone, blood and brains bursting out in all directions. Then I raised my bone-weapon and slammed it through the skull of the ghastly Grigori leader. Her sleepy eyes snapped open, rolling around in their sockets trying to see and understand what had just happened. Her wings flapped maniacally, her head pinned by my pressure on the spear, arms and legs jerking in frantic spasms, her brain already dead, her body slow to realize. As her twitching corpse flailed about me her second winged pet became aware of what was happening and shot toward me, its neck snapping out like it was spring-loaded, wicked beak clamping down through the air and snapping closed where my arm had just been.

I stomped my foot on the Grigori queen's neck and yanked my weapon free, snapping her vertebrae and ending her struggles, spinning around as I did to shove my bone-spear into the side of the still attacking Ingonghu. The reptile's mouth clamped down hard on my shoulder as the spear impaled it through the stomach, to explode out its back. Blood gushed over my hands in warm rivers, as the Ingonghu viciously chewed my shoulder, probably clenching more from the pain in its gut than any actual attack. Fortunately it couldn't hold on long, died quickly, and fell into the water at the base of the throne.

My shoulder hurt like hell, my left arm already weakening as my fight was just beginning. The attack had sent a signal to the other Grigori and they all leaped into the air, circling overhead, hissing like furious, broken steam engines. The room had darkened from Zash's plugging of the holes in the roof, but I could still see by the dancing light of the flickering fire he'd obviously set. Smoke was already filling the upper areas of the chamber, which caused the Grigori flyers to panic and shriek.

"Into the water!" I yelled to the remaining women, and they all moved quickly, diving, slipping, falling from their little islands to dip below the pool's red surface. "Get low, and move toward that wall!"

They did as commanded, staying remarkably calm as panic began to spread rapidly among the Triassic bat-things circling above them. Fear and terror could obviously shut down the superior intellect of a Grigori as easily as it did a human.

One or two of the dominant race slammed into the flaming debris covering the escape holes in the roof, but couldn't succeed in breaking through. One even caught fire, and fell screaming into the waters near the women. To their credit they avoided the thing as it thrashed and churned the bloody waters, and kept moving toward the wall I'd told them to hug.

"Over that wall is a ladder leading down to an escape hole!" I shouted to the closest women, one of them an Angara.

They nodded, quickly and efficiently clambering up what had been until recently the Grigori box seats. They deftly hefted their pregnant bodies over the ledge, then turned around, the first helping those behind, then leaving those women to help the next in line as they themselves disappeared behind the stone wall, hopefully exiting to safety.

Finally the terrified Grigori attacked. They certainly hadn't heard or understood my instructions being as deaf as they were, but they could plainly see the women moving toward some kind of escape, an escape they had to hope would work equally well for them.

I thrust up my bone spear to stop the first attacker as she swooped over me toward one of the women at the top of the wall, its speed and momentum causing it to rake along the length of my weapon, open its own gut and spill its contents over several of the frightened females. Its nearly empty body fell in a heap on two of its former victims, and they bravely kicked the carcass aside, then continued their escape.

I climbed up on some of the lower stones, scrambling higher so I could have a better angle to protect and serve. I knocked aside another attacking beast with just my fist, then found myself slammed backward by two panicking Grigori whose crazed claws shredded my weakened and already damaged arm, and digging into one of my legs. I stabbed ferociously with my bone weapon and eventually managed to sink the thing into one of the Grigori's eyes, but then it's head jerked back in pain before it died, taking my knife with it, and suddenly I was unarmed. Unarmed and fighting for my life against a second enraged beast.

Its open maw was pushing toward my face as I shoved back with hands about its neck, but its legs were doing the most damage, clamped about my torso, extended claws digging deep into my soft flesh where it'd already been torn open back in Emibi. The thing's force jammed me back against one of the women who turned to see my struggle, and valiantly smacked the Grigori in the face, repeatedly punching the thing in an eyeball. But still it wouldn't let go.

It was strong, and strengthened all the more by panic and mad fear. I was weak and getting weaker. My only advantage had been surprise, and that was long gone. Now the battle was speed and strength, and I was clearly outclassed. Not only were these damn things probably smarter than me, they were tougher and quicker. Dominant race, for sure.

As I pushed, as the woman punched, joined by others who were doing the same, the battle was clearly being lost. At least by me.

"Go!" I told my helpers. "Save yourselves!"

The woman who had first come to my defense stopped punching and stared at me with a surprised, hopeless, saddened expression, glanced around quickly at the others, then up at the rest of the circling, screaming, diving Grigori. She touched the shoulder of one of the other pregnant females, a monkey-woman with a tail like those that had captured me when I first arrived in Pangea. Slowly—reluctantly—continuing to watch me struggle—they all backed away, toward the wall.

I watched them scramble to safety with concerned, fearful glances back in my direction, saw my fate in their eyes, and smiled. I had achieved something in my lifetime. I had saved a generation to come for these women, and perhaps even freed them to return to their homes. Maybe they would talk about the stranger who had fought for them—not just the humans—but for all the females at risk that day. Maybe it would lead to understanding. To change. To cooperation, and a better life for every sentient being in Pangea.

Or maybe not. But it gave me hope, and a sense that my coming death had more meaning than if I'd died a janitor at APL.

GRIGORI BETRAYAL

I I turned and continued to push with what little strength I had against the Grigori's neck, but I was losing, and the thing could sense it, now. It spasmed and attacked with renewed strength, its jaw snapping less than an inch from my nose. I was going to die. I was never going to see Nova again. Her, or Milton, or Zash, or the outer world, my mother, my sister... no one and nothing. All anyone would ever know is I might have been inside Milton's mole, and maybe I'd died deep in the darkened shaft somewhere, miles below APL.

But none of it mattered as much as never again being able to see Nova. To prove to her how much I loved her and how sincerely I believed that she was the most beautiful thing inside and out that I'd ever known. She might live a lifetime never realizing how much I'd really loved her.

Suddenly an arrow split through the Grigori head and stopped a hair's breadth away from my right eye. I jerked back in surprise, and the Grigori fell limp in my grip, its claws releasing my torso, its body now nothing more than a sack of lifeless goo.

I shoved it aside and through the thickening smoke saw a Chutanga man—not Zash—waving to me from a hole in the ceiling. He smiled, then shoved a torch into the face of an approaching Grigori. As the thing flew off in terror, the Chutanga notched another arrow and took aim at a different flying beast.

I stood and saw Zash and two other Chutanga men fighting fiercely beside me on the rocks and in the pool, protecting the last few escaping females. Arrows flew, spears impaled, dark, green bodies fell on all sides.

As fast and as fiercely as it had begun, it ended.

We stood quietly in the middle of the carnage, looking around carefully for survivors. An Ingonghu spasmed limply over at the pool's edge, and one of the Chutanga men sloshed through the red waters to crush its skull. As he did, Zash moved closer to me and put a hand on my shoulder.

"Are you all right?" he asked.

"Why?" I said, smiling. "Don't I look all right?"

Zash grimaced back at me.

"No, actually, you look awful."

"You say the nicest things," I said, laughing. "Who are your friends?"

"Sen, Bana, and Chá. Friends of mine. Better friends than even I knew."

He smiled at the two walking towards us.

"Thanks," I said.

One of them waved me off, dismissing it as nothing.

"Always happy to help a man too stupid to help himself."

I laughed. "Yes, looking back, diving into a den of Grigori may not have been the smartest thing anyone's ever done."

"Maybe now you'd like to go out and stick your head in the mouth of a Latha?" Zash asked, laughingly.

Before I could even ask what a Latha was, the third Chutanga stuck his head over the wall leading to the ladder, a stunned expression scarring his face.

"Zash!" he said, insistently. "You have to come see this."

Zash looked at me, curious. I just shrugged, and we followed the other man out of the amphitheater.

WE WERE ALL STUNNED to see her. She must have been hidden back in the deeper shadows of the tomb, cowering behind the others, or just low and mixing in with the crowd. She was nearly a foot taller than her equally pregnant companions—all of them eight or nine months along, I could now see—her dark, golden skin and long, sun-lightened blonde-brown hair making her all the more striking and noticeable. How could we have not seen this Chutanga woman before now?

Zash was less surprised than the others. The Grigori had not honored whatever treaty had existed between them and the Chutanga tribes. They were not only taking Chutanga slaves, they were eating them, and their unborn children.

"Will your chief listen to you, now?" I asked.

"He will," said the snarky Chutanga named Chá, "or he will no longer be chief."

As the other Chutanga men stepped forward to learn the woman's name, and tribe, Zash pulled me aside out of earshot of the others.

"Thank you, Brandon," he said, softly. "You forced me to do what I should have done years ago."

"I can be annoying that way."

Zash laughed, then quickly became very serious.

"You need to get on your way to finding your woman," he said.

"I do," I agreed. "Or do I need to get back to Emibi to save Milton's mate, Elia, and their child? God, I wish I knew how much time had passed since I'd left them."

"How much what?"

"Exactly."

Zash stared a moment, and then shook his head, utterly confused.

"I'll have to risk it," I said. "First I'll get Nova safely to Sa Fasi, and then head back to Emibi. Maybe some of the Nyala will help me." I held up my well-chewed arm. "But I'm not at my best for wandering in the wilds of Pangea."

Zash placed a hand on my shoulder.

"I will come with you," he said. "To Sa Fasi, to Nova, and then to Emibi. I owe you that much."

I held up a hand.

"You have a wife and child that need you. I can find Nova on my own. And she has a kingdom. She's a princess, after all."

He stared at me intently giving me no indication of an answer either way.

"Suri can give you creams that will help you heal," he said, finally. "She is our tribe's medicine woman in training."

"Thank you," I said, looking at the device in my hand. There was only one dot—purple. Captured. "And then I'll *really* have to be on my way."

Again Zash stared at me, long and hard, saying nothing. Eventually he lowered his eyes and *did* speak.

"I understand," he said, sadly.

MY BELOVED NOVA

WITH NO STARS TO GUIDE ME it's little wonder I became confused and lost in the labyrinth of hills.

Suri had given me the creams Zash promised, and hugged me goodbye, sadly. I'd kissed the little one, gotten a sweet smile in return, then Zash and I made our strange trek back to the shore of his island. He provided me with fresh supplies, an animal skin 'fanny-pack' carrier for my 'GPS', weapons like a knife, and a bow and arrows, and his canoe.

As I'd climbed in the little boat, I searched the nearby trees for Nala's body, but I couldn't see anything. Maybe we were on a different part of the island. I felt her loss, momentarily, then shoved the canoe into the sea.

I waved goodbye as he stood on the shore. He watched me for a long time until I could no longer make him out clearly on the sand. I had finally set off in the direction of the purple dot. Purple. Captured. My Nova—or whoever it was—had been taken by Angara and was now on her way back to Emibi. I, however, would reach them long before they arrived at the Grigori city.

Unfortunately Mother Nature, or whatever passes for her in this bowl shaped world, decided to intervene. The straightest path between me and the purple dot never turned out to be very straight. Rivers, rocks, hungry creatures, tangles of brush, and sheer cliffs kept intervening, making my passage more difficult than I could have ever imagined. The purple dot kept moving closer to Emibi while I never seemed to get any closer to the purple dot.

Worse, an uncountable number of new, blue dots had begun moving in my direction from Emibi. A blue cluster, more like. I have to assume they were keeping track of whether or not the red dots turned purple—and stayed that way. Given that I and an errant plesiosaur had killed all my original blue dots, whoever decides such things had apparently felt it necessary to send a larger hunting party for a second go.

All I could do was pick up my pace, stop eating, stop sleeping, and make every effort to reach Nova as fast as possible. In a world with no time, time was of the essence. This meant I was rapidly exhausting myself under the never-ending heat of the noonday sun, and growing weaker with each step. If I did have to fight any Angara in order to free Nova, it wouldn't be a battle I was likely to win.

Topping a low hill I ran headlong into another blockage in my path, a steep decline filled with twisted, spiky brambles and the sounds of some pig-like creatures living within them. I climbed a tree to see the best and fastest way around this latest barrier, checking my GPS against the surrounding terrain when something odd happened. The purple dot stopped moving, and suddenly turned back to red, with a single blue dot moving hurriedly away from it.

Then just as abruptly that blue dot also disappeared.

What the hell had just happened?

Had Nova—or whoever it was—found a way to kill her Angara captors? Had someone—or something—killed them for her?

It seemed most likely that the group had been attacked by one or more of the endless numbers of dinosaurs that roamed freely around this savage land, a drifting death that had descended on the slavers, unintentionally freeing their captive. So what did that mean for the remaining red dot? For Nova? I watched with sweating helplessness as the dot remained lit, held still, then finally began to move back along the way it had come, back in the direction where Zash had told me Sa Fasi lay.

It had to be Nova! She was alive! And free again!

Suddenly my strength returned. I searched the decline and found a clear path leading down into the valley below—a wide savanna filled with grazing ankylosaurs—dropped quickly from the crook of the tree I sat in and began a near run down the slope. Keeping my eyes perpetually on the hills where Nova had to be, I hurried past clusters of the curious, armor-backed dinosaurs, nearly tripped over some smaller grass eating bipeds, and raced across the flat plain that separated me from what I hoped would be my final climb to the woman I loved.

A few hundred yards up that slope I checked my GPS and watched as the screen suddenly jerked, and the purple dot that indicated me became suddenly very close to the other red dot, as if some satellite somewhere were updating its information, recalculating perhaps because I'd been traveling faster and further than either of us realized.

From somewhere above me a hissing noise caught my ears, a horrifying sound that reminded me of the pterodactyls I'd heard in the Grigori temple. Rounding a slight outcropping of rock I saw it was a pair of the winged rats cautiously beating the air, practically hovering in and down on something I couldn't see on a ledge not far from me. A spear occasionally jabbed into view, forcing the flying beasts back, but they quickly regrouped, circled, and descended again, and again. Fearing it was Nova in danger, I scrambled quickly over stones and roots on a serpentine path in her direction.

In some distant time an earthquake had shifted dramatically along a fault at this point and ripped the planet, creating the path on which whoever was being attacked now fought, while also forming a wall that jutted straight up about ten feet to block my progress. I searched frantically as the Ingonghus continued their attack, and found a few random vines and a fallen tree that offered a sort of bridge upward. I leaped on it, grabbing the vines for support, and tested my exhaustion and balance by racing as fast as I could manage along the long dried pine.

The trunk of the fallen tree stopped a few feet below the path's ledge, so I had to jump to get up there, losing my spear in the process. Heaving with almost the last of my strength I hauled myself over the lip, and stood on the narrow precipice with a young, dark-haired girl—bloody and naked—cowering on the narrow platform, her face buried behind one of her arms, as she angrily stabbed out at the attacking monsters with the spear in her other hand.

The pterodactyls had withdrawn and flown off, but were circling again, lower this time, and I watched as one folded its wings for a fast dive on its prey. I dove with my knife just before the creature's open maw reached the frightened girl. The stone blade plunged into its skull just behind the eyes—a lethal jab for which I was grateful because I'd been aiming for its heart. With twists and jerks it died quickly then rolled off the ledge, disappearing from our lives.

But there was still one more.

The second Ingonghu had followed its brother, darting fast toward the girl, but my sudden appearance must have startled it because it veered to one side, and then arced off and away from us, back into the sky.

I made use of the moment to check on the girl, and watched as she raised her eyes over her forearm in astonishment. Very slowly she lowered that arm to reveal her astonishment. The expression she showed would be difficult to describe, though it was plainly as complicated as my own—because the wide eyes looking back into mine were the stunning, sea-blue eyes of my Nova. Nova the Beautiful.

"Nova..." I said, the emotion nearly overwhelming me.

"Brandon?" she whispered, and I couldn't tell if she were pleased, surprised, horrified, or all of the above. "How did you find me?"

"I..." I began.

"Not now," she interrupted, pointing behind me. "Ingonghu."

Once more the beast was sweeping toward us, so quickly that I had no time to unsling my bow. Its open mouth rocketed toward me like two massive blades pointed at head and heart, and all I could do was duck slightly to one side and punch the hideous thing in the face. This time I hit him exactly where I wanted, and with a hiss of pain and rage the reptile was knocked in a heap on the ledge where it scrambled frantically trying to right itself. Very quickly it jerked itself upright, dove off the path. I hoped it was done with us. But within seconds we saw it rising up in the distance, making a graceful sweep over the treetops on a curve that would bring it right back to where we stood.

I quickly nocked an arrow in the bow Zash had given me, preparing for another attack, and as I did I looked down at the woman I loved so much it hurt, to catch her stealing a loving glance at me; but as soon as she saw my eyes on hers, she immediately turned away.

"Pay attention to your work," she said, snippily.

"Come on, Nova," I said, smiling. "I know you're glad to see me."

She turned furiously and glared directly into my eyes.

"I hate you," she said, "and if you don't pay attention to that Ingonghu I'll be hating your *corpse*."

I couldn't help myself. I smiled again, and turned to meet the winged reptile/bird/fantasy creature—whatever the hell it was to the palaeobiologist establishment this week. To me it was now—as to Nova—an Ingonghu. The cruel bloodhound of the Grigori. The long-extinct pterodactyl of the outer world.

This time I met it with a weapon it had never faced before. I'd selected my longest arrow, and with all my remaining strength bent the bow until my weakened arm fairly vibrated with the strain, resting the very tip of the shaft upon the quivering thumb of my left hand, I waited, waited, as the great winged beast plunged once more toward us. A hundred yards away... fifty yards... twenty... my arm shook horribly.

I loosed the arrow straight for it's open mouth—and prayed.

I didn't see where it went. And the thing just kept coming. I had missed, and now we were dead.

The Ingonghu slammed into me and knocked me across the tiny ledge, one of its beaks impaling my shoulder. I fairly flipped backwards over Nova, and slammed directly into the cliff face where the two of us collapsed—man, and dinosaur—me about to become its next meal, it to dine—first on me, and then on Nova.

But neither of us moved.

The head of the Ingonghu lay still, beak jutting through my shoulder, its eyes filmy and unmoving. A little freaked, I pushed the thing's nose out of my wound, shoved it aside, and stood quickly away from it.

I turned toward Nova, who knelt nearby, staring at me with wide, fearful eyes. Her expression betrayed her real feelings. She had been terrified—for herself, yes, but mostly for me.

"Nova," I said lovingly, feeling overwhelmed just to be near her again.

"I hate you," was her only reply; but it sounded less sincere than it had before.

"You hate me?" I asked, smiling, and not believing her.

"I do," she said, tears forming in her eyes. "I really do."

I stepped closer, gently, patiently, holding my arms out to my sides. She stood and backed away, only stopping when she reached the edge of the precipice.

"Can I take your hand?" I asked.

She moved both behind her back.

"I want to hold it over my head, then close to my heart," I said, "and never let it go."

She tried to stay angry, but I saw her face melt, and one tear slipped free of a lid and trickled along her cheek.

"You can't have me, now," she said, trying to sound defiant, but only sounding deeply sad. "I belong to Gudra, The Ugly."

My heart collapsed, and I can only imagine my face did as well, because with those words, her expression fell as far as mine, and she turned away from me.

"I'd gone home," she said, sadly. "To Sa Fasi. After we had escaped from the Angara in that tunnel, Hajah tried to rape me, but I beat him senseless, and ran. He laughed and laughed, but he didn't follow. Without him I made my way back home; because of Gudra I wouldn't enter the villages, or let any of my friends or family know I'd returned. I was too afraid of what would happen when Gudra found out. So I circled the tribe, watching for some sign that might tell me what to do, trying to decide if I should just leave as I'd done before. But I knew the Angara would be coming, and I didn't want to face them alone.

"My father and brother would do what they could to protect me, but I didn't see either of them as I circled my people's caves. They must have been out looking for me. So—unsure what to do—I lived in a fissure beside a valley not far from Sa Fasi that my tribe rarely goes to, just trying to think of an answer."

That explained why the red dot hadn't moved. Not because she'd gotten home, but because she was too afraid to finish the journey.

"Eventually one of Gudra's brothers saw me when I got too close to my father's cave, he told Gudra, and Gudra came after me. He chased me for miles and miles, across many different lands, and then I ran right into the Angara who were looking for me. They took me prisoner, and then took their time heading back to Emibi, not realizing the danger they were in. I actually tried to convince them to move faster—told them Gudra would kill them all with only one hand, and they just laughed."

"But he found them, and he *did* kill them" I said, at last understanding the sudden disappearance of the three, blue Angara dots on the GPS.

She nodded. "He went after the last one and I ran. But…"

"He'll be back soon," I said, feeling the exhaustion of the recent fighting and my torturous journey to get here.

Again, she nodded. More tears trailed down her cheeks, and fell to the earth below. A fearful rain of tears.

"He will kill you, Brandon," she said quietly, but with complete certainty. "And he would have the right. He took my hand. I struggled, but he's so strong, Brandon. So strong. He raised it, and held it aloft before the Angara, then to his chest."

I swallowed hard. Because I'd been ignorant. Because I hadn't known...

"I am his wife, Brandon, because he did what you would not."

I tried to take her in my arms but she slapped me away, lowering her eyes and crying a torrent. I was devastated. Lost. We both were. All this time I'd thought of nothing but Nova, and how I would make this stupid, insignificant custom work *for* me instead of against me. And now... now it was even more against me than before.

"It can't mean anything," I said. "Just because he did it in front of some Angara..."

"It is custom, Brandon!"

"And then he *killed* the Angara!" I snapped. *"This is ridiculous!"*

"He followed our customs!" she snapped back, turning to glare in my face. "And it has meaning because he *gives* it meaning, and he will kill you to protect his commitment to that meaning just as he did the Grigori servants! You cannot beat him, Brandon! I don't love him! I will never love him as I..."

She paused. Her cheeks reddened beneath her liquid filled eyes. I took her shoulders in my bloody hands and plead into those eyes.

"I love you, Nova," I told her, my own eyes moistening. "I will never love anyone the way I love you. I will *die* without you. I didn't know your custom. I would have done it then, would do it in front of anyone, a million times had I only known..."

"And he would still have *killed* you," she said, turning her head and resting her wet cheek against my chest. "I would rather know you live, than be tormented with the thoughts of your body being eaten by worms while Gudra forces himself into me. It will keep me alive through anything to know that you, too, are alive, and perhaps happy, somewhere else."

"I'll never be happy without you," I said. "I'll fight for you. Is that allowed? Can I kill him and take you back?"

"What kind of bizarre customs do you have on your world? No, Brandon, you cannot kill a man and take his wife. And as proud as I am of your bravery and skill, you would have no chance against Gudra, anyway."

"We can run..." I said.

She clutched at my chest like a little girl, and thought about it. I reached my hands up to hold her, and slowly, inevitably, she melted into my embrace, resting her open mouth against my chest, and kissing me, gently. Very slowly her arms went around me, to cling tightly. I returned her squeeze, and felt the love flow between us, once again.

"We could," she whispered, with finality. "For a little while, anyway." Her hands caressed my back, my bare behind, my thighs, and then returned to my shoulders, gripping me fiercely, almost desperately. "At least it would be something."

"I love you, Nova," I said.

"And I love you, Brandon," she replied, her voice breaking with fear, and sadness. "So, so much."

And so we ran. She had just come up from the valley I'd passed through, so we continued on up the hill and over, our only goal: to move faster the Gudra.

But I already knew there would be no escaping him. He would find us. And he would kill me.

"HE CAN'T BE FAR behind me now," Nova said. "He's a master tracker, so we will have to move quickly and carefully to escape him. When he comes he will kill you—rape me for leaving him—and carry me back to his cave."

"Okay," I said. "Can we stop dwelling on how severely outmatched I am against Gudra."

"At least you'll be dead. I'll still be alive, with his dick stuck up my ass."

I laughed, and she did, too.

"Perhaps we can go to the sea," she suggested. "If he catches us there, I can throw myself into it as he kills you."

"Seriously," I said over my shoulder. "Enough with the 'he's going to kill you' crap, all right? I'm a resourceful guy. You never know."

She laughed a little, and I just shook my head. All this negativity was beginning to get to me. What kind of monster *was* Gudra, The Ugly?

"We'll go on until it gets dark," I said. "And then tomorrow…"

"Until *what* gets dark?" Nova asked. "What's a 'tomorrow'?"

I stared at her for a second, then shook my head.

"Never mind. It doesn't… how odd." I said to myself. "The word is in the vocabulary, but not the meaning."

Before long we found a rift in the cliff which had been widened and extended by an endless age of rushing water draining through it from the plateau above. It gave us a rather rough climb to the summit, but eventually we stood on a level mesa that stretched back for several miles and melted into the mountain range. To one side lay the broad inland sea, curving upward into the horizonless distance where it merged with the paler blue of the sky, so that for all the world it looked as though the sea lapped back to arch completely over us, briefly disappearing beyond the oversized sun, and then back down the other side. We were alone atop a sea of blue.

Not far ahead lay a dense forest, but to the left the country was open and clear to the plateau's farthest edge. We chose open and clear, and had turned to resume our journey when Nova touched my arm. I turned to her, thinking that she was about to finally admit that she loved me, too; but I was mistaken.

"Gudra," she said, nodding toward the forest.

I looked, and there, emerging from the thick darkness of the wood, came an immense whale of a man. He was still too far off and covered in shadow for me to distinguish individual features, but I didn't really need any clearer picture to know that I was doomed. The man must have been seven and a half feet tall, and built like someone who ate steroids with every meal.

"You're right," I told her. "He *is* going to kill me."

"I *told* you," she said. But her voice was fearful, not triumphant.

"Run," I said to Nova. "At least I can earn you a good start. Maybe hold him off until you've gotten a few miles away."

"Brandon," I heard her say through tears and sobs.

I couldn't look at her. Couldn't bear it. So, without a backward glance, I moved forward to meet The Ugly one. I was going to my death for Nova's sake, and I could think of no better cause.

As Gudra stepped further from the shadows I began to understand how it was that he'd earned the title of 'Ugly'. Apparently the fight with the bear had not been an easy victory. It—or something else even meaner—had ripped away the entire left side of his face. The eye was still there, but in an open socket, held in place by scarred muscle-tissue and tendon. His nose, and all the flesh from the center of his lips outward was gone, so that his jaw bone and teeth were exposed, and apparently grinning from within the horrible disfigurement.

From what was left of his features I could see that at one time he may have been as handsome as any young man, and probably admired and desired by many women. Being mauled might have been part of what made him brutal and angry—all the angrier to find his mate running away with someone else. But there was more than possessiveness in his expression.

Both eyes moved rapidly side-to-side from Nova, to me, then back again. For all Nova's beliefs and thoughts that Gudra's motives for marrying her were entirely selfish and borne solely from a desire to become chief of the tribe, she had obviously missed the fact that he did, indeed, feel *something* for her, and he didn't like what he was seeing between us. It amped up his fearsomeness to a terrifying level.

Abruptly, he broke into a run, and as he advanced he raised his tree-trunk of a spear. I quickly knelt, nocked an arrow and struggled desperately to steady my aim as best I could. My arms shook horribly from exhaustion and fear, the arrow tip refusing to stay in place on my vibrating thumb. My trembling combined with his movement made it impossible for me to target, and so I whispered a silent prayer and just let the damned missile fly.

I missed completely. The useless projectile sailed harmlessly over his shoulder and into the forest beyond.

Shaking more than ever, I tried to reach back for another arrow, but there was no time. The spear was going to impale me unless I moved, and so I did. I dove to one side, and the carved, stone tip ripped through the air where I'd been kneeling and dug deep into the dirt behind me. I thought it might buy me a minute or two as he struggled to free the thing from the ground, but I underestimated Gudra. He jerked the thing—not only out, but directly my way, throwing off several pounds of dirt and grass, and aiming the spear deftly between my eyes.

I rolled away and down but the spear still carved a piece of flesh off the bridge of my nose. Falling away from the man-monster, I rolled up on one knee, and checked on my fast-moving enemy. Behind him I saw Nova standing there, still, watching with horrified eyes.

"Nova!" I yelled. *"RUN!"*

But she didn't move.

"Brandon," she said, plaintively, and the obvious loving sound in her voice infuriated Gudra. He may not understand her imposed 'slave-language', but he couldn't miss the emotion behind those words. He jabbed the spear at me again so fast I almost didn't see it, or move in time. As it was he still ripped open my cheek.

I screamed and fell to one side, and Nova screamed as well.

Gudra jerked the spear again in my direction with terrific velocity and while the blade tip missed, the shaft didn't. The impact to my skull knocked me to my chest, and I once again understood the phrase 'seeing stars'. Intense white light filled my vision and blinded me, then sparkled away to reveal Gudra raising his spear above his head to jam it down through some tender part of me—probably my face. It was hopeless. I was exhausted, starved, wounded, and slow—and Gudra was ten times the warrior I was.

I looked at Nova, her nude body so lovely and delicate. Her face so indescribably beautiful. She had loved me so intensely, and so sincerely, that I would have given anything at that moment to feel her against me just one more time. She was worth any battle, any agony.

Almost against my will, my upheld arm moved slightly to the left as the spear came down, pressing lightly against the point and widening the angle of Gudra's thrust. It slammed downward just a few inches to my right—not far from me, but enough that it missed. It dug so hard into the dirt behind me that the ground shuddered—and the spear snapped. In that moment, I realized my advantage.

Apparently I'd internalized more of the high school training I'd gotten in fencing and martial arts than I'd realized. Never enough to become a threat, or particularly proficient, but apparently enough to remember something that was now going to save my life. Use your enemy's power against them. With minimal force you can widen their angle of attack, and avoid ever being touched.

Gudra's surprised face was now so close to me that I was able to punch him hard in the raw, exposed eye. The pain was obviously severe.

He shrieked, and fell away from me, stumbling around and covering his injury.

I pulled my knife, and stood, unsteadily, took a wobbly step toward him and encouraging him to attack. Growling like an animal he did, red with rage, moving so quickly he almost got me before I could move. But I did move, a little to my left, and as his overbalanced weight flew past me, I jabbed my knife hard into the fleshy part of his upper arm. It was a tactic I should only use once, as Gudra was likely to catch on, but a wound like that was already balancing out the fight.

I began to think I had a chance.

My agility would save me, and because Gudra lacked control, my depleted condition was less of an issue.

Slightly less.

He attacked again, I ducked beneath his raised arm, and stabbed upward into his stomach as he practically flew over me. Apparently I missed any vital organs, because he immediately wheeled to come at me again, only to find his quickness rewarded with another punch to the face, followed instantly by an inch or two of sharpened stone in the muscles of his other arm.

For the first time since our meeting, I saw something that gave me hope. Fear in Gudra's good eye.

It was a duel of strategy now—the great, hairy man maneuvering to get inside my guard where he could bring those giant muscles to play, while I continually moved just enough one way then the other to avoid being grasped. I remembered a judo-studying friend of mine once telling me that all the fancy karate moves in the world would only work until he could get hold of his enemy, and then they were dead. If Gudra ever got me in his crushing grip, that was *my* fate, and I knew it. So I had to keep dancing around, avoiding those monstrous, grasping hands.

Every brain cell was frantic with the task of keeping Gudra at arm's length. Three times more he rushed me, and three times more I blocked his knife blow with my forearm, as my own knife found soft places in his body—once penetrating a lung with a wound that instantly foamed and sprayed with each of his now desperate breaths.

He was dripping with blood by now, and the internal hemorrhage induced fits of coughing that brought a steady red stream through his hideous mouth and missing nose, running down his jaw, neck and chest, covering it with pink froth. If it was possible, he'd become even more hideous, but he was far from dead.

As the duel went on I continued to gain confidence. I hadn't expected to survive beyond the first attack from this monstrous engine of rage and hatred, and I think Gudra had felt the same. His thoughts had gone from utter contempt of me to a grudging feeling of respect, and perhaps even some recognition that he had at last met someone who could stand up to him—if not beat him.

Whatever the case, the fight had to end soon, because I was about to, and if I passed out before finishing Gudra, Gudra would finish me.

The Ugly One charged again, but instead of trying futilely to stab me once more with his knife, he instead dropped the weapon and grabbed my blade with both hands, wrenching the thing away from me.

I was entirely unprepared, and now unarmed. I'd given it a valiant go, but it was over for me. With no way for me to inflict damage. It was only a matter of waiting me out until I collapsed from injuries and exhaustion. I was done.

Gudra flung my blade far to one side, into some bushes and stood motionless for just an instant glaring into my face with such a horrid leer of malignant triumph that the look alone nearly kill me—then he sprang for me with his bare hands.

As he came roaring like the massive bear he was, I ducked under his outstretched arm, and came up with my right to plant as clean a blow to his jaw as any ultimate fighter has ever landed on any opponent. Two of his exposed teeth exploded away from the jaw, and down went the great monster to sprawl on the ground. He was so surprised and dazed that he lay there for several seconds before making any attempt to rise. As he did, I stood shakily over him with fists ready.

But my knees were shaking with exhaustion, and suddenly, unexpectedly, gave out on me, dropping me to my knees. I managed to keep my fists up, but my arms were fairly vibrating with fatigue, and I knew they'd be useless to defend.

For what seemed like forever Gudra just lie there in front of me, his good eye turned toward me, staring at me, his breath heaving in ragged gasps, lid drooping over his one, covered eye. Then his expression softened, and he looked over at Nova, whose own eyes were only on me, tears dripping, face anguished.

"Gudra, please," she said. "*Please*, don't kill him!"

Finally, with a deep sigh, the massive man looked away from her, momentarily seeing nothing, until he turned his gaze back to me. He didn't move. Didn't breathe. He simply stared for an unusually long time.

Then slowly, agonizingly slowly, he reached behind his back, and for the first time I noticed the pool of blood that had been spreading out across the sand and grass.

Nova saw it too, and gasped.

Gudra rose, unsteadily, and I watched as he lifted himself off the shaft of broken spear that had stuck in the ground beside me, earlier. Dark red fluid coated the wood like candied apple. As he rose from his knees, Gudra gripped the piece of spear tightly, and slowly drew it from the ground. Holding the dripping thing loosely in his massive hand, he just stood there for a long, long while, staring at me, breathing frothily. Finally he began staggering my way, moving nearly at a snail's pace. His leisurely speed fooled me into thinking I might defend myself against him. But before I could react he shot out a hand and grabbed my shoulder tightly, holding me in place, the bloody spear-point aimed directly at my heart.

Time stopped in the timeless Pangea. I waited for the death I had foolishly thought he wasn't fast enough to deliver, but in reality I was the one who was no longer fast enough to escape. Then—instead of impaling me—he glanced back at Nova.

"Please, Gudra," she said, crying. "I know you can't understand me, but please! *Please!* I love him. I *love* him."

I saw her words land harder than any blow I'd delivered in this fight. He lowered his head, destroyed, then lifted it back up with painful slowness to glare at me. After a minute of unblinking intensity, he turned the spear shaft around, and rested it against his solar plexus, holding it there, as if waiting.

I looked up at him in surprise, not sure what was happening.

Slowly, almost imperceptibly, a smile formed on the good side of his face, and Gudra nodded. I was being given the honor of ending it. As slowly as he had smiled, I reached up and took hold of the spear, and he let go as my fingers closed about it's sticky shaft. I obliged, intending to make it quick, and pushed as hard and fast as I could manage. But it wasn't fast, or hard enough. I had nothing left.

Very slowly he put his other hand on mine, and forced the spear in, and up, directly into his heart. Then he dropped to his knees, frozen there for a moment as I stepped aside, and finally forward onto his face, dead.

Nova was whispering my name. I could barely hear her. I turned to her and saw her grateful, hopeful eyes. I smiled. The world swam and flowed and grew suddenly dark, then light again, then dark once more. I pitched face down into the dirt at her feet, knowing I would only stop loving her when I died, just as Gudra had.

OUR GARDEN OF EDEN

I AWOKE WITH Nova's arms around me.

Every inch of me ached. I had bandages covering almost my entire body, but I felt no pain. My lovely, loving cave girl was holding me as I slept. As *she* slept.

I lie there a long time, with her head on my chest, then slowly so as not to wake her, pulled my hand up to hold her shoulder. I stayed like that, almost perfectly content, staring up at the dancing leaves of the trees that shaded us from the constant, scorching, noonday sun. Strange birds drifted past in the azure of the sky, and insects that probably hadn't been heard on the outer world in millions of years chirped and clicked from every direction. A small brook splashed nearby. I supposed that was how she'd cleaned my wounds and bandaged them. My brave, resourceful beauty.

Somehow she had pulled me near to the mouth of a small cave, but not far enough in to actually hide us. I became aware of the world, my mind coming into focus, and became nervous about being exposed, wondering how far away our inevitable Angara trackers were.

Hurting more than I ever thought I could, I leaned down to kiss the tangle of raven hair on her head, and—smiling—fell back to sleep.

When I awoke I saw Nova kneeling near the stream, soaking grasses and strips of hide. She still wore nothing other than hide sandals and a few stone and string bracelets, and though it hurt just to think of it, I longed to feel her lovely, bare body. Her skin was a deep, golden brown, and I remembered how soft and magical it was to touch. She bent over, oblivious to my stares, her breasts pressing against her knees, her long hair flowing magically with her deliberate movements.

She turned and shook out the things she'd been—I don't know—washing, or rinsing—still unaware that I was looking at her. Her breasts jiggled with her gentle movements, and I was surprised to find my body responding in ways it probably shouldn't given that my blood was more urgently needed elsewhere.

At last she glanced my way, and we smiled at one another, happily. She stood and walked over to me, her movements so sexy that the affected part of me sprang to life in a way that surprised us both.

"Well," she said, noticing. "I guess you really *do* think I'm pretty."

"There's never been anyone prettier," I said, smitten. "On your world, or mine."

She smiled more broadly, averting her eyes shyly, blushing a bit, then finished her journey toward me. She knelt down in the grass beside me to remove some red-stained bandages, and replaced them with the ones she'd been washing in the river. Her eyes bobbed back and forth from her work to my silent erection.

"Stop that," she whispered. "You're not well enough…"

"Says you," I replied, and pulled her lovely face to mine, kissing her softly.

She backed away, studied my eyes, nearly laughed, then shot another quick glance at my hardened flesh.

"I'm not going to see you survive against Gudra just so I can kill you with love," she said, very clinically and coldly.

"Kill me with love," I said. "*Please* kill me with love."

She laughed—a pleasant, musical sound—and finished re-wrapping a particularly nasty cut that ran the length of my ribs, up under my right arm. Some of my injuries I didn't even remember getting. Had all these been from Gudra?

After she was done bandaging, Nova placed her hands on her thighs and looked me over. She smiled gently with both her lips and her eyes, and I could tell that some of the fear had left her. Some.

"You are very handsome," she said, warmly. "I had forgotten how much I enjoyed looking at you."

Now it was my turn to laugh.

"I'm glad you think so," I said.

"As glad as I am that you think I'm beautiful. You really do think I'm beautiful?"

"I really do."

She shot another glance at my still solidified shaft, then looked away again, shyly. After a moment she glanced its way once more, this time with obvious desire in her eyes, and reached out quickly to brush her fingertips down the length of it, very softly. Just as quickly she removed her hand, and lowered her eyes nervously. After a bit, she looked up at me and smiled again.

"Did that hurt?" she asked.

I shook my head. "Felt good," I answered.

More shy smiles from her, more lowered eyes, and then another hungry look at my appreciative member. She reached for it again, touching it so gently it almost *did* hurt. Ache. Her fingertips started at the tip, and moved slowly, sweetly, down the upward facing underside, all the way to the bottom. Then she leisurely moved them back up the side, with slightly more pressure, this time.

"Tell me if I'm hurting you," she said with concern.

"Believe me, Nova. You're *healing* me."

She giggled, girlishly, and pressed harder as she stroked back once more to the tip. Then she very slowly pressed her fingers down and outward until her palm was against me, closing her grip tenderly, but firmly, around my grateful flesh.

"I missed you," she said, and I heard her voice crack with sadness, "and the way you loved me."

She lowered her eyes, and I thought I saw a crystalline drop fall into the grass where she knelt.

"You said you hated me for what I'd done," I reminded her, gently. "Or hadn't done."

"I knew then it was because you were telling the truth about where you were from. But for my whole life people have made fun of me because I wasn't pretty. And here was a man who everyone else had believed was lying to me just so I would let him put himself in me. So it hurt."

I was crushed. It was inconceivable that any woman as lovely and kind as Nova could not see how amazing she was, but clearly I was a stranger in this strange land. I saw the genuine suffering that had been a lifelong part of her, and began to understand how she would be all the more hurt when I'd done—in the eyes of those around us—the wrong thing.

"I realized then that people would always wonder," she said, "wonder if you were with me only so you could have my lands, or be king of Sa Fasi, and I knew that as I grew wrinkled and gray and the love diminished between us, your eyes would shift toward other, more attractive women, and I would begin to wonder the same thing."

"The love will *never* diminish between us. It will only deepen."

I tried to sit up, which was a mistake, and settled for grabbing her free hand, the one closest to mine.

"I will *never* think anyone more beautiful than you, Nova. *Ever.*"

I pulled her hand toward me, and kissed it, then drew her down to me. She came without releasing her grip on my spear, and kissed me with such longing, and such passion, that I nearly cried.

"I don't care about being king," I said. "I don't care about your lands, or your money, or your stuffed animal collection, or anything else. I only care about you."

The smile returned to her face, and my heart soared. She turned and rested her cheek on my chest and I felt tears moisten my skin.

"Why would I—or anyone—collect, and stuff animals?" she asked, laughingly.

"It's hard to explain," I said. "I just mean that I could live my life right here with you in this cave, under these trees, beside this stream, and die without ever wanting more."

Her fingers squeezed mine, so tightly.

"I love you, Nova. With all my heart. With all my soul. If you never want to return to your tribe, I will hold your hand up, and then to my heart before everyone you know. I will go with you wherever you want to go, do whatever you want me to do. If you want me to be your lover, your guardian, or your slave, I will be. I will carry your water, wash your hair, clean your feet... whatever will keep you near me."

She laughed, and kissed my chest.

"You would clean my feet?" she asked.

"I would, Nova. And nothing, not wrinkles, not gray hair, not death, will make anyone more beautiful to me than you."

There was a long silence between us, the only sound was her sniffling, the only movement her gentle rubbing along my erection.

"I love you, Brandon," she said finally. "So much. More than I ever thought I could love anyone. You were the first man to look at me with the kind of genuine adoration that only my father ever showed me. He, too, believed I was beautiful."

I pulled her close, not understanding. This world was so strange on so many levels, and yet it was starting to feel more like home to me— more than my own home ever did—and all because of this amazing, wonderful, *beautiful* woman.

"What happened to our loincloths?" I asked.

"I needed them for bandages."

"Oh," I said, touching the leathers around my waist. "What's this goo?"

"It's the medicine you got from the Chutanga woman. Remember? You told me how to use it."

"I did?" I said, wearily. "I guess I... do I... how did you get me here? To this cave?"

"I tied you to some branches, then trapped two small horses, and tied the branches to them. They did most of the work."

I smiled, and felt such a warm glow. What a woman. I was so proud of her, so glad to have her, and amazed at her resourcefulness.

"You saved my life," I said.

"You saved mine," she said, squeezing my dick firmly. "In so many ways."

She turned her head up to face me and I kissed her soft lips with all the passion I could muster, our tongues slipping lovingly over one another. She nibbled my lower lip, and then bit a little harder on my chin, playfully.

"How sore *are* you, exactly?" she asked.

We both laughed, though I stopped quickly because of the pain.

"I'm willing, if you are," I said, unconvincingly.

She raised her eyes to mine, and I could see her consider it, then change her mind.

"No," she said, grinning. "I would kill you."

I laughed, and winced. "Yes, you probably would."

"Your spear would spit inside me, you would tense with pleasure, and burst open every wound."

"What a way to go," I said.

"Sleep," she whispered. "I would prefer you live so you can pleasure me often, and without dying."

I laughed again and realized she was probably right as razors of agony shot through my ribs and stomach.

She moved away, stood and stared down at me.

Her lean, nude body was so tempting, and my staff hardened once more, throbbing with illicit thoughts of her. She noticed the slight movement and scowled.

"Stop that, Brandon!"

"I can't help it!" I said. "You don't understand how beautiful you are."

She huffed, and put her hands on her hips, trying her best to be angry, but rather obviously delighted with my carnal interest. The sudden motion made her lovely breasts bounce, which didn't help at all, especially when she caught me looking at them.

"Close your eyes, if it's a problem!" she snarled.

I did as commanded.

"Doesn't help. I can still see your gorgeous body in my mind."

"Ooooh!" she howled, laughing slightly. "You're hopeless!"

I heard her footsteps shooshing through the grass away from me, giggling as she went. It was a heavenly sound.

"I'll go find something for us to eat. Maybe if I'm out of the camp, you'll stop thinking about how amazingly gorgeous I am."

"Not likely!" I called after her.

"And leave your penis alone!" she yelled. "If you can't handle putting it in me, you'd better not go pulling on it all by yourself!"

I laughed again, instantly coughing and groaning from the lance of pain, and the sudden opening of a wound or two.

"Serves you right!" she called back from somewhere off in the forest, laughing hysterically.

I smiled to myself, and lie back to finally rest.

"That girl," I said to no one, as I drifted almost instantly into sleep. "Please don't let me lose her again."

HUNTERS RETURN

I SUPPOSE IT WAS possible I was sleeping less. I'd heard that happens to people living near the North Pole when the sun never sets for months. Their bodies become confused and they stay awake for weeks at a time. Or maybe Suri's medicines were simply wonders of primitive science. Whatever the case—I'd only slept twice since the fight with Gudra, and was nearly healed. So the time that passed had to be at least two weeks, right?

I opened my eyes groggily from my latest period of slumber and saw Nova cooking over a small fire between me and the little brook. She was still wet from the stream, apparently having bathed, or swum, or maybe just fallen in. She was holding her hair back from the licking flames, and sprinkling something over a fish on a spit while humming quietly to herself. Once the seasoning was complete she turned the tiny trout to keep it roasting evenly. I rubbed the sleep from my eyes, and just lie there, watching her work.

For years men's magazines like Playboy had made a fortune by posing women erotically, wearing lingerie and heels, but for me there was nothing sexier than my naked Nova just being herself in our little camp. Her happiness was infectious, and her joy for living made me higher than any drug. Her comfort with walking around nude was sexier than any G-string, or airbrush, or pair of heels could have made her.

As I watched, she tested the fish, decided it was ready, pulled it from the fire and turned back to me.

Seeing I was awake, her eyes lit up with electrified love.

"Good waking, sleepy man," she said with a radiant smile. "I have something for you."

She walked toward me and I felt my 'little friend with a mind of its own' spring happily to life. Nova noticed and chuckled.

"Well, good morning to you, too, little one," she said.

She stepped beside me and put one foot on either side of my chest, giving me a delightful view of her best parts.

"I think you're well enough to eat, now," she said, grinning.

"Eat what?" I asked.

"Eat... *fish*," she said, holding it out, clearly confused. She held up her stick and pointed at it. "See? Fish."

"Well, you're offering me more than fish," I said, pointing between her legs.

She covered it quickly.

"You can't eat that," she said, grinning.

"Oh, can't I?" I said, reaching up to cup her ass and pull her to my mouth. She squealed with surprise.

"Brandon!"

I was used to women who shaved and preened, but there was something feral and lusty about plunging my lips into the recently washed fur of a natural woman. I kissed her playfully, and then quickly found what I was looking for between her heated lips—that tiny pink knob of hardened, delicious flesh. I rubbed it gently with the tip of my tongue, and she purred, happily.

"Ooooooh!" she said, with surprise. *"Brandon!"*

I felt her hands grip my head and grasp my hair, her knees wobbling just a little. I pulled her ass more tightly to me and went to work, hearing her voice trill upward in pitch and volume. Then I let go with one hand and plunged my fingers deep into her moistening fissure, applying pressure on the inside, opposite my tongue.

She nearly screamed.

Her thighs were shaking against my ears, her voice warbling and I knew her head was back, eyes closed. Very quickly her hips began to buck, her grip tightening in my hair, and I knew she was there. She called out repeatedly as she came—not my name, not any name, just the simple noises and cries of pleasure.

After she'd finished and started to sag against me, I helped her down onto my lap, guiding myself into her, dropping her down on my thighs to drive my hardness into her. Then I began to move.

"Oooooh, Saraja!" she cried.

Suddenly her eyes and mouth fell open and she stared at me with red cheeks and dilated pupils. Her hands still gripped my hair, and with a sudden surge of pleasure she yanked my face to her neck and held me there tightly, as if afraid of falling. I felt her hips explode back and forth with movement, and given how wet she was and amazing she felt, I didn't last long. As I drove deep for my final thrust, she clutched my head more tightly to her neck and wiggled her hips frantically. We

206

finished—breathing heavily—and I grabbed her hips to gently roll her over beside me.

As she lie back, she loosened her grip on my scalp, and stared at me with wide, amazed eyes, and open mouth. She looked at me as if she'd never stop loving me. I'd never seen anything sexier in my life.

"What did you do?" she asked.

I just shrugged.

"No," she said, genuinely wanting to understand. "I have pleasured myself, but that was… beyond…"

"You've done so much for me." I said. "I just wanted to repay you."

"You did," she said, in a whispery voice. She pulled me down and hugged me sweetly. "Oh, you did, you did."

She laughed and held me as though she wanted to make me a part of her. But I already was.

"I love you, Brandon," she whispered.

"I love you, too, Nova."

I WAS STILL A little weak from my injuries, and Nova insisted we stay put a while longer, just to make sure I was ready to travel.

"Sit back," she said, approaching me with another tasty thing she'd prepared over her fire. "Tell me what you think of this?"

Her cooking was truly masterful. I'd never imagined cave people making anything other than simple, raw meals, or overcooked meats as Nala had done, but Nova knew of many flowers and grasses that added flavor to the meals she prepared, and her little masterpieces could have rivaled a Top Chef.

"I'm sure it's as incredible as everything else you make," I said as she once again straddled me.

She squatted down and knelt to rest on my hips, holding out the meaty morsel between us. Before officially offering it, she reached down and guided my once again erect member inside her.

"I never knew dinner could be so much fun," I said.

"Nor I," she admitted, sighing as she settled around me. She shivered a bit with delight, then continued. "This is the haunch of an orthopi…"

"Orthopi?" I said, confused. "The little horse? I hope it's not one of the little guys you used to drag me up here? I'm very grateful to those little horses."

"Then be even more grateful that he tastes so good," she said, offering me a bit of the meat.

I made a face, but tasted it anyway. It *was* good. Incredibly good.

"Damn, Nova," I said, smiling. "I bet that orthopi is actually grateful you made him so tasty."

"I killed him quickly," she said, matter-of-factly, "more quickly than some other predator would have."

She took a bite herself, and seemed pleased with her work. Then she shifted her hips a little and gave us both a thrill.

"I would be happy to die this way," she said, smiling. "Take this as my last memory into the paradise on the other side of the sun."

"Is that what you believe?" I asked. "That there's a paradise on the other side of the sun?"

"It's what some people of Pangea believe. I *like* to believe it. Or did. Now *this* feels like paradise to me."

She shifted her hips and laughed as my face melted with pleasure.

"Is it paradise for you, too, Brandon?" she asked.

"It's become my new definition of the word," I said.

We chewed silently, as Nova made small, sexy movements with her hips.

"Then why don't we stay?" she asked.

I stopped chewing as I realized she was serious.

"Here?" I asked, looking around.

"It's well protected," she said, explaining quickly. "The valley mouth is so narrow that large animals can't get in. The cave provides shelter if it rains, or gets too hot, and no one would ever find us here. We are not on an easy path either to the valley or the sea."

She rocked her hips again, and stirred me around inside her.

"Keep doing that and I'll never be able to deny you anything," I said.

"How about another ride on your mouth?" she asked.

"Your wish is my command."

"After we eat," she amended.

She fed me another piece of horse meat and I chewed along with her. She smiled at me through greasy lips. Who would have ever thought *that* could be sexy?

"What about your family?" I asked. "Wouldn't you miss Sa Fasi?"

She shrugged, and I could see she was hiding something.

"I no longer speak the language of Sa Fasi, so what's the point? I have the slave language, now."

"Your family wouldn't care. Your father. Your brother."

She shrugged again.

"Why do you want to stay here, Nova?" I asked. "Really."

She looked down at the bits of bone and meat left in her hands, nibbled away at a tiny piece, then tossed it rather expertly all the way into the river. She slapped her hands, wiped them clean on her bare thighs and leaned back—all without ever looking me in the eye.

I was in no hurry for her to talk. I could have sat there forever staring at her naked body straddling mine, her suntanned breasts so soft and lovely in repose.

But I was concerned for her.

"Nova?" I prodded.

"I never cared before," she said suddenly, still without looking at me. "I never cared if I lived or died. It happens. Usually quickly and unexpectedly in Pangea. At times I wished it *would* happen."

She looked at something far away, farther than the woods she was staring into, remembering some old pain, probably of being unattractive and unwanted in her tribe.

"And now I want so very badly to do nothing but live," she said, turning finally to stare me in the eyes. "Live with you, forever, preferably with your spear always inside me."

She wiggled her hips rapidly, smiling, and I smiled, too. But her smile fell quickly.

"People die—even in Sa Fasi, Brandon," Nova said, sadly, "We become food for the dinosaurs, then shit for the worms. Our lives are a blink. Most of us try to live with no regrets because regrets are a waste of what little life you are given. Run, sing, and die fighting for one more breath to laugh with, one more heartbeat to love with."

She leaned forward suddenly and took my face in her hands, kissing me passionately. As she did, she thrust her hips back and forth so hard and rapidly that she brought me very close to a finish. Then she stopped abruptly and stared into my eyes from only a few inches away.

"I never thought I would love, and now that I do, I want our hearts to beat together forever, Brandon," tears formed in her eyes. "I want to live long and die first so I never have to feel anything but how wonderful it is to be with you. We can do that here. We are protected. We can live safely, and raise babies who will also be safe, and grow old beside us… no Grigori, no Angara, no…"

The look in my eyes must have told her something, because she stopped talking and stared at me silently.

"Brandon?" she asked. "What's wrong?"

"I…" I began, nervously, then looked around. "I had a pouch. With a silver thing in it."

"I used the pouch. But I have the silver thing."

She stood instantly and I slipped out of her. She ran inside the cave and rooted through a pile of things she'd put there, found the device and returned quickly. She knelt beside me and looked at the screen as I explained.

"This is a thing the Grigori use to find us," I said. "It's how the Angara tracked you." I pointed. "These red dots are us. You, and me."

She traced the contour of the map on the screen.

"Is this…" she began, struggling to understand, "I have seen others make drawings like this in the sand. Is this the Usuyasa Um?"

"I think so," I said. "I don't know the names of places I only know that this is a map of Pangea. Or part of it. Emibi—the Grigori city I was trapped in—is over here near this bay. This island is where I went with Zash. These are the mountains we came through where you and Hajah escaped."

"Yes," Nova said, getting it. "Sa Fasi is here." She pointed.

"When I was looking for you, I used this. I saw your red dot near Sa Fasi, not moving, and occasionally disappearing. I didn't know what that meant. Maybe you were hiding in caves."

"How does the dot know where I am?" Nova asked.

"I'm not sure," I said, as I looked up at the sky. Satellites seemed out of the question. "When the Angara gave us the common language, they also put a thing inside our heads that tells them where we are."

She touched her forehead, shocked and a little afraid.

"How do we get them out?" she asked.

"I don't know. Milton was working on some ideas. It might be easier just to deactivate them, somehow. Break it so it doesn't send a signal anymore."

"If we can, will my language come back? Will I be able to speak to the people of Sa Fasi again?"

"Interesting question," I said. "I don't know."

I looked at the device once more, front and back, and saw that the cluster of blue dots, which had been following me, were very close, almost beside us. I felt like an idiot for not remembering to check the damn thing sooner.

I took Nova's cheek in my palm.

"I love you, Nova, and I will treasure every moment with you. But we are *not* safe here. Not while these things are in our heads. These blue dots are Angara who must be very close, practically on top of us. We have to go."

She looked momentarily horrified, then saddened, but recovered quickly and smiled.

"Then we go," she said, standing.

I stood beside her and took her hand, intending to move quickly and head immediately out of our little Garden of Eden. But we were stopped by something that shocked us both into immobility.

Standing in the mouth of the cave, as if having just arrived from somewhere inside, stood a man, naked, and tall.

No, not a man, though he looked almost like one.

He was reptilian, nude, skin covered in patterned greens and glistening textures, my height, or bigger; he stood straight and perfectly still, his eyes focused unblinkingly on mine and mine alone.

"Hello," he said.

THE SERPENT MAN

"YOU ARE NOT FROM PANGEA," the newcomer noted, staring directly at me.

I said nothing. Nova moved closer to me, and put an arm around my waist.

"You are not from here," the reptile man said, "are you?"

"No," I admitted, and Nova glanced at me. "No, I'm not."

"He's from Pasadena," she said.

He scowled, apparently not recognizing the name, and slowly nodded.

"We have not had one from outside Pangea since… well… there is no longer any real measurement of time, here, so it's difficult to say. Before the end of recorded history."

"You mean the beginning of recorded history," I corrected.

He stared a moment, then slowly shook his head.

"No, I don't."

We stared a moment longer, he and I, in unmoving silence. Something twitched behind him, and for the first time I noticed his tail. And small wings.

"Who are you?" I asked.

"Someone who wishes to assist you," he said, holding a hand out in front of him. He turned his palm up, and a red ball appeared there that I hadn't been aware of before. "There is information contained inside this that will help you defeat the… defeat the Grigori."

I stood for a while, just staring at the reptile man, then turned my attention to the thing in his hand. It was metallic, about the size of an orange, and entirely smooth. From where I stood it looked like nothing more than a glass sphere; a Christmas tree decoration.

"But... you're a Grigori. Aren't you? A male?"

He nodded. Nova gasped, and moved further behind me.

"We won't need help defeating the... your people," I said, confidently. "We have their reproduction manual, and will simply hunt and kill the rest."

The reptile man shook his head.

"They have knowledge you don't," the new arrival said. "They control Pangea in more ways than simply with those devices in your heads, and in your hand. You *need* this."

He again offered the red ball. I looked at Nova, who returned my stare with equal amounts caution and concern. Neither of us knew whether or not to take his offering. To trust this being.

"I assume it's not dangerous," I said. "You've been watching us for a while, and could have killed us at any time before now, I'm guessing."

His only reply was a slight smile.

"It's not dangerous," he said, simply. "Take it now. Consume its knowledge at any time that is comfortable for you. We offer it only as an aid. Things did not go as planned, and need to be corrected. I think you might be the one to do the correcting."

"What are you..." I began, but he cut me off.

"It's your choice whether to take our assistance, or not. But as long as you do not consume it, the Grigori will have an advantage. They will know things that you do not. Things that can kill you."

Nova looked at me, and decided for us. She stepped forward and cautiously took the sphere, then returned to my side. The reptile man stayed where he was. Curious, she and I examined the sphere very carefully. It seemed to have no buttons, or seams, or any other distinguishing marks.

"How do we...?" I said to our supposed benefactor.

But he was gone.

"What do we do?" Nova asked.

"Take it with us," I said. "We'll decide later. Besides, I don't know how to use it, do you?"

"He said 'consume' it. Does that mean eat it?"

"I can't imagine it does. How would we eat it? And anyway, we need to get going. Is there anything you want to take?"

Nova looked around the little camp, and shook her head.

"Only memories," she said, smiling.

I returned her smile, took her hand and guided her toward the river, both of us paying more attention to the sphere, and the still empty cave than where we were going. We each had both feet in the creek that flowed beside our camp before we saw the Angara hunters on the other side, each of them astride a dinosaur.

"Oh, shit," I whispered.

"You!" The tallest of them said in obvious surprise.

"Kiga?" I said, amazed, pulling Nova's hand and moving her back toward camp, out of the creek, and away from the Angara. I smiled at the big panther man, and tried to be charming. "I didn't think you went hunting anymore."

"You know him?" Nova asked, shocked.

"I do," I said.

"So many slaves escaped in the carnage when the enraged Nyame crashed through that wall," Kiga said, smiling at me, "they had little choice but to send me. I always had a feeling that you were smarter than you pretended to be. And yet, somehow I still liked you. Had I known it was you I was trailing, I would have stayed home."

"You can always go back and pretend we never saw one another," I said, smiling as broadly as him.

He shrugged, and laughed.

"They'll only send someone else. Someone who will probably kill you. You made the Grigori very angry, and worse, you made them frightened. I've never seen them like they are now, the way you left them. They're enraged, and terrified at the same time, taking it out on the other slaves—*and* the Angara—forcing us to search endlessly for this book that you took."

"With any luck, it's been burned by now."

He sighed. "Then it will be bad for us for a very long time."

"Escape them. Start over. If you all rise up..."

"There's no escaping them while they have these," he said, holding out his own GPS and urging his mount forward.

"Maybe before they do I'll find some way to get the thing that tracks me out of my head," I told him. "And whoever they send will never find me."

Kiga stopped. He was just the other side of the little stream.

"What are you talking about?"

I held up the tracking device I had stolen, and showed him.

"Where did you get that?" he asked.

"Off a far less friendly Angara," I answered.

"And far less alive, I'm sure."

"He wasn't very nice to me."

"A mistake I won't make. What are you talking about—what thing in your head?"

"This tracking device works with something the language thing puts inside our skulls when you capture us. The two pieces talk to each other, telling you where we are."

Kiga looked at his own device as if the thought had never occurred to him. I supposed it hadn't.

"Why don't you sit down and have something to eat," I said, "and we'll have ourselves a little talk. A rest break, some food, some laughing, and some understanding. Just to rejuvenate us before we start our journey back."

Kiga stared at me for a moment, turned to his soldiers, the closest one of which just shrugged, and looked at the still burning fire, sniffing.

"Smells good," he said.

"Orthopi," I told him. "And my mate, Nova, is a cook who makes it worth taking the time to focus on a meal."

Kiga and his men all glanced at one another. The apparent lieutenant shrugged again, and casually dismounted, as the others followed his example. They tied up their dinosaurs, and crossed the stream, taking seats on the soft earth, and a nearby fallen tree, close to the fire.

"So tell me about the thing in your head." Kiga said.

"These things in *our* heads," I corrected, indicating all of us, and moving to take a seat near the fire with Nova. "I'm willing to bet they're in your heads, too."

CONVINCING KIGA

"SO THE MAGIC IN IT," Kiga said, indicating the silver box in his hand. "Is that it sees—not us—but the implanted bead."

"Yes," I said. "As long as those are there, you and I can speak the same language, and the Grigori always know where we are."

"Can we take the bead out?"

"I don't know. Would you want to?"

Kiga thought about it, and looked at one of the other Angara, who stared at him, hopefully, but said nothing. So Kiga turned back to me.

"I have an easy life in Emibi," he said, thinking it through. "Because of my injuries, I am warm and generally safe. Crazed, enraged Nyame aside."

I laughed, and he smiled, pleased to have amused me.

"You could still be safe in Emibi," I said. "But do the Grigori have to be there?"

Kiga looked panicked and stood suddenly. The others appeared equally afraid, and glared at me.

Kiga searched around us, examining the skies, moving around the campsite as if waiting nervously for something—something that would come from above. At the center of the clearing he turned and focused on me with fierce intensity.

After a moment, he stared down at the device in his hand.

"What you said has gotten people killed," Kiga told me. "The Grigori cannot hear us, but they still seem to know things…"

He glared at me intently, thinking it through.

"They seem to know when someone means them harm," he concluded.

"Even if they understood what I just said," I told the large Angara, "it was *me* who said it, and it will take them a long time to reach me. In the meantime, just think about how nice it would be to live in Emibi without Grigori."

Kiga said nothing.

"And then think about something else you should know," I said.

I stood myself and walked carefully around so that I was facing Kiga, making sure I stayed more than an arm's length away.

"Do you have a mate, Kiga?" I asked.

"I did," he answered, somewhat confused by the question. "But the Grigori took her to serve them in another city."

"Perhaps," I said. "Perhaps not. Was your wife…" I hesitated, knowing this could go either well, or very badly, knelt beside him and spoke quietly, kindly. "Kiga, I don't know how to ask this without upsetting you. Was your wife… pregnant?"

He scowled and bored his eyes into me angrily. The question had again surprised him.

I proceeded to tell him about my experience in the Grigori temple, and the Angara woman I'd seen there. He said nothing—only stood silently, staring at me with a bubbling fury. When I'd finished my tale, explaining that the Grigori would continue taking pregnant women to eat—including Angara women—the other Angara stood and spoke with obvious concern.

"Kiga! My mate is with child!"

Kiga said nothing, and never stopped glaring at me. Even though I'd been careful to put enough space between us, I'd underestimated the older Angara. His hands were around my neck before I could blink. His fingers so strong and brutal, I nearly blacked out instantly. I heard Nova scream, and Kiga snarl.

"*You LIE!*" he said, unable to face the idea that his wife and child had probably been eaten.

"Do I?" I choked. "You said… yourself! The… human who… helped you. The… Grigori… ate *him*!"

His grip never loosened, and I began to black out.

"They… *like*… human… flesh!" I struggled to get out. "But… *prefer*… unborn… babies…"

I couldn't finish. My eyes flickered with sparks and stars and I felt I was looking at Kiga through a long, dark tunnel. Nova was on his back, biting his ears, and I was falling. Falling.

Fading.

Black.

GOD, THIS GETTING knocked out shit was getting old.

I opened my eyes and found Nova over me, tears in her eyes, pressing moist skins against my face. I sat up quickly and looked around, saw Kiga sitting on the log facing away from us while another Angara spoke to him frantically. The rest of their group huddled around, listening.

"... if he is telling the truth we cannot do *nothing!*" said one.

"I will not see what he described happen to *my* mate! To my *child!*" said another.

"*How can we fight the Grigori?*" Kiga yelled, suddenly, silencing them all.

"You won't have to do it alone," I said. "I have friends in the Chutanga who will help. And I hope to have friends soon in Sa Fasi..."

"You are about to become *king* of Sa Fasi," Nova said.

I stared at her, open-mouthed. I couldn't believe what I was hearing, although the subject had sort of floated around us for a while.

"Yes, Brandon," Nova said, smiling. "Didn't you realize? You'll be able to order the tribe to do whatever you wish."

My mouth worked open and closed, but it wasn't really sinking in.

"Will they follow him?" Kiga asked. He had turned to face us and I saw one of his ears was a ruined, bloody mess. Damn, Nova! That girl *must* love me. "It's one thing to *take* control. It's another to actually *have* it."

"They will!' Nova said, proudly.

"But to follow me willingly, they'll need some time to get used to me," I said. "The point is, Kiga: we can take Emibi, and move one city at a time. I don't know how far distant the Grigori can communicate but it's communication is difficult for them, and it's possible the first city can fall without the others knowing. Possible. And if it is, then each new city will bring more of the races of Pangea to fight by our side without word of the danger being spread. Bust however it works, before long Pangea *can* be united, and the Grigori *will* fall."

"Big words for a naked man living in a garden."

"Have you got a better offer?" I said.

"I just want to save my mate," the other Angara said. "Anything more is *your* war."

A few other panther men nodded, murmuring agreement.

"No, the rest is *yours* as well," I said. "You fight, or they will find you. Maybe not *this* child, but the next will be eaten along with your mate. Maybe the Grigori won't care that they've been discovered, and just be more open about their dietary interests. This need they have to consume unborn children and mothers borders on the obsessive, for whatever reason. So they're still going to take your women—at the very least *some* of your women—and they're still going to use them for fine dining, because once you've tasted the forbidden fruit..."

Kiga said nothing.

"We found a Chutanga woman in the temple, " I continued, "and you know the Chutanga are supposed to be off-limits. The Grigori know no restrictions. Unless you get rid of them, they *will* eat your wives!"

"Once word gets out, it will be harder to control the Angara," Kiga said.

"Harder, but not impossible unless you *fight*," I said. "*That* is your only option. But know this: we *can* win. Together we are stronger than they are, and we know that not all their magic is really *magic*." I held up the device. "It's mechanical. Technological. It is something that can be stopped, blocked, and conquered."

The little campsite fell silent for a moment while the Angara considered my words.

"I will fight with you," one of the Angara said. "I am Garga, and I will fight by your side."

I smiled, as did Nova. She took my arm, obviously proud.

"Is it possible my mate and child…" Kiga began, but lowered his head, and simply shook it. "I will fight with you, Brandon the Mack. Not that it will do either of us much good."

"You will do me the most good," I said, surprising him. "You are liked and respected in Emibi. You can get me to the queen… and if you do, we can take Emibi with a single stroke, then make that city our base from which to make war on the other Grigori cities."

"I HAVE TO GO BACK to Emibi," I told Nova, "right away, after I get you home. With or without the men of Sa Fasi. I have no idea how long I've been gone, or how long before Elia is taken from Milton. I need to help them, before the war, if necessary."

"Brandon,…"

"I *have* to, Nova. Milton's my friend, and he needs to know what they're planning to do to the woman he loves, and the child he so desperately wants."

She leaned her head against my chest. I felt her reservation, and reluctance. But eventually she put her arms around me, and hugged me sweetly.

"Then you must go," she said.

"I'll take you back to Sa Fasi, first, and then when this is all over," I told her, pulling her chin up so I could look into her sad eyes, "we'll come back here, to our little Garden of Eden."

She smiled.

"I will hunt you down if you don't."

I smiled back. "I know you will."

Nova lost her grin, lowered her head, her eyes hidden from my view. She sniffed, and began to shake her head.

"You are so stupid," she said, sadly, then threw her arms around me and held tight. "You think you know everything, and you know nothing; you're going to die, and I'm going to lose you."

I held her tightly and cooed in her ear.

"Sssssshhh," I said, softly. "I'm not going to die. Not while I have you to protect me."

"But I'm not going to be there! You're leaving me in Sa Fasi!"

"I thought you'd prefer to be home with your family while I made this trip."

She shook her head against my chest.

"Fine, then," I said. "Come with me. But not until I can claim you in front of your father, your friends, and Gudra's brothers."

"No man claims me," she said, smiling. "But if you want to *accept* me in front of everyone, then I'll let you."

I laughed, and Kiga moved closer.

"I've spoken with Garga and the others," he said. "A few don't want to wait to go back to Emibi. Their wives are well through their pregnancies. I'm not sure how much further I can go on, anyway, because of my pain, so I will head back with them."

"I really need you to help plan the attack on Emibi," I said.

"Sa Fasi is not much further," Nova promised.

Kiga considered, then looked over at Garga, who held up his hands impatiently, palms to the sky. Kiga turned his eyes down, seemed to wince at some ache or other, and sighed.

"All right," Kiga said. "But I will need to rest before long." He grinned, charmingly. "I am not the Angara I used to be."

"None of us are what we used to be," I said.

WE CROSSED A WIDE, but shallow river, passed over the mountains beyond, and tracked carefully through a deep, and tangled wood, until we finally came out on a vast, level plain that stretched away in all directions, curving upward into distant forests and azure ocean.

"I stayed here in these woods while deciding what to do about Gudra," Nova said.

"Where?" I asked. "In a cave?"

"Once. Mostly I slept in trees. I didn't want to go too deep because these forests are haunted. Everyone knows you should not go into them."

"Why?" I asked.

"It's a bad place. Many people who suffer some severe pain, or other come here to commit suicide. Others get hopelessly lost and die alone."

I stepped closer to the darkened wood and saw no difference to any other forest we'd gone through.

"Sometimes," I said, "back where I come from, heavy magnetic activity or other kinds of natural energy could make a place *feel* dangerous. It often seemed to affect people, mentally. Can you show me the cave where you stayed?"

Nova looked nervous, and hesitated.

I smiled at her and held out my hand.

"I'll be with you the whole time," I said, trying to sound comforting. "Along with Kiga and…"

But Kiga shook his head.

"Everyone knows about this forest," he said firmly, adamantly refusing to move.

I have to admit, I was shocked. It was the first time I'd encountered any real superstition since coming to this stone age world. Nova had always been open to ideas, and willing to learn. But even now, though she took my hand and moved forward with me, I could tell she really didn't want to.

"There was a time when your dot disappeared from the GPS device," I told her. "And if these forests have some kind of natural magnetic activity, maybe that's why. Maybe we can find a way to block the effects of the things in our heads."

"The cave I used is there," she said pointing, and halting. "I went there because one of Gudra's brothers had gotten close, and I was afraid he'd find me. Otherwise I wouldn't have gone so far into the forest—or the cave."

She hesitated, and I didn't want to make her go any further. But I *had* to go on. There was a definite prickly sensation in the air, and even I began to feel a bit nervous.

I moved closer to the cave, and the energetic sensation increased. My skin felt as though it had a mild electric charge running through it. I turned back to Nova.

"I can definitely feel something weird," I told her. "How far into the cave did you go?"

She looked at me oddly, then shook her head and pointed toward her ear.

"Nik tiagga shok fon."

I stood completely still and felt momentarily lost. She didn't understand me, and I certainly didn't understand her. The common language we'd shared was gone. I looked around frantically, searching for an answer. There was nothing obvious—rocks, mud, plants, weird insects. All the usual Pangean stuff.

I knelt closer to the earth and noticed the stones seemed to be shinier, and more metallic looking. I picked up one of the smaller rocks and studied it. I wasn't a geologist, but I'd be willing to bet it contained some kind of magnetized metal.

Maybe.

I took the stone back to where Nova stood.

"Do you know anything about this type of rock," I asked.

She only shook her head.

"Nik tiagga shok fon, a la solanda."

The idea that I couldn't be understood by Nova startled me, and scared me more than a little. I glanced over at Kiga, who was as surprised as I was that *he* couldn't understand me either. He pulled out his GPS device and looked at the tiny screen. After a moment of adjusting, he pointed at the thing and looked at me, shaking his head.

"Ashaga tudok ma. Nazzennzi, ta."

I pulled out my device, and saw that all dots had vanished from the screen. I smiled at the others, all thoroughly confused, then carefully tossed the stone aside almost to where I'd picked it up, but where I could see it and retrieve it if needed.

I looked at the GPS. All the dots had returned.

"How about now?" I asked, looking around at all of them. "Can you understand me, now?"

Nova breathed a heavy sigh of relief, and nearly laughed. She grabbed me and held tight.

"Yes, Brandon. I can understand you."

Kiga smiled, as well.

"The Grigori can no longer follow us," he said, understanding the implications.

"The downside is, we can't communicate," I told him. "But we'll work around that. For now, this is big."

I told them what we were going to do, and how we might be able to make this work for us, and they all understood. I grabbed the rock and we headed off again toward Sa Fasi.

WE CROSSED THE OPEN savanna beyond the white cliffs and headed toward what Nova called "the Mountain to The Clouds" that flanked the indescribably blue waters of the Usayasu Um.

We were halfway across the immense plain when we saw two enormous Brontosaurus-like dinosaurs approaching from a distance in the direction of Nova's home, Sa Fasi. They were immense beasts, forty or fifty feet long, with tiny heads at the end of very long necks that must have been a good twelve to twenty feet above the ground. The lumbering behemoths moved very slowly, but their strides covered so much territory that they were getting closer to us at a very good clip.

Eventually we could see that each animal had at least one rider. Nova gripped my shoulder knowing I couldn't understand her while I held the magnetic rock, and smiled as she stepped forward holding up a hand, and waving.

"HOOOO! Hilleeeyyaaaa! Shenk Novaada no turon!"

One of the riders answered her in return, with a wave and a smile, leaning out to be seen from behind one of the others, laughing with delight.

"Shenk Novaada no turon, Naga!" he said, and I felt a twinge of jealousy.

But not nearly as much as I did when Nova leaned forward in shock, recognized the speaker, and her voice went shrill with joy and excitement.

"Naga! Naga aiala sobroto!"

Squealing in a way that would have been unintelligible in any language, she ran over as the huge, muscled, stunningly handsome man dropped from the back of his dinosaur and ran over to her. I was nearly ripped apart by confused emotions when she leaped into his arms, and he hugged her naked body a little too tightly for my tastes, then swung her around in an enormous circle, laughing with her, and kissing her forehead and cheek.

"Come over here," I heard her say. "I want you to meet Brandon, my mate!"

I guess she'd gone far enough from the magnetic stone to escape its affect. The tall, handsome 'dude' looked at her with a scowl, and spoke something that obviously expressed his confusion at no longer being able to understand her. She just waved a hand and shook her head, motioning for him to come with her and be patient.

"Brandon, this is Naga mia sobroto," she said, getting back to within range of the stone at precisely the wrong moment.

This is *who*? I desperately wanted to know. *Who*? An old friend? Classmate? Preferred sex toy?

I glanced down and saw that—unfortunately for me—there was a lot to this guy. The next size up in loincloth might be called for.

Nova spoke to me in more of the language I couldn't understand, then waved it off when she realized I wasn't getting a word of it. She turned back to the big, tall, handsome dude and spoke exclusively and rapidly to him. He seemed very excited to hear everything she had to say, and I watched her mime many of the exploits we'd shared over the past—well—God only knew how long. Then he explained what *he* had been doing while *she* had been away—pleasuring lots of grateful women, no doubt. I just shook my head and glanced at Kiga. He gave what is apparently a universal expression for 'fuck if I know' and just shrugged.

Nova then took the rock from my hand and explained it to her gorgeous friend, walked a good distance away to set it down, and returned.

"And now you can't understand me, can you?" she said to him, giggling.

Playing his part, he held his hands out, palms up, and shook his head. Nova just laughed harder, which made him smile, then she took his hand and leaned in under his arm, placing an affectionate hand on his chest, which made my blood boil.

"Brandon, this is my little brother, Naga," she said, and I almost instantly calmed.

"I hope incest is frowned upon in Pangean society," I said, smiling.

Nova's face registered surprise, then she glanced at Naga, stepped back from him and laughed so hard I thought she might pass out. Then she looked at me with the sweetest, most loving expression I've ever seen on another human face.

"Brandon," she said, walking over to me and putting her arms around my neck. "You're *jealous*."

"Maybe," I said.

"Oh, my God, you really *do* love me," she said, quietly.

"Was there ever any doubt?" I asked.

She kissed me sweetly, and softly, and I felt her whole heart blend with mine.

"No," she said, with delight. "But I still like that I mean so much to you."

"Always."

She kissed me again, until Naga cleared his throat, and Nova stepped back from me, holding out an arm to the group.

"Brandon, Kiga... this is Naga, The Mighty, and his friends from the tribe of the Hilleya. They tame and ride the giant Hilladi, and were just going out again in search of me."

She smiled warmly at her brother.

"They came far for him," she said, proudly. "All the way from their home at the edge of the Place of Endless Dark."

"The Place of Endless Dark?" I asked.

"The country which lies beneath the Dead Ball," replied Nova; "the Dead Ball which hangs forever between the sun and Pangea, casting a constant shadow over the land... the Place of Endless Dark."

I had no idea what she meant, obviously, because I'd never been to that part of Pangea.

I noticed a pleasant, focused look from a woman on the back of the dinosaur Naga had dismounted, and wondered if there might have been more than Nova as a motivation for coming all this way to assist her brother.

"I'm going to get the stone, now, Brandon," Nova said, sweetly. "I'm going to explain to Naga and the Hilleyans your plan for fighting back against the Grigori, so you won't be able to understand me for the remainder of the trip." And here, she fixed me with a sly grin. "Try not to be *too* jealous."

I gave her an amused sneer as she walked over to get the now annoying rock, and Naga stepped over to me, threw an arm around my shoulder and smiled right in my face, saying something that probably amounted to "Welcome to the family!"

After a journey, which, for Pangea, was fairly uneventful, we came to the first of the Sa Fasi villages. It was built into the face of a giant cliff and consisted of between one and two hundred carved-out caves. As we neared the base of the mountain, dozens of Sa Fasi—or Nyala—they lived in Sa Fasi, they *were* the Nyala—it was confusing—began climbing down ladders or lowering themselves on ropes with cheers of delight and greeting. As the happy tribes people surrounded their beloved princess, delighted to see her so appreciated, I slowly backed away to give her space, and was surprised to hear someone call my name.

"Brandon!"

Turning around I was absolutely floored to see Milton, and Bruk coming up behind me.

"MILTON!" I yelled, grabbing the old man and hugging him tightly. "How the hell did *you* get here?"

"We found the skins you hid, and used your plan!" he said, proudly.

"But, Milton…" I said, grinning, meaning to give him some serious shit about his easily changing morals, but he interrupted me with an explanation that horrified me.

"They took Elia," he told me, tears welling in his eyes.

I nearly fainted. I'd taken too long, and it had cost my friend the woman he loved, the child he *would* love.

"They said they needed to care for her, because of her pregnancy, but I began to worry that they had other plans in mind—one of the books contained some very unsettling things, Brandon, they…"

Tears were streaming down his cheeks and I was agonizing along with him. If I'd hurried. If I hadn't had to fight Gudra. If I hadn't delayed with Nova in our perfect little garden…

I took hold of his shoulders and swore a promise I hoped, more than believed, I would keep.

"We'll find her," I said. "Milton, I swear to you…"

"Brandon, I think…"

But he didn't finish. He saw the look of horror in my face, realizing it wasn't because of Elia… it was because of who was standing behind him.

Hajah.

"What the fuck is *he* doing here?" I snarled.

Milton turned to see who I was glaring at, and instantly tried to calm me.

"He discovered our plan," Milton said quickly. "We had to bring him or he said he'd expose us."

"He was actually very helpful in our escape," Bruk said. *"Never stick your arm down the throat of an Araga when it's licking you."*

Without another word I walked straight for him. He had the good sense to back away, because I immediately grabbed an axe out of the hand of a man from Nova's tribe.

"Brandon!" Milton called, following me.

"I'm going to split his fucking skull," I said, as Hajah turned and ran.

I was about to chase him down when the murmur of the crowd grew beyond the general excitement of Nova's return, and even my attempted murder, into something darker, and more fearful. One woman screamed.

Because something entirely unexpected had just arrived.

A flock of Grigori stood at the edge of the plain. No one had seen them fly in, nor had anyone noticed the arrival of their immense Angara guard.

Nova had told me the Nyala people had never been conquered precisely because you could only approach their villages from across those expansive grasslands. It couldn't be done without being seen. Even if you were flying.

And yet, here was an army of Grigori, and Angara soldiers.

Several dozen Ingonghu swirled about the enemy legion, and a few dropped to the ground in a loose row, very near the queen, my queen, the one who'd crawled around inside my mind and tried to rip it open.

She stared at me directly, leaped quickly into the air and covered the distance between us in less than a second. No more than five feet from me, she continued to stare at me intensely, took a few jerky steps to one side, then the other, never removing her furious gaze from mine.

Suddenly a knife-like pain split my skull, and I went to my knees, dropping the axe. Nova screamed and ran over to kneel beside me, but there was no comfort she could offer to reduce the suffering. It was the Grigori. Not just invading my head with thoughts, but outright attacking me.

You are the one who stole the book. AND you are the one who killed your betters in the Chutanga temple.

"I dispute the term 'betters'," I said.

Nova looked around, wondering who I was talking to, then saw I had locked eyes with the Grigori queen. She grabbed the stone I apparently still held in my hand, and threw it aside.

"What's happening, my love," she asked. "Who are you talking to?"

"The queen," I said, still staring at the thing whose mind was squirming around inside my head.

"She's *talking* to you?"

Where is the book? the voice splitting my brain demanded.

"I have no idea what you're talking about, you ugly, reptoid bitch," I snarled. "Now get out of my skull!"

No. Give us the book, or I will kill you and move on to the old man.

Fighting the searing agony behind my eyes, I stood, and glared at the hideous beast. She was fully four feet taller than me, and I'd already seen how quickly and viciously a Grigori could move when provoked. But there was something in her eyes, something in her 'voice'. She was scared, and her decision to 'speak' to me again only made that more clear. Touching the mind of a human was obviously distasteful—perhaps even painful. It's why they preferred to do their talking through the Angara.

"I will give you nothing," I said, holding out my hands in invitation. "Now, kill me if you can."

She moved so fast and so savagely that I barely got out of the way in time. Her mouth snapped with a loud, searing *smack* in the air where I had just stood, and she wasn't done. As I rolled to one side, in a direction away from the now screaming Nova, the Grigori queen followed me, biting and rending the spaces I had just vacated instants behind my frantic movements.

She'd caught me off guard. She was much faster than I could have imagined and it nearly cost me my life. Thinking fast I saw Naga moving in with a spear. Leaping and dodging to avoid the Grigori's attacks I danced his way and yanked the spear from his grasp, then turned just as the Grigori reached me and closed her fanged mouth around my upper torso.

Shoving for all I was worth, I jammed the spear into the roof of her mouth where it broke through and out the top of her beak, right between her beady, orange eyes. Shrieking in pain, she chewed on me with her lower jaw, snapping the bottom of the spear, and opening some of the wounds I'd gotten from Gudra. Blood seemed to be flowing out of me in a torrent, and I genuinely feared for my life.

But so did the Grigori fear for hers.

The bottom of the spear had wedged inside her mouth, and until I died, she was trapped because I held onto the thing with all the strength I had. She could not open her mouth to dislodge me, she couldn't close it enough to kill me.

Stalemate.

I watched as her eyes darted about fearfully, waiting for someone to come to my aid—or hers. To one side I saw Bruk preparing to step in, and I was fairly sure that Naga, and Nova were planning the same.

The queen knew she was dead. And more. Garga stepped forward, axe in hand.

Even the Angara. She said. *They all begin to look upon you as a leader.*

The thought surprised and confused me, but I had no time to consider it.

Without warning I was in the air, and the Grigori was carrying me as easily as I would carry a doll. Her massive wings beat the wind ferociously, and glancing down I saw the other Grigori and Angara move in to attack the people of Sa Fasi, the Brontosaurs' of the Hilleyans charging forward, and my beloved Nova in the middle. I cried out in terror. The upsetting vision ripped me in two, and was shrinking so fast that in seconds I could no longer see it—except in my horrified mind.

"*Brandon,* NOOOOOOOOOOOOOO!!" I heard Nova's distant voice scream.

227

THE DREAM ENDS

THE GRIGORI FLEW AS IF possessed. Sa Fasi became a colored blur far below, the plains blazing by beneath me, then the forest, then the mountains. In what seemed like no time I saw Emibi—at least I think it was Emibi—appear in the distance, and very quickly it wasn't in the distance anymore. We were flying through the gates, over the heads of humans and Angara, so fast I couldn't see how we didn't crash into anything. Then the queen skidded to a stop on the broken, concrete street, falling forward, and cracking my skull on the smooth surface.

But I held on.

Again, she stood and looked around for help from others. But none came. No slave moved, no Angara offered aid.

The terrified Grigori queen pounded me once more into the concrete, but I held fast, so she took once more to the air, flying crazy-fast into a tunnel, down long, darkening corridors, down, down, down, into a shaft that could have housed an elevator and seemed to go deep, deep into the depths of the planet. Deeper than I'd known you could go. I wondered if we would come out on the outer surface of Earth.

Then suddenly she landed, hard again, in a small chamber.

She lifted herself, and me, stumbling toward something that looked like a computer terminal that filled a wall. Very rapidly her fingers tapped a keypad beneath a reflective surface, and a door behind me opened with a swish. The queen lurched forward, still clamping her mouth tightly around me, and we entered a room filled with electronic equipment far more sophisticated than the little GPS devices.

Moving very quickly the Grigori raced to a lighted panel, tapped in more instructions, then stepped quickly over to a flat pad in the center of the room, slamming me on top of it.

LET GO! She commanded.

"NO!" I yelled.

She smashed me down again, even harder, over and over and over. I felt myself weakening.

LET GO! She repeated, so angrily my skull nearly exploded.

"NOOOOO!" I shrieked.

More slamming, but instead of releasing the spear and doing as she wanted, I jerked the shaft, then shoved it upward, hard, ripping the hole in her top beak even wider. Now it was her turn to shriek.

The two of us stopped struggling and lay on the pad at a complete impasse, both of us breathing hard, both of us bleeding profusely.

You won't die. Just let go. She said. It sounded almost like a plea.

"No," I answered, simply.

I won't harm you. I just want you to go away.

"Well, too bad."

I could feel frustration and fear from the Grigori. Her wings lifted purposelessly, then settled again. With her exhaustion her mind relaxed its control over me. My head began to clear. I looked around at the room, amazed at the sophistication of the equipment surrounding me. Screens and monitors filled with images of Pangea—the Place of Endless Dark, the Chutanga Islands, a metallic sphere in space, the plains of Sa Fasi, where a massive battle now raged. Brontosaurs, mounted Angara, pterodactyls, and Grigori, all fighting for their lives.

I guess in my astonishment I must have loosened my grip because the Grigori suddenly sprung away, and though the spear was still lodged in her mouth, she moved fast and was free of me. In a split second she was standing at a panel near the pad, her fingers wiggling, and not realizing what she was doing I stood where I was, crouched and ready for another attack.

But it didn't come. Instead my world hazed and blurred, and suddenly I was standing on another pad—a different pad—inside a different room with different equipment, and different lighting.

There were men in lab coats, one wearing glasses, all staring at me.

"Brandon?" a familiar voice said.

I turned to that voice, and saw the last person in the world I expected to be standing there.

"Lena?" I said.

She was plainly as stunned to see me standing there as I was to see her. I looked around trying to understand, but I couldn't. What had happened? Where was I? Was this APL?

No answers came, and only questions rained down on me.

Had I ever left APL? Was I part of some experiment? Had I...

"Nova?" I asked.

"What?" Lena said.

"Nova." I felt tears forming in my eyes. "Where's Nova?"

My mind reeled at the horrifying thought that I had been part of some holographic experiment, or test, or mind-fuck, and that none of it had been real. That the woman I loved so passionately, so fiercely, hadn't been real.

"Brandon," Lena said, gently. "Where did you come from?"

I looked at her. And it hit me. I had been there. And now I was back.

"Pangea," I said. "I came from Pangea, and I need you to send me back. *SEND ME BACK!*"

The look in her eyes said everything I needed to know. Nova was real, I had been inside the hollow sphere of the Earth... but Lena had no idea how to return me to that world. To *my* world.

To Nova.

"YOU HAVE TO FIGURE it out," I said over a cup of coffee. The first I'd had in almost a year, apparently. "You have to send me back. The Grigori were attacking... Nova... Elia is pregnant and they're going to eat her. I have to help. You can't tell me there's no way back to them."

"Brandon," Lena said, patiently. "I don't know if *any* of it is even *real.*"

"It is real. It is. Look at my wounds. My scars."

"But you could have gotten those any number of ways. And if we're following the logic of your story, we an understand you. You're not speaking any alien, Grigori, slave language."

She was right. I hadn't considered that. I was speaking English. And being understood.

"You fell through Milton's floor into my lab and landed on that pad... activated it somehow. It was terrifying. The drill spinning, grinding, wires sparking and exploding everywhere, and then... you vanished. There was that all enveloping, blinding flash that you described as well, and you were gone. We had no idea where you were, or what had happened. You were both just... *gone.* Maybe you went into some kind of entertainment device..."

"Like a video game?" I asked.

"It's more likely than that the Earth is hollow."

"No," I said. "No. It wasn't a... it was real."

She said nothing.

"Where did the pad come from?" I asked.

Lena sat opposite me, and the technicians she now apparently worked with all stood or sat around the room paying complete and focused attention.

"We found it in the Yucatan," she told me, "investigating the asteroid collision that killed the dinosaurs."

"The dinosaurs aren't dead."

"Yes," she said, tentatively. "So you said. Brandon, are you sure about what happened? Your wounds are incredible, but maybe..."

"I know. You don't believe me. But I don't care. I just want to get back to Nova."

She looked hurt.

"Who's Nova?" she asked.

"My ma—my wife. Nova is my wife."

Lena stared at me silently and I thought I saw real pain in her eyes.

"Just send me back," I said. "I have to get back to her. She was right in the middle of a *war*..."

Still, Lena said nothing. I set down the empty coffee cup, and walked back to the pad.

"Just turn it on. Send me back."

"Brandon, we don't even know how it works..."

"Please," I said, hot tears in my eyes. "You can't tell me there's no way back to her. Please, Lena."

She only stared at me, silently, as did all her technicians.

"Please?" I begged.

A. P. L. HAD APPARENTLY DECIDED I was incredibly valuable—too valuable to let wander around unsupervised, and though the cops wanted me downtown and booked for manslaughter, they had apparently been outranked. I was a prisoner inside Lena's office at APL. I wanted to see my mother. See my sister. Let them know I was alive, but no one would let me call or leave.

All I ever saw was the inside of that one room, the two cops, a rotation of APL guards, some nameless high-ranking agent who never said a word, a couple of technicians, Dr. Lena Mizellier, and her husband, or ex-husband—I was never entirely clear—Dr. Iain Pompaneau.

Not that I had any satisfying answers for them, but they kept hoping that maybe some memory, or recalled moment would click things into focus about the pad and what it was really for. I was telling them my story for the eight hundredth time when Dr. Pompaneau, the doughy prick who was really in charge of the pad thing, asked me to go over the part where I'd been sent back to APL one more time.

"I've told you," I said.

"Tell us again," he said.

"I'm not going to tell you anything different than I did the last time."

"Really?" he shuffled through some papers. "Because you've told it differently *every* time. Once the Grigori queen slammed your head four times. Once three times. Another time she bashed you into a wall. At the end she activated a panel on the wall. In three earlier versions she wiggled her fingers near the pad on which you stood."

"Really?" I said, surprised. "But… I'm telling you the truth."

"We know you are," Lena said.

232

"Especially about the parts where you had sex with Nova but not with Nala," Pompaneau said, snarkily.

I glared at him, confused by his remark, then looked from him, to Lena, but she wouldn't make eye contact with me.

"Lena?" I said.

"Brandon," she replied, still not looking at me, "you have to understand our point of view. You see a play called *Beasts* and then you enter a world where you become—and fight with—beasts. We looked into it. The play has a lot of parallels to your story. Lost in a strange world. Speaking different languages. Animals that strip you naked. Having sex in front of an audience…"

"I'd… forgotten about that," I admitted.

"You even used the word 'danced' at one point when talking about your actions avoiding the Grigori," Pompaneau said with a sneer. He was entirely too pleased to be taking me apart. "So let's start this over, one more time. State your name, please."

"Fuck you," I said.

"Brandon, please?" Lena said.

"Why are you pushing me?"

"Brandon," she repeated. *"Please! It's the only thing keeping you out of jail!"*

I sighed heavily and closed my eyes in frustration. I felt tears over a dead man I'd hated enough to kill.

"I didn't mean to do that. I am *so* sorry I killed him—my God what I would do to get it back, but I was defending myself. He kept hitting me, and hitting me, and…"

I looked around and saw no one cared. No one except Lena, who seemed near to tears, herself.

"You know what?" I said, quietly, barely containing my anger, my sadness, my fear, my horror, my guilt, my raw, frayed emotions about Nova, and if she was even real, if I was I insane, if I was I not, "Bruk was real, and Bruk was right. *'Life is short, then you die.' 'Life is a race that no one wins.' 'Live before you die, because you will die.'"*

No one said anything in reply, so I continued.

"My name is **Brandon Mack**," I snapped because I *couldn't* contain it any longer. "I *went* to Pangea, I *fought* dinosaurs, I *befriended* Bruk, and Elia, and Kiga, I *loved* Nova, and you know what? Life *is* too goddam short. I told you about it, already. Several times. And I am done talking about it."

I fell silent, determined to say not another word. Everyone waited for a while, until they realized I was serious, then Pompaneau wiped his face with his hands, and moaned.

"And you think you have that choice?" he asked through his fingers. "That you can just stop talking?"

I said nothing. He lifted his head and scowled at me.

"You belong to me, Mack," the fat prick said. "Whether you speak again or not… until *I* say otherwise."

I leaned back in my chair, with an expression of 'who gives a fuck' branded into my face.

"You want to see your mother again?" he asked. "Your sister?"

That got me, and he knew it.

"You have to go through me. And to go through me, you have to talk. You have to tell your story again."

"And what's my ultimate end, here? At what point am I done having to talk to your fat ass?"

"Is that a serious question?" the prick asked, irritated.

"Yes, it's a serious fucking question!" I yelled.

"Brandon, calm down," Lena pleaded. "I'm begging you..."

"Fuck you, calm down! I need to get back! There is a real urgency here that you do NOT seem to understand..."

I guess I'd gotten a little out of control, and now it was time for the cops to get involved, because the local policeman who'd first figured out I was still hiding in Milton's machine over a year ago leaned forward into the light, with his best 'good cop' routine.

"Mr. Mack, this is important. We need to..."

"This is *NOT* important, okay?" I snapped. *"NONE* of this! You just *think* it's important! That all this *bullshit* is important! But it's not! Your little jobs, your little worries about bills, about fashion, about Netflix, and Wi-Fi... about what dumbass restaurant to go to! I have very little time, okay, and you are *wasting* it! Nova needs me, and I need to get back to her!"

"Tell us about Nova?" Lena said, plainly trying to get me back to calm.

"Oh, fucking hell," I said, more frustrated than ever. "I *told* you about Nova."

"Help us to understand..." Good cop said.

"Screw your understanding! Let's go back to the pad..."

"There *are* some inconsistencies in your story that..."

"You disappear for nearly a year..." Pompaneau interjected, apparently feeling he was the only one who could get this back under control, "just *vanish* with a billion dollars worth of equipment to God knows where—then suddenly *reappear*, without that equipment—claiming you were *inside* the Earth, which—contrary to all known laws of physics, astrophysics, and common sense—is *hollow like a frickin' beach ball and filled with dinosaurs...*"

"I claim nothing. I told you what happened, and you don't believe me. The problem is on your side."

"You think all that really happened?"

"I KNOW it happened!"

And that's when the jackass laughed at me. Just... fucking... laughed.

"Jesus, man, seriously?" he said, condescension dripping from every syllable. "And you can't see how maybe your story is just the *teensiest* bit unbelievable? How you went off and lived some wild fantasy life in a land of eternal sunshine, and panther men, and monsters, and evil, flying lizards... a place where you met some sexy little slut named *'Nova'* who liked to run around naked, and play with tiny horsies, and tyrannosaurs, and your *dick,* especially..."

And that was it. I'd had enough. I shoved my end of the table, which was exactly opposite Pompaneau's, slamming it directly into his fat chest. Something cracked and he screamed, falling backward a bit until his body had slipped partly under the table, and his chin was resting on its surface. I kept on shoving until his lard ass was pinned against the far wall of the interrogation room and pressing against his neck.

He gurgled and choked out more screams, his face pale and horrified, as I came quickly around the table for him.

"NO!" he yelled. *"Please! Don't hurt me! DON'T HURT ME!"*

I stopped only a foot or so away from him, my fist raised, fully intending to pummel him into unconsciousness, or worse. He was lucky I came to my senses and stopped before showing him how short life could really be.

"So..." said the 'good cop' with a grin, "tell us again how you didn't *mean* to lose control and kill that kid."

I turned to him, and felt my face fall. I had—by once again acting on instinct—made my situation infinitely worse.

THE TRUTH

TWO GUARDS STAYED to keep an eye on me, but the others had all finally gone, leaving me alone with Lena.

"It's okay," she said to one of the guards. "You can wait outside."

The men looked at one another, looked at me, then did as she asked. And just like that, we were alone, her standing nearby, me slumped over the table I'd tried to ram through Pompaneau's chest, handcuffed to a chair. I shook my head and rested my forehead on the polished surface. How had I become my own worst enemy? I was never going to get back to Nova. If Nova was even real.

"She has to be real," I whispered to myself, surprising both Lena and I that I had even spoken.

The room became quiet again for what seemed to me a really, *really* long time before she finally sat in a chair beside me, put a hand over the back of mine, and spoke.

"I'm starting to believe in your Nova," she said.

I continued my silence, my forehead still pressed against the table, then finally, reluctantly, spoke.

"Really?" I said, not convinced.

"It's hard to accept that there could be such passion tied up in a hologram, or an hallucination. You talk about her with such… love."

I lifted my face, and stared at her, wanting to believe. The prevailing hypothesis was that I had fallen onto some lost, alien artifact that provides a holographic entertainment experience for the user—after somehow disintegrating said user and uploading their physicality and consciousness. It didn't answer all the questions, like how I was scarred, or why something as complex as a disintegration process was needed for 'entertainment'. But it made more sense to them than that I'd been inside a hollow Earth. Go figure.

Lena smiled at me, and I returned a weak smile of my own. She patted my hand and stood, taking up her purse to go.

"Would you like to stay with me, tonight?" she asked. "At my place?"

"They'd allow that?" I asked.

"Well… there would be guards outside. But only outside."

I studied her, and realized it was a sexual offer. I shook my head.

"You know…" she said, treading carefully, "Iain and I are officially divorced, now. For some time, actually."

I stared at her blankly. Hadn't she been listening to my story? Hadn't she heard everything I'd said about Nova? Repeatedly?

"Thanks," I said. "But, no. They've brought me a cot. Not that I'll use it."

She stared a long time in silence. Then her eyes showed a deep sadness.

"You should sleep," she offered, sounding genuinely concerned.

At last she walked away from me, across the office, and opened the door to leave. She paused with her fingers on the handle.

"It does make me wonder if you could have loved me with that same intensity," she said before exiting, and closing the door behind her.

I sat in the dim light and silence for quite a while, trying to understand everything that had happened to me. Nothing made sense. Nothing made *more* sense. I'd been there. To Pangea. I'd really known an actual woman named Nova.

Hadn't I?

I stood and walked over to climb atop the pad for maybe the thousandth time since my return, dragging the chair I was cuffed to with me. Standing quietly atop the center, I tried to think of anything that might get it to work. I searched the room and scraped through my brain once more about my last moments in Pangea. Closing my eyes I fought away memories of Nova screaming up at me, terrified for me, afraid of losing me—the thing she'd told me she feared most.

This room had a pad, but none of the equipment from that other room—the one the Grigori queen had sent me from. I'd seen her activate things, and then watched as she …

"Oh, my God…" I said.

I ran to the exit, stumbling with my ball and chain wooden chair, and threw the door wide. Lena was at the far end of the hall, nearly out the building in the direction of the parking lot. She turned at the sound of her office door banging against the wall. Both guards were still there, turned and pulled their guns from their holsters, pointing them directly at me.

"*LENA!*" I called, cocking my head, summoning her toward me, then ran back inside to stand once more on the pad.

I shattered the chair against its surface, still cuffed, but less constrained, and jumped over the links so my hands were in front of me as the guard ran over, gun still drawn and pointed at my nose.

"Hey, *hey!*" he said. "Stop that!"

I ignored him, and knelt, pressing my palms and fingertips to the smooth, polymer surface of the weird pad, replaying my last moments in Pangea before the Grigori sent me home.

Lena raced back in through the door with more guards behind her, their guns also still drawn.

"Tell him to stop doing that!" the guard nearest to me yelled, speaking to Lena, but aiming at me.

"Come around here to the opposite side of the thing," I told Lena.

"Why?" she asked, doing so.

"When I arrived, you were all on *that* side, and I was associating it with the same side the Grigori had used. It wasn't. This is."

I pointed to where she was walking.

"Get off of there!" the guard yelled.

"In a minute," I said, hoping I'd never be getting off the pad, ever again.

"But the sides are all the same," Lena said, ignoring the man with the gun, stopping where I'd told her. "There's no difference."

"No, there is!"

"Get down from there," the guard snapped, stepping closer and pointing angrily. "*Now!*"

"It's like you told me once last year," I said to Lena, calming my voice, hoping it would settle the guard, "about sifting through the information from WISE, sorting out all that satellite imagery. Finding difference in a lot of things that look the same. It's easier to see from my angle up here, but you'll get it. Look carefully."

She did, touching its smooth surface, bending over and examining it from the side.

"It's slightly raised," she said, getting it.

"That's the control panel," I told her.

She pulled her hand back like she'd been burned.

"Are you sure?"

I smiled, and nodded.

"Listen!" the guard yelled, now focusing on Lena. "Stop messing with that thing. Stop doing what he tells you! I mean it!"

"But how do we turn it on?" she asked me, ignoring him.

"It's already on. It was on when Milton and I fell on it while we were inside the mole, and somehow activated it. This is the remote pad. I'm guessing it's *always* on. We were wishing we had controls that we don't need." I pointed at the panel. "Touch it in the lower right hand corner—your right hand corner—as if you're going to pinch it, then hold your fingers there, and draw back like you're pulling a string."

"How do you know that's what I'm supposed to do?"

"Because that's what the Grigori did."

She looked up at me, startled.

"You remembered."

She looked at me strangely, and I wondered if she was *really* starting to believe me, or was simply humoring me. Whichever it was, it didn't matter. She pulled her fingertips as I'd told her to. The cop had stopped focusing on me, and was watching her, carefully.

The panel lit up, and she gasped. So did he.

"Oh, Jesus," the guard said. "I mean it, lady! Stop what you're doing!"

"Don't listen to him. Keep pulling. About a foot up. I was watching the Grigori carefully, waiting for it to attack me, and after all those buttons it pushed on the wall, I didn't realize it was still operating controls of a different kind on the pad itself. Sensor controls."

Her fingers reached a point about a foot above the panel, and all around me the pad ignited with light, just as it had back in Emibi.

"Son of a bitch," the guard said, his hands beginning to shake. He pointed the gun right into my face, and seemed on the verge of hysteria. "Get off that thing or I *will* shoot you!"

"The pad in Pangea is the main control," I told them both, "This is just a receiver, or a sender. That Grigori probably had a number of pads it could send me to. That's what the other controls were for. She probably thought she was sending me to wherever you found this one."

"The bottom of the Gulf of Mexico," Lena said.

"Where I'd be dead and out of her hair. If she had hair."

The guard, apparently tired of waiting, cocked his pistol.

"How do I turn it off," Lena said.

"No!" I said, my eyes darting nervously between her and the security guard. "No. Now form a flat palm and push all the way down to the panel."

"What," she said, aghast? "No, Brandon, I can't. This is the discovery of a lifetime! We have to make plans, we have to organize..."

And that's when the guard shot me. He hit me in the shoulder. I'm not sure if that's what he was aiming at, but it was effective. I screamed and fell to my knees.

"Lena, please!" I said, my eyes dancing between her and the nervous man with the gun, now shakily aimed at my eye. "Milton needs me. *Elia* needs me."

She stared at me, and the reality rushed in on her, quite suddenly. It was all true. Everything I'd said was true, on some level, even if it was just some kind of game machine. Her eyes locked on mine in abject wonder, and I thought I saw the beginnings of more tears.

"Nova needs you," she said, almost in a whisper.

"And I need her," I answered.

Lena smiled at me, sadly, very sadly, and formed her hand into the palm shape I'd told her to.

"*STOP!*" The cop snapped, leaping up onto the panel. "*DOWN ON THE GROUND! LADY, STOP WHAT YOU'RE DOING!*"

"Send me something back," Lena said to me, quietly, "so I'll know. Know you're safe, and..."

"*GODDAMMIT!*" The cop screamed, grabbing me, pressing the gun to my temple, and cocking it again.

"That it's real?" I asked Lena.

She nodded.

"Promise," I said.

Lena pushed her palm all the way to the control panel, as the guard pulled the trigger.

I KNELT IN THE CENTER of a different pad, in a different room. Different in all ways. Different than Lena's office. Different than the one the queen had sent me from back in Emibi. The guard still had his gun to my temple, the shots having somehow not harmed me. He no longer seemed to be aware of my presence as he looked nervously back and forth at our weird surroundings.

Slowly, overly excited because I was actually back—really and truly back in Pangea—I stepped down from the pad and began to laugh.

"Where..." the guard asked, "where the hell are we?"

"Pangea," I laughed.

"It looks real," he said.

Forcing myself to focus, I checked my bullet wound, which hurt like hell, but didn't seem to be mortal. Ignoring it, I—like the guard— took in the room.

There were great grooves dug deeply into the floor, and a massive hole in the wall. I spent a minute or two wondering what had happened here when it dawned on me that I was in the room Milton's mining machine had been transported to when the pad first brought us here. The rumbling mole had apparently slipped off the impenetrable surface of this pad's alien polymers, and careened about the room before boring straight into a wall. Control panels that once filled that partition were now nothing more than useless scrap metal, rent plastic, and shredded wiring. When Milton and I had thought we were digging into the Earth, we were actually digging out of a subterranean room deep beneath Pangea.

If I followed that trail, I would wind up in the exactly spot where we'd first come out on the surface of this crazy world.

The place where I'd first met Nova.

Excited, and desperate to get back to her, to Milton, to Bruk, to Kiga, and all the rest, I was about to run into the mole-made fissure when I realized it was impassable. Most of it had either been filled in behind the efficient digging machine, or become blocked when the earth above it had collapsed. I would have to find another way to the surface, and back to my friends.

I'd just begun searching the room for a corridor, or stairs, when the guard stopped me short.

"Is that outer space?" he asked.

I turned to him, and saw he was looking up. I raised my own eyes to the place he was studying, and was awed. The entire ceiling of the room was made entirely of a transparent material, filled wall-to-wall with a mind-blowing view of the blackness of space.

Space.

Stars. Asteroids. Planets. I could see movement through the window, a small tumbling rock to one side, and a shift in light that indicated we were orbiting a star. But it couldn't be. Milton had been so certain. We were inside the Earth. The Earth was *hollow*.

"You idiot," I said to myself. "You aren't inside the Earth. This is a Dyson sphere! You're inside a goddam spaceship!"

"I'm not an idiot," the guard said, irritated.

"No, I…"

I heard a small noise behind me, and spun instantly. Just entering the room through an open doorway was a Grigori; dark green, sleek and just as ugly as I remembered. It looked around, surveying the damage, and didn't notice us at first.

"Holy, mother fucking…" the guard said, as the Grigori turned, noticing him.

It moved so fast neither of us had time to react. Fortunately for me, it went for the guard, first. His sudden scream was stopped cold in his throat as his head snapped away from his body. Blood sprayed over me, over the walls, the floor, the pad, the panels, and the Grigori was on him, ripping, snapping, chewing, shredding until the guard's body was nothing more than meat and ruined blue cloth.

Satisfied that the guard was no longer a threat—as if he ever was—the Grigori bitch turned to me, fury and rage still clouding her eyes.

I clinked my handcuff chains, and just smiled.

"So what happened next?"

"Well, I've just gotten a few of the other security recordings forwarded, the last that were made before the electronics in the room failed. Or were shot. Maybe they'll tell us something."

"Bring 'em up."

Onscreen, Lena backed up away from the alien pad, and essentially collapsed into a chair, her eyes like balloons, mouth so wide you could practically see down her throat.

She sat silently, just staring at the thing in disbelief. The guards were all near, weapons still drawn. One of them moved closer to her.

"Where did he go?" he asked her, quietly.

"I..." she said, considering the question, "I don't know."

"Is he in another room?"

"No," she answered, her voice barely audible. "I don't think he's even in this building."

She looked lower, at the center of the pad.

"Or maybe he's inside that thing," she said. "I have no idea."

"Like a trap door?" the guard asked.

"No," she said, and nearly laughed. "No, I don't think so."

There was the sound of a door opening in the distance 'Good cop' Officer Ransom raced back in, entering the video frame near the pad with the agent whose name no one could ever remember, mostly because he never talked to anyone. Both were carrying cups of coffee.

"We heard shots." Ransom asked. "Where's Mack?"

"I don't know," Lena said, absently, still staring at the pad.

Ransom studied her a moment, then looked around the room. Not seeing Mack anywhere, he turned his attention back to the pretty female astrophysicist.

242

"What do you mean, 'you don't know'?" He said, confused.

"He got on that thing," one of the guards interjected. "Then she waved her hands all around, the whole place lit up, and Mack just fuckin' disappeared along with Germaine."

Ransom's eyes widened, as did the agent's, and the two of them stepped closer to the device.

"It worked?" Ransom said. "For real?"

"For real," Lena repeated.

"So… what does that mean?"

"I don't know, yet. So far all it means is that Brandon is gone."

Ransom's face fell, anger slicing through his normally 'good cop' demeanor. He set his coffee cup down and walked around the machine to glare at Lena.

"All right, Dr. Mizellier," he said. "I need some answers."

"You what?" she asked, as if suddenly becoming aware that he was even in the room.

"I let it go because I didn't want to compromise you in front of your husband, or your ex-husband, or whatever he hell you two are these days, but you need to start leveling with me."

"What are you talking about?" she asked, already knowing what he was talking about, and becoming nervous.

"I'm talking about a half hour of missing time in Mack's story!" he snapped, "I'm talking about how you and Pompaneau are the only ones who know about this damned weird, alien pad-thing, and then I come looking for Mack because he killed someone, and you and Mack had a relationship neither of you mentioned, and then he vanishes because of the pad! *Twice!*"

There was a stunned moment of silence while Lena considered exactly what he was saying.

"You think…" she said, horrified by his logic, "I helped him escape… *last year*," she shook her head, disbelieving, "*and* just now… with this… this *device*? Because of our… because we'd had… a relationship."

"This goddam facility has cameras *everywhere*, so when Mack's story didn't gibe with the sequence of events I checked some of those security recordings…"

"I got Mack's MRI back," Pompaneau said, entering the room, seeming excited, though daubing his lip where he'd bitten it when Mack slammed the table under his chin. He waved a manila folder in his other hand. "They actually *found* something inside his skull. Can you believe it?"

Ransom stopped leaning in toward Pompaneau's ex, stood and faced the newcomer. Then he turned his eyes back to the attractive scientist he was fairly certain had helped Brandon—*both* times.

"Do you want me to discuss this in front of him?" he asked Mizellier, walking toward his laptop near the interrogation table.

"What's going on?" Pompaneau asked, sniffling blood.

Ransom grabbed his case and waited, not taking his eyes from Lena's. Not blinking. She, in turn, never took her eyes off Ransom.

"Show him," Lena said, quietly. "I don't care."

Ransom seemed surprised, then turned to Pompaneau.

"You know," Ransom said, as it sunk in. "About her and Mack. That's why you were being such a dick to the guy. You knew he was banging your wife."

"Of course I knew." Pompaneau said, grimacing at the expression.

"Did you know she helped him escape?" Ransom asked. "Both a year ago, and just now?"

Pompaneau was stunned.

"What?" he said, turning to her in shock. "You helped Mack escape?"

She glared at him, furiously, as Ransom set the laptop down, opened it, and the screen glowed into life. There was a folder already open on the desktop, filled with files.

"Why?" Pompaneau asked his wife.

"I didn't," she began, intending to argue that she didn't really think it would work, that she hadn't really believed in 'Pangea' or 'Nova' or any of it, but she couldn't. In the end, she had believed, and she'd activated the pad.

"Not originally," she continued. "Not back then."

"But now?"

She turned away and said nothing.

"Are those security recordings?" Pompaneau asked Ransom.

"They are," Ransom said, still staring at Lena.

"And Mack is on some of them?" Pompaneau wanted to know.

"He's in all of them," Ransom replied, still not looking at the man. "And so is Dr. Mizellier."

Pompaneau stared at the list of files, their tiny icons showing frozen moments of Mack and Lena, mostly in her office. Many of the images appeared to be two people very close together.

"Let's have a look." Pompaneau said, clearly uncertain.

"No!" Lena said.

Ransom still stared only at her, unblinking. Pompaneau, on the other hand, couldn't stop staring at the files on the laptop.

When Lena finally continued, her voice was cold, emotionless. Just stating facts.

"No, " she said. "There's no point. He'd broken it off with him many weeks before all this began. Once he learned I was... once he learned I'd been lying to him about not being married. It has nothing to do with any of this, other than that it was clearly another of the stress factors that led him to kill that boy."

"He didn't know...?" Pompaneau began, barely able to speak.

"No. He didn't. I liked him. He was smart, and funny, and..."

"Manly?" Ransom offered. It seemed an odd, personal kind of observation, but it was true.

"Yes," Mizellier said, the passion evident in her voice. "We began having sex not long after he came to work here—he didn't know I was married. When he found out from Milton, he broke it off."

Pompaneau stared at her for quite a while then slowly pulled his attention from her, reached out and double-clicked on one of the files. It opened quickly and began to play. It was a high resolution QuickTime, shot from somewhere overhead in the room they currently occupied. Mizellier was wearing a lab coat and high-heel boots, but nothing else, leaning back across a desk as Brandon, pants around his ankles, mouth bent down, sucking passionately on one breast, thrust himself into her.

"You're such an *animal*," Lena was shouting on the recording. "Oh, God, I love the way you fuck me, like an animal!"

The room was still and silent, no more sound from the QuickTime other than Lena's passionate screams, and Pompaneau's suddenly labored breathing.

"I never meant to hurt you, Iain," Lena said, her eyes filling with tears. "The guilt was killing me."

"Oh, clearly," Pompaneau said, pain pouring from every syllable as he watched her being pleasured on her desk in ways he knew *he* had never pleasured her. "It's just tearing you up, inside."

"You told Mack the night he disappeared that you were getting a divorce," the agent asked. "Didn't you?"

Everyone turned to him, amazed that he had finally spoken. Mizellier looked up at him in surprise.

"Yes," she admitted.

"We checked, of course," he told her, taking a casual sip of his coffee. "Your conversation was picked up on one of the videos from the night he disappeared. You were waiting for him. Hoping to get him back from that Jessica chick, weren't you?"

"Yes."

"It's why you were all made up," the agent continued, "and why you weren't wearing anything under your lab coat *that* night, either."

She stared at him in silence.

"You weren't wearing anything under your lab coat, except the boots, were you?"

"Is that relevant?" she asked, angrily.

"No," the agent said, grinning darkly through the foam that covered his lips from whatever it was he'd gotten from Starbucks. "I just like thinking about it."

"He was about to become a college boy," Ransom, the cop, said, "and therefore worthy of you."

"It's not like that," Lena said, surprised by the accusation. "I just... I... it was timing, and..."

She stared, and angered a little, realizing she didn't have to dignify the accusation.

"I was hoping things hadn't progressed very far with Jessica," she said, quietly, looking down, remembering that night. "I realized how I felt about him. Getting into college was just coincidental, and an excuse to make contact after we'd agreed to avoid one another. But I guess he felt leaving out those little details would help me, somehow. He obviously didn't know that Iain and I had divorced while he was gone, and… I don't know."

She paused, remembering the heightened emotions of that night, a year ago.

"I told him I loved him, and wanted him. He… just looked at me as though his world had ended. I didn't understand at the time. I expected him to leap into my arms, but he only went pale, and walked away."

"And then you helped him escape," Ransom said.

"*I didn't help him escape!*" she snapped at the detective. "We didn't even have the pad out, yet! It was still mostly trapped inside all that concretization! I didn't even know what the damn thing was! *None of us did!* The mole crashed through the floor—ceiling—whatever—shattered the stone, and activated the pad somehow! You were there, Ransom! *You started this whole fucking mess when you shot at him!*"

"**HE** started it when he **killed** that boy!"

"*Brandon was a good kid who was hurting! A good MAN who held it together longer than I would have, and only fought back when that asshole kept beating on him! And you investigated it! You fucking KNOW that!*"

Ransom stood silently, staring at the auburn haired scientist. She glared into him from behind her glasses for a solid minute, then turned away, and folded her arms across her chest.

Ransom scowled at her, trying to decide if she was being sincere. Eventually he shook his head realizing he didn't care.

"Where…" the policeman asked with barely restrained fury, "*is* MACK?

"Why do you care?" Lena asked. "Wherever he is, it's out of your jurisdiction."

"*DAMMIT, woman, where did you SEND him?*"

"You know as much as I do."

"*EXCEPT HOW TO GET HIM BACK!*" Ransom snapped.

"Or how to get back the billion dollars worth of government equipment he stole," the agent offered, sipping his coffee, and staring at the pad. "You think it really is just some advanced game system? Or is he actually in that Pangea place?"

Pompaneau snorted derisively.

"That's not even a possibility," Lena's ex said, less snarky, and more angry. "Mack lied about that, just like he lied about everything else. The existence of a 'Pangea' defies all known laws of science. It *can't* exist."

Suddenly the pad ignited again, bright light exploding upward and out from its center, then fading away just as quickly. Everyone flinched, and stepped back from what had appeared on its smooth surface.

Mizellier gasped. Ransom stared in horror and disbelief. Pompaneau whimpered.

"Hoooooly shit," the agent said.

EPILOGUE

"And that's it? That's all we know?"

"Yes sir. The cameras in the room stopped working as the Grigori and the guard appeared on the pad. Electrical interference of some kind, or damage from the guard's wild shots. Our agent ran from the room to call us as we'd asked him to, and by the time he'd returned, Mizellier, Pompaneau and the cop were all gone."

"And the Grigori?"

"What Grigori?"

"Ha. Okay. I guess you've answered my question. So what next?"

"I don't know. Nothing, unless one of the security guards remembers exactly what Mizellier did to turn on that device."

"Is that likely?"

"I don't know. After what happened to that guard, part of me hopes not."

"Yeah. I know what you mean."

ABOUT THE AUTHOR

Michael Kace Beckum gained his love of
the "Swords and Romance" genre primarily
because of Frank Frazetta covers
featuring—predominantly—bad-ass,
naked cavegirls fighting dinosaurs.
It's still his preferred reading to this day.
Perhaps that's why he lives alone.

Printed in Great Britain
by Amazon

26704944R00145